Neglect

A NOVEL

KIM WOZENCRAFT

ARCADE PUBLISHING • NEW YORK

Arcade Publishing books may be purchased in bulk at special discounts for sales promotion, corporate gifts, fund-raising, or educational purposes. Special editions can also be created to specifications. For details, contact the Special Sales Department, Arcade Publishing, 307 West 36th Street, 11th Floor, New York, NY 10018 or arcade@skyhorsepublishing.com.

Arcade Publishing® is a registered trademark of Skyhorse Publishing, Inc.®, a Delaware corporation.

Visit our website at www.arcadepub.com.

10 9 8 7 6 5 4 3 2 1

Library of Congress Cataloging-in-Publication Data is available on file.

Cover design by Kai Texel

Print ISBN: 978-1-5107-6439-2
Ebook ISBN: 978-1-5107-6440-8

Printed in the United States of America

For Sasha, Dash, and Max
With love always

PART I

PART 1

ONE

THE VOICE COMES IN DISTORTED, as though bubbling through water. A woman's voice, shouting from an unfathomable distance. "Can you hear me?"

Erin lies dormant. The voice calls her name, but the sound echoes, sinking through huge rolling swells from somewhere far above. Erin's eyelids spasm. Light bits strobe, flaring like flame on a match head: sulfur yellow, brilliant orange, splinters of blue.

"Wake up." Tremolo voices emerge, *"her BAC was twenty-nine . . . maybe we should get a doctor in here . . ."* Bits of garbled sound gather speed as they Doppler past and evaporate.

"You have to wake up." Hands slip under her back, jostling forcefully.

Erin retches awake, brain function at reptilian level. Her eyes won't open. She is blind to her surroundings but back in her body, fully and horribly in her skin, as though she has donned a heavy, gelatinous coverall. Arms push their way farther beneath her. "Come on now." Hands shift and prod. "Sit up."

She can't move. She doesn't know if she's trying. Fingers pry open her eyelids. Dark blurry figures hover next to her, shadowy aliens gathered to observe a newly discovered life form in some low-budget sci-fi cult film. More hands, gripping her arms now. They push her upright. Something liquid sloshes inside her skull. The room mirages into view.

1

She is lying on a hospital bed. Curtains hang close. Someone has put blue paper hospital garb on her, but she has no recollection of when or how. She can't find a single memory. It's as if she has just this instant materialized.

Shame floods in, heavy, silver, and with it the vague realization that something has gone terribly wrong. This is not the right ending to the story. The actual doing of the thing was reckless, mundane, happening in a seeming instant after she'd slogged through all those months—eons—of lacerating indecision. It was such a simple task.

And she has failed. How utterly pathetic.

She hates herself.

She despises everything around her.

The people whose job it is to categorize incidents of this sort, to fill in the blanks on forms, will label it An Attempt.

A cry for help.

Erin's eyes close again. She feels herself lowered back onto the bed. The liquid in her skull settles, congeals. The voices move away, one of them saying disgustedly, "She's stable. Let her sleep it off."

TWO

Eddy snaps his battered wallet shut and stuffs it into his back pocket, the dark blue denim worn thin where the wallet always sits. Not that he expects the jeans to last long enough for the pocket to actually rip. A seam will split or the denim will rip randomly, opening a six-inch tear in the middle of the thigh. It's the same with his work gloves. They don't last. Nothing lasts.

He pushes his shaggy black hair out of his eyes and grips the fuel pump nozzle, jamming it into the feeder pipe. Listening to the gasoline gush into his truck, he spots the New York Lottery sign on the double glass doors of the plaza entrance. Eddy plays only Lotto, twice a week, buying his tickets at the local Mobil station on Thursday for Saturday's drawing and on Sunday for Wednesday's pot. His strategy maximizes hope, allowing it to last for days instead of hours. In the early online ads—gray animations—a featureless creature resembling a bathroom pictogram walked up to a counter and handed over its dollar while a chyron scrolled across screen proclaiming *let the dream begin*. Eddy knows his gamble isn't about winning against astronomical odds. It's about relief, a chance to get through the next few days riding on a one-dollar bet that life can change instantly and permanently for the better if only the right numbers come up, if only he gets, for the first time since forever, lucky.

But he's not at the local Mobil station tonight; he's at a large service plaza off the New York Thruway, on his way to a delivery in Jersey. Nick should be with him, but lately Nick has been coming up with reasons he can't come along on the hauls. Nick is fine with running Eddy out front on their deliveries. Eddy slings the nozzle back onto the pump, his angry gesture startling a young woman filling her Jetta nearby. He shrugs an apology, jumps in his battered pickup and pulls over to the main building.

Inside is an amusement park food court. Fast food concessions line an entire wall. Dunkin' Donuts and Starbucks compete with one another from opposite ends of the mall while colorful vending machines and coin-eating electronic games flash and whir between them. Paul and Lindsey would love it. Eddy feels a small pang of guilt: it's been a couple of months since he's taken them anywhere. He should make an effort, even if it means he has to deal with Erin when he picks them up. He spots the lottery stand near the main register of the souvenir shop. He deserves to win. It's his destiny. His heritage.

The Hill family has been in Granite County since before America was America. Eddy's ancestors, if his grandfather is to be believed, received a patent with an appended Queen Anne's seal deeding them a hundred acres in southeast Granite County. The family milled the timber, built their home. Built two barns and a silo. They raised cattle and chickens and hogs, grew corn. But farmsteads require maintenance, as do houses, and ever-rising property taxes took a larger bite each year. As time passed, they were forced to sell off acreage bit by bit, even as middlemen sucked all the money out of milk, until there wasn't enough land for sufficient profit. A persistent drought reduced them to seeking factory work, all in the space of a few generations. When Eddy's grandfather died, his legacy was only what was left of the farm and a large collection of arrowheads, picked up over the years of clearing and plowing land. Eddy's not sure where it went. And anyway, nobody talks much about the Esopus tribe that preceded the colonists.

He picks up the pencil attached to the counter by a dirty piece of string and eyes the Lotto slips. Select the winning six from numbers from one through fifty-nine. He breaks his high school graduation year up: 19-9-8. He needs three more.

After emancipating himself from the tedium and drama of high school with a Regent's diploma, Eddy stumbled around the county for a year or so, picking up construction jobs when they were available. Many of his friends had left for college, taking out loans with vague and distant due dates, but four years feels like eternity when you're just out of high school. Like some of the other graduates who couldn't manage going away to study, or didn't want the debt, Eddy signed up for an evening class at Granite County Community College. But even if he took two classes each term, an associate degree was years away, and there was no way he could afford to go full time. He had to make a living. And he found sitting in classrooms tedious beyond belief. What use was algebra? Whatever you did to one side of the equation had to be done to the other; achieving the solution required symmetrical manipulation of the numbers on either side of the equal sign. That concept was irrelevant outside the world of mathematics. In real life, the word equality was just something that sounded good on parchment.

He preferred being outdoors and, like most carpenters, knew geometry from every necessary angle. Geometry was applicable. He found odd jobs through word-of-mouth, working as a roofer, learning his way into construction. Building things felt good, but he listened carefully when the older guys complained about the work being hard on the back, hard on the hands, hard on the joints.

When the opportunity finally presented itself, he'd gone to work at Schraden, a large plant at the north end of the county that manufactured high quality hunting knives and enjoyed the benefit of military contracts from the federal government. The factory was in the same large industrial complex as IBM. Many of the kids who'd gone away to college never really came home, stopping in after receiving their degrees to grab the last of their belongings and head to cities, where there were jobs and opportunity. Those who did come back to stay found decent employment at IBM or at the other major employer in Granite County, St. Martin's Hospital. The numbers weren't huge: Eddy's entire senior class comprised 143 students.

He pencils in the bubbles over six and twenty-five: the twins' birthday. The guy behind the counter tires of waiting for Eddy to finish the ticket, reaches up and straightens the cigarette packs in the overhead rack.

One more number. Two if he plays the extra. Eddy knows he's over-thinking it. It's not the stock market; research is irrelevant. He closes his eyes and holds the pencil poised above the slip. He'll darken in whichever bubble it lands on and hope for the best. Odd, the memories that arrive randomly, at unpredictable moments. He's in the bleachers at a varsity girls' basketball game, admiring the way Erin moves on the court, athletic and graceful, and he knows as soon as he sees her eyes narrow that she'll take the shot. He's seen it every time, just before she takes a long one from outside the arc. She sinks the three-pointer. The bleachers erupt with cheers. It's because of her that he goes to the games.

Dumbass. He opens his eyes. The pencil point is on four. Erin's old jersey number. Odds are like that: predictable in hindsight. He'd started any number of times to ask her out after a game, but wound up stammering some lame phrase like, "awesome shot on the buzzer" instead. He tried to convince himself that it was only a high school crush, but that didn't make it hurt any less.

He hands his Lotto slip to the clerk. Nothing lasts. The clerk takes Eddy's dollar bill carefully, avoiding any skin-to-skin contact, and hands Eddy his printed ticket. Eddy pockets it and heads for the Dunkin' Donuts. He'd been playing Lotto the day Nick rolled back into his life, which is what has led to him being here today, on another run to Seaside Heights in quest of the almighty dollar.

Eddy isn't thrilled at the direction that chance meeting with Nick has sent him in, including here and now, playing Lotto at a thruway rest stop, but he hadn't been happy the day Nick bumped into him either. Still married to Erin, then, but not happy at all. That day, out of nowhere, on two-week's notice from the Army Reserves, his wife was shipping out, headed overseas. When he got the news, he'd been ready to give up and join the ranks of men who go out for a pack of cigarettes or a loaf of bread and never come home. He loved his kids, but not enough to take a job mopping floors at night or stuffing French fries into cardboard containers. That crap wouldn't solve the financial problems he and Erin faced, it would only stretch out the pain as they moved toward the inevitable. And then she'd gone and joined the Reserves to bring in extra cash.

The day Nick reentered his life, Eddy had been standing at the Mobil station counter, pushing last Saturday's ticket into the blue plastic scanner and hoping for the triumphant blare of electronic trumpets.

The machine remained silent.

He was crumpling the flimsy paper when a large hand slapped against his shoulder, squeezing tight. Eddy jumped sideways, his hands tightening into quick fists before he recognized the guy yanking his chain.

"Eddy! How you been, brother?" The voice didn't go with the large man clapping Eddy on the back as though they were best friends. Eddy hadn't seen Nick for a long time, maybe even a couple of years. He'd heard that Nick had taken off for Jersey, probably running his latest multi-level marketing scam, or else just laying low, hanging around some beach town spending other people's money. Since high school, Nick always had some big deal on the horizon. Still, they went way back. All the way back to Granite Elementary.

"Hey," Eddy said. "Same old, same old. Living the dream." He tossed the crumpled Lotto ticket into the trashcan near the counter.

"You're looking good, bruh. Staying in shape, looks like." Nick still had that weird, uncertain grin, like he was trying to get the punchline to a joke everyone else was already laughing at. "Glad I ran into you. Got time for a beer?"

Eddy's back ached from splitting wood all day and life, thanks to Erin, had once again kicked him in the teeth. A beer sounded pretty damn good.

It was happy hour at the Visser Kok Inn, which on Monday through Thursday served mostly local clients, but was increasingly dealing with an invasion of weekenders during summer and autumn months. The allure was local: fresh trout, seasonal vegetables, and craft beer. Authentic. The hip city dwellers were enamored, too, of the owner-bartender, Big Gordy, whose silver beard draped across his ample belly nearly to his belt. It was a wizard's beard, and legend had it that Gordy made millions importing Columbian cocaine in the seventies when it was still a suitcase business, before the cartels got involved and things turned ugly. He bought the Visser Kok when it was still a farm, converted the large main house to a bar and restaurant and video rental store. The racks of VHS boxes had been tossed years ago, replaced with additional dining tables shortly after Y2K came and went with little more impact than the bleating of billions of plastic noisemakers and a slew of hangovers, failing to tank either the internet or the international electronic banking systems of the world.

They were in a back corner, dark and cool, far enough away from the bar to have a little privacy. The clacks and dings chirring from an old-school pinball machine and a billiard game faded beneath the wail of Merle Haggard. The bar was slowly filling with men in soil-smeared coveralls and sweat-stained T-shirts, wearing baseball caps dusted with dirt and mortar, the bills smudged with cement-colored fingerprints.

"Check this out." Nick eased something across the table, hiding it under his smooth, chubby fingers. Eddy slipped it into a pocket without looking, recognizing from the feel that it was a small baggie of weed.

"Thanks, man."

"Don't thank me," Nick said. "I'm looking to expand my market."

"Really." Eddy had friends, plenty of acquaintances from his factory days and from working construction, guys who liked to catch a little buzz on the weekends. His weekender firewood customers sometimes asked about the local market, but so far Eddy had stayed away from dealing. Not that he respected the laws against cannabis; he didn't want the nagging doubts that come with doing something illegal.

"So, what do you think?" Nick raised his bottle of Arrowood Stout Pig as if examining a test tube in a lab.

"I don't know. Not looking to run into Johnny Law."

"No, man, the beer."

"Oh. Yeah, it's excellent."

"Homegrown organic hops." Nick took a slow, deliberate sip, savoring. "A little side gig and a man could afford more of the niceties of life."

"I could use some niceties," Eddy said. "I'm about to be six months without a wife."

Nick raised his thick eyebrows, waiting for an explanation. Eddy told him that Erin was, that very evening, being deployed overseas.

"What?" Nick rocked back in the booth, his bulk shaking the wooden structure. "She fucking enlisted?"

"Yeah," Eddy said. "She's been in the Reserves the past year and whatever. Claimed she was doing it for the family, just gonna earn a little extra cash. It was okay for a while, just a weekend a month once the training was done."

"I feel for you, brother."

"Now she's getting on a plane to Afghanistan."

"Where are the kids?"

Eddy explained that Erin's sister, Tanya, had flown up from Dallas to take them to see Erin off. Eddy wanted nothing to do with it.

"Tanya. Haven't seen her since she took off after graduation. Damn."

"Yeah. She got the hell out. Fine by me."

It was a six-month deployment. Eddy wasn't sure how he was going to deal with the kids, much less with running a household, without his wife around. Maybe he should've agreed to let them go stay with Tanya again, like they had when Erin was at basic training. But Texas was too far away, and he didn't much care for Tanya anymore. The years in Dallas had made her a little too slick, kind of uppity, different from the way she'd been in high school. Not that he'd ever really noticed her much back then. She'd gotten pregnant, finished up in night school, and moved away with the baby's father. And now she was his sister-in-law. It made it easier that she lived so far away.

Nick hesitated. "She's not, like . . .?"

"They've got her driving trucks. Convoys."

"They named County Rt. 85 after that kid who got killed last year. Damn. Can't remember his name."

"I try not to think about that shit." Eddy took a long, slow pull off his beer.

"Was it Iraq? Afghanistan?"

"You're asking me?"

"He graduated from Granite High." Nick shifted forward, still fond of their alma mater. "Played football."

"Go Bobcats."

"Remember that extra point I blocked? That was a game. Man."

"Who can forget." Eddy tried to sound interested. "What's it been, fifteen, twenty years?" Nick had blocked a crucial extra point, saved the game, got the team to Regionals.

"His parents seemed real proud though, in the newspaper. To have that kind of honor. A parade and all."

"Saw it on Facebook." Eddy picked at the label on his beer bottle. There was no sense trying to tell Nick that he didn't want to think about where his wife was headed at that very moment, or why she'd decided to jump off and do her patriotic duty in the first place. The Army Reserves. In wartime. Talk about a gamble. But it was always wartime, it just didn't feel like it because the thing had been going on forever.

"Is that grounds for a divorce?"

For a moment, Eddy thought Nick was serious, then he laughed. "Don't get me wrong," he said, "I love my kids, but I didn't sign up for this."

"You'll do fine." Nick chuckled. "Just don't let them start calling you Mommy."

Eddy dropped his voice to mimic the ad announcer, the guy who did every lottery ad he'd heard in the last several years, saying, "Hey. You never know."

"I heard it was a mortar." Nick drank and smacked his lips. "Damn. It's bugging me. Wish I could remember his name."

Eddy drained the rest of his beer, stuck out his hand. "Good to see you. I gotta run."

"Hey, buddy." Nick pulled his bulk out of the booth and clapped Eddy on the back, leaning in to whisper. "Let me know if you change your mind. It's good money."

It had taken a while, but eventually Eddy did change his mind. Erin had been three months into her deployment when he called Nick and said he was in, and now here he is, two years into this gig, his relationship with Erin in shreds but that can't be helped, and he's out here doing the work while Nick sits home watching TV and stuffing his face with popcorn. Eddy pays for his coffee and almost veers back into the souvenir shop to grab something silly for Paul and Lindsey, some kind of stuffed animal or maybe matching sweatshirts, but decides against it. He doesn't want to answer questions from Erin about what he's doing. He doesn't want to so much as speak to her. She'd come back different, spent the first four months after her return drinking. She had no business going in the first place, but there it was. She'd done it on her own, without asking him, without even thinking about it seriously. Their marriage had been in trouble and both of them knew it. What was the point if they weren't making life easier for one another? And then just—boom. She enlisted. She could say whatever about promises made by the recruiter, but any idiot knows you don't put your life in the hands of the government and count on luck to keep you safe. Maybe it wasn't all Erin's fault, but most of it was. He couldn't help it if there weren't any real jobs left, and it's hard to pull yourself up by the bootstraps when you can't even afford a pair of boots.

Back in his truck, he grabs his phone from the console and dials the number that used to be his landline. It rings in the house where he used to live. He'll pick something up for the kids on the return trip, drop it off this weekend. The phone rings and rings. He can picture it, hanging on the pale green wall in the kitchen, next to the key rack that used to hold his keys. He and Erin had built the house. They'd been early in love then, the future shimmering with promise like some eye-popping mirage in the desert.

The phone rings and rings and rings. Earlier that day, Eddy's girlfriend, Megan, who he lives with now, told him a friend of hers thought she'd seen Erin coming out of a liquor store in town. That can't be good.

Eddy tries once more but there's still no answer. He decides to call Nick and ask him to drive over and check in on the kids. It's only a couple of miles away.

When Nick answers, Eddy hears a ball game in the background, but ignores it and asks Nick to drop in and check on Lindsey and Paul. The TV sounds cut off abruptly. Nick assures Eddy that his kids are fine.

"They're eight years old and no one is answering the phone." Eddy keeps his tone even, picturing Nick on his butt on the couch. "Hey. I'm out here, you know. For both of us. Just do it, would you?"

"Okay buddy," Nick says. "Okay, I hear you."

"Call me back."

"Where are you?"

"Halfway there," Eddy says.

As he merges back into the speeding parkway traffic, Eddy wonders if Nick will really drop by the house, or just watch another half hour of the ball game and then call him back to say everything's fine. Nick's not the most reliable guy. If he was, he'd be here right now instead of at home sitting on his ass. Next time they're face-to-face, Eddy's going to have to talk to him about their arrangement.

THREE

It is already Monday morning and already hot outside. Barb Copley does not want to get out of bed. She wipes a crumb of black mascara from where it has lodged at the edge of her right eye and flicks it toward the waste basket in the corner of the bedroom. The room is not to her liking. The house isn't either, but it was left to her last year when her father died of a heart attack, and the mortgage payment is a lot lower than the rent she was paying at the time. She'd intended to save money to put her sons through college, but it's too late to scrape together anything substantial, and she's still bent on getting her BA in psychology herself once they graduate high school. She wants to be a therapist. She wants to help people. She'll have to take on more debt. She catches her thoughts, berating herself for letting early morning turmoil erupt in her still half-asleep brain.

Above the bed, the ceiling fan whirs, the motor emitting a low, irritating buzz. Barb's sky-blue polyester nightgown is glued to her skin with perspiration. At least the office is air-conditioned. Even this early, her ankles are swelling, her feet throbbing, her knees and hips and lower back aching dully. She vows to go on a diet. Again. She vows to buy a window unit for this room.

She lies staring up at the fan and thinks about calling in sick, but she has barely ninety days on the job. She's determined to put in at least a year; anything less will look bad on a résumé. She thinks about another day in the Walmart-sized Granite County Department of Social Services complex, another day in that garbage can of a car, another day dealing with screaming kids and crying babies, drug-addled adults and, worst of all, another day of her boss, who is on the countdown to retirement and doesn't give a damn about anyone or anything. Mrs. Hattleburg has nineteen years under her belt. She is an unpleasant woman whose every word is delivered in a tone of utter and complete exasperation. The only person in the office she speaks to with even a hint of kindness is Bob Steele, a man ten years her junior who carries himself like an FBI agent even though he's only a caseworker in Preventive. Preventive takes over after the dirty work has been done, so Mr. Steele deals primarily with parents who've managed to get through enough programs to be considered for family reunification. Barb envies the position.

She sits up and looks over at Roy, who's still fast asleep. She wonders what he dreams of. He's a good man, a decent guy. He takes her out to dinner; they go to the movies now and then, and he doesn't complain about watching romantic comedies. He's shown her two sons how to spend Sunday afternoons watching football on TV instead of hanging out inside a digital reality for entire weekends, blowing things up onscreen and getting popcorn grease all over the controllers. Most weeks he takes out the trash without having to be reminded.

Barb glances down at her hands, now folded in her lap, or what there is of a lap, which makes her think of dieting, which makes her think of food, which makes her hungry for breakfast though there isn't really time. She'll have to pick something up at the deli on the way to the office.

Watching Roy sleep as she dresses, she feels as if she has missed something, that some secret knowledge, something rudimentary and essential, has eluded her. He is kind enough to be a substitute dad and he never has said anything about the way her weight ballooned less than a year after they signed the paperwork and exchanged vows. They met when Barb was at her lowest weight since high school. He knew nothing of the ups and downs she'd gone through, the dieting, the fasting, the starving. Their marriage ceremony, a second for both of them, was attended by Barb's sons and a few of her and Roy's friends. There were tax benefits to being married, and Barb was able to put Roy on her health insurance plan after they made the relationship official at Our Lady of Perpetual Mercy.

Dressed for work in a long, loose-fitting summer skirt, Barb walks tenderly down the too-narrow hallway toward the kitchen, wondering if there's chocolate anywhere in the house. On occasion, she unexpectedly discovers a forgotten box of sweets hidden in some dark corner of a cabinet, causing simultaneous elation and dismay.

She's pretty sure she's got some black and white cookies stashed behind the row of canned vegetables in the pantry. She's on the verge of abandoning the search when the kitchen phone trills. The phone, a slimline wall model that belonged to her father, doesn't have a screen, much less caller ID. But at this hour, unless it's the school nurse calling to tell her to come get one of her boys, she knows who's at the other end of the line.

∞

Barb stops en route to get gas station coffee and a bagel. The coffee is surprisingly good. She finishes the bagel and wipes cream cheese from the corner of her mouth as she pulls into the driveway, wads up the plastic wrap from the bagel and tosses it onto the rear floorboard. She gets out of the car and walks past a beat-up Toyota station wagon, trundles up steep wooden steps to the front door. She knocks. A chipmunk scurries around the front corner of the house, sticking close to the concrete foundation. She knocks again. She walks around to the side of the house, but the windows are too high up for her to get a look. She goes back to her car.

She turns the ignition to roll down the windows, wishing she'd gotten more than just a bagel on the way. God. The world is full of assholes. And paperwork. That is her job: 1. deal with assholes; 2. fill out forms about dealing with assholes.

Forty minutes now she's been waiting. She picks up the clipboard from the passenger seat, makes sure she's at the correct address. The clipboard contains all the forms she'll need, if she winds up needing any, if this guy even bothers to show up. On top, the DIR— the Domestic Incident Report—the reason she's here. The Granite County Sheriff's deputies were here last night. They sent the kids home with friends and filed the report. And now she's stuck with the follow-up. She stares down at the page.

INCIDENT NARRATIVE
COMPLAINANT: EDDY HILL

Patrol responded for a reported Domestic Dispute at 21:10 hours on August 15, 2016. The caller Eddy Hill stated that a neighbor had called him on his cell phone concerned about his children because she had seen the mother in the back yard and she appeared to be smoking marijuana. Eddy Hill said he was at work, on a delivery in New Jersey, and he tried to call his children but had gotten no answer on the phone. He asked his friend Nick Thomas to go by the house and when Thomas went to the house, he and the mother got into a fight when she refused to let him in the house and demanded that he leave the premises immediately. Thomas called Hill to tell him that the ex-wife was intoxicated and wouldn't let him in the house and Hill then called the Sheriff's Office.

Upon arrival the parties were interviewed separately, and it was found that the suspect, Erin Hill, was intoxicated. Two children, Paul Hill and his twin sister Lindsey Hill, were present in the home in an upstairs bedroom. Patrol decided that given the mother's current intoxicated state, it would be best to release the children to family friends for the night. Both Paul Hill and his sister Lindsey Hill were released to friends of the family. A DIR was filed and NYS Child Abuse Hotline Registry was notified.

Barb sets the clipboard aside. She eyes the house, the woods surrounding the yard. She wonders who the mysterious neighbor might be who called this Eddy Hill and told him his wife was smoking pot in the back yard. Barb can't even see any neighboring houses. The woods are too thick this time of year, foliage everywhere. And really, what kind of snoopy neighbor does that? Was she creeping around in the woods in the dark, spying? Barb wonders momentarily if any of her neighbors have seen her and Roy sharing a joint on their back patio, which of course they don't do unless the boys are away on a sleepover somewhere. She doesn't dwell on it. It doesn't really matter, and it doesn't matter if some neighbor nearby is a restless busybody. The father called the cops, the cops filed the DIR, and now it's up to Child Protective Services—in the person of Barb Copley—to follow up. Cue the trumpets.

Barb would like to know why she's not meeting the father here, if he's the one so concerned about his kids. Why didn't he come get them last night? People are weird. People do stupid stuff every day. But really. Where the hell is dad and why is she meeting a family friend to make sure the children are not being neglected? Because Mrs. Hattelburg, that's why. So she'll meet this guy Nick. They'll check on mom, who's probably inside the house right now, sleeping it off, too zonked to answer the door. The place is decent, well kept, not like so many of the other houses she gets sent to. She's still new enough at this to be shocked at the level of poverty she encounters. Though she errs always on the side of caution, she feels like this case will require only her initial follow-up report and that will be that. A matter of minimal paperwork. Mrs. Hattelburg told her early on to be aware that some of the calls she would get would be about nothing but vengeance, one parent reporting another just to put a former spouse into the Child Protective Services system. It was one of the pitfalls of anonymous reporting. Still, she doesn't want to make any mistakes.

She'll give it another twenty minutes. It will be the first case she's handled solo where she hasn't taken the kids away, or at least she hopes it pans out that way. Already her caseload is staggering. She has dreams, or nightmares, about Domestic Incident Reports. Thousands of them, thousands and thousands, stacked into mountains and towers of paperwork forming a haphazard skyscraper made of nothing but paper, looking like something out of Dr. Seuss.

This isn't what she anticipated when she applied at the Office of Children and Family Services. She'd been thinking desk job: food stamps or medical assistance or something easy like that, but Child

Protective Services was the department with a position open. Saying no would've put her on a very long waitlist. And twenty dollars an hour was a very good starting wage in Granite County.

Finally, a pickup truck pulls up the driveway, a sleek, sparkling black Dodge Ram with tinted windows. The kind of truck her husband would drool over. A heavyset man with longish brown hair, in jeans and a golf shirt, gets out and slams the door. A kid, maybe ten or eleven, in cargo shorts and a tank top that looks like he slept in it, gets out of the passenger side. Barb can see the kid is scared. Scared and covering it with anger. She uses the car door to pull herself out of the driver's seat. She can be light on her feet, once she's on them. She's always been a good dancer, even with the weight.

The man swaggers up and plants himself in front of her, uncomfortably close. Barb dislikes him instantly.

"She still here?" His tone is weighted with authority.

"I knocked earlier." Barb asks the man for his name. The kid bolts toward the front door and lets himself in.

Barb wonders momentarily if she should have tried the door, if she would have entered had she found it unlocked. She doubts it. No sense inviting trouble.

"He lives here," the man says.

"I gathered. I need your name." Barb retrieves a pen from her bag.

"Wait a minute. I don't want to get dragged into this."

"You already are."

"Nick Thomas." He spins abruptly and walks toward the door.

Inside, Paul rushes into his mother's trashed bedroom. Barb enters just as he kneels next to the bed, his face twisted with fear. A woman lies on the floor. Passed out. Or worse.

"Mom?" Paul reaches slowly, touches his mother's shoulder. "Wake up, Mom. C'mon."

Nothing.

Paul looks up at the woman standing in his mother's bedroom. Barb presses her clipboard tight against her chest, feels something drain out of her spine.

"Mom? Mom?!" He's shaking her shoulder now, about to cry, whispering, "Mom. Wake up."

Barb stands frozen. Nick moves in, pulls Paul up by his shoulders and tucks the boy close against him, heading toward the door.

"Paul. Come on, buddy." Paul strains against him, looking back helplessly as Nick urges him toward the door. Paul shrugs loose, ducks and breaks away, yelling now, "Mom! Mom!" his face contorted, tears flowing as he lunges toward his mother's body. Nick grabs an arm and hoists Paul off his feet, carries him out, the boy's cries echoing down the hallway.

Barb cannot move, cannot breathe. She is standing in a stranger's bedroom, staring down at a woman's body, possibly a dead body, sprawled on the floor like a carelessly tossed rag doll. An empty vodka bottle lies on its side near the woman's hand, an empty pill bottle tossed not far from it.

She knows CPR; that was part of the ludicrous bit of training she'd gotten before they printed her badge-embossed business cards and sent her out on her first solo case. She's still a trainee. It says so right on her card. Child Protective Services, Caseworker Trainee.

Still holding her breath, she sees, finally, the barely visible rise and fall of the woman's chest, and the slightest bit of pulse under the skin of the woman's neck. She takes out her cell phone and dials her office. The call drops before connecting. In the clutter surrounding her, Barb finally spots a landline on a small corner desk, half buried under papers. As she picks it up and dials, she notices a bright blue paper sticking out from the mounds of white paperwork on the desktop. She picks it up.

It's a foreclosure notice.

Barb stares at the woman on the floor and listens to the phone ring and feels a brief flash of gratitude. Even though this job sucks, at least she's got a steady paycheck.

When the call finally connects, she tells Mrs. Hattelburg the mother is unconscious on the floor.

"Unconscious?!" Mrs. Hattelburg's voice hits Barb's ear like a chicken squawk and she jerks the headset away. Mrs. Hattelburg screeches again, her voice blasting from the earpiece. "Call an ambulance! Wait! Never mind. Just stand there and do nothing. I'll call the goddamn ambulance!"

FOUR

Hands grasp Erin's arms. She is pulled to her feet. Suddenly upright, she teeters shakily, unable to balance, unable to fully control her limbs.

"Let's go now. Up up up! Someone is here to see you."

The hands urge her forward, gliding her across the floor. She floats across something that feels like water to a place that seems far away. The hands take her across the never-ending hospital room, toward a small oak-veneer desk. Later, Erin will recall her return to consciousness as the feeling that she had been dragged back from existing as nothing more than a volatile crumb of carbon—a lingering awareness floating at the dark edge of oblivion—not to a hell comprising nine circles, but to a maze with no exit.

Approaching the desk, she sees a woman's face, plain and chubby. The skin on the face is coated in some kind of oily base, dusted with pale powder. The cheeks are streaked with an odd shade of pink blush that pulls the pores of the skin into stark relief. The face is framed by straight hair, not natural blond but that platinum color that is neither blond nor brown, neither silver nor gray.

The face tilts to one side and the entire room leans with it as the floor slides beneath Erin's paper-slippered feet. She staggers; her arms flail, bending in the air like thick whips. She does not fall down.

"Easy now." The nurse's voice comes from behind her, the nurse's hands guide her into a seat. "There we go." Puffs of air squish from the nurse's shoes as she walks toward the blinding doorway and disappears into the light.

"Mrs. Hill? I'm Mrs. Copley." The face belongs to a woman holding out a business card. "Department of Social Services." Erin sees something embossed and badge-shaped on the card before she folds her hands over it. Her hands are back. She can see her fingers.

"First, your kids are okay."

The words slap Erin, knocking her sodden brain into a whirl, thoughts and memory spinning in tight furious circles of utter confusion. Lindsey. Paul. Her heart thumps wildly; her entire body floods with heat and panic.

Her children.

What has she done? The enormity of it crashes over her, a huge wave of dread and remorse washing in cold, solidifying instantly. Her children. She is stuck in a freeze-frame. She does not know where she is. She does not know where *they* are. She does not know how she got here. She has to get to them. Now.

Suddenly she is standing in a corner of the room, observing herself—a young mother in blue paper hospital scrubs facing an overly-made up platinum-haired woman in a long floral printed skirt. The woman is talking.

Just as suddenly Erin is back in the chair and facing the woman, unable to breathe as the immensity of her action, the sheer unmitigated thoughtlessness of it, consumes her. She has to get out of here. Immediately. Where are her clothes?

The faux oak closet is locked. Erin rattles the door helplessly. The other Erin is still at the desk, dazed, frozen. There are two of her and she doesn't know which one is real. But what is very real is that she needs out of here and to do that she needs her clothes because *she has to get to her children.*

"Mrs. Hill, please come back here and sit down." The woman directs her comment at the ceiling. Erin follows her gaze. No one is up there.

Erin slams a hand against the closet, jiggles the handles frantically.

"Mrs. Hill? I need you to sit down." The woman's tone smells malicious, its threatening odor seeps into Erin's nostrils. She snorts, trying to clear the scent. "Seriously," the woman says.

Erin finds herself seated once again at the desk, helpless. She is a ghost, still hovering in deep space, in the place they pulled her out of after dressing her in these blue paper scrubs.

Barb Copley retrieves her clipboard from her bag, observing the contortions of panic on Erin's face. They should think about consequences, these mothers. They all seem so stunned, so surprised when the state steps into their lives. It's as if they have no understanding that choices matter, behavior has consequences.

Erin tries to calculate the distance to the door, but it's impossible. The target keeps moving, one moment seeming close enough to touch and then magically retracting until it appears almost minuscule.

Her children are not okay. Her children cannot possibly be okay. She has failed them and now she is locked in a hospital. She has failed everything. It doesn't matter how hard she tried, it doesn't matter that she had good intentions. She could not provide for them, not by herself, and their father would not help. They were always so angry, asking her why, why, why, until she reached the point where she could no longer fabricate believable lies. She could no longer console them, which left her enraged. Not at them of course—they're children. But at herself. She is stupid and pathetic. She has to make it up to them.

"Mrs. Hill?" Mrs. Copley settles her clipboard in her lap. "I'm Mrs. Copley, from Child Protective Services."

Child Protective Services? Erin tries to absorb the words. She has heard of CPS, but only in passing. She's never had occasion to pay much attention to any of that. She doesn't really know what they do. The room spins slowly, like one of those restaurants stuck atop a huge spire, a giant, slow-moving merry-go-round for adults. Her children don't need protection; she is their protector. Whenever they were frightened, she assured them she was their mama bear. And they believed her.

"I'm doing the investigation on what happened at your home." Mrs. Copley holds a pen poised above a form. "There has been a removal."

"A removal?" Erin's body fills with static, a low-voltage electric charge that runs to the tips of her toes.

"Your children have been removed."

"What does that mean? Where are they?"

"It means they've been removed from your custody. Right now it's temporary."

"Right now? Where are they? How long have I been here?" Erin breaks into a sweat. Her lungs hang in her rib cage like two sodden sponges.

"They brought you in yesterday around noon." Mrs. Copley tilts her head, as if trying to grasp a difficult math equation. "The ambulance? You don't remember?"

"Where are they? Right now. Where are they?" Erin wants to scream. She will scream until the scream itself spits her out and she's back in her house and with them, making an afterschool snack. She will scream until she wakes herself up, until all of this goes away. She sits paralyzed by the grimace on Mrs. Copley's face, a tight, knowing expression that terrifies her. She can see Mrs. Copley's heavily-painted lips moving, but the sounds seem to evaporate as they travel through the brightly-lit room, arriving broken, distorted . . . temporary emergency custody . . . your ex-husband . . . we might have to opt for foster care . . ."

Erin hears the sound of waves crashing against a rocky shoreline. Their voices come to her, the squeaky tones sounding as though they're standing right next to her, practicing Spanish. *Dónde está la playa?*

"Mrs. Hill?"

Erin blinks rapidly, trying to pull her scattershot attention back to Mrs. Copley.

"Thought I'd lost you. As I said, there will be a hearing to determine whether to continue the temporary order giving your ex-husband emergency custody or place the children in foster care."

They can't be with Eddy. Eddy walked out on them. They've barely even seen him for the past year. He doesn't even know them anymore. Erin is hit with an image of a sedan with blackwall tires, a state vehicle pulling to a curb in an unfamiliar neighborhood, and Mrs. Copley escorting her crying children to the front door of a house inhabited by strangers.

"I want you to know I'm on your side. Children need their mother. I'm a firm believer in that. But I need your cooperation. I need you to be honest with me. The Agency . . ."

What language is this? Removal? Agency? Erin's brain seizes up. She cannot think. She cannot reason.

"Mrs. Hill?"

Erin tries to look as if she understands what Mrs. Copley is saying.

"The Agency will do everything it can to reunite you with your children, that's our mandated function. Provided you cooperate."

Cooperate. Anything. Whatever they ask. Anything.

"We'll be doing a full investigation. I just want you to know that if, at any point, I find out you haven't been completely honest with me, the Agency will request a Permanency Hearing." Erin's blank expression betrays her lack of comprehension. "If the Court rules in favor of the Agency, your children will be *permanently* removed from your custody. You will be allowed no contact whatsoever. Forever."

Forever. The word hits Erin like a brick. Mrs. Copley sits back and shifts her clipboard on her lap, as if she were remarking on the weather or complaining about traffic. "You won't be allowed to have so much as a school picture."

"Forever? Until I die?" Erin is crystallized by fear. One tiny tap, one flick of an index finger, and she will shatter.

"Yes. Well." Barb is tempted to comment on the reason Erin is hospitalized, wondering briefly if the situation is ironic, but holds her tongue. She's always had difficulty grasping the difference between irony and sarcasm. "It's a lot to take in, I know."

Erin feels warm liquid draining from her nostrils. She reaches toward it.

"Wait." Mrs. Copley plucks a tissue from a box on the desk and offers it.

When Erin takes it from her face, the clean white tissue is stained with blood. She presses it back into place and holds it there. That is when she realizes that none of this is happening. She is still at home, in her bed. Her children are in their rooms sleeping. This is only her mind playing its twisted games: sins of the past. She will wake up at some point and deal with the hangover.

But Mrs. Copley keeps talking.

"My mandate is to look out for your children's best interests. To make sure they are properly taken care of until things can be resolved. I'm sure that's what you want, too."

Erin removes the tissue. The blood is real.

Again she presses the tissue to her face. She does not want to stammer. She used to stammer, for months after she came home. Her tongue would break off the front part of the word she was trying to say and spit it out again and again, always more pieces of the same sound, over and over, until her mouth could finally get the last piece out and the rest of the word would follow. Sometimes it still happens.

The pressure against her skull takes all the weight out of her head, makes it feel as if the thoughts clotted inside might float out and disintegrate. She needs to go to her children. To explain. They have to know how much she loves them, how sorry she is. She stares at the tissue, splotched generously, like some remnant of a discarded Rorschach test printed in glorious Technicolor red.

"I have to be somewhere by noon." Mrs. Copley checks her watch. "I don't have time to explain the entire procedure right this minute but I need you to sign some forms."

Her words gush forth in an indecipherable stream. The roar that had been so hushed when Erin first returned to consciousness grows louder—louder and louder—until it drowns the words. Erin tries to hear, but can only see Mrs. Copley's lipsticked mouth, in close-up, as though Erin has been trained to read lips. Two thick red worms tangle into a dance, right where Mrs. Copley's mouth should be. Mrs. Copley talks and talks and talks, but still Erin cannot hear. She watches the nightcrawlers dance and tries not to cringe.

Erin feels a vibration in her throat. Her voice makes sounds.

Mrs. Copley eyes her through spider leg eyelashes, thick with black mascara. The lipstick worms coil into a perfect O before curling into a polite smile. Mrs. Copley begins asking questions; she writes on her form on the clipboard in her lap. Erin presumes from the caseworker's sympathetic nods that she is responding appropriately.

Mrs. Copley says please call me Barb. Mrs. Copley says cooperate fully. She says it several times. Mrs. Copley says she can help, she wants to help, but to do that she needs Erin to be honest. She keeps saying that. Be honest. Be honest. Be honest.

"I need to be with my children." Erin chokes. She blots at her nostrils. Blood has dried on her upper lip. She licks it and dabs with the tissue, trying to clean her skin. "I'm okay now. I need to be with them." The taste of the blood is reassuring.

"Sign here. I'll help you however I can."

Mrs. Copley puts the clipboard on the desk in front of Erin and holds out the pen. Erin takes it and signs the form. Mrs. Copley separates copies: the yellow copy from the blue one, and the green one, and the white one. She hands the yellow copy to Erin. Erin struggles to fold it. She sees their faces, hears their voices.

Mommy? Mommy?

Her stomach is gone; her lungs have disappeared, and where her heart is supposed to be there is only a small quivering animal, thumping spastically against the thick wire mesh walls of the trap in which it is caught.

FIVE

Fatima stands in the lending section of the library, surrounded by thousands of dusty, randomly shelved books. She's not looking for a specific title; she's waiting for something to speak to her. She's *browsing*. She likes that word, enjoys the connotation of leisure that drifts from it as she says it quietly to Bashir. A head taller than her, with deep blue-green eyes, he raises his eyebrows and gives a hint of a grin to acknowledge her use of a new word.

"I remember this one." He pulls a ragged-edged, jacketless hardcover from the bookshelves in front of them and offers it to her: *Popular Proverbs & Sayings.*

Fatima takes the book.

"Over 1,500 sayings." Bashir speaks easily in English, the language having become second nature for him. "You might find it useful." Fatima understands enough of what he says to make sense of it. She's intent on learning to speak it as well as he does. When no one else is around, Bashir practices with her, helps her with correct pronunciations and syntax.

They are quiet friends, secret friends, as they must be. Whenever anyone comes into the lending area they quickly separate, moving down the rows of books as if they don't even know one another. Sometimes Fatima wishes Bashir were not so handsome, wishes she could run a hand through the thick, dark brown hair that falls in a gentle wave across his forehead. But attractive as he is, that's not why

28

she comes to the Kabul Public library every Wednesday. She is there to learn.

The sudden sound of footsteps at the end of the aisle startles them, and Fatima sees fear cross Bashir's face as he moves quickly away from her and grabs another book, cracking it open and pretending to read, glancing covertly from the pages to see who's approaching.

When Fatima realizes the two young men marching down the aisle are her brothers, she's at first relieved but quickly grows alarmed—she can't imagine how they would know to find her here and why they have bothered to track her down. Their grim looks deepen her unease. Has someone died?

They don't say anything. The older one takes the book and chucks it at Bashir, who fumbles it almost comically before pulling it to his chest, watching silently as Fatima's brother takes her firmly by one arm and wheels her toward the exit. The younger one takes her other arm and together they drag her down the aisle and out of the loaning section, leaving Bashir staring after them, clutching the book of proverbs and hoping Fatima doesn't get beaten. Or worse. He has not heard good things about her father and brothers.

On the street outside the library, surrounded by the noise of traffic and assaulted with afternoon heat, Fatima listens stoically as her brothers interrogate her, asking her when she was planning to leave and where she and Bashir thought they would run to.

"Nowhere," she says. "This is crazy. Whoever told you that is lying." She tries to explain that Bashir is not the reason she goes to the library, but they cannot hear her over all their sputtering about honor. Who does she think she is to bring this kind of shame on her family? Does she have no morals?

They locate a police officer, a puffy-faced man in his mid-thirties whose uniform is growing too tight for comfort. He looks like he's already had a long day. He listens to Fatima's brothers and, on their word, arrests her for *zina*—a moral crime. He takes her to jail.

Sometime later—Fatima does not know how many days pass—she stands before a judge. He tells her he's doing her a favor by sending her to prison. If he lets her go free, her father will surely kill her.

SIX

_____

The fuselage is crammed with soldiers. Rows of five seats run from the front of the large cargo hold to the rear, where an open-top wooden crate is piled high with the troops' overstuffed duffle bags. Every seat holds a soldier. More troops fill the side-facing seats that line either wall of the fuselage from front to rear. Erin was lucky enough to get an aisle seat. Next to her, Candice sleeps, her M4 resting against her thigh, barrel down. Like Erin, Candice joined the reserves to make some extra cash. A single-mother receptionist at a dentist's office on Long Island, Candice has a quick laugh that reveals impeccable teeth. She likes to have fun. She's also savvy enough to know that she should rest as much as possible on this flight. Erin closes her eyes, but all she can see is her children's faces.

When Erin had stopped at the hospital to say goodbye to her father before reporting for deployment, he tried to talk her into heading across the border. Lying in bed waiting for a liver, he looked at her with his sad blue eyes, the whites tainted yellow by disease. "You're too pretty to go to war," he said. She wondered what he would have become if he hadn't managed to duck the draft. Not that she faulted him. She didn't know much about what happened in Vietnam, but it sounded like a disaster. She wanted to tell him that she hadn't joined the reserves to spread democracy. You can't spread something that's already in the throes of suffocation, unable to breathe beneath the weight of all that money. He looked weak and tired. She told him she loved him and got out of there, wondering if he would make it for six entire months. That was the moment reality hit: she was going to war.

The troops boarded the plane right after the ceremony, which took place in a huge hangar, large enough to hold a couple of C-130s and then some. Erin sat in a sea of camouflage before commanders lined up on a portable plywood stage, a massive American flag splayed on the wall behind them. She searched the bleachers framing the hangar, row upon row of gathered family members, masking their fear with patriotism. Tanya had promised she would be there. She'd said she would bring Lindsey and Paul.

Erin searched for their faces and tried not to listen to the angry voice in her brain berating her for her idiocy, for her impulsivity. The only excuse she could come up with was desperation, which wasn't actually an excuse, only an observation. She'd been doing what she was supposed to do that day, one of the zillion things mothers are responsible for: shopping for school clothes. Considering her state of mind, it was a miracle she'd even managed to get out of the house. The Goodwill store was a long shot for locating clothes the twins wouldn't be ashamed to wear, but she always started there.

The roar of the powerful engines leaks through the disposable earplugs the troops were issued upon boarding the plane. The cabin is uninsulated; the noise level necessitates Army-mandated ear protection. Erin pushes and twists the foam buttons, tries to reassure herself that Lindsey and Paul will be fine.

Unable to find more than a few pairs of jeans in the kids' sections, she'd paid quickly and walked out of Goodwill, picturing the bills piled high on the desk at home. She hoped her car would start. She hoped that when she got home Eddy would not be there. The night before, he'd rolled in at two in the morning, drunk and muttering something about a metaphysical encounter with a deer standing in the middle of the road. "It *saw* me," he said. "It was like a mystical exchange, like it was delivering a message." He sprawled on the couch. "We *communicated*."

Erin followed him to the couch, trying to remember the last time she and Eddy had actually communicated. She hadn't planned for it to be that night. She'd known it was coming, and probably Eddy did too, but she had no plan. It was as if something external took over her brain and made her say the words, at last, out loud.

"Eddy." She didn't sit down. "I want a divorce." He yawned and stretched out on the couch, turning his back to her and settling in silently. She went back to the bedroom alone. She managed to doze in snippets, never falling fully into slumber. Deer sleep that way, rarely for more than a half hour at a time, often with their eyes open, ever alert for predators.

The C-17 powers through the sky, buffeted by occasional crosswinds. Erin forces her eyelids to stay closed, though sleep is out of the question. They're still hours away from their destination.

The Armed Forces Recruiting Center was located a few hundred steps from the Goodwill Thrift Shop, conveniently close to the poverty shopping experience. Exhausted from the sleepless night, angry that she had to scrape change from her wallet to pay for the jeans, Erin stared at the posters taped to the windows of the storefront. It looked almost like a travel agency. But vacations are for people with full-time, benefit-bearing jobs, like the one she'd taken at IBM when she returned home after college. The one she'd lost, along with thousands of other employees in and around Granite County who found themselves instantly jobless when the corporation, with little warning, closed its plant. The entire county, and several contiguous counties, were devastated. Erin had been fortunate, to a degree. She found a position teaching English as an adjunct at Granite Community College, though the job came about only through lucky timing. She'd showed up in person, résumé in hand, the week before the English Department Chair was leaving for an extended trip to Mexico. His technical writing teacher had quit just that morning and would not be returning in the fall; the Chair wanted to fill the position quickly, before he left the country. He handed her a textbook and asked if she could teach it. She thumbed through it and said yes. She got the job. But the job didn't pay. When you added up the hours logged working, she could probably make more flipping burgers.

She unlocked her car and tossed the Goodwill bag onto the seat, still gazing at the recruiting office storefront. Last night had shaken her badly. She and Eddy were no longer friends, no longer confidants. Increasingly, she'd found herself drinking more than she wanted to, late at night, grading papers after tucking Lindsey and Paul in and assuring them that Daddy was working and they would see him in the morning. She couldn't see a way forward.

Standing there in the parking lot, gazing at the posters in the recruiting office windows, she decided she owed it to herself and her children to at least check it out. The marriage seemed doomed and her job didn't pay enough for even the basic necessities of life. She never knew from one semester to the next whether she'd be offered a course, or three if she was lucky. Three was the limit; as long as adjuncts taught fewer than twelve credits per semester, the organization wasn't required to offer them health insurance, and adjuncts were the bulk of the institution's academic employees.

The Army recruiter made it sound like joining the Reserves was just the ticket for someone in Erin's situation: a chance to make some badly needed extra income, a chance to enhance her skill set and increase her job prospects. The odds of ever being deployed were extremely low. The Army was pulling out of Afghanistan. All equipment had to be out by the end of next year and the only troops remaining after that would be advisors. After completing basic and advanced training—paid training—Erin would probably just spend one weekend a month on a nearby base. She would most likely never even leave the US. It was a two-year contract, and a regular paycheck, for working one weekend a month.

Erin had never been super patriotic. She was tired of the stack of bills on the desk. She was tired of rice and beans for dinner. Even after last night, she held on to a vague hope that the man she married was still there somewhere, buried beneath the anger and indifference that seemed to have consumed him since he lost his job. More than anything she wanted to work things out for Lindsey and Paul, and she hoped maybe Eddy would appreciate her more if he experienced what it was like not to have her around, even if it was only one weekend a month. And if he didn't, if the relationship continued its downward trajectory, then at least she was doing something, taking an action.

She heard what she wanted to hear from the recruiter and let the rest slip past her like a cooling breeze on a summer afternoon, the kind that goes unnoticed until it dissipates silently and the heat from the midday sun once again bears down. Erin did not stop to consider that she might be sent off to a war zone. War was not real to her, and denial had always been her go-to. As she was signing the papers, a young guy who looked about fourteen walked in and announced to the recruiter that if the Army would provide dental services, he was ready to join. He'd grown up leaky-roof poor, and his teeth were starting to fall out.

When Erin arrived home that evening with the plastic bag of jeans from the Goodwill store and her signed-and-dated enlistment paperwork, Eddy blew up. He told her she was out of her mind. She explained that she was trying to keep enough money coming in. He wanted to know what the hell was he supposed to do while she was away at basic training. Ten weeks? And there's even more training after that? The twins had taken to their rooms, as they did whenever the fighting erupted. Erin had gotten good at stepping back, leaving the room, walking away from Eddy's anger and going silent, sometimes for days. Though they never spoke about it, both of them knew that, worst case scenario, there would be a time when the twins would be grown and the marriage could be dissolved without breaking their children's home.

Eddy's work situation didn't improve drastically, but he found odd jobs and picked up sporadic construction gigs here and there. Except for his late nights, which continued unabated, things were manageable. In addition to her one-weekend-a-month Reservist obligation, Erin worked at a landscaping company in the summer months, pulling weeds and digging holes and planting flowers at the stately second homes of weekenders who lived a few hours south, mostly in Manhattan or Brooklyn. She continued to teach what courses she could get at the college though, hour for hour, that job paid less than the landscaping gig. Since the plant closures, there simply weren't enough jobs to go around in Granite County and, short of taking a crowbar and prying one of the professors from his desk, Erin had no shot at a permanent teaching position. Enrollment was down, state funding was down, everything, but everything, was down, down, down.

She told herself it would work out, though the dismal day-in-and-day-out of marriage to a man who no longer seemed to want anything from her but childcare left her feeling heavy and disoriented, as if she were coming down with a flu.

The orders arrived almost a year and a half into her enlistment. Against all odds, her unit was called up.

The plane's ventilation system is already taxed. Packed to capacity with humans, the fuselage reeks of fear: the odor of nervous, sweaty soldiers, most of them male, mingling with the scent of metal, high-impact plastic, and the aroma of spent jet fuel.

At the deployment, a colonel who was the picture of military spit-and-polish, square-jawed and sharp-nosed with wide shoulders and flawless posture, had taken the stage to praise the troops seated before him. His voice was resonant, his words echoing off the metal walls of the cavernous hangar. Erin wondered if the Army had called him out of central casting.

"You are ready," he intoned. "You are well-trained and proficient. Physically and mentally prepared. These last six weeks have tested you, and you have made me proud." Erin couldn't focus. There was still no sign of Tanya and the twins. And no matter how the colonel waxed lyrical about readiness, she didn't feel at all ready. In spite of the deployment training, she felt she had learned just enough to get herself seriously hurt. Or worse. She tried to believe the colonel's words, but his message was lost to her as she snuck searching glances at the crowd.

"I have watched with pride as this unit coalesced into a team, ready for the task that lies ahead. Make no mistake, it is a difficult task you face. . . ."

A tiny bird swooped in through the sun-glare of the giant hangar door and perched at the edge of a steel ceiling beam just inside the building. Erin remembered discovering a robin's nest in the overgrown lilac bush at the edge of the back deck, the serene curve of the eggs resting inside, the soothing turquoise blue of them. And her sense of wonderment when she peeked over the deck rail one morning to see four golden-orange beaks resting on the edge of the nest, gaping, waiting for their mother to feed them. She'd run to get Lindsey and Paul from the teepee the three of them had built out of beech saplings and an old bedsheet. The awed looks on their faces when they saw the hatchlings had filled her with a simple joy that lasted even through a hectic dinner of burned fish sticks. A couple of weeks later, the birds disappeared, leaving the empty nest resting hidden in the large green leaves of the lilac. She assured the twins they would find another one next spring.

Finally, she spotted them: Tanya and Lindsey and Paul, the twins looking nervous and uncertain, Tanya out of place in her designer clothing and impeccable make-up. Erin's sister was beautiful, and put-together, and confident. Seeing Lindsey and Paul sitting next to their aunt, Erin wished she'd been able to talk Eddy into letting them stay with Tanya during the deployment. She'd thought he was considering it, but in the end he'd refused to agree. It seemed to Erin, as the months of his unemployment mounted, that he couldn't bring himself to do anything that might make her happy. Increasingly, she found it difficult to remain sympathetic to his situation. Her husband had let the world win: he had become a total dick.

The bird dropped from the beam, free-falling until it lifted its wings and caught air, sailing out into the sunshine. Erin watched it go as she snapped to attention with the gathered troops to receive the chaplain's blessing. The band played a stirring military tune that she had never heard.

The troops were released for one last visit with family before loading onto the bus that would take them to the plane. Erin made her way through the milling families. When she reached them, Lindsey and Paul looked up at her and the fear in their eyes almost buckled her knees. Those adorable faces. Lindsey's lop-sided glasses. Paul's attempt at a wink.

Nearby, Candice was laughing and kidding around with her nine-year-old son as if she would be back in a few hours. Erin envied her confidence. She pulled Lindsey and Paul close, squeezing until Lindsey said, "Mommy, that's too tight." Erin released her, smiling in spite of the tears leaking out of her eyes.

"Hey," she said, trying to sound light, "I'll call as soon as I can. Be good for Aunt Tanya, and be good for your dad, and be good at school."

"When are you coming back?" Paul tugged hard at his trimmed brown hair and struggled not to cry.

"Right after New Year's." Erin hugged them again. "Easy peasy. I'll be back before you know it."

"Mom?" Lindsey steps back to look her in the face. "Promise you'll be careful. Okay? Promise?"

Erin held out her pinkie and Lindsey looped her little finger into it. "I absolutely positively totally and completely promise. I will be very, very careful." Erin squeezed them both once more and stood to hug Tanya, whispering, "I fucked this one up good, didn't I?"

Tanya pulled Erin close, into the aroma of her perfume.

"What are you wearing?"

Tanya laughed sadly. "Flowerbomb. Maybe I should send you a bottle?"

"No need. The Army's providing weapons." They giggled nervously and said "I love you" at exactly the same moment, but neither of them dared to call jinx. Tanya took the twins' hands, Paul on one side and Lindsey on the other, and led them to join the crowd of families moving toward the hangar doors, where they watched Erin march past in troop formation, out through the doors, and into the hazy glare of someone else's world.

A prod in her ribs yanks Erin from sleep and there is Candice, smirking furtively. Sergeant Drake stands at the head of one aisle taking stock of the troops, an impassive mask on his tanned face, his pale blue eyes scanning the rows of soldiers.

Candice leans in close to Erin's left ear. Erin loosens an earplug.

"Look at him," Candice says. "Is it just me, or does he seem nervous?"

Drake, wiry and unpredictable, keeps his blond hair high and tight, and likes to remind his troops, when they are sweaty and exhausted, that his Patronus is the jaguar. Erin looks, but doesn't see anything unusual in his demeanor. During training, there were days when he was encouraging and helpful, and other times when he seemed to despise the entire world and take his loathing out on the unit. All Erin knows right now is that whatever the man says to do, she will do and do it fast and do as good a job of it as she can. He's pulled two tours, one in Iraq and one in Afghanistan. The fact that he's survived makes her want to trust that, mood swings and all, Drake knows what he's doing.

"Where are the flight attendants?" Candice says, again leaning in, "I want some peanuts."

"I want a vodka tonic." Erin chuckles, not because anything's funny but because she appreciates Candice trying to lighten things. If Candice is scared, she's doing a great job of hiding it.

Candice nudges her and Erin sees Sergeant Drake watching them, an amused grin on his face. He turns his attention to the Air Force crew members manning the cabin, who are standing up now, pulling flak jackets on over their flight suits, buckling on helmets, adjusting their mics. Sergeant Drake pulls his helmet on and makes sure the troops follow suit. They're entering a combat zone. Drake walks the aisles to make sure the soldiers are helmeted before returning to post himself at the head of one aisle, eyeing the troops expectantly, a grin playing at his mouth. He slips into his seat and buckles in.

And then the lights go out, plunging the cabin into infrared darkness. The C-17 flares into a descent and nosedives so hard that Erin has to brace herself against the seat back in front of her to keep her head from slamming into it. Candice stifles a shout, grabs Erin's arm but quickly lets go to slap her own hand against the seat in front of her, pushing against the suck of gravity. Erin keeps one arm flexed against the seatback; with her other hand she grips the butt end of her rifle. The adrenaline surging into her bloodstream prickles and burns.

Even through the earplugs she hears the roar of straining engines as a lone helmet skids past her ankle from somewhere behind her, tumbling down the steeply inclined aisle until it bounces off the front cabin wall. Hit by sudden vertigo, she sucks in a breath. There are no windows; it's impossible to get her bearings as the massive plane hurtles earthward.

They have barely slowed, but Erin hears the high mechanical whine of landing gear deploying. She focuses on the cockpit access stairs at the front of the fuselage, trying to get a sense of which way is up. It's not helping. She closes her eyes, but still the tilt and sway of the plane rises through her body from the seat, from the floor. Nausea spreads through her, emanating from her stomach in waves, and then just when she thinks she'll either puke or pass out, the front of the plane rises, the floor levels out, and a hard, heavy thunk jolts the fuselage as the wheels hit concrete. The C-17 settles its weight on the landing gear as they speed down the runway. Erin gasps her relief and grips her rifle tighter, rubbing a thumb over the hard plastic butt. The roar of reverse-thrusting jet engines fills the cabin as the pilot slams on the brakes, rocking the soldiers forward in their seats as though they are davening, bowing in prayer to a higher power.

The feel of wheels rolling across solid earth knocks most of the vertigo out of Erin and she gulps her relief. The plane comes to a stop. The lights come on.

No one says a word. Relief at landing in one piece mingles with fear of where they have landed, of what might be waiting for them outside the aircraft. From somewhere in the rows behind her, Erin hears soldiers being sick. Until this flight, some of them had never even been on a plane.

Sergeant Drake jumps up quickly and faces the troops, that same bemused expression on his face. "Secure your weapons and basic load!" he commands. Then, sounding almost friendly, "Welcome to J-Bad!"

SEVEN

S he is not having a heart attack. She is not losing her mind.

"Please, God, not now." Tanya says the words slowly, quietly, using everything she's got to keep her throat from seizing up. She inhales, counting to six. Exhales, counting to four.

"You are fine," she says, again out loud. She reaches into the open drawer of her antique walnut dresser and plucks a pair of socks from the impeccably neat rows that fill it. Each pair is carefully rolled, the rows organized according to fabric and hue.

She purses her lips and breathes very slowly, focusing on the breaths instead of on her out-of-control heart, which feels as if it is beating to the rhythm of galloping stallions. She grips the pair of socks, holds it against her chest as though preparing to execute a Heimlich on herself—or maybe commit hara-kiri. Shit. She can't even laugh at her own joke.

She concentrates on the rise and fall of her rib cage. Her palms feel sweaty; she squeezes the socks tighter.

It's a panic attack. She knows this.

It's only a panic attack.

Only.

"This too, shall pass." She enunciates each syllable. Her throat goes tighter.

She bows her head and whispers, "Hail Mary full of grace, blessed art thou amongst women, and blessed is the fruit of thy womb. . . ."

By the time she finishes the prayer, the clock on the dresser shows that seven digital minutes have been eaten away. Time warp. She prayed the short prayer, the less-than-a-minute-long prayer. She doesn't recall what she thought about after that. *Blessed is the fruit of thy womb.* One day after Mass, when they were still young enough that none of it made any sense, she and Erin had dissected the prayer, arguing over what exactly the fruit of the womb was. Erin said pears, but Tanya had been certain it was peaches. They agreed that it couldn't be apples, because that one had been used in the Garden of Eden story. She realizes with alarm—but no longer panic, thank God—that her Estimated Time of Departure is now. She has to leave her home. She has to go to the airport.

There is an obscene number of socks in the open dresser drawer. Tanya has enough socks—and belts and shoes and jackets and dresses and earrings and bracelets and necklaces and all the rest of it—to wear a different outfit to work every day of the week for several months on end. She doesn't wear outfits to work. She wears a uniform.

She remembers vividly her mother's predictable dinner admonition from so long ago, when she used to sit next to Erin at the kitchen bar and try to find a place to hide the impossibly huge mound of soggy peas her mom had heaped next to the Shake-n-Bake pork chops: clean your plate, people all over the world are starving.

Yes, well, you can't eat socks, and Tanya knows all about hunger. She starved herself for most of her freshman and sophomore years in high school before realizing two things: She could not save the world, and she would never again reach size 0. Not if she could help it. In her head, she talks back to her mother: People are hungry because they don't work as hard as I do. They don't earn a living because they don't try hard enough. Willpower. There's always a way.

If she is proud of anything, it's that she has always done for herself. She's worked hard and raised her son and managed to do well. She'd survived the high school pregnancy, taking night classes and falling in love with her baby when he arrived the month after she graduated—with honors. Her big mistake there had been to believe the father, to marry him and move to Texas when he got a job as a baggage handler at Renegade Airlines. It was a relief to escape the prying eyes and gossip that had seemed to follow her around Granite County, and city life agreed with her. She'd always felt constrained somehow by small town existence. But the biological father—that is how Tanya thinks of him now, because he hadn't been able to figure out how to be a real father—hadn't liked it much when Tanya went to work as a flight attendant. Four years into the marriage, when Stephen was going into pre-K, bio-dad took Tanya out to lunch to tell her he'd been having an affair with her best friend. For two years. And he wanted a divorce.

Several years later, Tanya found her soul mate, a kind and generous man who truly loved her and who accepted her love openly. Things were finally good. A late-night phone call turned it all upside down: Tanya's sweetheart had hit a bridge abutment outside of Houston, doing approximately eighty miles per hour. Zero blood alcohol. No sign of drugs. He'd apparently lost control of his car. An accident of distraction, or maybe misjudgment. Tanya had been with him for three years by then. She had never known him to exceed the speed limit. Funny how easily the entire world could change with a single, solitary loss. It had been like that when her brother was taken, too.

And now this, her sister. Why all these catastrophes, people she loved chucking them at her like emotional hand grenades? This one—this one—has sent her spiraling to the place where panic floats about her like an invisible vapor, searching for a way in, seeking one minuscule opening.

She yanks shut the zipper of her carry-on and grabs it from the bed. The Whys tumble around in her head like socks in a clothes dryer, gathering small electrical charges that glue them together with static cling until it becomes one giant ball of Why. At the bottom of the stairs, she parks the bag, composes herself and heads for her son's room.

Stephen has his headphones on, his attention on his wall-mounted flatscreen. She motions to him; he hits the controller and pulls off the headphones.

"Hey Mom."

"Time for me to go, hon."

"Okay."

"You'll feed the dogs?"

"Got it covered."

"I left a check for registration on the counter."

He runs a hand through his shaggy red hair and does the almost an eye-roll thing, but not quite blatantly enough that Tanya can be sure.

"Twelve credits. Minimum."

"Mom. I'm looking for a job."

"And you're going to register. You can't hang out and play video games for the rest of your life."

He flexes the headphones, gazes at the frozen warrior images on the TV screen.

"I've got a band. A real band with real gigs."

"Fifteen credits, preferably."

"Jesus. A full load and a band? Not gonna work."

"High school is over, Stephen. You are going to college. You're smart. Use your brain."

"My brain tells me if I do what I love, the rest will follow. You've heard me play. You know I'm good. I just need time."

"Stephen . . ."

"What the hell good is a degree, anyway, unless I want to spend my life in a cubicle, which I def do not want to do, just so I can buy a bunch of shit that I don't need and don't even really want—"

"You like your computer. You like the phone? The video games? You like your guitar, don't you? And your car? Those things cost money."

"That's all I need."

"You need gas for your car and insurance for your car, you need food, someday you'll need a house, maybe?"

"Not feeling the aesthetic, Mom, the house in the burbs, the—"

"I have to go. At least twelve credits. We'll deal with the rest of it later."

He leans in for a hug.

"Love you Mom."

"Love you too. Register. This afternoon."

"I'd like to be excluded from that narrative."

"Funny, Stephen. Very funny."

Stephen leans against his bedroom doorframe and watches his mother wheel her carry-on down the short hallway and across the spotless white tile of the kitchen floor. He waits until he hears the front door latch and lock before sitting down again. He clamps on his headset and clicks into Xbox Live—*Call of Duty: Black Ops*. That shit's savage. The host, kyotosan, is in Tokyo, where it is already 1:00 a.m. tomorrow; dingbat is on from Melbourne; zipit2 shows to be in Toronto; and there are a couple of guys from Kansas whose tags Stephen doesn't recognize. Possible noobs. Possible easy kills. Kyotosan speaks really good English, so good that he sometimes affects a Texas drawl just to jack with Stephen, but he keeps it low-key. And the bro is deadly, as in major skills at online modern warfare.

Mom's headed out of town and his room is equipped with enough electronic technology to rival Mission Control at NASA. The afternoon is *lit*.

∞

Outside, it's sweltering. Tanya stows the carryon in the back seat of her Jeep and jumps behind the wheel. Light a cig. Start ignition. Set A/C on arctic.

She pulls away from the curb on the quiet suburban Dallas street lined with homes built in the forties. She'd bought before the neighborhood became a place to be. Now couples were buying with the intent to raze their lots and erect McMansions. Tanya hadn't exactly led the charge, but she'd gone to the meetings and done her part to prevent the residential equivalent of pornography from springing up in the neighborhood. She bought here because she liked the individuality of the houses, the mature shade trees on the lawns, and because it is seventeen point five minutes, plus or minus traffic, from her door to the airport.

Barely down the street, she calls Stephen to reiterate that he has to remember to feed the dogs. The dogs are helpless. The dogs depend on her, and have since she rescued them. Yes, she'll call when she gets in. Yes, she'll call again to remind him to feed the dogs. Just out of high school, her son doesn't know which direction to go. He refused to apply to any four-year universities, insisting that he needed to live at home. Except for music, video games, cars, and girls, everything, especially school, is just plain boring. They'd compromised: he agreed to enroll at the community college a few miles away.

Tanya assures him she'll give his love to Aunt Erin. She'll call and let him know how things are. She hasn't exactly told him what's going on, only that her sister needs her.

She could drive this route in her sleep, and has done so more than once during the sixteen-plus years of her employment, many of the trips involving 4:00 a.m. check-ins. She stubs out her second cigarette, telling herself she has got to quit smoking, and soon, as she cruises toward Employee Parking.

She checks her makeup in the rear-view mirror. "Here's your airhead flight attendant, ready to smile and put up with attitudinal passengers: Another beverage, sir?" She wonders whether she can actually do this for another ten years. And what will her pension plan look like? It was looking very pretty until last year, when the stocks tanked.

Wearing khakis and a light blue Renegade Airlines sport shirt, she slips on her ID card and hurries through the metal detector at the employee check-in. Her worries must be showing on her face: the security man gives her a tight, sympathetic nod and sends her carry-on through with barely a glance at the X-ray screen.

The first flight is packed and she has to fly jump seat, taking one of the foldout crew seats bolted to the cabin wall at the rear of the plane. She passes the forty-minutes flipping through a magazine and chatting with the on-duty flight attendants. It's all she can do to hold a conversation.

Oklahoma City to St. Louis: she gets a window spot with two vacant seats next to it, spends the bulk of the fifty-five-minute flight staring out at the tops of clouds and trying not to cry.

On the leg from St. Louis to Chicago she thinks if she has to sit still another minute she'll start screaming, so she gets up and helps with the beverage service. Walking down the aisle with a trash bag, collecting the cups and peanut wrappers, she smells the collective breath of the passengers, exhalations of peanuts and alcohol. It could nauseate her. Sometimes it does. She hasn't had a drink since the night she got pregnant with Stephen and is certain she'd gag if she tried to choke down a single peanut, particularly the trademarked honey crisp kind she has served now to thousands of passengers.

During the final leg of the trip, Chicago to Albany, the sun goes down; the 737 slices through nighttime sky. In the darkened cabin, Tanya manages to doze, drifting one thin layer away from true sleep, in the zone where sounds are so intensely magnified they seem to be coming through a digital theater sound system. The constant low hum of conversation competes with the steady whine of the jet engines, pierced by occasional laughter, a fussing baby, and the staccato rattle of ice punctuated with the plastic clatter of someone spitting ice cubes, one by one, into an empty cup.

EIGHT

The bus coughs to a stop and the troops disembark, some still disoriented from the abrupt C-17 landing. Erin moves in a haze of jet lag and dust, following behind Candice as the unit trudges toward the barracks. She lugs her bag past a huge yellow excavator that claws at a long, low building, ripping and smashing, flattening a now empty barracks into a scrap heap of splintered plywood, two-by-fours, and roofing tin. The excavator pulls back noisily from the rubble of the smashed bee-hut, rolling on its huge metal treads like some giant mechanical grasshopper. A gang of soldiers in tan T-shirts moves in with claw hammers to dismember and sort the remains. The roar of an F-15 taking off erupts into the air and the newly arrived troops' heads turn in unison, watching the fighter jet arc out toward the snow-covered crowns of the Hindu Kush. The mountain peaks look fiercely jagged compared to the gentle swells of the Catskill Mountains back home.

Sweat trickles down Erin's face as the sun beats down on J-bad, the base a sprawling affair of concrete, metal, plywood, and sand. The backpack chafes at her collarbone and her socks are like sponges. The air feels like the blast of heat that would hit when she opened the door to pull out a tray of cookies but smells instead like a mixture of excrement and smoldering hair.

Inside the barracks, Candice moves fast, chucking her backpack onto the single bunk against the back wall of the tiny room and throwing herself next to it on the bare mattress.

"I hereby claim this territory for Puerto Rico!" she shouts, breaking into a laugh.

The other woman assigned to the room, a beast of an athlete with curly bright red hair, had led everyone, every time, in every PT challenge they'd gone through in training. Sergeant Drake tagged her as Original Ginj before the second day of training was done, and the name stuck. She seemed to like it.

"Coin toss?" Ginj pulls a quarter from her pocket and balances it on her thumb, tails up. Flips it.

"Tails," Erin says.

Ginj lifts her hand from the coin and pockets it without a word. Tosses her backpack onto the upper bunk, gives Erin a fierce-friendly glance as she climbs up after it.

"Okay bitches," she says. "I should have just volunteered for this shit. Y'all too old to be going up and down bunks." She unzips her backpack and starts pulling things out.

"Whatever." Candice breaks out a bottle of water, sizing up the gray-painted cinderblock walls, the small desk crammed opposite the bunk beds, the concrete floor. "Explain your bad luck any way you want."

"No such thing as bad luck." Ginj pulls a bottle of moisturizer from her backpack, examines the directions on the back of the blue plastic bottle. "I hope this stuff works. They said the water here is merciless, shit'll dry you out like a prune."

Erin sprawls on her bunk, tired and dazed, stares up at the crisscross metal mesh that holds the upper bunk mattress in place a few feet above her face. Travel fatigue presses onto her body like a full-length lead X-ray apron.

"Hey, Hill," Ginj says, leaning down over the edge of the bunk, bugging her eyes out comically. "You some kind of fucking introvert?"

"Don't be throwing shade!" Candice laughs. "She's like a professor. Teaches English, or some shit like that."

"For real?" Ginj makes her green eyes even bigger. Erin offers a weak nod, so tired she can barely move.

"Shit." Ginj cracks a grin. "I got my GED and got the hell out of high school. Anyway, I seen you on the rifle range, girl. You was flexing out there for sure."

"Beginner's luck," Erin says.

"Don't short yourself, bae." Ginj smiles, upside down, at Erin. "You can shoot. And you must at least be kinda smart."

"If I were smart, I wouldn't be here right now."

"Depends, don't it? I'm right where I wanna be." Ginj laughs and disappears from view. The bunk creaks as she settles herself to finish unpacking. To Erin, Ginj's recklessness feels dangerous. Someone has scratched a peace symbol into the black metal bunk frame holding the mattress above her bunk. She lies there listening to Ginj dig things out of her duffle, and wonders if the soldier who etched the symbol was being sarcastic, and whether she made it home alive.

NINE

Tanya steers Erin's decrepit Toyota past the St. Martin of Tours brick entry facade, recently defaced by large, ugly spray-painted red letters: TRUMP 2016. The August sun bakes cars sitting in neat rows in the freshly paved parking lot. The hospital, a massive white brick building set on a hilltop, has been enlarged and modernized with a curved glass addition that sprouts from its left side like a giant glittering angel wing, and a gleaming, round, glass and steel front entrance. The building looks new and big, nothing like Tanya remembered it. But she'd been a kid when their mom brought Erin to the emergency room for stitches after Erin gashed her knee in a bicycle fall. Their mother seemed more angry than concerned that afternoon, driving in grim silence, but she was often like that, her mood set at a low but consistent simmer, betraying a certain level of frustration even when she was smiling.

A large red-on-white sign next to the revolving front door proclaims *This is a tobacco-free campus.* Immediately, Tanya wants a cigarette. She wants a cigarette and she wants to know where Lindsey and Paul are. She wants to know why Eddy thought it was okay to send her a text that said *Erin in St. Martin psych ward thought u should know* and then ghost her. When Tanya called the hospital, the admissions coordinator was apologetic, but could only confirm Erin had been admitted. Tanya had used one of the employee flight passes she'd stashed away for a vacation to come to Erin's aid.

The door to Room 214 stands open. The window in the opposite wall reveals the purple and green peaks of the Catskills in the distance. Beneath it sits an empty bed, perfectly made-up, the corners tucked impeccably, military style. Maybe Erin is up and about.

Rounding the entry, Tanya sees another bed, near the front wall. Beneath the blanket, her sister lies motionless. Tanya wants to cry, seeing Erin in this place. Erin, the athlete, the smart one. Erin who never seemed to need anyone or anything, sailing through high school without studying, doing everything right. The basketball star, the shooting guard who could reliably arc the ball into the net for long three-pointers. Fearless Erin, the one who navigated around their father's episodes without shedding tears. Episodes. That was Erin's code word for Dad coming home from his favorite bar too drunk to make it any farther than the living room couch. And she treated their mother's indifference as though it were a ticket to freedom. Erin, in Tanya's younger-sister eyes, had always seemed invulnerable. Tanya had tried once to talk her into moving to Dallas, coming on board at Renegade Airlines, but instead Erin had fallen in love and married Eddy. And then went into that awful desert.

She thinks about calling their mother but second-guesses the impulse. Mom had been ready for a kid-free house by the time Erin and Tanya reached middle school, when their brother Daniel was a high school freshman. The second time their father went back to drinking, she had simply lost heart. It showed on her skin even, which lost its shine, taking on the dull semblance of a faded kitchen counter. She cooked her children's meals and got them where they needed to be until they were old enough to drive. They learned not to expect more than that. She worked as a secretary at a real estate agency. She did crossword puzzles and watched Jeopardy on TV. Her husband lived in a bottle, leaving her outside and alone, staring through the glass at what was left of him. She would never risk happiness again. As soon as Tanya, the youngest, was out of the house, their mother moved from Granite County, New York to Somewhere-in-Arizona to work as an administrative assistant in the office of a retirement community. She sent Christmas and birthday cards to her children, signing her name with big, looping letters.

Erin doesn't stir when Tanya sits next to her. Tanya puts a hand on her shoulder.

"Erin?" She shakes gently, taps lightly. A long, jagged sigh escapes from Erin's lips.

"Hello? Erin?" Tanya shakes harder, squeezes Erin's shoulder. "Wake up." She lets her hand slide down Erin's slim, muscular arm, feels total slackness. She lifts the wrist. In addition to the clear plastic hospital bracelet with its crimped metal fastener is a bright yellow one with red letters: fall risk. The hand hangs limp. Tanya squeezes it, pats it firmly. "Erin. Come on." Tanya brushes Erin's hair off her forehead.

Erin raises her head a few inches off the pillow, then falls back onto it, mumbling. Tanya waits patiently as, very slowly, Erin manages to roll onto one side and pull herself onto an elbow. Her face is a blank; her head wobbles, swaying to the rhythm of intoxication. Tanya leans in to hug her, holding her for a long moment before helping Erin slide into a sitting position, slumped against the headboard.

Erin battles to keep her eyes open. The room twists and warps and rolls. She recognizes Tanya and wonders if it's a hallucination. She tries to push herself upright.

"Tanya." Erin's tongue is thick in her mouth; it takes a moment for it to let go of the N and get the rest of the name out.

"Hey." Tanya doesn't like the artificial cheeriness in her voice. She tugs at a pillow to scoot it behind Erin's back, revealing a folded yellow sheet of paper on the mattress. She props Erin upright and picks up the paper.

The document header—*Granite County Department of Social Services. Child Protective Services*—makes it clear why Eddy hasn't returned her calls.

"Erin? When did you sign this?"

Erin struggles to stay awake. Her words come out slurred. "You came all the way up here?"

"Of course. Who got you to sign this?"

"Thank you, Tanya. Thank you." Erin pats around on the blanket until Tanya realizes what she's searching for and slips her hand into Erin's. "Thank you," Erin whispers.

Tanya puts the paper in Erin's hands and Erin squints at it, turning it slowly and clumsily, as though contemplating the intricate folds of an origami figure. She has a vague recollection of a woman sitting at the desk across the room, but the memory is a blur, like a low-res YouTube video flickering on a shattered phone screen. She drifts off again, sleeping sitting up.

"Erin. You have to wake up." Tanya takes the paper back and examines the signature, an illegible scribble.

"I keep not remembering." Erin's eyes open slowly. The room tilts and shimmers; she squints against the brightness. "Where am I?"

"In the hospital." Tanya feels frustration building. "I need you to wake up."

"Where are the kids?" Erin's head wobbles on the stem of her neck like an unbalanced gyroscope.

"With Eddy." Tanya holds up the paper. "This says you've agreed to it."

Erin takes in a stuttering breath, then her eyelids droop again and she slides down under the covers, falling back asleep.

Tanya feels her anger rising. She's trying to forgive her sister's utter selfishness. Because that's what it was: selfishness. Fuck the world, it's all about me, and I can't cope so I'll check out early and leave you all to deal with it. Tanya can't take the thoughts any further than that. To do so would mean admitting just how totally pissed off she is.

On her way out, she tosses the paper onto the desk, angry at whoever got Erin to sign it. Tanya has been doing drug and alcohol work for the union for years. Anyone can see that her sister is way too medicated to understand what is happening or communicate her legal intentions.

∞

In her sister's backyard, Tanya sits on a stone bench in the shade of a peach tree, holding the fruit she has just plucked and staring up at a bird she does not know the name of. Its back is brilliant blue, contrasting sharply with the pale shades of the peaches hanging from the tree. Tanya is used to buying rock hard fruit in the massive Albertson's Supermarket not far from her suburban home. The peach is close to ripe, but still too firm to eat. She remembers a summer when she and Stephen were up for a visit, how they'd picked peaches from this tree, the kids eager to bite right into the fruit, especially Stephen, who'd never even seen a real peach tree up close before and was astonished that he could pluck something edible off a tree right there in the backyard. Erin explained that the peaches needed to rest for a day or two in the big bowl on the kitchen table, where they would ripen to perfection. When he was finally allowed to eat one, Stephen had practically danced around the kitchen, juice dripping down his chin, surprised and delighted by the flavor, the texture, and the fact that he had gotten the fruit straight from the tree. It seemed miraculous.

It's beautiful out here, green and peaceful and quiet. Robins peck their way diligently across the lawn, hopping comically. The air is clear; a warm breeze flows across Tanya's arms, tickles her neck. She does not want to go back to the hospital.

Erin has all this: a home in the country, surrounded by nature, two beautiful children. Why couldn't she just get over it? She's not in Afghanistan anymore. It's done. Why can't she learn to look forward instead of backward? Tanya knows the importance of avoiding self-pity. It was Erin who had taken her out that night, to an amazing bonfire in a meadow surrounded by woods. A few kids had brought guitars and drums. Others had brought too much beer and too many bottles of harder stuff. But with a hangnail moon in the sky and the scent of wood smoke hanging on the aroma of new spring growth, the evening felt magical. She remembers seeing Erin dancing with Eddy near the bonfire as she was led to the edge of the meadow, an arm around her waist. Among the partiers was a guy who'd graduated the year before, who had no issues with luring a drunken junior into the woods and refusing to stop even when Tanya realized through the haze that she was on her back, pinned to the ground, her jeans shoved down to her knees and him on top of her, thrusting hard and heavy, grunting obscenely, "God, I love you." What were the chances? What were the chances that Tanya, who before that night had never had more than a sip or two of beer, fearing it because of her father's repeated downfalls, would fall prey to the drunken lust of a boy she barely knew? What were the chances that one seriously nonconsensual sexual encounter would end with pregnancy?

Tanya turns the peach in her fingers, examining, appreciating. It is gold and yellow and orange, almost red in places, as though it is blushing. The chances were excellent. One hundred percent possibility. The accidental encounter, because that's what it was—an encounter, a small and dirty *incident*—had altered the course of her life. It had taken her into motherhood and marriage, and how totally fucked up was that, to marry the guy who loved her so much that he had fucked her while she was too drunk to consent. But Tanya refused to let herself be his victim; she adjusted her recollection of the event to one that she could live with. They'd both been drunk, they'd both lost control and, together, they would raise the child who had been conceived that night. What kind of idiotic thinking had that been? But through it all, Tanya had never once said *oh poor me, how could this happen to me*. When the baby arrived, her fears of doomed motherhood fell away, and she was in love instantly.

She rubs a thumb across the soft, fuzzy peach skin. *You are what you eat.* You are what you believe. You are what you do. But she doesn't know what to do, and her uncertainty gnaws at her like some kind of rodent working away at an exposed tree root. Helplessness is not a situation Tanya handles well. She's a woman who does everything in her power to hold on tight, control her life, take actions that lead to positive results. And she needs to get a grip right now, before the damage is critical. If she allows it to persist, it will lead to panic. It will lead to not being able to breathe.

She picks up her phone and shoots a text to Stephen: *Dogs okay? Sprinkler system working? Miss you. Love ya.* She is determined not to bug him about school while she's away. He'll still be able to register when she gets back, but she wants him to take responsibility. She scrolls through her texts, her emails. Still no response from Eddy. She can understand if he's mad at Erin, she's mad at Erin too, but really, he doesn't have to be a jerk about it. She's their aunt.

She dials his number, expecting yet another invitation to leave a message.

"What's up?" The edge in Eddy's voice startles her. She wishes she'd blocked her caller ID.

"Erin's okay." Tanya gives him a moment to respond. "I thought you'd want to know."

"I'm busy, Tanya. What do you want?"

"I'd like to talk to the kids."

"They're not here." Eddy explains that they're on a play date. He assures her they're okay. Tanya asks for his address. He says he took a place in Leverton but doesn't offer a street or number. It's a half-hour away. Tanya suggests that she drive over that evening, but Eddy says that isn't good.

"So when's good? Eddy, I just want to see them."

Silence.

"Eddy?" Nothing. Tanya eyes her phone. *Call ended.*

"Prick." She says it into the phone, as if he's still receiving a signal.

The bluebird in the peach tree launches itself skyward, the force of its departure bending the slender shoot it was perched on sharply downward. The bird sails toward the woods as the branch whips up and down rapidly, its arc diminishing with each recoil as though it is reluctantly waving goodbye.

Tanya pockets her phone and heads indoors, wondering if she and Erin had inherited from their mother some kind of genetic predisposition to marry dickheads.

TEN

The scream of a departing fighter jet roars overhead as Erin spoons Rice Krispies from a single serving cup filled with luke-warm milk that has quickly turned the Krispies into mush. She huddles in the shade of her M35A3, a two-and-a-half-ton cargo truck that can churn across the beat-up Afghanistan roadways carrying ten thousand pounds of whatever the Army loads onto it. Erin's heard stories of the trucks carrying twice that weight. It's a monster.

The unit has been on stand-by since just after midnight. After sleeping part of the night in the front seat of the truck, Erin was released with the rest of the unit to catch a quick nap in the barracks, but they were called back out shortly after sunrise. Drake is in one of his moods, striding around and poking into everyone's business, and Erin is doing her best to stay out of his way, trying to hide next to her truck.

Ginj appears out of nowhere and plops down cross-legged next to her, resting her rifle across her thighs. Erin noticed early on that Ginj seems to have the ability to make herself almost invisible, able to dodge around and disappear at will.

"God, I wish we could just go already."

"It's a lot safer here than outside the wire."

"That's my point. I wanna get out there." Ginj peels the wrapper off a protein bar. "And I miss my dog."

"Don't you want to go home to her?"

"Fuck it, I could be home right now and my house blows up from a gas leak."

"I'm betting there's not a war going on in your neighborhood."

"Don't be so sure. Anyway. I don't want to spend my time sitting around on the base. Let's hit the road already, is what I say." Ginj picks up a handful of gravel and pokes through it as if she's looking for precious ore. "What are you gonna be for the Halloween contest?"

"Nothing."

"You could be a judge then."

"And vote for you?"

Ginj grins, nods emphatically.

"Testing my ethics? Who are you going as?"

"Maybe Raven."

"From *X-Men*?" Erin slurps another spoonful of lukewarm cereal.

"She can metamorphize, like change herself into other creatures. Plus she's blue."

"Metamorphose."

"I bet you're a hard grader." Ginj chuckles.

"It's the worst part of teaching."

"Unless you're a sadist, which, in my humble opinion, a lot of teachers are."

"You know what they say. The rich get educated. The poor get tested." More than once Erin has considered pulling Lindsey and Paul out of school, joining the homeschool scene. She wonders what costumes they'll concoct for Halloween, whether Eddy will get into the spirit. The physical distance between her and her children leaves her unsettled and restless, wondering almost constantly where they are, what they're doing, feeling the ghostly tug of the umbilical cord. "I think my kids like Halloween even more than Christmas."

"I know I do." Ginj wads up the protein bar wrapper. "I hope the party's good. I'm bored as shit."

"In this place? Boredom is a gift."

60

"It's like, I pictured like people getting shot and helicopters and bombs and all that, but I kind of somehow thought it would all be happening at once. And sorta constantly, you know?"

Erin shakes her head, going after a single remaining piece of puffed rice stuck to the side of the white plastic cup. "Like a video game."

"Yeah, kinda, I guess. Now that I'm here the whole thing seems kind of stupid."

Erin nods. Every morning when she wakes up in her bunk, she's hit again fresh with the realization that she hasn't shown much ability to function in the world. She's missing something; she just doesn't get it. What good are book-smarts if you can't navigate life? And how else could she have gotten herself here?

"Maybe you could fake some kind of psychological problem. Get discharged. Sent home." Erin is thinking it wouldn't be a big stretch and, even if it were, Ginj strikes her as one of those people who knows how to get one over on the earnest and unsuspecting fools of the world. Like herself, for instance.

"Hells no, I'm still down with being here. It's not like a bunch of cool shit was happening in my world. But seriously, it's like what if, all of a sudden, some fucking army from another country shows up in your hometown and starts like blowing shit up? Wouldn't you be pissed?"

"Ginj. It's tribal. They've been fighting since forever."

"It's all just weird, not like I thought it would be. I think I'm home-sick or something."

"I know I am."

"I thought it would be more exciting."

"Let's just try to get home safe."

"That's not what I'm saying. I wanted to get in the mix. I just like, literally can't even."

"Can't even what?"

"That's all. I just can't even." Ginj scrapes up another handful of gravel, picks through it. "It's confusing as fuck."

"My brother was killed in the towers."

"Damn."

"One minute he's settling in at his desk for another day at work and the next. . . ."

"See? Ain't no hiding." Ginj throws a fistful of gravel at the dirt. "It's random, sister, totally fucking random, and right now I just want to get outside the wire, where something might actually happen."

ELEVEN

The mountains aren't real. The gentle rolling swells of blue-green push against a backdrop of pale blue sky, framed by dark brown aluminum window molding. Erin touches the cool glass in an attempt to confirm that the view is not merely a digital image, a computer screensaver.

The sound of footsteps at the doorway startles her. The man standing there is tall and slender, with reddish-brown skin and sharp features. From India maybe, or Pakistan.

"I'm Doctor Patanjali," he says. "It's good you're up and about."

"I need to go home." Erin tries to walk steadily across the room, wishing she had said hello instead of blurting out her panicked desire to escape the hospital.

"I'm sure you do, and that's good, but we have to make sure you're well enough."

Erin tries to conceal the fact that she's shivering. It's unbearably cold in the room.

"You very nearly succeeded in taking your life." The doctor tilts his head and looks at her sideways.

"I was overwhelmed." Erin fidgets with the yellow bracelet on her wrist. She stops when she sees the doctor watching. "I handled it badly."

"That, I think, is an understatement. I cannot simply let you walk out of here."

"But I'm okay. This isn't where I need to be."

63

"Not forever, no. But we have to wait and see. You were overseas?"

"Please. I should be home. For my children."

"You are not suicidal?"

"Not at all."

"You are telling me this, but I think maybe you're not so okay. You tried to kill yourself. The next time you might not be so lucky."

"There won't be a next time, I promise. I lost it, okay? It's over."

"You've seen someone, before, for the PTSD? For the alcoholism?"

"I had a year. A whole year of sobriety. I lost it. It won't happen again. Please let me go."

"I'll let you know tomorrow. But before I release you—if I do—I will have to know that you have appointments for at least two follow-up sessions with a therapist. You have a therapist?"

"It's hard. Dealing with the VA, you know." The VA. The joke. Just like in any medical setting, it was luck of the draw. Dr. Kloeten's answer to everything had been *suck it up*. Don't give that shit space in your head. Get over it. "I'll get the appointments," she says. "Just please let me go home."

"I'll check on you again tomorrow. We'll see how you're doing."

When he's gone, Erin goes to the desk and takes out the hospital paperwork, which includes a brochure: *Your Rights as a Patient*. She scans the pages, underlining the sections she might be able to use for her argument.

Back when she was drinking, she thought she had it under control. She thought no one knew. She never went to the local liquor store. Instead she picked and chose, plotted and planned. She knew where all the stores were, in the neighboring towns and the several scattered around Granite proper. It's amazing how many liquor stores there are in a town of twenty-three thousand people. Liquor stores and churches. Sinners and saints. She had scheduled her errands around buying alcohol. She'd known she should stop, and did sometimes, for a day or two. Until her life fell apart and she got sober for real. For a whole entire year that is now down the tubes and for what?

When she finishes examining the brochure, there is only a scribbly mess of phrases that mean, essentially, that she is fucked. She shoves the booklet back into the drawer. She cannot think. She cannot construe, deduct, rationalize, or deny. She can only hope the images cascading through her brain do not go bloody on her.

Maybe she really has lost her mind. None of this is real. It's a dream, a nightmare. She will awaken, head throbbing, and drag herself to the kitchen to see if there's any booze left in there. Just a shot or two so she can make it through the morning.

Because after this?

She is done.

Certain of it.

She will never drink again.

She laughs out loud. Yeah, right. But she tells herself again, like a thousand times before, she will never drink again.

A pigtailed nurse in a bright pink smock leans through the doorway. "Something funny?"

Erin pretends not to have heard her.

"We're going outside. If you'd like to get a little rec."

Erin follows pigtails down the corridor to a yellow steel door equipped with a panic bar and marked with large red letters: EMERGENCY EXIT ONLY. ALARM WILL SOUND.

A lanky guy in his twenties, arms and neck heavily inked with images of skulls and daggers and planets, bangs against the panic bar as the patients gather in a clump near the door.

"I wish somebody would fuckin' hurry their ass up and unlock this bitch!"

"Hey. There's no need for that." The nurse walks to the door and pulls a set of keys from her smock. "Patience is a virtue."

"Whatever, I guess I don't got none of that, just open the fuckin' door, would you? I need air. Fresh air. Not the fuckin' shit circulating up in here. Air's fuckin' rank."

Erin wants to tell him he doesn't have the first clue about what really rank air smells like. The smells from the base invade her olfactory nerves, as real as the first moment she stepped off that bus. Burning trash, burning sewage, burning bodies. She shakes her head, trying to dislodge the odor. She brings her hands up to her face and inhales the scent of sanitizer, with its whiff of alcohol.

The nurse keys open the door and the patients jostle through. Erin lets the others push past her, wondering if it's legal to keep an emergency exit locked. What would happen if there was a fire? Have any of these people seen what happens when a missile strikes its target?

When she steps through the door, the sun hits her for the first time in days; she doesn't know how many. The heat feels good on her skin. She squints against the brilliant light, inhales deeply, hoping to smell green and blue and yellow, but what she breathes is city air, stinking of petroleum products and concrete, tar and hot tires. But it's an improvement. It comes with no memory attached.

The terrace is two stories up, a concrete rectangle stuck against a corner of the white brick hospital building, enclosed on the other two sides and on the top by chain link. They are in a cage. *Put me in the zoo.* She used to read it with the twins, that one and so many others, until they began reading to her, and finally reading for themselves. She will not think about it.

A netless basketball hoop is attached to the narrower of the brick walls. White plastic lawn furniture, streaked gray from rain and spotted with mold, is scattered about the terrace. A basketball appears. Erin sees the other patients tossing in shots. She hears good-natured bragging and taunts. They're having fun, making the best of a bad situation. It reminds her of the hoop on the base, where the soldiers would gather some evenings to show off their skills and make bets in three-on-three games. *No no, you should not be in the zoo. With all the things that you can do, the circus is the place for you.* Are they having fun, or just pretending? She can't tell.

"Here you go."

The ball shoots toward her, thrown hard and fast. Somehow she slaps it down before it hits her face. She tries bouncing it, struggles to keep it from escaping and is hit by a wave of dizziness as the orange hoop blurs and tilts.

"Shoot." Tattoo Guy moves under the goal.

Erin tosses the ball. It sails two feet left of the backboard and pings against the brick wall.

"Gotta love the meds," Tattoo Guy says. Everyone laughs. Erin does her best to join them.

∞

At lunch, she eats slowly and deliberately, even though it's typical crappy hospital food that tastes like salted cardboard. But she knows the nurses are tracking her for intake. She will show them she has a normal appetite. Normal is her ticket out of here.

After lunch, she is back in her room when a nurse she hasn't seen before enters to tell her it's time for Group.

"I would prefer not to," Erin says quietly.

The nurse sighs loudly and props her fists on her hips. "Four words, dear: attendance is not optional."

The dayroom chairs are pulled into a large circle. Erin sits closest to the door. Identifying options for a quick escape is the number one priority in any unfamiliar building. Even though this escape would be only as far as the locked steel door of the unit, she needs at least the illusion of a plan.

The therapist, an earnest young man with a soul patch dripping from his bottom lip, asks who would like to speak first.

"Me, yeah, no problem," Tattoo Guy spits. "I got plenty. How'm I feeling? That's what this is about, right? In a word, *angry*." He leans forward, one heel jittering against the linoleum, his knee bobbing up and down. "This is what I learned in school—not history, not geography, not reading, not math. I learned how to hate. I hate. Everyone and everything, myself included. Hate fuels me, it consumes all my energies. I fucking *hate*."

"Why?" The therapist shifts uncomfortably. "What does it give you?"

"This hatred state of mind? What's the reward?" He stills his leg. "A sense of control," he says calmly. "A sense of power. And—most important—a million little reasons to stay fucked up on drugs and alcohol."

Erin feels it seeping into the room, rolling across the dark linoleum like vapors from melting dry ice, creeping up the walls. He is right, his hatred is a force, invisible, dagger-shaped particles of it scattering randomly throughout the room, mingling with the oxygen and leaving her afraid to breathe.

"Can any one of you motherfuckers tell me one good reason I shouldn't be free to be exactly who I am? This is America, goddamit! So fuck off."

Erin pulls herself into a ball and tugs a blanket around her, leaving only her burning eyes exposed. She wants to pull the blanket over her head, hide her tears.

"You!" Tattoo Guy says harshly, aiming his words at her. "What are you looking at? You can't shoot worth a shit, you know that?"

"Hold on," the therapist says. "Let's take a moment and calm down."

Erin hides in her blanket. She has seen enough hatred. She has felt enough hatred, all the way up to war. She does not hate anyone else in the entire world. She keeps her hatred small, directed solely at herself. It has taken her years to fine-tune it, to reduce it to a simple self-loathing that is at times a distinct creature living inside her head. She has asked it, on occasion, why it hates her so much, but it refuses to answer.

∞

Tanya arrives that evening to find Erin sitting up in bed, a blanket around her shoulders, her face still drained of color.

"Feeling any better? You look tired." Tanya feels the tremble in her sister's arms when they hug.

"Did you see them?"

"They're fine. You don't have to worry."

"I have to get out of here."

"Calm down. I talked to Eddy on the phone. They're fine. They love you, Erin. They want you to get well." Tanya assures herself that she's not really lying. She did talk to them on the phone, finally, when Eddy relented after three callbacks. They hadn't mentioned Erin at all. They'd said they were having a good time with their dad. But they hadn't sounded certain; they hadn't sounded happy. They sounded like kids who instinctively knew that their survival was tied to saying what the grownups wanted to hear.

When it's time for meds, Tanya helps Erin to the nurses' station, holding onto one arm tightly and keeping the other around Erin's waist. She feels Erin's arm tense beneath her grip, worries Erin might collapse on the long journey down the hall.

The station nurse is pleasant, offering a plastic cup of apple juice with the pills. Erin downs them complacently, but Tanya knows it's only because her sister fears being caught if she tries to fake taking the pills. And that would mean more time in the hospital.

"I'm getting out tomorrow?" Erin puts the empty paper cup on the counter.

The nurse flips through pages on a clipboard, runs her index finger down a list of patient names.

"There's nothing here, and I'm not aware of any scheduled releases."

"He told me probably tomorrow."

"Dr. Patanjali told you that?"

Erin nods.

"I haven't received any paperwork. Why don't you go finish your visit, and I'll see what I can find out."

The hospital socks have grips on the soles, but still they slide on the polished linoleum floor. Erin feels almost as if she's walking on ice. Back in the room, she wraps herself in her blanket. She has been freezing since she got here.

Tanya doesn't think Erin is lying, but doubts that the doctor said what Erin heard. She can't imagine a professional would think Erin is ready to be released. Still, there's the insurance situation. In her stints as a flight attendant union rep, Tanya has dealt with the quandry many times before. The hospital says the patient needs more time, more care, but the insurance company refuses to pay. And so, for the patient, it's *ready or not, out you go.* More than once, Tanya has found herself at a funeral because an insurance company said no to an extended stay in rehab.

"Erin? What were his actual words? Can you remember?"

"He said if you'll stay awhile, and I make follow-up appointments, he'll release me."

"But I can't."

"Just tell him. Please. Tell him three weeks."

"I don't want to lie."

"You're not. You could stay, right? If you had to?"

Tanya feels like she's being taken hostage. She thinks being home might be better for Erin, but she's not at all sure, and she really can't stay. Not for three weeks.

"Please get me out of here."

"I want to know you're okay."

"I am. I'll make the appointments. I'll follow up."

"You absolutely promise."

"I promise." The hospital drugs, coming on strong now, make Erin woozy. There's no stopping it. "Have you talked to them? Are they okay?"

"They're fine, Erin. How bad was it? How long?"

"The woman from CPS said Eddy told her they don't want to see me, they don't want to talk to me on the phone."

"You know that's not true." Tanya sees the tears leaking from Erin's eyes, so bloodshot that the whites appear pink.

"Erin. How long?"

"Will you make an appointment for me? I have to have two appointments to get out of here. Two of them. Dr. Kloeten." She and Eddy had seen Kloeten for couples counseling a few months after Erin returned. She had to scrape to make the copay, but she'd still had her military benefits then. Kloeten will have to do. He meets Dr. Patanjali's requirement.

Tanya waits for an answer to her question.

"I drank when I first got back, okay? And then I stopped, about a year ago. Trying to save the marriage. But it didn't work. It made it worse. And I wasn't drinking at all when this," waving her arm around the room, "happened. It got me in a single day. I lost it."

"You weren't when I was up last Christmas, were you?"

"No."

"I didn't think so. You seemed fine." Tanya tries a laugh. "Not like college, right?" More than once Tanya had picked up the phone and known right away from the slur in Erin's words that her sister had drunk-dialed her again.

"College was college," Erin said. "You couldn't go to a party where there wasn't . . ." She pushes herself into a corner of the bed, crying openly now. Tanya was right about Christmas. Erin had worked hard to seem fine from the moment her feet hit American soil, for the entire past year and a half. She'd gotten off to a rough start, lots of soldiers did, needing to blunt the hard, sharp edges of returning from a war zone. But during Tanya's last visit, Erin had managed to limp through the holidays without any crutches, putting on a happy face while Tanya, aware that Erin was barely scraping by, bought the Christmas tree and put gifts beneath it.

"You'll call Kloeten?" Erin wipes at her eyes.

Tanya moves to sit next to her, wishing to God that Erin had picked up the phone and called her, wondering if she could have done something, anything, to prevent her sister's fracture.

TWELVE

Erin peers through her night vision goggles out the dust-caked windshield, gripping the steering wheel, her insides miserable from the constant bump and sway of driving over mile after mile of rudimentary roadway. Misting rain on the windshield is a dirt magnet, gluing a fine film of grit to what was already cloudy glass. The wipers swipe back and forth rhythmically, leaving a line of dust-mud at either end of their arcs, angry eyebrows of muck. The cabin stinks of old sweat and damp cammies and worn out rubber and dust, everywhere dust and sand. It's in her nostrils, on her tongue, in her ears and her hair. She longs for even a whiff of the mushroom loam smell of the woods but can't begin to conjure the memory. Ginj peers out the passenger window through her goggles. Outside is nothing but black.

They had spent the rest of the day on stand-by, loitering near the trucks, trying to sleep, waiting for the order to move out. It came after dark.

Erin follows the truck in front, is followed by the truck behind. Fourth position in the convoy, which bumps along at an excruciatingly slow speed, the MRAPs and cargo trucks and flatbeds strung along the roadway like a caravan of huge mechanical snails, crawling, sliding along the mud slicked road, if it can even be called a road. The Mine-Resistant Ambush-Protected vehicles carry the combat troops: infantry or military police, sometimes Special Forces, there to defend the convoy against ambush. They're in Blackout Drive; Erin keeps

72

her eyes trained on the two tiny infrared markers on the bumper of the truck in front of them, constantly scanning the side mirror for the markers on the vehicle behind.

"You awake?" Ginj leans forward to get a look at Erin's face.

"Yeah, yeah, I'm fine."

"I wish something would happen."

"Ginj. You're gonna jinx us."

"Okay, I'll stop wishing, like it makes a difference. I miss Louise."

"You keep saying."

"Best dog ever. Did I tell you she's a Beagle?"

The markers of the truck in front go suddenly askew; the vehicle stops dead.

"Hold up, hold up!" Ginj stiffens, grips her M4 as Erin brakes hard, jolting the truck to a stop, checking her mirror. The Hummer behind has halted. Erin cuts the wheel hard and pulls to the opposite side of the road as the convoy goes into herringbone formation, alternating vehicles pulling to opposite sides of the road, spacing to minimize damage and maximize defense against attackers. The radio spits static and a voice inside her helmet says, "Jaguar 1, Jaguar 1, this is Rooster 3, we're good, no IED, repeat, no IED."

Drake's voice fills her helmet. "Rooster 3 copy that. What's the problem?"

Erin checks the side view mirror, sees the glowing red markers of the vehicle behind her. Through the mucky front windshield, covered with heavy netting, she sees the markers of the vehicle in front of her have gone askew, the left one two feet higher than the right.

The radio crackles again. "Front right wheel. We're in a hole."

"Seriously." Ginj snickers.

"Hey, at least it wasn't us."

"Ha! Like you'd ever hear the end of that."

Through her goggles, Erin sees a shadowy Sergeant Drake and the gray-green images of troops assembling around the stranded vehicle, studying the situation.

"This shit makes me freaky," Ginj says quietly, peering out the passenger window. "You feel 'em? Sitting out there? Watching? I feel it. I've got a sense about these things. I'm telling you."

Drake's voice comes through Erin's earpiece. "Bantam 1, Bantam 1."

She acknowledges and Drake replies, "Your winch operational?"

"Affirmative."

"Pull your vehicle up here."

"Copy that."

Drake guides Erin to a stop a few feet behind the disabled truck. His voice again, jokingly. "Wenches with winches! I like it."

Ginj shoots Erin a look that cannot be seen because of the goggles covering Ginj's eyes, which is fine with Erin. Ginj's eyes can be frightening sometimes, as if they've disconnected from her brain, leaving a vacant space where judgment should reside. Ginj's left boot heel taps a slow beat on the dusty floorboard as Erin opens the door. She leaves the truck idling and steps down into the muck.

Three hours later, the convoy is moving again, bouncing over the rutted roadway. Erin maintains her distance from the vehicle in front while Ginj peers into the black countryside through a pair of night vision goggles that are much nicer, and more expensive, than the military-issue pair she had on earlier. Erin doesn't ask where she got them. They're still a long way from their destination, Forward Operating Base Shank, where they will load up equipment for transport back to the US. They're seriously behind schedule.

At least the rain has stopped. Erin feels the strain in her eyes and hears the strain of the engine as they hit yet another section of uphill roadway. She maintains her distance from the truck in front, a safety measure to prevent a rocket or IED taking out more than one of them in a single shot. Ginj has calmed down, at least for Ginj. She cradles her rifle in her arms, hugging it loosely, almost protectively. They drive in silence.

Erin tries to keep her mind on the road, which isn't difficult. They're on pavement now, yes, but the road is narrow, hardly designed for military use. In another couple of months, it will be impassable due to snow. She hopes the sappers didn't miss anything when they swept for explosives. Those guys. She doesn't know whether they're exceedingly brave or just crazy. Either way, she's thankful they're around. She grips the wheel tight, releases, grips again. It strains the fingers, this driving in darkness, hour after relentless hour.

The roadway is empty but for the convoy of military trucks and the MRAPs escorting them. She knows how to drive in darkness. Upstate New York gets dark like this: earth-dark, nature-dark, no streetlights, no building lights, no man-made lights of any kind for miles at a time. She remembers taking Lindsey and Paul outside one bitterly cold winter night, snowsuits over pajamas and knit caps pulled snug on their heads, bundling them with her in a sleeping bag on the back lawn. They lay there staring at the sky, shivering until their body heat warmed the sleeping bag to a tolerable level. The stars hung overhead, glowing orbs dotting the nothingness of infinity. Soon enough, it started. First, a single spectacular streak across the blue-black night. And then another. And another. And then a shower of beautiful white arcs tracing across the midnight heavens, flares of golden pink light as meteors rained down from space. Even talkative little Lindsey had been stunned to silence by the magnificence in the sky.

She should be with them. She wonders what they are doing right this moment, feels more strongly than she did even when she first stepped off the plane carrying her rifle and backpack that she is someplace where she is not supposed to be. It's still yesterday in New York.

THIRTEEN

Damn, it's hot out here. Gavin Costa loops an index finger into the collar of his suit coat and flips it over one shoulder. The Victorian that houses the office is painted in historically accurate shades of green and lavender. A fresh coat of lacquer shines on the artfully hand-painted sign posted in the clipped green front lawn: *Costa, McConner, Hakeem, and Frankel.* The hedges are trimmed.

Gavin trots down the wooden steps and heads left on the sidewalk, barely pausing at the corner traffic light before ignoring the red signal and jaywalking across the intersection. It's sweltering out here. He'll put his jacket on when he reaches the court building, ten minutes away through downtown Granite. Passing the square, he sees the noon regulars, a knot of men and women smoking and drinking coffee near the basement steps of the Old Stone Church. A historic landmark, the massive Renaissance Revival building rises up from the midst of the graveyard that surrounds it. The dates carved into the weathered headstones are from the seventeenth and eighteenth centuries.

From the opposite side of the street, keeping his distance, Gavin recognizes a tall young man, barely out of his teens, in slinky Nike basketball shorts and a Knicks jersey, throws a nod in the kid's direction. He still isn't sure how he managed to talk the court into releasing the youngster to his mother on a personal recognizance bond. His Honor had seemed to be in an exceptionally jovial mood that day, as had his normally dour court clerk. Maybe they'd both gotten laid. Maybe they'd got laid together. Who cares? The kid was out and, from all appearances, doing the right thing. Good for him. Fifteen years out of law school, the whole of that time spent practicing at his father's firm—one of the oldest in town—Gavin takes his breaks where he finds them and never questions a gift of beneficence from The Bench.

The scent of a garlicky stir-fry wafts through the screen door at Mo Pho Express and Gavin picks up his pace, realizing that he hasn't eaten since last night and anyway he has no appetite whatsoever, thanks to the bump of cocaine lingering in the back of his throat, the post-nasal drip from some clean white flake that he's thinking he should really steer clear of for a while. He's not about to wind up standing outside the church across the street. Fuck that. Not going there, buddy. Anyway, he's not even close. First thing every morning he throws on his sweats and laces up for a mile-or-two run, depending on his mood and how much he drank the night before. Once in a while he goes three. Sweat out the toxins. And he does eat well. He's not one of those meat and potatoes only guys, like his father.

His father. It's nearly 1:00 p.m. and the old man hasn't yet showed his face at the office. Not a good sign. Gavin loves him, sure, but damned if he's going to stick around till Daddy croaks and then step into his shoes and rustle paperwork for the next thirty years. Jesus how boring. Yeah, sure, he went to law school because his father wanted him to, but also because he wanted to do something decent with his life. Help people out, maybe do some environmental defense work, or criminal justice reform, something like that. But here he was, stuck in Granite, population twenty-three thousand, more or less. Married and divorced in the space of eight years, with a three-year-old daughter he sees on weekends. His father's heart attack sent Gavin's life into a detour a few weeks after he sat for the infamously difficult New York State Bar exam. In the recovery room, seeing a new appreciation for mortality in his father's post-anesthesia eyes, he promised that he'd come on board officially as soon as he was licensed to practice.

And he'd done a good job, more or less, while the elder Costa recovered from a triple bypass and his mother fretted and worried about his dad. But he'd also gotten roped into a marriage he wasn't sure he wanted and certainly didn't expect to happen so quickly. Catholic pressure: MaryAnn got pregnant, probably on purpose he realized too late, but Gavin stepped up. Since the divorce, she had perfected the art of being a spiteful, bitchy ex-wife, and he hates her for that, mostly because she's so effective at reminding him what a deceitful, cheating dick he is. Like he didn't already know. Fuck it. So what if he's not that eager to step out of his comfort zone, so what? Just . . . fuck her, too.

Heading up the crumbling pavement that leads to the glass front entrance of the Family Court building, Gavin sniffs deeply and runs a handkerchief across his nose. Jesus, he's got to get out of here. New York City is a few hours south. He could commute at first, ease out of his Granite life quietly, slip away gradually. But, just at the moment—this coke-fueled brain-buzzing moment—he doesn't want to give too much thought to precisely what's holding him back.

At the entrance, he studies the aluminum door handle suspiciously, hoping it's not slimed with God-knows-what from some drug addict who hasn't washed his hands in a month. Jesus, when was the last time anybody washed these windows? Pathetic. Maybe he should run for mayor, get shit done. Fix the potholes, get Code Enforcement to board up that row of abandoned houses off Maple Avenue. Trim back the trees so drivers could actually see stop signs before cruising obliviously through intersections. Where the hell had civic pride gone? Probably the same place as high school civics courses and civil political engagement, tossed carelessly onto the smoldering waste heap of history. Fuck running for office. It's no-man's land. He pulls on his jacket, thinking *it's just another day in paradise*, and yanks open the door.

FOURTEEN

Fatima walks like a man, having practiced enough now that it is second nature; she no longer has to think about it. She goes unnoticed on the sidewalk, her head and face covered by her *shemagh*, her shoulders broadened by pads in her longish suit jacket. Her trousers are baggy, her boots worn and unpolished. She is just another nobody, striding down the street as if, being male, it is her God-given right to do so.

Her father still claims to believe that paradise is a place full of fruit trees and pure flowing water, with pavilions full of virgins restrained there for the pleasures of the righteous. Fatima spits at the thought of him. She doesn't think about what her father might do if he knew where she was or what she'd done. Or her brothers. She pleasured a guard to get out of prison. To escape. Two blocks down the road from the bright green doors of Badam Bagh prison, just as the evening call to prayer was blaring over Kabul, she ducked into an alley and vomited until nothing else would come from her stomach. She did not say a prayer.

That was two months ago. Her family, her father and two brothers, for all they know she is still locked in Badam Bagh for committing *zina*. Not once did they visit. Not once did they respond to her letters. It doesn't matter. In a way, prison was freedom. At least while she was in there, they couldn't sell her off to be married. Now they would want to wait, until her punishment was finished and she was released

79

and they could try to get a better price. Let them wait. Let them wait until she is gone far from here, untraceable.

The street is still crowded, has been all day. The sun is disappearing behind the Ninjai Ghar peaks on the western rim of the city. Fatima winds through knots of pedestrians who loiter at stalls, considering the purchase of chicken or lamb, eggplant or melon, in the Pul-e Khishti Bazaar. On the evening street, drivers fume in their cars, backed up on the busy avenue. She doesn't slow as she passes the open-air shops.

She has money in the pocket of her suit coat. She did not grow up a thief, but she has become a good one, very fast. Some of her methods she learned in the prison, some of them she has developed on her own. One afternoon while she was still locked up, a guard delivered a package to her. Bashir had somehow managed to send the proverb book inside the walls. To her. She'd read it over and over, dissected it, and one of the proverbs became her mantra. *Necessity is the mother of invention.* Fatima repeats it to herself first thing every morning. She repeats it to herself every time she hears the call to prayer. She repeats it whenever the bombs go off, whether the bombs belong to the Taliban, to ISIS, or to NATO troops and the Americans. This country is all she knows, but she also knows that she has done nothing wrong. Her mother would understand, her mother who died giving birth to an infant who would have been Fatima's sister if the baby hadn't died also. Fatima was twelve. Every day, she misses her mother and she misses her baby sister. She misses Bashir, too, but has not contacted him since she escaped from prison. She goes nowhere near the library.

After her mother died, Fatima took over the running of the household, and she'd done a very good job of it. She's done nothing wrong for her entire life, has brought no dishonor to her family. She knows this, she is certain of it, so who cares if a judge said she was guilty of *zina*. She is guilty of nothing. She feels bad about stealing, but prison has changed everything, has required that she learn to negotiate the world from a place of higher consciousness than merely following the rules. Necessity is the mother of invention. A friend of a friend of a friend has a motorcycle for sale. She is not sure where she will go, but she knows she is not staying here, where biology is destiny, and destiny, if you are female, is pain.

FIFTEEN

The names of the classes are insulting on the one hand and laughable on the other: Muffin Club. Dual Recovery. Art and Insight. Funky Fitness. Journaling for Life. Like some kind of sleep-away camp schedule for the mentally ill. Erin fingers the yellow paper on the desktop, wondering how many of them circulate through the CPS system each year, imagining stacks and stacks of them, enough to wallpaper an entire room. She tosses the form aside. The nurse sitting opposite her flicks at a blond curl with her pen, frowns and taps the pen against the clipboard in her lap.

"You need to choose. What about the meetings?"

"But I'm not going to be here."

"We have to see about that. In the meantime, you can choose or I'll choose for you. You should start attending meetings."

Erin doesn't want meetings, doesn't need meetings. Jesus Christ, she's over it. Can't these people just wrap their goddamn indoctrinated heads around the fact that she should be home with her children?

In the fog of the first months after her return, at the point where she was tired of the hangovers, tired of having to drag through the days until it was time to make dinner and she could drink, she'd gone to a meeting. Since she'd come home, Eddy mostly left early and came in late, after the kids were in bed. He never had much to say. She didn't know how long she could keep doing it, but she functioned, tiptoeing around his hostility. She got the kids off to school and picked them up after. Lunch boxes packed. Dinner served. Clothes washed. They were the reason she didn't just walk away. They were the reason. She worked landscape. She wrote stupid little blog posts that had not-so-subtle links for camping gear tucked into the sentences, earning twenty-five bucks per post. Eddy began complaining that she was drinking too much, too regularly. She needed to get a grip. He had a grip, he said. He just smoked pot every day, which made it easy not to drink. Nothing addictive about that. After one particularly brutal hangover, Erin considered the possibility of quitting. Even if AA hadn't worked for her father, she thought she should at least check it out.

Fearing to be seen in Granite, she went to a meeting in the next town over. A man talked about the morning he'd woken up next to a box of limp, rusted lettuce in a dumpster behind a restaurant, clutching a half-full bottle of Two Buck Chuck. When he realized where he was, he emptied the rest of the bottle into his belly and went looking for more. By midmorning he was in the county jail.

Erin left the meeting feeling a sense of relief. So she had hangovers. She wasn't sleeping in dumpsters. She would stop drinking, that was all. Though the man's story had bolstered her determination to stop, it also reassured her: she was not actually an alcoholic. A problem drinker, possibly, but she was only a few months back from war. Not a real alcoholic. She was admittedly having a rough time adjusting, but she was nothing like that guy. And she does not believe that some Higher Power, which is obviously a euphemism for God, is personally interested in her welfare and that if she gets on her knees and asks, then He (oh, yes, it has to be a He) will magically lift the desire—make that the compulsion—to drink. The God she encountered in Afghanistan had given her ample evidence that He didn't give a shit about anybody or anything. His job was to punish: randomly, ruthlessly, and with malice.

"I have to turn this in." The nurse is waiting, not-so-patiently, for another choice.

"Anger Management," Erin says finally, watching as the nurse circles the words and waits for the next choice, waits for Erin to say *Meeting*.

Erin scans the page, searching for something, anything, that will placate the nurse.

"You know, usually in a case like yours they like people to stay for at least two weeks. Sometimes thirty days. It might be good for you."

Erin feels her insides shrink.

"It's safe in here. There's no temptation."

"I don't feel safe in here."

"There's no alcohol. You'd have time to get yourself together before going back to the stresses you were under."

"I'm done drinking. And the other stuff I just need to deal with, which I cannot do from in here."

"The other stuff isn't going to disappear. It'll be waiting for you when you get back."

"I know. So why procrastinate?" Erin realizes her tone is growing sharp. "I appreciate your help. You have all been very kind to me. But what I need right now is to let my children know I love them and I'll be there for them."

The nurse sighs loudly, losing patience.

Erin tells herself to shut up and follow the rules. "The Open Meeting. On Saturday."

The nurse circles the words triumphantly and pats her chart. "I'll make a copy of this and return it to you. Right now, it's time for WRAP. I'll meet you in the dayroom."

"But, my sister's on the way."

The nurse pauses at the door. "If she gets here on time, you'll still have almost an hour with her. Right now? The dayroom. Wellness Recovery Action Program. Don't be late."

∞

Waiting for the elevator, Tanya hears her phone chime from somewhere inside her bag, the ringtone like an accompaniment to the scattering of fairy dust. She digs, wishing she could remember to change

84

the setting. The caller ID says only: Granite County. The elevator doors open. Tanya steps away and answers the phone.

"Tanya? Barb Copley. Child Protective Services. I thought you should know. The Court has called a hearing in the matter of custody for today at two o'clock. If there's any way Erin could be there it would be good. She's still in the hospital?"

"I'm just going in to visit. Don't you like, bring her there?"

"That's not something we handle."

"But I don't even know when they're going to release her." Tanya tells herself to calm down. She will remain courteous: honey catches more flies than vinegar.

"I'm just making sure you're aware."

"How can they have a hearing if she can't be there?"

"They'll appoint someone from the Public Defender's office to appear for her."

"That doesn't seem fair."

"It's the law. The Family Court is required to hold a custody hearing the day following an emergency removal. The judge says we're already several days late. It has to be done today."

"Erin should be there," Tanya says firmly.

"The issue we're dealing with today is whether Erin can function reliably as a mother."

"She's been functioning, as a single mom, ever since Eddy walked out on the family. Six months after she got back from—"

"Well, he seems to have stepped up when it counted most."

"Maybe if he'd stepped up with some damn child support we wouldn't be—"

"I don't handle support. That's a different division."

"But—"

"Look, the hearing's set. It's at the Family Court building on Lexington Street. Two o'clock. Just try to get her there."

∞

Gavin scans the packed waiting area, silently recalling a line from one of the many books he's read, something about "the cognitive load of poverty." He doesn't recall the author, and who cares, anyway. It's a no-brainer; it hardly takes a study to know it's practically impossible to make effective decisions about the long term when the short term is right there in your face, snarling like a wolverine. He quashes the empathy welling up inside him; it won't make his day any brighter and it won't help the people bent dejectedly in the waiting area chairs. Where the hell is his client? He's certainly not here.

The lawyer lounge is a ten-by-twelve room with a cracked brown leather couch and a couple of unmatched office chairs crammed into it. A bulletin board hangs on one wall, not quite squared, and a white plastic folding table holds an aluminum forty-five-cup coffee urn. Someone has made a sign, handwritten in Sharpie on the back of some form or other: *Flavors du Jour—Beaned for Alimony Double Shot Cappuccino, Splitsville Skinny Mocha Supreme, Grounds for Divorce Caffè Americano.*

At one end of the couch sits Todd Bagley, a chunky man in a tweed jacket and bow tie who keeps his thinning brown hair snugged in a scraggly ponytail, which he tucks under his suit coat before entering a courtroom. Gavin finds the gesture pretentious, believing as he does that the difference between consciousness and self-consciousness is awareness of ego.

"Counselor," Gavin says. Bagley lowers his print copy of the *Granite Daily Ledger* and nods a silent greeting before returning to the sports section. Gavin doesn't know the guy beyond to say hello when they bump into each other here in the Family Court building, or down the street in the City Court building, or across the street in the County Court Building. He's seen him once or twice at the Couillard House, a restaurant that operates out of the stone house built by its namesake in the 1750s, now on the National Register of Historic Places. It's a place to be seen in town. Somehow, even in a town this size, they've never met as adversaries in court.

Gavin neither wants nor needs any coffee but he goes to the urn anyway and grimaces as the muddy liquid oozes into the Styrofoam cup. Every aspect of Styrofoam disgusts him—the smell, the feel, the sound it makes against skin, the way it taints the flavor of whatever food or beverage it contains. No environmental awareness at all, whoever ordered these. Maybe he *should* consider a run for mayor. But the politics. The knocking on doors. The speeches. The fucking public. Maybe the Natural Resources Defense Council. Do some good. Make the world a better place. His brain spins with possibilities, but then out of nowhere he's hit with a sudden lethargy and thinks first it's the result of pondering the difficulties of being able to effect any kind of lasting or meaningful change in a world that feels to be spinning off its axis. Then he realizes it's only the coke wearing off.

He puts down the coffee and heads for the door, almost colliding with the stumpy Court Bailiff who appears from nowhere, filling the doorway.

"Judge needs a lawyer." The bailiff folds his arms across his chest. Bagley remains hidden behind the newspaper, making it clear that he's not interested. "In Courtroom Two." The bailiff tucks a thumb into his gun belt. He has the loose lower lip of someone who regularly chews tobacco. "Right away," he adds.

Gavin squeezes past him into the hall, calling back to Bagley, "I'm meeting a client. This one's all yours," before slipping around the corner. He's on the rotation at the Public Defender's Office, and when it's his turn, fine. But he is most definitely not looking for an emergency court-appointed gig today.

In the men's room, he enters a stall and pulls a small vial from inside his suit coat. He likes this jacket, a Madison fit poplin in pale green. Brings out the blue of his eyes, or so said Chrystal—that was her name, right? Yeah. Chrystal McClain—right before she practically ripped it off of him and then went after his belt buckle. He almost pops a chub thinking about it. When was that anyway, night before last? Last week? He remembers seeing some kind of ivy vines painted on the pastel wall above her headboard. Fuck. And she's with the Department of Social Services now, too, in a county prosecutorial role. Not the kind of person he needs as an enemy. He's got to get his shit together. At least he should call her and say it was fun.

He taps a bit of powder into the black plastic cap and snorts a bump, repeats the process in his other nostril. Before he's done stashing the vial, he feels the pleasant warmth of the drug spreading from the center of his brain, flowing down his spine and into his limbs. He feels light again. Strong. Confident. Ready to make a custody deal with whoever makes an appearance from DSS Legal. Hopefully it won't be Chrystal. Hopefully his client will show up. Fucking baby-daddies. You need a license to drive a car, but not to have a kid. He gets it, God-given right and all that. But some of these guys? Christ. If the idiots at DSS would distribute free condoms, maybe they'd have fewer child support cases to deal with. He resolves to take his daughter someplace special the next time he sees her.

He checks his nose in the mirror, runs his hands through his hair, going straight back with it, adjusts his wire frames. The suit color isn't as pleasing in the ugly fluorescent light above the sink, seeming an almost putrid shade of green. He straightens his tie and checks again in the mirror. Yeah. Okay. Pushing forty but still got it. Wait. Is he? Did he turn forty last year? He can't remember. Never mind. Thirty-nine, forty, whatever. No big deal, right?

He exits the men's room to see the bailiff standing outside the door, again with arms crossed.

"The Court requests your assistance." The bailiff is not happy.

"What about Bagley?"

"He's already in there. He gets the kids. You get the mom."

∞

A lidless cardboard cigar box holding a cell phone and set of keys glides forward on the conveyor belt and disappears into the stainless-steel X-ray machine. The uniformed Court Officer standing on the far side of a tan plastic Magnatron gate grips his black plastic SuperScanner, clearly bored beyond reason. He jerks his head to motion the woman standing in front of Erin to step through the metal detector. Erin, woozy with medication, waits her turn. The nurse returned the patient's belongings prior to discharge approximately a half hour ago. Standing in line just inside the front doors of the brown brick Granite County Family Court Building, Erin feels that through-the-looking-glass distance the human brain creates to facilitate ego-survival in moments of severe emotional distress. But it's not like this place is new to her. She's been here countless times since Eddy walked out, filing petitions for child support, always to no avail.

A neon pink paper taped to the wall on her left declares YOU MUST BE DRESSED APPROPRIATELY FOR COURT! *Shorts, tank tops, and skimpy clothing are not allowed. Cell phones must be turned off before you enter the courtroom. No food or drink is allowed. No chewing gum is allowed in the courtroom.*

Erin is in the clothes she had on when EMTs loaded her unconscious body into the back of an ambulance: black jeans, a cut-up gray sweatshirt, and black foam flip-flops. Maybe she is dressed appropriately enough for court. She has no cell phone with her. She has no chewing gum. She hugs herself tightly, trying to stop shaking. It's freezing in here.

Next to her, Tanya exudes confidence almost to the point of aggression. She is perfectly made up, not one auburn hair out of place, best-dressed in the building. She has donned her armor and war paint; she is prepared for battle. She removes bracelets, rings, a necklace, puts the cascade of custom-made gold jewelry into the cigar box. She adds her key-clasp and cell phone to the box, hefts her Louis Vuitton bag onto the belt. Fuck all y'all with your navy-blue uniforms and bad haircuts.

Erin is thankful for her sister's warrior attitude as they pass through the metal detector one after the other, the Court Officers eyeing them with a mix of suspicion and indifference. The clock on the wall says

1:58. Tanya has worked a miracle, getting Erin released and speeding her to court in time for the hearing.

"Follow the red line down the hall and upstairs." The sergeant's voice is nasal and flat. Instead of navy blue, like those of the rank and file court officers, his shirt is white, with golden chevrons on the sleeves.

Trembling, feeling as if she might pass out, Erin walks next to Tanya, following a strip of red tape on the linoleum as it makes a right turn into a shorter hall and leads to a steep flight of dirty gray safety-stripped stairs. She is dizzy and out of breath by the time they reach the top and make a U turn into a small waiting area. Another Court Officer, seated at a high desk near the top of the stairs, stares into space, apparently hypnotized by boredom. Men in ill-fitting suits mill about near the closed oak double doors at the opposite end of the room. Several young women sit next to each other against one wall of the narrow room, one of them filling out paperwork.

"Sit here." Tanya puts her bag on a chair. "I'll be right back."

Trying to convince herself that she is cold, not shaking from fear, Erin watches Tanya approach the pasty-faced Court Officer posted outside the Courtroom door. There is a brief exchange before Tanya returns to sit next to Erin.

"They'll call you when they're ready. I can't go in."

"Why not?"

"He says he doesn't know. It's just how they do it."

The wiry Hispanic Court Officer at the desk snaps out of his trance and begins leafing through a stack of papers, pointedly ignoring his surroundings. Erin hears footsteps coming up the stairs, the sound of shoes scuffing against safety strips, and another Court Officer, also in his twenties, a tall Black man with his hair cut in an impeccable high fade, saunters from the stairwell.

"What's happening?" He posts himself next to the desk.

"Nothing." The seated officer gives a shrug. "You in charge."

"No way, bro. You da man, you da man. I'm just the man standing next to the man."

The seated one smirks. They see Erin watching them. She looks away quickly, afraid of their attention.

The hum and buzz of conversation comes to her ears as a dull, hollow reverberation. Near the looming Courtroom doors, behind a counter topped with a scratched Plexiglas barrier aged to the color of urine, a sharp-dressed Court Clerk holds the phone receiver pressed between cheek and shoulder, listening and shuffling papers. He picks up a staple remover and expertly plucks a staple from papers, reorders pages, taps them smartly against the desktop and, knowing precisely where he has left it, reaches for his stapler, slips the corner of the paperwork into its jaws and squeezes.

Erin hears the slow-motion rip of metal staple prongs piercing the pages as the sharp metal points slice through fiber and screech against the metal grooves that bend them into place behind the last page. Her auditory receptors have gone into overdrive, courtesy of PTSD.

Slow steps, slow and heavy, start up the stairs behind the wall against her back, and the sound of breathing, and it's all going slo-mo. Erin's spine fills with ice as she realizes it is someone with a gun, a terrorist coming up the stairs. Coming to wreak havoc, coming to spray bullets from an AK47. She is certain of it. She knows it even as she realizes her thoughts are not rational because yes, she is aware that her brain's neural pathways are a skein of narrow, dark back alleys all leading toward treachery and death, but, in the moment, she cannot help but believe.

The footfalls grow closer, shoes scuff against safety treads—scratching, sandpaper steps— the breathing louder, labored with the effort of climbing, climbing.

Erin cannot move.

Shoes on carpet now, about to round the corner.

It feels like blood is running from her ears.

A swirl of skirt as Mrs. Copley, heavy and out of breath, emerges into the room and brushes past, heading for the Courtroom doors. Just then, Eddy appears from around a corner and Mrs. Copley smiles broadly, offering a cordial hand, seeming happy to see him.

Erin's heart thunks erratically as Mrs. Copely, flanked by Eddy, speaks briefly to the Court Officer guarding the big oak double doors.

"Oh my God," Tanya whispers, leaning close to Erin. "He looks older."

"You've been away for a while."

"And thank God for that." Tanya shrugs. "Do you blame me?"

"Of course not," Erin says. "But I've missed you."

Erin wants to look away but can't. Eddy says something to Mrs. Copley that makes her laugh. He's charming her.

When you've seen an actor at work over the course of several years, seen the different roles played, you come to know when he's hitting the mark and when he's just saying the lines. Mrs. Copley, though, lacks the benefit of experience. She nods sweetly at Eddy and hobbles across the carpet, stopping in front of Erin, who feels now as if she's seated on a slowly moving subway car with Mrs. Copley strap-hanging in front of her.

"I'm so glad you could make it." Mrs. Copley smells vaguely of cheeseburger.

"I'll get them back today, right?" Erin wants to stand, but she's afraid to try.

"Nothing will be decided today. This is just a conference, to determine where to place the children until things are a little more . . . settled. Oh. I have some paperwork." She digs in her bag. "I didn't have a chance to get by the hospital."

She hands Erin a form, so thick with pages it's more like a booklet.

"The sooner I have it, the sooner we can get you some help." Mrs. Copley snugs her large knock-off Gucci bag against her belly. "Make sure you check all four boxes for the types. Were you working? Did you have a job?"

Erin doesn't answer. Yes. She had a job digging holes and planting flowers. She wonders if she still does. How do you call the boss and say *sorry I disappeared.* I had a . . . what did she have? What do you call it? How do you explain? She's not even sure what day it is, and she seriously doubts she still has a job.

Mrs. Copley points out the box for *Services, including Foster Care*. Erin looks at Tanya. This isn't happening.

Tanya snatches the form and stuffs it in her bag, startling Mrs. Copley. "We'll deal with this when we get home."

"Oh. She's not going back to the hospital?"

"They released her." Tanya stands and offers her hand. "I'm Erin's sister. Nice to meet you in person."

"Tanya." Mrs. Copley shakes hands before shifting her eyes back down to Erin. "They released you?"

A man in a light green suit approaches, nodding at Mrs. Copley before turning his attention to Erin and Tanya. "Sorry to intrude," he says. "I'm looking for Erin Hill?"

He leads Erin to one of the three tiny conference rooms that open onto the waiting area. Erin takes a breath and holds it, hoping it will stop her trembling, or at least mask it a little. She can't blame this on the room temperature, but she still feels as if she's freezing, and now acutely confined by the walls of the small room. The Public Defender puts a folder full of papers on an old metal desk and sighs loudly.

"Gavin Costa," he says, extending a hand. Through a haze, Erin sees his sharp blue eyes shining behind wire-rimmed glasses. She feels her hand enveloped in warmth, realizes that her fingers are icy, so cold they're probably blue. She tries to say hello, but no sound will come out.

"Don't go anywhere," he says. "I'll be right back." He ducks out of the room, closing the door firmly behind him.

There are six chairs, three on either side of the room, two of them upholstered in legal green, that dark shade found in courtrooms and law offices. The colors of law, the leathers: there's the green, always the green; there's the maroon; there's the deep blue. There are sometimes the black, the brown, and the tan. There is no brightness in any of the somber tones.

Erin isn't sure how long she waits before Gavin comes back, sniffling loudly, wiping his nose with a handkerchief.

"Excuse me," he says. "I think I'm coming down with a cold. So you just got out of the hospital?

Erin nods.

"Okay. Sorry for that. Do you have to go back?"

"No."

"And you're looking at charges of Neglect. What happened?"

"I made a mistake."

"What kind of mistake?"

Erin hears her voice say the words, but it doesn't feel as if they are coming from her.

"First attempt?" Gavin stops writing, looks up from his notes.

"First?"

"Have you attempted to kill yourself before?"

Erin shakes her head. She can't imagine going through that kind of pain ever again and the way the lawyer asks the question—so matter of fact, like it happens all the time—unsettles her tenuous composure.

"Are you all right?"

"Yes."

"Do you want them back? Your kids?"

The walls shift, closing in. Who is this man, asking her this huge question as if he's inquiring about how she takes her coffee?

"Of course I want them back."

"Good." He shrugs and gives her a tight smile. "Some people don't."

"I love them," she says. "I'm their mother. I have to make this right."

Gavin asks her a series of quick questions, piecing together a brief narrative of her circumstances, preparing for the hearing he's about to walk into on a half-hour's notice.

"Okay," he says finally, gathering his papers. "I've got what I need."

He leads her back out to the waiting area. She rejoins Tanya while Gavin jokes with the Court Officers posted at the podium.

"So where are we?" Tanya speaks quietly. "Who's he?"

"My public defender," Erin says.

"Maybe you won't need him after today. I'm sure when they realize what's happened—"

The courtroom doors open. The Court Officer emerges.

"Attorneys only. Hill. Attorneys only."

The lawyers approach and the Court Officer waves them inside. Mrs. Copley hurries over, speaks to him briefly. He waves her in and backs into the courtroom, pulling the doors closed. There is a loud click as the latch falls into place.

The waiting area is suddenly silent.

"Okay, something is just seriously not okay here." Tanya is on her feet again. "Why aren't they letting you in?" The Court Officers watch her until she realizes there's nothing she can do and sits back down.

After the thrum of multiple muted conversations that had filled the rectangular space, the room feels now as still as a house in which, due to unanticipated system overload, the main circuit breaker has suddenly switched, shutting off the power in order to prevent damage from fire or explosion. Behind the Plexiglas, the clerk continues to staple papers and put them in In-Boxes, Out-Boxes, To-Be-Filed Boxes, on autopilot, working efficiently.

Erin stares at the Courtroom entrance. She doesn't know how long. Twenty feet away from her, Eddy shifts in his chair and runs a hand through thick black hair gone shaggy around his ears, taps his navy-blue baseball cap impatiently against one knee. She can't believe she ever loved him.

A sound comes through the courtroom doors. At first, Erin is not sure whether it's real or she is imagining it. And then it comes again, louder. Unmistakable.

It is a sound made by a group of people.

They are laughing.

∞

Gavin leaves the conference room ajar but speaks quietly. "You're going to need letters. From people who have letters after their names."

"People with degrees?" Erin isn't even sure what questions to ask. That one sounded stupid. Does he mean professionals, does he mean influential people, what does he mean?

"It's very simple." Gavin digs in his coat pocket. "You're about to be arraigned on charges of Child Neglect. I will, of course, plead you Not Guilty. Your former spouse's Temporary Emergency Custody of the children will be continued until the next hearing. For now at least, they will remain in his sole custody."

"It's already decided?"

"The judge made it clear that's what she wants. And for the time being, you are not allowed to have any contact with them."

"Wait, you all just went in there and made a decision and that's it? How can they do this? He walked out on us. They can't just come in and take my children away and give them to him."

"Erin. Listen to me. The alternative is to place them in foster care. Believe me, you don't want that. At least this way, they're together and they have their father."

"And I can't see my own children?"

"No contact whatsoever. Don't even try to call them. You'll have to arrange visitation through Child Protective Services."

"Are you serious?"

"Look, I don't know how you wound up in the system. But you are in the system, and right now you should concentrate on doing what you have to in order to get your kids back. When we go in there, let me do the talking."

At the conference room door, he produces a business card from his jacket. "I'm sorry to do this to you, but I'm leaving for vacation tomorrow. If something comes up, call the office. They'll try to help you out. But honestly I don't think anything will change before I get back. I'll only be gone a couple of weeks."

Erin takes the card. A couple of weeks? She feels herself collapsing onto a chair. It is legal green in color, the same almost-gray shade of green that is the color of the ink on the reverse side of a one-dollar bill. The side that says: IN GOD WE TRUST.

PART II

PART II

SIXTEEN

At the small pine table near the window, Erin pours a pill out of her prescription bottle and forces it down with coffee. The chemical taste lingers. One of the many side effects listed on the pharmacy print-out is *suicidal thoughts or actions*. She distrusts the medication and the doctor who prescribed it.

Tanya sips her coffee and stares at her reflection in the black window. Dawn is hidden, sunrise nowhere close. "You'll get them back," she says. She sees dejection etched in Erin's face and wonders if she should put off her return flight, but part of her cannot wait to get out of here. She rests a hand on Erin's, prying the prescription bottle from Erin's fist and placing it next to the salt and pepper shakers on the table. "I want to say I can't believe he did this to you, but unfortunately I can." She vows to phone daily, stay in close touch. "You're too nice, Erin. You should have divorced him years ago."

Erin envies Tanya's practicality. In spite of Tanya's disdain for lying and liars, she understands life in a way that Erin doesn't. Tanya knows better than to take things literally, a practice Erin never quite got. They had both been raised to be honest, to be nice. Their parents, their teachers, their coaches, all of the adults in their lives had trained them to be sincere and amenable. Girls. Be nice. Be courteous. Be good girls.

As the sky lightens behind the hills, they encounter a caravan of trucks traveling convoy style. Erin speeds past it, wanting to get it in the rear-view mirror quickly. She falls in at a courteous distance behind someone who's in a hurry, and after that the drive gets easy, the thruway practically empty. Tanya talks about Erin bringing the kids down for a visit when things have settled.

"I wish I could bring them right now," Erin says. "Just all of us pile in the car and drive straight there."

"They'd chase you," Tanya says. "They'd drag you back. Eventually." She cracks a window and lights a cigarette. "That Mrs. Copley? She's really something. You saw the way she was looking at him?"

They'd both seen it, waiting outside the courtroom. Mrs. Copley was crushing on Eddy, and he was playing the charmer.

"Let's hope she comes to her senses," Tanya says, "if she has any. Or that Eddy gets tired of playing hero-dad and decides to give your kids back. Like he's capable of being an adult."

They pull to a stop at the passenger drop-off area. Standing in the brisk wind, surrounded by the smell of damp concrete, Erin holds Tanya tightly. She's afraid to let her go, afraid of what might happen, of what she might do or not do when left here alone. She hears Sergeant Drake's voice, the thing he said before every convoy: *Failure is not an option.* But all the troops knew, even as he said it, that failure was an ever-present possibility, even if they were fighting for their lives.

"You're gonna be okay." Tanya snaps up the handle of her carryon and gives Erin a last hug.

"I'll try." Erin bites her tongue to hold back tears. They both know Erin isn't at all okay, but hope she is okay enough, for now at least, not to be confined in the hospital. "Thank you for coming up. Thank you for getting me out of there."

"Hey," Tanya says, "what are sisters for, if not to spring each other from the loony bin? You will be okay. You will. Find your sense of humor. Hang on to it."

Tanya disappears through the sliding glass doors, leaving Erin feeling like a kid who's just realized she's lost on the playground, scanning her surroundings for mom in that instant just before panic sets in.

∞

Approaching the thruway interchange, Erin pays close attention. There's a tricky spot—a twisted maze of multiple highway lanes where it's easy to wind up on Interstate 90 headed for Schenectady instead of south on the thruway. She has driven some of the worst roads in Afghanistan. In the dark. Expecting attacks at any second. The next thing she knows, she's on Interstate 90, headed toward Schenectady.

She drives the several miles to the first exit and corrects course, stopping briefly to set the map app on her phone. Navigate to: Home. A soothing British voice tells her where to turn, what lane to drive in, advises of upcoming tolls and approaching exits. There are no warnings of snipers lurking on the overpasses. At least not today, not yet. Is that funny? Has she found her sense of humor? She wishes Tanya hadn't left, though she gets it completely. Even she doesn't want to be around herself; why would anyone else?

Her eyes burn from lack of sleep, and then the tears start, trailing down her cheeks as she grips the wheel. She feels a shift in her head, and suddenly she is looking down from way out there in the Universe, and it doesn't matter at all that some woman is driving along the thruway at 7:00 a.m. on a Sunday morning, stunned and shocked and wondering if she has what it takes to survive another day.

The blare of a car horn startles her as a bright red Mini Cooper swerves abruptly and guns past, its engine blatting flatly. Erin white-knuckles the wheel and feels suddenly as if she's going very, very fast in this car. The speedometer reads sixty. Not even the speed limit.

The tires of her car hum on the asphalt. She struggles to stay awake, faint from lack of sleep, the medication, and emotional exhaustion. Traumatic aftermath. She can't keep her mind out of the courtroom, can't stop hearing the judge reading the Order into the Official Court Record, her face puckered as though she were at a civic club luncheon, seated next to someone wearing too much perfume.

The British voice intrudes: "In one hundred meters," it says, "you will have arrived at your destination."

SEVENTEEN

The air buzzes with the confetti of multiple conversations, people laughing and joking in the packed church fellowship hall. It's not what Erin expected. There are all kinds of people, from suits to bikers. A few she recognizes, some by sight, some by name: neighbors, community members, people you see at the places you ordinarily go, just living your life. Working, if you're lucky, and running never-ending errands: the grocery store, the library, the bakery, the farm stand at the edge of town, various school functions. Though they give her welcoming nods, she's mortified.

She finds a spot in the back row, against a wall, where she can see all three exits from the large rectangular room. Tattered posters set on the windowsills on either side of the table list The Twelve Steps and The Twelve Promises. The word GOD leers at her. The word SURRENDER makes her want to flee. Her father once told her he'd practiced the steps, though Erin would not otherwise have known.

Two men take places at the simple pine table set in front of the audience. One of them raps his knuckles sharply against the tabletop. "Welcome to the Take Time Group of Alcoholics Anonymous. My name is Bill, and I'm an alcoholic."

A chorus of enthusiastic voices responds loudly, "Hi, Bill!"

Erin cringes at the volume of the unexpected response. At the table, Bill recounts his story, laughing and joking.

The AA people frighten her, telling her she has a brain disease, and that the disease is capable of making her do things she doesn't want

102

to do. She can't know when it will hit: she might be driving down the road and suddenly one night the disease will force her to reach for the turn signal in her dark car, knowing by rote memory where the signal arm is and where the entryway curb cut is, forcing her to make the turn and park in front of a liquor store. Entranced by the disease, she will enter and buy some booze, and the next morning she will wake up in a jail cell or a mental institution or sleeping next to a stranger or lying in a gutter in an unfamiliar town, wondering how she got there.

Even right now, while she sits listening attentively, her disease is outside in the parking lot doing pushups. Her only hope, her only chance of survival, is to come here and share as if her life depends on it. Because it does. She is familiar with the concept of "uncontrollable impulse," but this seems to be more than that. This disease is a complete and utter negation of free will.

She could pretend to go to the ladies' room and sneak out the side door. No one would miss her. The voice of authority in her head reminds her sternly that she *has* to be here. It's not enough to be sincere; she must prove to the judge that she is sincere. Mrs. Copley said the judge likes to see initiative, that it would be a good idea for Erin to get proof she is going to meetings every day. She suggested Erin could have someone sign a paper verifying the date and time of all meetings attended. When Erin asked for the form, Mrs. Copley said she didn't have any. She wasn't sure where Erin could get some. She wasn't even sure there was a form. Erin made up her own form, two per page, thirty copies, with lines for signatures. Mrs. Copley said first names would be fine, since the program is anonymous. The situation seems ill-thought out. Erin could sign the home-made forms herself, and no one would know the difference. There is no chain of custody, no procedure for handling the evidence. Regardless, Erin will take Mrs. Copley's instructions literally and get signatures after every meeting. Whatever they demand.

Sitting in the back row, she has a million reasons why this will never work. She is certain the Court's requirement has sent a wrecking ball into the theoretical wall separating church and state. She's here because the State of New York, County of Granite, is forcing her to come here. And what's here is religion, with all its glorious fearmongering.

∞

Erin feels sad for the woman behind the desk, her office-pale skin bathed in fluorescent light. The carpeting in the dreary waiting room is rancid. But the paychecks arrive and you survive another two weeks, and that has to be enough. Even though Erin feels sorry for the receptionist, right now she would be grateful to have her job. Then again, working here might lead her back to drinking. Her salivary glands activate at the thought of a shot of vodka, reminding her that she is not a fan of her own autonomic nervous system.

The door next to the receptionist station opens and Dr. Kloeten sticks his head out, displaying a thin combover. Erin reads dismay in the downward curve of his mouth before he flashes a quick grin and brushes a hand across his mustache, as though swatting away the smile. He is probably the last person she should be seeing for therapy, but she will abide by Dr. Patanjali's orders and see someone who treated her before she was hospitalized.

In his office, Dr. Kloeten swivels to face her, crosses his legs and links his hands over his knee. Erin feels like she is watching a scene on TV, a sitcom involving a delusional psychologist. It's the pose. She hopes the pulse in her neck doesn't show.

"So," he says. "It's been a while."

She tells him what's happened since she last saw him—since the sweltering afternoon when she had been stupid enough to think that couple's therapy could save the marriage. Some months after her return, those stunningly slow months after her return. The sleepless nights. The fights. The drinking. The not drinking. The appointment here.

"I was surprised to see your name on my schedule."

"Doctor's orders. I've been in the hospital."

Erin tries to hide her discomfort, but there's always uncertainty when seeing a therapist. She tries to reassure herself that although Dr. Kloeten may look like he can read her mind, observing her placidly, nodding thoughtfully, he can't. He's just some guy in gray slacks and Hush Puppies who obtained a degree and hung out a shingle. Whether he actually knows what he's doing is anyone's guess. But she has to keep her guard up, watch her words; one stroke of his pen and she could be back inside the hospital.

One of the platitudes Erin hears often at meetings is *Keep it simple, stupid.* She explains to the doctor that she just plain lost it and found herself in a place so dark that she couldn't see any way out. She couldn't even think how to ask for help; asking for help was not an option when she had made such a godawful mess of everything.

Dr. Kloeten offers the tissue box. Erin plucks one out, wondering why he's offering but, before she can fold it away, the floodgates open. She'd hit a wall, couldn't deal anymore with the pressure, the constant, relentless pressure. Nothing helped but alcohol. She'd lasted several months after she and Eddy had come for counseling, not drinking, working landscape and trying to find another job, trying harder to fight the nightmares, the flashbacks, the anger—no, the rage—the interminable nights of terror. The harder she fought, the worse it got, but surrender was not an option.

Erin sits sobbing as Dr. Kloeten looks on. She is sure he'll never understand. She's not even sure she can. "I started drinking again," she says.

"Ah," he says.

She cries silently, unable to talk, remembering the unseasonably hot November afternoon near the end of the landscape season. They had a couple of weeks more at best. All day long, sweating and ferrying wheelbarrows heavy with mulch, shoveling and shoveling, Erin kept flashing on the day Eddy finished the roof on the house. Their home. She had come outside with tuna fish sandwiches and iced water for lunch. He was standing up on the roof peak, shirtless, muscled, his skin brown from all those days in the sun. When he saw her, he crouched his way down the roof, nimbly working the angle to get to the ladder. He gulped down some water and kissed her neck, his lips cold against her skin, and then took her hand and pulled her toward the woods, grinning.

He said he would love her forever. He swore he would always protect her.

The lost promise of that day was all she could think about, pushing the wheelbarrow up steep hills to the back garden of the estate they were working. Load after load, shoveling, hauling, shoveling more—*I will love you forever. I will always protect you.* Where was he now?

Driving home covered in sweat, a layer of mulch dust coating her clothes, her skin, in her ears even, she decided she deserved a beer. Her muscles ached. She'd worked hard all day. She deserved it. *I will always protect you.* But he hadn't. He'd stopped loving her, had no interest in protecting her. Maybe financial desperation hadn't been the only reason she enlisted. Though Erin hadn't recognized it at the time, perhaps she had hoped the Army could teach her how to protect herself. Instead she had learned that there is no real protection. And that even in a dangerous world ruled by people whose grotesque self-confidence only partially masks their human stupidity, what she most urgently needed to protect herself from was herself. Her own human stupidity.

Dr. Kloeten waits patiently, his face a mask of indifference. The awareness dawns on her gently, quietly. She is mentally ill. She'd always been afraid of the term, conjuring as it does visions of lunatics running amok in the asylum. But her recognition and almost instantaneous acceptance of this fact lightens her, silencing the awful voices in her brain that make such a habit of berating her.

Erin composes herself. "I guess I didn't believe I was really an alcoholic."

Dr. Kloeten nods knowingly; he's heard it before.

She had drunk the beer and gotten in the shower, scrubbing the sweat and mulch from her body. And then the next day, she bought two. After all, she'd had a beer the day before and nothing bad had happened. So, two. Two beers. Perfectly reasonable. And then a few weeks back on the wagon. And then she bought a bottle of wine. And the next week, a bottle of vodka. She cleaned up before Tanya came to visit for Christmas. And then drank alone on New Year's Eve, after Tanya had gotten on a plane and after the kids were in bed. And it went like that for months, Erin functioning, drinking secretly, cherishing the few blessed hours where her brain wasn't in complete turmoil. Needing a drink or three or four to get to sleep at night. And then she was down the rabbit hole and there was no way out, there was only the certainty that yes, yes she was an alcoholic and this was how she would spend the rest of her life until she died a miserable alcoholic death. And she loved her children too much to put them through any more of it.

"I just really, really need my children," she says. "I can't even explain how painful it is. It's instinctual. It is ripping me apart. Physically. Inside. And I'm not drinking. I know I won't drink ever again. Okay? I lost it. But I know I can't drink again. Ever. I get it."

She hears a long sigh from the doctor as he uncrosses his legs and leans on his knees. He says quietly, "I really don't think I'm the best fit for you in this case. Situations like this, truthfully, Erin, I don't know that they'll be able to forgive you, and things didn't go so well the first time around, when I was seeing you. I can give you some names. I have a couple of colleagues who might be willing to see you."

Erin thinks she has misheard him. *They will never forgive you?* What kind of doctor would say that? He couldn't have said that. It's her own mind, making things up, hearing what it believes is the truth, manifesting her worst fears.

"But I need to be in therapy or they won't let me have my children."

"I understand," he says.

"I can't even see them. I can't even talk to them on the phone."

"I just don't think I'm the right one to help you." He turns to his desk and picks up a small yellow pad, scribbles some names on it. "I think the first one is your best bet," he says. "Come. I'll walk you out."

∞

Erin arrives promptly for her 10:30 a.m. appointment at the Department of Social Services. Mrs. Copley must document Erin's compliance with her Treatment Program, which consists of going to meetings, maintaining sobriety, completing Early Recovery, and getting any needed counseling. She has sent Erin here for a drug and alcohol assessment to help determine the extent of counseling needed. Now that Dr. Kloeten has taken himself out of the picture, Erin will have to find a new doctor.

She finally spots an open seat in the large, crowded waiting area that seems perfumed with the competing smells of old floor wax, Bubblicious gum, assorted body washes, and fruit-scented hair products. A young Hispanic father sitting nearby holds a sleeping infant, his eyes full of wonder. Anyone can see it: he's mad infatuated. Eddy had been that way, too, at first, a proud father of newborns. Erin takes out her phone and scrolls aimlessly. Opens apps, closes them, pretending to pay attention.

One hour and fifteen minutes she's been waiting. The full-time, fully benefitted, pensionable employees at the DSS are setting a fine example for society's losers and fuckups. The clients must be prompt, or their appointments are cancelled. The clients must be civil, or they are ejected from the building. The clients must do everything they are told or they will not receive benefits. Erin considers picking up her yellow plastic chair and throwing it across the room. Perhaps that would remind them that there are actual human beings out here who deserve to be treated as such. She plops back down, feeling stupid for expecting anything useful from a one-size-fits-all government operation. Still, it's frustrating to watch how slowly the employees move, as if lethargy is a job requirement. Erin has always been a hard worker and has little patience for slackers. But who is she to say? Maybe these folks have it right: show up, do the absolute minimum required to keep your job and get through the week: the eagle shits on Friday.

In the rooms, they say one must guard against self-pity. *Poor me. Poor me. Pour me a drink.* She's been living on peanut butter and jelly since forever.

She's about to walk out when her name is called. She follows a woman dressed as a cross between a punk rocker and a corporate secretary to one of the interview rooms that line the puzzle of hallways in the huge DSS building.

The woman introduces herself but her name sails past Erin. "What we're doing here is a drug and alcohol assessment to determine if you're in need of treatment for any issues." The Drug and Alcohol Lady licks her index finger and separates some pages before picking up a pen. She wants Erin's story. Erin tells it, and even as she's starting out she has a feeling today will be easier than some of the other times. Today she is lucky. Or maybe it's just that she's told the story enough that it has stopped hurting her, at least the way it used to. The Drug and Alcohol Lady asks questions and makes notes.

"Have you been drug tested?" She holds her pen poised above a form.

"I thought you were doing that today."

"We're not set up to do that."

Erin recalls Mrs. Copley telling her to expect a drug test when she came to the appointment. "I was told I would be tested here."

"We're not set up to do drug testing."

"So how do I get it?"

"You can make an appointment with your personal physician. Fill this out please." She writes something on her paper and hands Erin the same form Mrs. Copley pressed on her at court. Erin doesn't mention that she has no personal physician, and she definitely doesn't have money to pay for testing.

"I've already filled out this form." Erin pulls the application for assistance from her bag and pushes it across the desk. She has checked the box marked *Services, including Foster Care,* but has drawn a line through the words "*including Foster Care*" and written "*Do not want,*" next to it, as well as her initials. "I need a drug test. Mrs. Copley said—"

"I've explained it to you. We don't do that here. I'll send my report to the court. And to Mrs. Copley. And you need to get a drug test."

∞

It is the kind of building that might house a clandestine government operation, the kind you would drive right past unless you were looking for it. Nondescript, unobtrusive, and ugly. Single story brown cinderblock. Narrow, inoperative, burglar-proof windows spaced across the front. The building is home to Causeway Aftercare, which provides comprehensive addiction recovery programs to private and public agencies. Erin is here for the Early Recovery Program.

A middle-aged man who reminds Erin of Peter Griffin from *Family Guy* is the only one in the room when she arrives. An eclectic collection of chairs forms a rough circle around the center of the otherwise empty room. Erin takes a seat near a back corner, in a wobbly desk chair upholstered in a shade of teal that reminds her of the last time she visited her father, in the hospital, just before she deployed. She wonders how many people have logged hours here. Maybe her father sat here, in this very spot, during one of his several sobriety attempts.

"First night?" Family Guy is stone-faced, his voice monotone.

Erin nods. "Yours?"

"Hopefully my last." He leans back, adjusting his white USA baseball cap. "I just want to get my license back."

Group members trickle in, falling into the seats carelessly to show just how much they don't want to be here. For most of them, it's about one thing: The Certificate of Completion, awarded after ten sessions unless the counselor leading the group decides otherwise. Rumor has it that it's difficult to get out with just ten sessions due to the fact that Causeway Aftercare gets paid by the number of attendees at each session. It's financially expedient to tack on a few extra sessions here and there.

The silver-haired counselor arrives wearing faded jeans and a sports shirt topped with a leather biker vest and takes his place at the front of the room, easing into his chair as if entering a chilly swimming pool.

"Without recovery," he says, his voice like fresh-washed gravel, "you will die. It's only a matter of time. And often, not very much time." He pauses and eyes them one by one before explaining that he's been in recovery for twenty-six years. It's a process.

Erin can't connect to that: at what point do you pass from being in recovery to being recovered? There's no end game, no goal line. The war against your own mind goes on until your heart stops beating.

"For those just joining us, this is a ten-week program," the Counselor says. "I encourage you to participate like your life depends on it. When you complete this program, if you do, this is your reward." He holds up a green paper, which appears to have been printed from a generic Microsoft Word template. Forgery would be easy. "But if you're lucky, your recovery will go on for the rest of your life. Seriously, folks. There is no middle ground."

Mrs. Copley said she was almost certain the Court would give Erin her kids back when she completed Early Recovery. So Erin will stick it out, get her legitimate green piece of paper, and take it to Court.

"Okay," the Counselor says. "Who'd like to start?"

Erin tries to picture him in a jungle. He said he was in Nam. She wonders if he saw combat, but she won't ask. She'll keep her head down, participate as if she's a government worker: at the level needed for successful completion.

A hand goes up. A voice says, "My name is George, and I'm an alcoholic and addict."

Everyone says, "Hi, George."

When they are finished saying how their days went and how many days of sobriety they have, the counselor gives them a lecture about how to avoid slipping. Erin tries to pay attention, but her thoughts keep drifting to Lindsey and Paul, living in Eddy's rented house twenty miles away, taking hour-long bus rides to and from school. Eddy insists they do not want to see her or talk to her. Mrs. Copley says patience is the best route to take. Erin has to give them time to come around.

When he finishes his talk, the Counselor passes around badly printed handouts, a written exercise that looks like something from junior high school. He tosses out a few statistics intended to scare the shit out of anyone who's even thinking about picking up.

After the Counselor finishes scaring them, they say the Serenity Prayer and Erin files out the door with the others, homework in hand. One down. Nine to go. Nine more weeks.

EIGHTEEN

The blatting thrum of a departing helicopter beats the air in the distance as Erin wipes sweat from her forehead and climbs into another battered MRAP, this one an Oskosh Assault. Candice leans in through the opposite vehicle door, spray bottle in one hand, disposable towel in the other. "They coulda told us we'd be doing fucking car wash duty."

Erin sprays the passenger seat and wipes. The inside of the vehicle smells something like the inside of an overused ambulance after a particularly busy shift: metal and plastic, dirt and sand, sweat and blood and puke and piss. Combat.

"Jesus . . . *apesta aquí!*" Candice ducks out of the vehicle, lifts her face to the sun and takes a deep breath before leaning back in, laughing. "Hah. Stinks out there, too."

Erin chuckles, continues scrubbing, going to work on a large stain on the seat back. "How clean do we have to get these?"

"Ain't no getting these things clean. Just wipe it down. Drake'll tell us if it's not good enough."

Something moving on the floorboard catches Erin's eye. She leans down to see a crushed, crumbled chocolate chip cookie, under attack by an army of desert ants. "Candice."

Candice leans in close, bracing herself on one arm. The desert ants move quickly on long legs that hold their bodies well above the black thermoplastic maze of the floor mats. Swarming over the cookie, they grab crumbs as large as themselves in their mandibles, scuttling in a perfectly ordered line across the ridges and gullies of the floor mats before disappearing into some hidden space near the running board.

When she worked landscape, Erin always dug carefully, and whenever she found an earthworm she picked it up and put it someplace safe. Though there was pressure to work fast, she could not make herself plough through a garden carelessly, without regard for the creatures living in the soil. The insects amaze her. "Look at them," she says, marveling at the elaborate choreography, "Look how organized they are, how dedicated."

"That's why they call it an army, girlfriend. Get rid of them. You heard Drake. These vehicles gotta be like, able to pass a USDA inspection. No plant material, no creepy crawlers."

"I can't just smash them."

Candice eyes Erin like she's nuts and goes back to scrubbing.

Erin uses her rag to scoop up the cookie and place it carefully on the ground a few feet away from the MRAP, quickly dusting off the ants that have darted up her arm, targeting their landing next to the cookie.

Back in the vehicle, she gently drags one end of the rag across the floorboard, herding the confused ants toward the doorway, marveling at how quickly they move on their stilt-like legs. Lindsey and Paul would be fascinated. She tackles the stain on the door panel, scrubbing hard, as if to erase the now familiar homesickness brought on by thoughts of her children.

114

NINETEEN

The line of humans stretches out the front door of the Family Court building and around the corner into the parking lot. People thumb their phones, chewing gum conspicuously, an act of defiance. Processing people through the Magnatron, the Court Officers move robotically. Sitting in the waiting area, Erin wonders how long it will be before they are replaced by actual robots, and whether anyone will notice.

She picks up a *Ladies Home Journal* dated three years ago. Before Afghanistan. Sometimes she is slow to recognize anxiety creeping in, slowly filling her body with something resembling a mass of weightless dough, a translucent tan substance shot through with millions of minuscule bits of metal, prickling and burning. It is a frightening energy, one step short of crippling physical pain. All she knows right now is that something is very, very wrong, at a time when nothing can go wrong without serious consequences.

She thinks maybe she should go to the hospital, but that would mean missing the hearing. She could wind up back in the Psychiatric Unit. She might never get out and, even if she did, she almost certainly would never get her children back.

She would rather die. She waits, afraid to move. When she realizes what's happening, she stays very still, seized by a panic as quiet as snow, and waits for the monstrous, horrible entity that has invaded her body to go away.

To others in the room, she looks like a woman reading a magazine.

From the hallway, someone calls her name. Erin jumps, drops the magazine. Gavin, still tan from wherever he went on vacation, posts himself near the Magnatron in his sharp blue suit, exuding impatience.

In the conference room, he places papers on the metal desk and leans over them. "I guess I should say that I'm not happy to see you here."

Erin appreciates his sympathy. "I'm halfway through Early Recovery. I haven't even had a visit. I want them to come home."

"I know, and you have a right to see them. But first we have to deal with today. I'm sorry to be the one who has to break this to you." He rubs his eyebrows, pinches his nose. "DSS wants you to participate in Family Treatment Court. If you want your kids back, if you even want a chance to get your kids back, you have to agree to it, and you have to sign a contract."

Gavin had tried to get Bagley and the DSS attorney, who wasn't Chrystal, thank God, to agree to Adjudication in Contemplation of Dismissal, which would put Erin's case on hold for a year while she got her shit together and, if she did everything right, would result in dismissal of the case. He'd been reasonable and courteous at first. Gotten nowhere. They refused. So he shifted gears into his stomping, fuming maniac persona that sometimes got results when being civilized didn't work. Still, they said no. They wanted an admission from Erin. By the end of the discussion, he wasn't play-acting his fury. His disdain of the arbitrary nature of who got breaks and who didn't took him almost to the point of a contempt finding from the judge.

"It's a pretty harsh contract."

"Wait." Erin is not sure she's heard right. "What happened to Early Recovery?"

"This is separate. Additional. Under a contract. And if you don't live up to it, they have the right to expel you from the program, at which point the judge has the right to go back in and reopen the matter and make changes to her order."

"Jesus Christ."

"Erin. You have multiple issues. PTSD—"

"No. I was never diagnosed with that and even if I was, this is not right, what they're doing." The VA doctors hadn't given a name to her condition, beyond anxiety. It was almost impossible to get diagnosed with PTSD. The doctor she'd seen had as much as admitted that budgetary constraints limited the number of PTSD cases they could diagnose. Erin got the message right away. She shouldn't expect much in the way of treatment, not for an illness that was all in her head.

"And alcoholism," Gavin continues. "That's the whole reason you're eligible for Family Treatment Court."

"Ask my friends. Ask my neighbors. Ask their teachers. Jesus, this is insane."

"I get it. You're sober. Ask me, you're ready for them now. But." He pulls out a handkerchief and dabs at his nose.

Erin eyes him carefully. She attempts to make eye contact, wondering if he's tweaking, but Gavin keeps his head down.

"Look, it's nothing personal against you. They process a certain number of cases and they need admissions on a certain number of cases. It's about numbers."

"Lotto is about numbers. This is about my children."

"Lotto is about money. And DSS has to produce just like any other state entity."

"I'm not denying I fucked up. I'm trying to fix it. Look at me. I'm fine."

He doesn't take his eyes off the paperwork on the desk. "They're insisting you go into the Family Treatment Court program. If you want a shot at getting your kids back, you have to sign this contract and make an admission in court. It's the equivalent of a guilty plea. The only other option is to go to Fact Finding, which is essentially a trial. I can assure you, you don't want to do that."

"Maybe I do."

"No. Really. You don't." Now he looks at her, his jaw clenching repeatedly, barely controlled anger in his voice. "It works like this:

DSS writes up the language to be used in your admission. I haven't even seen it yet. But today is your day in court. We're on the calendar for Fact Finding and Disposition. We'll get a chance to read what you'll be admitting to just before we go into the Courtroom."

"Wait. This is the first time anyone's—"

"It's how it's done. And if, after reading the admission today, you decide you don't want to make it, you can demand to go to Fact Finding. But if you do, that hearing will commence at once."

"Like, today?"

"Like in a few minutes."

"All this is based on the word of one caseworker, on her report? Do I have any rights at all?"

"The short answer is not many. All neglect matters are heard by a Family Court Judge. There is no right to trial by jury." He could suggest that Erin file an Application for Return, but he knows that will only piss off the judge even more than she already is, and the DSS attorneys as well. He doesn't want to see Erin lose her children, but he can't afford to sour what relationships he has with the court and the agency, and certainly he doesn't have time to pursue this thing as if it were bound for the goddamn Supreme Court. The expedient route is to convince Erin to make the admission.

He sees her crushed look. "It doesn't matter," he says. "They've made their decision. And they redact any information they feel could endanger the people who made the statements."

"Endanger them? Me?"

"People do crazy shit, Erin. The caseworker summarized her findings based on her interviews and presented it to the DSS lawyer. That's how it works."

"And what if she got it wrong? What if somebody lied to her? How am I supposed to defend myself?"

"It's what we have to work with." Gavin presses one corner of the paperwork, as if trying to pin it into the desktop.

"Does she have legal training?"

"Who?"

118

"The caseworker. Mrs. Copley. Does she have investigative training? Does she have psychological training? Does she have any, I don't know, credentials? Because, I gotta tell you, this looks like amateur hour to me."

He hands Erin the contract. "You think I like this shit? You think there's a politician anywhere that's got the balls to say *hey, something's fucked up?* We've got a government agency that's out of control? Hah!"

"But she said just go to Early Recovery. Get your certificate and you'll get your kids back." Erin reads, growing angry at the increasingly insulting stipulations listed on the document. She slaps it onto the desk and shoves it toward Gavin.

"They have the right to decide if I have a *bad attitude?* And take steps to adjust my attitude? What the fuck?"

"Exactly." He leans toward her, speaking quietly, seriously. "If you choose not to sign, they'll proceed with the charges of Neglect, and we'll go straight to Fact Finding. At this point, I can guarantee the judge is going to find you guilty. And when she does, she can decide on the spot to put your children in foster care." He clears his throat. "I don't think they'll do that at this point. Your ex is here, right? He has custody right now?"

"He disappeared from their lives. Dragged me through month after month of trying to get child support. He's a goddamn liar. This is so fucked."

"He's probably better than foster care."

"To think I let him send me over the edge. I'm an idiot." Erin sees herself as a cartoon character, googly-eyed Mom Mangué, being methodically flattened by a giant yellow road roller, her ex at the wheel, laughing maniacally. She tries to laugh, but has apparently once again misplaced her sense of humor. She wishes Tanya were with her.

"If it's any consolation, I've seen worse cases. I had one mother whose ex told CPS she had a major pot-growing operation. CPS shows up, cops in tow, they find a single joint. One fucking joint. She wasn't growing anything. And the kids are there—these were happy kids, everything was good—but there was that joint, so CPS took the kids, put Mom in the system. It was a nightmare for her to get them out of foster care, because guess what? Dad didn't even want them. He was just pissed off because she had a new boyfriend. Kids loved the new boyfriend. Ex didn't like the new boyfriend. So he dropped a dime on Mom. Happens more often than you think."

"They can't just—"

"Yes, they can. And listen to me. If you sign, you're agreeing to stay in this program until *they* decide you can leave. Until you, quote, *graduate*. Who makes this shit up? If at any time they feel your progress is inadequate, they can kick you out. And I have to make you aware, legally, of what can happen. Be aware that this is worst-case scenario." He shows her a paper:

NOTICE:

IF YOUR CHILD IS PLACED IN FOSTER CARE, YOU MAY LOSE YOUR RIGHTS TO YOUR CHILD AND YOUR CHILD MAY BE ADOPTED WITHOUT YOUR CONSENT.

IF YOUR CHILD STAYS IN FOSTER CARE FOR 15 OF THE MOST RECENT 22 MONTHS, THE AGENCY MAY BE REQUIRED BY LAW TO FILE A PETITION TO TERMINATE YOUR PARENTAL RIGHTS AND MAY FILE BEFORE THE END OF THE 15-MONTH PERIOD.

Erin hears Mrs. Copley's voice: *You won't be allowed so much as a school picture.*

"Look, I've seen cases where people really do *not* have it together and are incapable of taking care of their children, and the court doesn't take the kids. We've all seen the headlines."

"So it's what, a total crap shoot?"

"At this point, and I'm giving you my best advice here, the fastest way for you to get your children back is to sign the contract. Show them that you're willing to do anything they ask."

Erin picks up the pen.

∞

Eddy sits next to Bagley, the bow-tied, court-appointed Attorney for the Children. Erin doesn't remember the last time she saw Eddy in a suit and tie. He has combed his hair. In a glance, she sees that he's hungover.

She takes a seat at the defense table next to Gavin, who has his handkerchief out again. A sudden buzzing in her ears almost deafens her. Erin bites her lip, wanting to call him on his allergy bullshit. He's got to be on something, maybe cocaine. The lawyer drug of choice, next to booze.

There's always a little hush when the judge enters a courtroom, something vaguely threatening in the air, as if unchecked power has caused a change in barometric pressure. It's goddamn serious in here. People's futures are at stake. And the person sitting up there behind the heavy oak desk on that platform may be competent—or may not. Privilege lingers in the room like microbes of disease, searching for a host to invade.

The judge's words come to Erin as if through a tunnel, the phrases reverberating hollowly, "And you freely admit that . . ." And "No one has coerced you to. . ." and Erin hears herself saying *I do. Yes, Your Honor, I do.* I admit to it all, everything you say. She shoots a look at Eddy and says loud and clear, in response to the judge's question: *I do.*

TWENTY

Lunch is something that resembles fried chicken and mashed potatoes, though the entrée doesn't taste quite like chicken. Erin sits at a long, laminated table laughing with the others as Candice pokes fun at her over the ant incident. The DFAC, with its wall-mounted TV, NFL posters, and condiment stations, resembles a low-budget sports bar, except that the patrons are almost all wearing camouflage.

"Yeah, and she's like, 'but I can't just kill them,'" Candice jokes, and Erin sees Ginj go suddenly quiet and lean in close.

"Are you serious?" Ginj grins at Erin. "I can't wait to kill someone. That's the whole reason I signed up."

"*Qiuen te mando?*" Candice says. "What the fuck attitude is that?"

Ginj sits back, takes in the stunned expressions on the women's faces. And cracks up, laughing from deep in her belly, her red hair glowing under the blue-gray dining hall lights. "Hah!" She shakes her head, snorts. "Y'all are so easy. Seriously."

"You ever killed anyone?" Candice leans toward Ginj. "Like, for real?"

"Me? Nah. Nothing human."

"*Ai jincha*, what then, ants? Spiders?" Candice smirks.

"Ha, ha, very funny. If you must know, I been hunting since I was twelve." Ginj makes a face at Candice. "Got my first buck when I was thirteen. What's *jincha*?"

"White." Candice examines her nails, as if inspecting a manicure. "Way, *way* white."

"I hope you ate it," Erin says.

"Duh. Of course I ate it. You kill it, you eat it. That's the rule. Hey Candice, you with us here?"

Erin follows Candice's gaze to the chow line, where a line of jacked Special Forces troops push tan plastic mess trays along the serving line railing.

"*Ai mami*, that view," Candice says. "Would you look at those perfect butts, all in a row like that? I want to run over there and quick along the line, squeeze those buns, one after the other."

The table breaks into laughter, Erin with them until she sees Sergeant Drake, who has quietly posted himself just inside the chow hall entrance. He does not look happy. He eyes Erin and jerks his head slightly, like *come here now*. Erin points to her chest. *Me?* He nods.

"Excuse me," Erin says. "Be right back. I hope." Candice and Ginj glance over, see Drake, and quickly turn their attention to the food.

Drake stares while Erin crosses the room, his expression undecipherable. She halts two feet in front of him, comes to attention.

"Sergeant, Private Hill reports."

"At ease." Drake squints suspiciously.

She assumes the stance, hands pressed at the small of her back.

Drake leans in. "What's going on over there?"

"Sergeant, we're eating lunch."

"What was everyone looking at?"

"The chow line, sergeant."

"What was so interesting about the chow line?" Drake leans closer.

"Sergeant, we were wondering, the chicken tastes a little off."

"Come on." Drake grunts. "You expect me to believe that?"

Erin can't think what to say.

He moves even closer, his lips inches from her ear. "Guys like that? You don't want to go near them, Hill. There's a reason they're called Meateaters. And it's not because they like roast beef for Sunday dinner."

"Copy that, Sergeant."

Drake steps back, an eyebrow raised, a smirk playing at his lips.

"The meal is fine. You know why it doesn't taste like chicken?"

"No, Sergeant."

"Because it's rabbit. Next time, read the menu."

Erin flashes on the afternoon Lindsey and Paul found an injured rabbit in the back yard and she wound up taking the kids on an hour-long drive to an animal rehab, the injured bunny wrapped in a bath towel between them, uninterested in the carrot Lindsey kept trying to feed it. That night, under her pillow, she found a card made of light blue construction paper with a rabbit drawn on the front. Inside, it said "Best Mom Ever."

"Private Hill!"

"Sir." Erin snaps to attention.

"I know what you ladies were looking at. And I do not like trouble. If there's *any* trouble, the merest *iota* of trouble, you're going to find yourselves on KP, or guard duty, or whatever the fuck else I can find to make your lives even more miserable than they already are." He does something resembling a wink, or maybe it was a facial twitch. "Watch out," he says. "I've got my eye on you."

Erin waits, unsure what to do or say, or what could even come close to being a proper response.

"Dismissed." Drake hikes his camos by the belt, folds his muscular arms across his chest. "Finish your rabbit and get back to work." He winks again, this time for certain.

Back at the table, Erin examines what's left of her meal. It hadn't tasted bad, exactly, before she knew it was rabbit. Candice waits until the sergeant ducks out the door before nudging Erin.

"So like, tell us," she says impatiently.

"He wanted to know what we were looking at."

"What a dick," Ginj says.

"Is he pissed?" Candice glances at the door.

"Who knows?" Erin pokes at her mashed potatoes. "He said he has his eye on me."

"What the fuck's that supposed to mean?" Ginj taps her white plastic fork against her mess tray. "That's just creepy."

"Maybe he means for promotion." Candice smirks.

"No seriously, that's fucked up." Ginj stabs at some green beans, stuffs them in her mouth.

"It kind of felt that way. But sometimes it's hard to tell." Erin shrugs.

"Not for me it isn't, and that sounds fucked up." Ginj looks at Erin through squinty eyes, like she's having trouble focusing.

"What," Erin says, "I'm supposed to file a complaint because I don't like the way he looked at me?"

"Guess not, considering the circumstances." Ginj shrugs.

"He also said the chicken isn't chicken. It's rabbit."

Candice almost gags. "You got to be kidding me!"

"Dude. I knew it wasn't chicken." Ginj takes a bite of the meat, chews carefully. "Yep. That's definitely rabbit. Knew it."

"Why didn't you say something?" Candice slaps her own forehead. "You actually eat rabbit?"

"I prefer venison," Ginj says. "Rabbit's a pain to skin."

Candice forks her serving onto Ginj's plate. "Enjoy."

Erin does the same. "I cannot eat a bunny. Sorry. Just can't." Erin and Candice watch Ginj slice eagerly into the rabbit.

"What're you two gonna do? Later on. When you're hungry?" Ginj grips her knife and grins at them. "Oh wait. I know. Chocolate covered ants." She wolfs a forkful of rabbit and bugs out her eyes, chewing maniacally.

"*Jincha*," Candice says, "I'll give you this: you got some *cajones.*"

TWENTY-ONE

The gray light of morning spills through the warehouse windows of Gavin's loft. He rolls out of bed and yanks on his sweats, suiting up to run before he has time to think himself out of it. It feels like a three-mile day. He reaches under the bed for his shoes.

Wait. Something doesn't feel right. Maybe he'll do two miles today. Two's sufficient. Pulling his left shoelace snug, he stops suddenly, ventures a closer look at the light hovering in the windows.

Shit. He grabs his phone from the nightstand, feels the beginning of a headache as he stares at the screen. Shit-shit-shit. He replaces the phone and massages his temples.

Fuck. It's not morning. The freaking sun is *setting*.

He's supposed to be at the fundraiser in half an hour.

He kicks off his shoes and steps out of his sweats. Christ on a cupcake. His suit coat is on the floor near the black leather couch all the way over in the center of the loft. Did he do that? He remembers lunch at Sashasan, and Chrystal suggesting they get sake.

Shit.

Okay. Okay it's not a big deal. He didn't miss any appointments. No hearings. He remembers telling her that his afternoon calendar was clear. And after that, the bar next door to the sushi joint. And after that?

His suit coat is all the way across the room. But there's no way he'll make it through the fundraiser without what's in his jacket pocket.

126

The Couillard House, built by hand out of limestone and pine, sits a couple of short blocks down Main Street from the Old Stone Church in the middle of downtown. Gavin circles the block twice before nabbing a spot near the entrance. He's lucky that way. He checks his tie in the rearview, grabs his jacket, and exits the car. He has to go back and retrieve his checkbook from the glove box. Part of his brain still thinks it's morning. At least the Advil worked.

He would have preferred to skip this scene, but his father wasn't up to going out and insisted that Gavin attend to show the firm's support for—as the elder Costa put it—the young Turk who, at the age of twenty-five, is hoping to unseat the Republican incumbent and solve the City of Granite's problems. He wants to be Mayor.

"It used to be that experience counted for something," his father said, his voice eroded by illness and age.

"Don't stress," Gavin said. He wished his father would take better care of himself. "He'll ride right in, on Hillary's coattails."

"Not necessarily." His father tucked a hand halfway into his pocket, an odd gesture that made him look a bit like Teddy Roosevelt posing for a photograph. "It's a very local election."

Rather than arguing, setting himself up for another of his father's increasingly rambling lectures, Gavin conceded the point and then claimed he had to hurry, it wasn't good business to keep a client waiting. His father's words came back to him when he got to the office and checked himself in the lavatory mirror. Did he still qualify as young? He looked young. He looked healthy. He would try to get more rest. Rest always helped. He hitched his cuffs and headed for the waiting room to shake hands with his newest client: another affluent father, hoping to shield himself from alimony. The discussion had depressed him to the point that, when the meeting finally ended, he'd called Chrystal and asked her to meet him for lunch.

Beneath the hand-hewn pine beams of the low-ceilinged entry, he scans the crowd, his radar up. Good. She's not here. Maybe their little afternoon soirée has her down, still, for the count. He takes out his checkbook and leans on the donation table to write, glancing eye-to-eye at the perky young woman manning the table. Is she twenty-two? Maybe twenty-three? She's hot, that's certain. *Half your age plus seven.* She's a few years short of that. Maybe several. Fuck the rule. Her shining brown hair falls over her shoulders in waves, and her playful brown eyes gaze at him like she's got a plus-one invitation to the most exclusive party in town. He signs the check with an exaggerated flourish. She thanks him energetically, practically gushing.

"My pleasure," he says. "Are you stuck here all evening, or do they give you a break?"

"I'm here for the next hour," she says. "Then I mingle."

He gives her a wink, then immediately wishes he hadn't, but she pulls her lips into a flirtatious smirk that kicks his confidence another notch higher.

"Find me," he says.

Ninety minutes and two Scotches later, he's got her, skirt up and panties down, against the wide pine paneling in the cellar of the stone building, in what was once the Couillard House slave quarters. She rides him hard, her lips warm and moist, her tongue finding his own as he thrusts deep into her and finds their rhythm. God, she's so wet, her muscular haunches flexing in his grasp as he quickens, and deeper, and feels her throbbing, closing tight around him, pulling him in and in and in until he explodes into her and they collapse against the wall, gasping.

They stay that way until their breathing settles and he eases her back to her feet.

"That was fun," she says, straightening her skirt. "Are you on Tinder?"

Tinder. Wow. "Uh, no," he says. "I like to keep a low profile."

"Dope."

Zipping up, he hopes to God that Chrystal McClain has not arrived upstairs at the bar.

TWENTY-TWO

Country & Western twangs through the building as Erin clomps across the plywood floor. Even her boots feel heavy. An orange and gold poster-board sign hangs on the wall near the billiard table: Happy Thanksgiving! She passes the pool tables and the gaming computers, winds through a narrow plywood hallway and adds her name to the list of soldiers waiting for phone or computer time. A young Afghan man sitting at the sign-in table tells her in heavily accented English that the wait is about two hours. He looks to be in his teens. Erin sees that he's been practicing writing in English on a lined tablet in front of him. The page is filled with doodles, and with words, among them "America" and "citizen" and "freedom." The word "liberty" appears several times, and the name "Fatima." The man covers the page with a forearm and smiles politely as he hands Erin a block of wood with the number 18 written on it in heavy black Sharpie ink. The wood has an oily sheen to it from all the hands that have held it, waiting to connect with home.

Erin goes to the bookshelves, unfinished pine, searches for something to read. The titles are mostly military history and thrillers. She wants to be home with her children. She's past the halfway point. And staying on the base is fine. Staying on the base is safer than being out in convoys. All she has to do is keep her head down and be alert. She tries to see the titles on the book spines in front of her, but the letters swim, illegible through the tears filling her eyes. She doesn't want to miss anyone as badly as she misses Paul and Lindsey right now. The ache in her chest moves slowly up her throat; she tries to gulp it back down. She grabs a book blindly.

She sinks into the cushions and cracks open the hardcover. Poetry. She has grabbed a volume of poetry, hiding in the shelves between the thrillers, and she remembers the day in class when one of her English teachers said, "The books you need to read will find you." It had struck her as slightly insane, but a good insane. She has repeated it to every English class she's taught. She can still hear the collective groan that arose whenever she brought up the topic of poetry in the classroom. She is struck suddenly by the absurdity of being here, thousands of miles from her children, for a cause she cannot comprehend, all because of one moment of desperation, one thoughtless decision. How stupid could she be? She cracks open the book and bends her neck to read, hiding out in the pages, hoping to conceal her tears.

Lines of text swim before her eyes. She sneaks furtive swipes across her cheeks with the back of her hand. She'd dumped most of her dinner in the trash, left Ginj and Candice at the table and walked to the rec center, needing to hear her children's voices. She's trying not to sink into a total funk, trying to stay positive. Some days it's really hard. Her back aches from spending hour after hour packing equipment into large plywood containers for shipment to the US, inspecting case after case of video equipment and electronics, making sure no insects or food are nestled inside the cases. She, Candice, and Ginj, along with the rest of the squad, have been assigned to Retrograde, maybe for the entire week. Any given day can result in an assignment that has nothing to do with her specialty. If there isn't any driving to do, Drake makes sure the unit is kept busy. No matter the task, unless she's outside the wire in a convoy, daily life on the base is Groundhog Day: one after the other, pretty much all the same. She spent most of today untangling and clipping cargo harnesses to container pallets. Her hands are sore and fatigued, and the repetitive nature of the task left her with too much time to think about how badly she missed her children.

When her number is called, Erin closes the book and winds through the plywood opening to a small room lined with phone stations, not completely private, but at least there are sheets of plywood between the phones. The room is raw, hollow, temporary. She sits down at the hammered-together desk labeled 18. It's eleven and a half hours later back home. They should be up now, getting ready for school. She summons a happy voice and picks up the phone.

Lindsey answers, sounding breathless.

"Hey, kiddo, it's Mommy. Ready for school?"

"Mommy! Mommy Mommy Mommy!" Lindsey squeals her delight. "Are you coming home?"

Erin tries to keep the tremble from her voice as she explains that it will be a few more months. Lindsey volunteers that they're going to Megan's house for Thanksgiving, since Erin won't be there to cook. Erin wonders if she's forgotten one of Lindsey's friends or if Lindsey has made a new one.

"She's a friend of Daddy's and sometimes we go over to her house after school. She's really nice. When are you coming home?"

"The end of January." Erin tries to maintain her cheerful tone. "Two more months." She doesn't know why she says that. To an eight-year-old, a month is forever. To an eight-year-old, new friends are full of possibility. She wants to ask questions about Megan but knows she shouldn't. She hears Eddy's voice in the background, telling Lindsey to come eat her cereal. "Is Paul there? Can I talk to him?"

"Yep," Lindsey says, and calls her brother to the phone. "Bye Mommy, I love you."

"I love you too, punkinhead. I'll call again soon."

Erin hears the shuffle of the phone being handed off, and then the sound of Paul's breathing. He was always stuffy in the mornings.

"Paul?"

"Hi, Mom. Where are you?"

"Still in Afghanistan." Erin tries a laugh.

"No, but where?"

"In the rec center, on the base. Where they keep the phones." Erin tells him there are videogames, too. He perks up at that. But he sounds down, unhappy. When Erin asks him what's wrong, his voice goes to a whisper. He doesn't want to go to Megan's for Thanksgiving. He wants his mom to come home. Erin tells him it's only once and promises to cook a feast next Thanksgiving.

"With my favorite dressing?"

"Whatever you want, with gravy on top." Erin asks how school is going.

"I'm on the basketball team."

Erin tells him that's awesome and promises to share the secret of her three-pointer when she gets back.

"I miss you," Paul says.

"I miss you too, hon. I'm sorry I had to leave."

Eddy's voice intrudes from the background again, calling Paul to breakfast.

"You'd better get going. Let me talk to Dad?" A shuffling sound again, and then Paul comes back on the line. "He says he can't right now. He's making breakfast and we're gonna miss the bus."

"Okay, doodlebug. Go eat. I love you."

"Love you too, Mom."

Erin puts down the phone and leans against the plywood wall, telling herself not to jump to conclusions. The day she was notified of the unit's deployment—drop everything, forget your life, make your arrangements, we're shipping out in two weeks—she'd been terrified. And then, for a few days, elated. Maybe, while she was gone, Eddy would remember that he loved her. That she loved him. That not-so-long ago they had a beautiful family.

She tries to think of the Megans she knew in high school, but no faces surface to connect with the name. She wonders if Megan is the one he'd been with before the deployment. Maybe that one was already in the past, replaced now by Megan, who apparently knows how to cook a Thanksgiving dinner for an entire family. Even if the family isn't hers.

TWENTY-THREE

When she hears car tires on the gravel driveway outside, Erin drops her handful of crayons, not even trying to catch them as they roll and scatter across the dining room table. Mrs. Copley didn't say she was coming today. But DSS can show up whenever they want and demand to be let in.

Still in her pajamas, Erin waits for the knock at the front door. At some point this morning she had pulled the kids' crayon box from the hall closet shelf that holds art supplies, vowing to organize her household. She doesn't want DSS to think she is incapable of keeping a decent house. They might decide she needs an attitude adjustment. She wonders what Mrs. Copley's house looks like, whether it would pass inspection.

She should get dressed. Mrs. Copley will not approve of her being in her pajamas in the afternoon. Fuck Mrs. Copley. Eddy still insists the kids don't want to talk to her. She can barely make herself call him anymore, dreading to hear what he says. Some days she knows he's lying. Some days she thinks he's telling the truth. The time between her appointments and meetings sends her mind in random directions, filling her with anger or despair, hurtling her into a future full of horrible circumstances. Her tears splat onto the rows of crayons on the thick oak tabletop. With each passing day, she becomes more certain that Dr. Kloeten was right. They will never forgive her.

Outside, a car door slams. Erin scoops up the crayons and pours them back into the shoebox, runs to pull on some clothes, smearing tears across her face.

When she steps onto the front porch, the sunny day stuns her. Indoors had seemed cloudy and gray. The trees have painted the hills in brilliant shades of orange and yellow and red, in gold and brown, and a hard night wind has scattered the first falling leaves across the lawn. Erin balks at the sight of a shiny SUV with black tinted windows. The man who rolls out of the driver's seat is in head-to-toe hunter's camouflage, so new it still has creases.

"Hi-how-ah-yah," he says.

Erin recognizes him then; it is Rico, the man who owns property adjacent to hers, up for his annual hunting trip.

"Fine," Erin says, lying as she walks toward him. She doesn't want him near the front door. They stand next to the car; Erin feels the heat come off the engine. A tall man gets out of the passenger side and comes around the front of the vehicle.

Rico doesn't introduce him. The man's camo is as new as Rico's, and he's topped it off with a wide-brimmed leaf-decorated hat. He looks uncomfortable, in the manner of people who try too hard to seem casual when they are completely out of their element.

Rico and his friend stand in her driveway like a couple of large, man-shaped houseplants. Erin wonders why they've bothered to come out of the woods, but it feels good not to cry. The people in the meetings say God will take care of her. Maybe this is a sign. Maybe God has sent these men here, unwitting Jehovah's witnesses, to free her from her tears. At the moment, she doesn't care. At least it's not DSS sitting in her driveway.

"You seen the fisher cat?" Rico asks, his dark eyes taking in Erin's curves. He did that the last time she saw him, years ago, when he came by to talk to Eddy about hunting. It makes her even more uncomfortable today.

Though she has never seen a fisher cat, she's certain she's heard one. The twins were still small, maybe four, and slept right through it. It was the middle of the night, several months after Eddy lost his job, and she hers. She had fallen into an exhausted sleep, bolting awake when she heard the screams. She called the sheriff's office immediately but couldn't tell the dispatcher where the sound was coming from, other than somewhere in the woods behind her house. The dispatcher asked for her address but Erin could tell she was not taken seriously.

"My kids saw one last summer," she says now. Paul and Lindsey had rushed into the kitchen breathlessly to tell her they'd seen some kind of yeti, or a wendigo or *something* out in the woods, and it had stalked them from up in the trees, leaping from limb to limb. It followed them most of the way home. But now she's not sure it was last summer. She can't remember how many summers she's been back. Time does that to her sometimes. Since her return, she suffers moments where she doesn't know what year it is, or when she went over, or when she got back.

"Hello?" Rico's smoke-husky voice sounds almost rude. "You still with us? You gotta be careful. They pounce."

"I've never seen one."

"They're dangerous, I'm telling you." Rico glances at his car. "You got a gun?"

Erin shakes her head. She tries to think of a way to ask Rico to leave, politely.

"You need one," he says. "You should have one." He waves an arm around. "Out here like this. By yourself."

Erin tells him she's okay, she doesn't need a gun. He asks if Eddy comes around much anymore, now that they're divorced. Erin wonders how Rico knows about it, and what else he knows.

"There's no telling when he'll show up," she says. She could have told the truth but doesn't want Rico to know. He has always struck her as creepy.

"How's the kids?"

Erin fights the tightening in her throat. "They're dealing with it."

"Kids are amazing."

"Yours?"

"My kids are assholes." He brays loudly, amused at his wit. "I'm thinking about selling though. The wife, the kids, they have no interest in coming up with me." He leans into his SUV and pulls out a brown leatherette rifle case, lays it across the hood of his car. "Take it," he says. "It's all yours."

Erin tells him she's never had a problem with animals. She doesn't need the rifle.

"The fisher, though." He zips the case open, slides out a 6.5 Mannlicher. "You know how to use this?"

Erin nods.

"Oh, yeah that's right. You went to, where was it, Iraq?"

Erin doesn't bother to correct him.

"Fucking ragheads." He points out the safety and shows her where to load the cartridges. She pretends to pay attention but can't stop wondering why and how Rico knows so much about her life, and whether he knows she was in the hospital, and if he knows that Eddy has full custody. Rico's visit strikes her as just plain weird. But he's a weird guy.

She tells herself to stop being paranoid and picks up the Mannlicher, feeling its weight. She steps away from them and shoulders the weapon, holding firm where arm meets collarbone, flexing the meat of her biceps against the shock pad on the rifle butt just to let them know she can handle the weapon.

"I really don't need this." She hands it back.

Rico zips the rifle back into its case and holds it out. "Take it. You never know."

Her children are at school and will not be coming home to her no matter how hard she pretends. They will be going to Eddy's house in the next town over. Eddy and Megan's house. She thinks of the many afternoons she spent consoling them in the months after Eddy left them, because Eddy said he was coming to visit but never bothered to show up.

"Take it," Rico says again. "I insist. I'd feel bad if something happened to you and I hadn't been a good neighbor."

Erin finds his tone threatening. She takes the rifle, hearing a chorus from the rooms: the Universe provides. She'll get rid of it later. Somehow. She'll hike over and leave it at his hunting cabin. He'll only be around for a few weeks. She holds the rifle case by its brown leatherette handle while Rico and his pal climb back into the black Explorer. She wishes they would hurry up. Finally the engine starts. Rico rolls down the window, shouts to her.

"Anyone asks, that didn't come from me. It fell off the back of a truck."

Erin chokes out a laugh. She doesn't believe for a moment that he's mobbed up. He works in some kind of administrative capacity in an office somewhere in New Jersey. Mortgage refinancing, if she recalls. Maybe she has missed an opportunity to refinance her house. She waves pleasantly as they rumble down the driveway, waiting until the car is out of sight before she goes back inside.

In her bedroom, she unzips the case and makes sure the rifle is not loaded. She lays it carefully on the bed, still wondering why she accepted it. This is the thing that frightens her: she hadn't realized she was saving the Xanax, but in hindsight recognized that she'd been hoarding the prescription, keeping it tucked away, safe and untouched, a hand grenade in an orange plastic bottle, waiting for her to pull the pin.

She has no appointments today. She needs to stay busy. She goes to her computer intending to search for a job, though she holds little hope. From the internet, she learns that the fisher cat is a large marten valued for its fur, found in North American woodlands. Fishers and mountain lions are the only regular predators of porcupines.

She understands why. She's seen a few porcupines up close, in the woods. The quills are quite beautiful, delicate and dangerous at once.

She'd heard once that if the quills pierce the skin and are not promptly removed they will work their way—over the course of several days or even weeks, sometimes months—into muscle tissue and eventually to internal organs. Should they penetrate the heart, the injury can be fatal. But the internet says this is not scientifically factual, that it is nothing more than folklore. The night Erin heard the scream in the woods, Eddy was out drinking with pals. It had become a regular thing.

She continues reading, trying to focus on the screen instead of the rifle on the bed. The fisher has a unique way of killing the porcupine. It repeatedly bites and scratches the animal's face until the creature bleeds to death, and then it flips its prey over to get at the soft under-belly. The fisher cat is known also for one of its calls, which is said to sound like a child screaming, and can be mistaken for someone in dire need of help. If she had known, the night she heard the screaming in the woods, about the call of the fisher cat, she might have recognized it for what it was and avoided the embarrassment of being dismissed by the dispatcher at the sheriff's office.

It hadn't sounded at all like a child screaming. She gets up and wraps the rifle in an Army blanket and places it on a high shelf in her closet, buried amidst sweaters and sheets. She secures the shells in her lockbox. It had sounded like a woman screaming, and Erin had mistaken it for the sound of someone being attacked.

She sits back down at the computer, still rattled. But at least the tears have not returned. It feels as if there's been a hemispheric shift; a distance has opened up—a small chasm between the left and right lobes of her brain—thwarting whatever relentless neural impulses were causing her to cry almost continuously, day after night after day. All she knows right now is that there is a weapon tucked away in her closet, and for the first time in a very long time, she feels at peace.

TWENTY-FOUR

The M35A3 is packed to the hilt with crates full of electronic equipment, stacked in around a generator that was never repaired after it broke down within weeks of arriving at Forward Operating Base Shank. Erin feels the weight of the load in the steering wheel. The contractors in charge of the repair effort claimed they couldn't obtain the right parts to get the thing running again. It sat, unused, for three years. Now it's going home to America with all the rest of the stuff too valuable, or too dangerous, to scrap or leave behind. The convoy got on the road by midnight, leaving FOB Shank under cover of darkness, headed for J-Bad. Erin is grateful that during the three days they were there, cleaning and packing the equipment, not a single attack happened. Shank was up close against Pakistan; the troops called it Rocket City.

Ginj, alert as ever, constantly scans the landscape through her night vision goggles. Her tendency to remain vigilant makes more sense to Erin now. Maybe Ginj really does want to kill someone, maybe the lunchroom joke wasn't a joke at all. Erin wonders how many are here for the same reasons she is—a paycheck—and how many enlisted for the chance to get away with murder.

"You know what I'm thinking?" Ginj twists in her seat, stretching. "My question is this. What the hell are they gonna even do with all this stuff once they get it back there? We been here what, going on fourteen, fifteen years?" She taps at the electronic tracker mounted on the dash. "How much you think all this shit costs?"

"Ginj. You ever think about going to college?"

"Me? Not really."

"Why not?"

"School's boring. And expensive."

"You finish up here, the government will help pay."

"Still boring."

"You're smart. You should go."

"Yeah professor, I'll think about that."

The vehicle in front of them swerves suddenly to the left side of the road and stops. Erin immediately pulls to the right as the entire convoy goes into the herringbone formation, alternating vehicles on opposite sides of the road, distance between them, on defense.

Ginj clutches her rifle tightly, shifts sideways in her seat, scanning the darkness outside. "Holy shit holy shit holy shit." She's practically singing. "What's going on?"

Erin sees nothing moving out there in the gray-black night vision haze; only the infrared markers on the vehicle bumpers glow red in the darkness. There's no movement anywhere. She tells herself to stay calm, stay alert, be ready for . . . she's not sure what. Ready for an attack. Every cell in her body hums with adrenaline-laced energy. She feels sweat above her upper lip and trickling from her armpits. What the fuck is out there?

"God damn it," Ginj whispers. "Where the hell are they? C'mon, bastards."

They sit, the truck engine idling noisily, Ginj craning her neck back and forth, back and forth, scanning for movement outside the vehicle. A message pops up on the dashboard Blue Tracker, the iPad-sized screen mounted in front of her. She leans forward, lifting her goggles to read.

"Oh fuck me," she says. "We're being rerouted to Bagram." She settles back into her seat. "Nothing ever *happens*."

"Does it say why?"

"Do they ever say why?"

Erin waits for the vehicle in front to move before pulling out after it. They ride in silence for a while, driving on paved highway across level lowlands. Slowly, but it's better than dealing with the mountains.

"Maybe I'll come here as a tourist someday," Ginj says. "Like they do now in Vietnam."

"Maybe you could study abroad. Get some life experience before you settle down."

"What, this doesn't count? And who says I'm settling down?"

"You don't want kids?"

"Not that I'm aware of."

"You've got time. You're what, twenty?"

"Nineteen. And why does everyone say that? Like, every time the subject comes up and I say I'm not sure, someone always says 'oh don't worry, you're young, you've got time.' Fuck that shit." She pulls out her iPod and plugs the jack into the truck's sound system. "I mean, the whole goddamn planet is imploding. I'm not sure bringing kids into this world is the best idea."

Erin has no argument.

"Did you think about that? What made you have kids?"

"I was in love and I wanted a family."

"Bae. That's so touching." Ginj grabs her water bottle from the floorboard. "You sure it wasn't just the old biological clock?"

Erin had always known she wanted to be a mom, though for a long time, until Eddy, she found the prospect frightening. But she hadn't heard any ticking when she said yes to his proposal.

"My parents divorced." Ginj chuckles.

"Mine too. Sometimes, after that, it seemed like my mom was just going through the motions, you know?"

"It's gotta be tough. But at least you've got a husband around to help. I bet you're a good mom."

Erin doesn't tell Ginj how bad things had gotten before she deployed. The man she had loved had disappeared, and it had happened so slowly that neither she nor Eddy realized it in time to do anything to stop it. Loss of self is like that, happening subtly, over

142

time, so gradually that although it is the most perilous of human losses, you don't notice it the way you would notice the loss of a limb, or even the loss of a paycheck.

Ginj digs in her backpack, hits a button on her iPod. The truck fills with the thump-thump crash of Imagine Dragons' *Radioactive*. Ginj taps her fingers on the butt of her M4, keeping time to the heavy bass beat as Erin joins her, the two of them howling "Welcome to the new age . . ."

The sun is still below the horizon, the sky coming up pale blue through the windshield when Ginj rips open a packet of Instant Folger's and holds it out to Erin.

"You're nodding."

Erin shakes her head hard, trying to pull herself out of the daze. She pours the powder onto her tongue, swigs from the water bottle Ginj hands her and her mouth instantly fills with bitter, practically gagging her.

"Good soldier." Ginj pats her on the shoulder. "Drive nice and I'll get you a donut when we get there."

Erin feels the caffeine rinse into her system and realizes she's been driving in her sleep. By the time the convoy pulls through the security checkpoint at the gates of Bagram Airfield, she has caffeine jitters. The scenery now seems familiar—concrete and concertina wire, gravel and plywood, sandbags and MRAPs and fighter jets—but this place is huge, a military Disneyland.

The convoy rolls past a staging area holding row after row of battered pickups and Humvees, doors unhinged or missing, tailgates gone, glass a thing of the past. Dozens and dozens of MRAPs and M-ATVs, hulking tanks, bulldozers and back-hoes, hundreds of vehicles lined up as if in formation, waiting to be shipped out.

The road takes them near a corner of the perimeter fence. Next to a large pile of gravel, a mound of trash has been pushed around an upright pole; it looks like a giant Christmas tree made of plastic trash bags and snarled barbed wire. Atop the chain link fence behind it, more plastic trash bags—black and white and blue—have snagged in the razor barbs of the concertina wire stretched along the top of the fencing, filling the wire with an almost solid wall of flimsy plastic film flapping spastically in the wind.

"Makes you feel kind of small, don't it?" Ginj leans forward to get a look at the Air Traffic Control tower.

The mountains, the Hindu Kush, snowcapped and jagged in the distance, watch silently. Erin cannot begin to imagine the struggles they've witnessed, the infinitesimal bits of bloody human folly that have, through the eons, passed beneath their gaze. The convoy pulls to a stop aside a long row of open-topped white containers set side by side for the length of a city block, maybe longer. The side of each container is labeled in black spray paint: Scrap B, Alk Batts, Liquid. At the end of the street are several tan metal shipping containers, doors wide open, and on the inside of the open doors more spray-painted labels: Medical, Office Supplies, Metal.

"Jesus," Ginj says, "they're never gonna get out of here on time."

"Isn't it always like that when you move? You think you've got it under control, and then you start trying to pack."

Sergeant Drake's voice comes through Erin's helmet. She follows his terse instructions and pulls the cargo truck up to the end of the row, where a crane waits, ready to lift the generator and place it next to the rows of generators already lined up for shipment. Hundreds of them, hulking rectangles of weathered, sand-colored metal casings holding heavy diesel engines, some that worked, some that didn't. They get out and begin unstrapping the cargo.

They're about halfway through when a soldier shows up to inventory the load.

"Y'all were supposed to go to J-Bad, right?"

"Yeah," Ginj says. "What's up with that?"

"No idea."

"You got any idea where I can go if I'm thirsty?"

"That," the soldier says, "I can help you with."

Pulling at a nylon cargo strap, Erin makes up her mind that whatever kind of trouble Ginj is looking for will not be part of her own evening agenda.

∞

Ginj fakes out the guy guarding her, popping a bounce pass to Erin without even glancing in her direction. Erin is relieved Ginj took her advice and came out to play some ball rather than hook up with the soldier who had access to alcohol. It wasn't worth the risk. She takes the pass from Ginj and dribbles easily, alternating hands, looking for a play. Sergeant Drake crouches in front of her, weight centered, arms wide, ready to move in whichever direction she goes. He guards loosely, giving her room because they're so far away from the goal, aiming to knock down her pass when she sends the ball in. Erin scans the alley beneath the goal. Ginj is covered, Candice doing a good job of guarding her. The other player on their side, a lanky Midwesterner almost as muscled up as Drake, stalks the free-throw line, waiting for a pass from Erin, who is outside the three-point arc. She fakes left, plants her feet and sends the ball toward the goal, catching Drake by surprise.

"Ha!" he shouts, spinning off, charging toward the goal to get the rebound.

Only there isn't one. Erin's ball swishes through the net clean.

Drake stops so fast his Nikes screech against the floor.

"Damn, Hill!" He props his hands on his hips, sweat running down his bare chest as he makes a tight circle, glancing at Erin with a mixture of disbelief and admiration. "Where'd you learn to do that?"

"High school, Sergeant." Erin back-peddles toward mid-court, wiping sweat from her eyes, enjoying the fact that she totally faked him out and nailed the shot, even if it's only a three-on-three pickup game. Ginj glides over and high-fives Erin as Drake's other teammate, a hulking teenager who moves as if he'd be a lot more comfortable on a football field, retrieves the ball and tosses it in to Candice. He's not outright laughing, but it's clear he likes it that Erin just owned the sergeant on the court. Candice dribbles toward mid-court to bring the ball back into play, not bothering to hide her amusement, even if she's not on Erin's team.

The next time Erin has the ball, Drake is on her like a shirt, hanging on her back so close he's practically hugging her: she's not getting past him. A couple of times she tries to pivot around him, but he moves right with her, like they're a unit; Erin can feel the heat coming off him and smell his sweat.

"C'mon, Hill," he says, almost whispering in her ear, "show me what you got," but it's not threatening, it's more like respectful. It's sport. He wants her to challenge him, though there's something in his tone that lets her know he's certain he'll prevail.

She tries once more to spin past him and drive to the goal, but that was never her strength. She was the Lady Bobcats' point guard, a legendary outside shooter in the Granite County Athletic League.

Erin whips the ball over to Ginj, who bulls her way up the right alley stripe and puts up a hook shot for the score.

"Jesus," Drake says, laughing. "If y'all could pack crap as good as you ball, we coulda had everything out of this fuckbake country a month ago."

Walking back to the tent with Ginj and Candice, Erin wonders uneasily what it might have been like to meet Drake under different circumstances. Maybe he felt the same thing she did when he was guarding her, in so close she could sense his strength as he stayed in tight, his body inches from hers and moving with her every step, almost as if they were dancing.

TWENTY-FIVE

One corner of the small, cinderblock office is cluttered with toys, baby carriers, boxes of toddler toiletries. Erin occupies the doorway, waiting to be acknowledged by the woman busy typing at the desk. On the wall behind her hangs a framed Associate Degree in Human Services from Granite County Community College, along with an assortment of cheaply framed certificates of completion from a variety of human services programs and seminars.

Finally the woman looks up, pushing black bangs out of her eyes. She looks about thirty and comes off as very laid back. Erin thinks she might be stoned. Or maybe it's something prescription.

She introduces herself as Cindy, the Family Treatment Coordinator, and apologizes to Erin for being unable to get to her at last week's Family Treatment Court session, Erin's first time attending. "Pardon the mess," she says. "I collect donations for the women who need a little extra help."

Erin finds Cindy's easygoing manner refreshing and thinks for a moment that maybe Cindy isn't like the others. But then Cindy ruins it by asking Erin to tell her story. And like every bureaucrat Erin has encountered since Mrs. Copley showed up at the hospital, Cindy emphasizes the importance of honesty. No one can help Erin unless she is absolutely honest about her drug and alcohol use and her mental health issues. Erin wonders why the agencies all insist on separating alcohol use from drug use, like it's a separate category. Just last week she got a mailer advertising an elegant hospital fundraising

147

dinner that listed a svelte vodka manufacturer as its major sponsor. She has no idea how she got on that mailing list, unless St. Martin's Hospital adds their alcoholic patients to their fundraising database.

Erin does her best to be honest, tries not to leave out any details, except the details she does not want to talk about today. She speaks only vaguely about Afghanistan. The Family Treatment Court will just have to trust that it was a nightmare. Cindy clacks at the keyboard. "I'm sorry to put you through it all again."

Erin knows by now that her best option is to cooperate. But she will do so only to the degree necessary. An entire industry has been created around drug and alcohol use and mental health issues, and business is booming. She wonders if Cindy would put in a good word for her if she were to bring a few of Lindsey's and Paul's old books here and donate them.

"I'm really sorry," Cindy says, still pecking away as Erin answers the same questions she's answered at every step of the agency-conveyor-belt process. "I have to get you into my computer system."

Erin nods. *You have to put me into your computer system. Just as someone put you into their computer system when you took this job, uploading your résumé, your application, your fingerprints, the results of your background check and whatever other details they required, and gave you a job putting other people— dysfunctional parents—into your computer system, only it's not really your system, it's theirs. The* Ubiquitous They *lurking behind the screens. You send packets of information skidding along the wires until they spill onto platters of aluminum or glass inside some distant plastic-and-metal storage device in a warehouse full of devices, a warehouse that hums electric.* Cindy's fingers plunk onto the keys. How do you enter love, or loyalty, or belief? They had all that, at the start, she and Eddy. How do you consign to electronic storage the look they'd shared watching Lindsey and Paul on stage in the annual Granite Elementary School Music Spectacular, singing "Yellow Submarine" as the middle school band squeaked and honked and banged accompaniment?

Cindy glides her computer mouse around the Granite County mousepad on her desk. Click. Erin offers yes or no in response to the questions. Click. Click. "Almost done," Cindy says. "Have you been diagnosed with any mental health conditions?"

Erin wonders why Cindy doesn't have access to the DSS files, why there is so much redundancy in this process. It's as bad as the military. She does not tell Cindy she has PTSD, even though the Drug and Alcohol Lady seemed certain of it. But Erin's military record will not bear that out. She answers the rest of Cindy's questions politely, courteously, until the loudspeaker blares, "ALL PARTICIPANTS IN FAMILY TREATMENT COURT TO COURTROOM TWO. THAT'S ALL FAMILY TREATMENT COURT PARTICIPANTS TO COURTROOM TWO."

"Just in time," Cindy says. "We're done."

Outside the courtroom, a dozen or so women wait, rebelliously chewing gum. For most of them, it's another day in the white man's world. They're used to it.

The Court Officer holds the doorknob as he counts heads. "Okay, spit out your gum, cell phones off." He opens the door and inspects each woman's cell phone as they enter the courtroom. Erin holds hers out, stiffens when she sees the Glock holstered on his gun belt. Mercifully, her brain conjures no flashback. She's just another mom, waiting for admission to this afternoon's shitshow.

She takes a place in the back row of the jury box, where the participants sit. The seats that line the back wall and opposite side of the room are filled mostly with strangers. Mrs. Copley is not there. Erin recognizes the Drug and Alcohol Lady from DSS. And the DSS attorney who stood fast in her conviction that she was doing the Lord's work, the one who could have agreed to Gavin's request to put everything on hold for a year while Erin got herself together instead of prosecuting her right out of the gate. Good for her. She's racked up another check mark in her personal Win column and helped DSS meet its productivity targets.

The woman next to Erin leans close, whispers, "I hate that bitch." Erin almost laughs out loud. In some odd way, the woman reminds her of Ginj. Maybe it's her fuck-it-all attitude.

The Court Officer locks the door and walks to the front of the courtroom. "All rise."

A door at the front of the room opens and the judge glides in wearing the flowing black robes of authority. She glances over the assembled parties and takes her seat at the imposing oak desk. The Bench. An American flag hangs limp on a stand behind her. The seal of the County of Granite, a blue circle with jagged gold rays splayed symmetrically around its radius, gleams on the wall behind her.

"Okay. Let's get started. I should state that we have a representative from the Office of the Public Defender here in case any of you feel you need legal counsel in the course of today's proceeding." The judge points out a tubby, balding fellow with oiled brown hair and thick black-rimmed glasses sitting against the wall opposite the jury box. He nods slightly. He does not appear happy to be here, but the court must cover its ass. Technically, this is a legal proceeding, and those who will be questioned today have a right to an attorney before incriminating themselves.

"Who's up first?" The judge glances down at her desktop. "Erin?" The judge spots Erin and points to the hot seat. "Come on up here."

Erin pushes herself up and walks to the center of the room. She hears her pulse somewhere in her head and reminds herself that this is just a room and these are just people and . . . *no*. No, this is not just a room. This is a courtroom. And there's a guy with a gun over there. And there's a woman in a black robe who is legally authorized by the State of New York to remove children from their homes. Forever.

"How are you today?" Her Honor props her chin on her fists.

Erin doesn't have the first idea of how she is, aside from seriously pissed off that she is here, that any of these women are here.

"Fine, thank you."

"How are things going for you?"

"Except for the fact that I haven't been allowed to see my children, things are going okay."

"Have you been drinking?"

"No. Not at all."

"Taking any drugs?"

"Only the prescriptions required by my treatment plan."

"Good, good. You need to make sure you comply with your treatment plan."

"I am doing that, Your Honor." Erin feels grateful for her military training. She knows how to courteously address authority.

"That's good. Keep it up. I'm going to give you some homework. For next week, I'd like you to write an essay about what it feels like for you not to be drinking. Talk about the changes you've made in your life since being admitted into Family Treatment Court."

Like so many of the students in her English classes had done, Erin asks how long the essay should be.

"A page or two will be fine. Do you have any questions about your treatment plan or procedures or anything else?"

"I'd like to see my children."

"You can talk to your caseworker about that. They'll take care of that for you."

"Thank you, Your Honor." Erin returns to the jury box. She knows when she's hit a wall. The caseworker says ask the judge. The judge says ask the caseworker. The Drug and Alcohol Lady says get your own drug test.

These people are going to keep bouncing her back and forth, back and forth, like she's a Ping-Pong ball and they're playing for a case of beer. The more people they can keep in their programs, the stronger their claim for a big piece of taxpayer pie at the county budget buffet.

Erin will go home and work hard on her essay. She will show the judge that she is sincere, and sober, and that Her Honor should let Paul and Lindsey come home. But she doubts it will have any impact.

TWENTY-SIX

After dinner at the Bagram defac, Erin walks along the main drag, wishing she'd waited for a bus. The weather has gone all strange again, a fine mist drifts down from the clouds that moved in as the unit unloaded the last of the equipment from the convoy. It was a long, slow trip over bad roads. Nothing had happened. Boring as hell, Ginj complained. The moisture dampens the smell of jet fuel, tamping it down near ground level.

For a while, Erin sticks to the main road, the pavement oddly smooth and hard under her boots. She hadn't realized how accustomed she'd become to walking on dirt and gravel. But after a while she tires of saluting officers—how much brass can there be on one base—and cuts down a pathway between a couple of plywood buildings, headed for a less traveled road that she's pretty sure will take her to the unit's assigned tent.

Dinner was better than she'd hoped for. The dining room was four times the size of the one at Shank, and tonight's options included a delicious macaroni and cheese, the top crisped to a crunchy brown. Ginj went with the beef stroganoff, which she renamed beef snot-enough due to the consistency of the sauce. She'd tried to persuade Erin to go with her to the Vulture's Nest for some kind of karaoke thing. Erin is glad she passed. Ten hours of driving has left her wrung out, her fingers sore from gripping the steering wheel, her back and shoulders one solid chunk of ache. Dusk is coming on fast and all she wants is sleep.

She adjusts the strap on her M4 so the rifle riding against her back won't rub a raw spot. The low-throated roar of a C-17 taking off fills the air, and she wishes she were on board, headed home. She tells herself not to think about it. Just walk. Go back to the tent, get some sleep. Like that's gonna be possible with all these planes taking off and landing.

"Private Hill!" Sergeant Drake seems to come out of nowhere. Erin stops, faces him, salutes.

"Sergeant." Two feet away from him, Erin smells the alcohol on his breath. No alcohol is permitted anywhere on base.

"Where you headed, soldier?"

"Back to the tent, Sergeant." She feels a tightening inside, realizes suddenly that she's wandered into an area between rows of plywood B-Huts.

He reaches out suddenly and runs a finger down the side of her face. She tries to dodge it, but feels the sting of his fingrtip on her cheek, the burn of unwanted contact. She steps back, scanning the area. Not a soul. A moment ago the base was swarming with people. She takes another step back, calculating whether she can escape if she runs.

"Sergeant, I need to get back to my tent."

"I'll walk with you." It comes out as a command.

Erin shifts her rifle and continues down the gravel path, Drake keeping pace next to her.

"Damn, girl, imagine us on a tropical island." He moves closer as they walk, inches away from her. Erin glances over. It's like a veil has dropped behind his eyes. His face is slack. No one's home.

She keeps walking, her breath coming short and fast. Still no one's in sight.

Drake asks if she knows why the convoy was rerouted, and when she shakes her head he says a C-130 crashed at J-Bad. The runway is still down, probably will be for days. Thirteen dead. Erin can't fully process the news. Mostly she is relieved that Drake's attention has shifted, however dreadful the focus. All she wants is to get to her tent.

"That's awful, Sir."

"Cut the 'sir' crap, Hill. It's just you and me now, talking." He presses closer, almost leaning on her as they walk the path between rows of B-Huts. "One of the loadmasters, we grew up together."

He trips suddenly, staggers and grips her arm. "Give me a hand."

Erin feels the lurch in his step as she holds her arm stiff, offering support. She can see a crossroad up ahead, where the narrow gravel walkway hits a larger base road.

"Now he's just gone." Drake tilts his head oddly, adjusts his cap. "Poof. Just like that."

"I'm sorry for your loss, Sergeant."

He straightens, seems to regain his balance and shakes his head hard, as if trying to jolt the alcohol out of his brain. "Fuck it," he says. "that's war." He veers off the path suddenly, pulling Erin with him toward the wall of a B-hut. He lets go of her arm and bends over, resting his hands on his knees and breathing heavily. She thinks maybe he's about to puke and takes a step back.

That's when he hits her. The blow staggers her backward and he's on her, on the ground up close against the B-hut, his forearm mashed across her face, the salt of his sweaty palm on her lips and the weight of him, the force of him thrusting drunkenly into her, the grunt and gasp in her ear and then he collapses and she's pushing him off and he's lying there, stunned and laughing quietly, almost giggling. Erin pulls up her pants, staggering, reeling, stumbling as she reaches for her pistol, fumbling with her leg holster, and just as she unsnaps it to pull the weapon he's on all fours and bolts up from the ground, charging, tackles her. Her head slams against the ground. The world goes black.

Pain wakes her. Throbbing, pulsing pain, radiating from her jaw, fills her head. Her fatigues and underwear are bunched at her knees. Her tongue is swollen and tender. She tastes blood. On her back, she chokes on a sob as she slides her pants up, fumbling with the buttons. God damn him.

154

She opens her eyes.

Pitch-black darkness. Her fingers crawl across concrete, stumble onto her M4. She pulls it onto her chest, locates her thigh pocket, extracts her flashlight. God damn him.

The beam cuts the darkness, revealing gray concrete walls. The light finds an octagon of black where the gray stops and night begins. She's inside a bunker. She sits up, reels from dizziness, folds arms across knees and puts her head down. Waits.

When it eases, she rolls onto all fours and slowly pushes herself up, holding on to the thick wooden bench that runs the length of the bunker. Her rifle in one hand, she uses the other to steady herself along the bench as she crouches toward the opening. It takes forever to get there.

At the edge of the bunker, she halts and takes a knee, again fighting dizziness. She hears a C-17 landing. She's not sure where she is exactly, but the runways are nearby.

She should have seen it coming. She stares out into the darkness, not wanting to remember, but remembering anyway: the night Eddy threw her into the bookcase, the day that dirtbag on the football team caught her alone in the gym and forced her against the wall so he could smear a spit-slimed kiss against her mouth, the night her father dragged Tanya down the hall by her hair when she announced she was having a baby. What kind of idiot is she, that she can't see this shit coming? It's going to happen. It's always going to happen. Why does she keep forgetting? How can she keep believing that somehow there is a set limit to the number of assaults that a woman has to endure in a single lifetime? Just when the fuck is enough enough?

Switching the flashlight to red, she emerges from the bunker into the night, choking against the shitty smoke-odor of burning trash just as another F15 screams toward the stars.

TWENTY-SEVEN

A tired, overweight, middle-aged woman with burgundy hair fried by frequent colorings calls Erin's name. She could be Mrs. Copley's sister, or cousin. Erin wonders whether county agencies attract women like this or the work itself creates them. The woman leads Erin down a maze of hallways, past tinted-glass cubicles masquerading as offices. Large, bright yellow arrows made of laminated construction paper point this way and that. Finally they stop outside an office. Burgundy lady knocks. The woman who opens the door, in her forties with dark blond hair pinned in an updo, has deep frown creases etched around her mouth.

"Come in, come in," she says. "Please. I'm Dr. Cuevas."

Erin edges around the side of the desk in the minuscule office, feeling like she is taking up too much space. The doctor motions for her to sit and then squeezes herself behind her desk, folding her thin body into an ancient leather desk chair. The room cannot be more than eight by ten. The large, cluttered desk barely fits, and Erin sits backed into a corner. But she's relieved not to be dealing with Kloeten.

"So," Dr. Cuevas says. She sits up very straight, as if holding a Yoga pose, and blinks rapidly. "Why are we here?"

What Erin wants to say is, "in the larger sense, I don't have a clue," but she knows better than to be a smart-ass. She is here because her treatment program demands that she get therapy for PTSD, even though she wasn't diagnosed with it when she was still in the VA

156

system. It's irrelevant. She no longer has military benefits, and the Drug and Alcohol Lady is a Licensed Mental Health Counselor who has decided that Erin has PTSD and needs treatment. So Erin has come to the Granite County Department of Health and filled out the paperwork to prove she is indigent. The questionnaire asked about all of Erin's income and expenses, including whether she had any dry-cleaning expenditures or valuable tools. She wonders whether they would take her tools away and sell them to pay for her treatment, if in fact she had any. Eddy took his tools when he left. She has a wrench and a hammer and two screwdrivers, one of each type. She didn't put them on the list.

Dr. Cuevas is waiting. Erin is forced once again to tell her story, only this time, just like each time she is forced to tell her story to someone new, it is a different story. It's not that she's lying; it's almost as if her story is a victim of circumstance. Depending on where and to whom Erin tells it, the story holds variation and nuance that turn it into something it was not when she last told it. Today it is the story of her time in Afghanistan, and after. She talks about the bloodiness, and the boredom, and the ache of being away from her children. She talks about the wounded, and the dead weight of stones that filled her for months, still fills her, but she talks of it vaguely, as if she only watched it on Netflix late one night. And she talks about the strain of returning, of coming home to a husband who had no interest in trying to salvage their damaged marriage. She does not talk about the terror, or the nightmares, or the flashbacks, or Sergeant Drake. She is in control. She is unemotional. Her voice sounds monotone, even to her. When she finishes, she does not need any tissues. Her head is clear, or so it would appear to anyone on the outside. Maybe it's something to do with the air in this building: there is an underlying sense of depression that permeates the place, as if the constant flow of poor and troubled humans in and out of these offices has released some kind of airborne sadness, a desolation that has filtered into the ventilation system and spread malaise into every corner of the building, filling the very air with a blue funk of dejection.

Dr. Cuevas sits expressionless while Erin searches for a way to break the silence, hoping that in the meantime some words of analysis or wisdom will come from the doctor. Finally the doctor says, very seriously, "You're seeing the nurse practitioner? For your medication?"

"I still have some left, from the hospital. But yes, I have an appointment."

"Good. Good." Dr. Cuevos waves some paperwork around. "So. You've been approved for twelve sessions. You'll come next week?"

Erin squeezes around the desk, thanking the doctor.

"And Erin? Just remember. Before every awakening," Dr. Cuevos inserts a quick, professional smile, "comes a rude awakening."

Erin nods and slips out the door, wondering if the doctor has any idea of a definitive point where rude stops and obscene starts, regardless of anyone's intentions. She only gets lost twice trying to make her way through the maze of hallways back to the waiting area. The yellow arrows are not reliable. She wonders if someone has tampered with them. Or maybe there are hidden cameras, and she has been unwittingly entered into a secret government study that utilizes medicated humans instead of rats.

∞

The church basement is packed, and you'd think it was a party. Instead of cocktails, the minglers clutch coffee cups. Erin sits in the back row, where they say you shouldn't sit. *Sit in the front row and share like your life depends on it.* Because yeah.

Erin tries to listen to the person speaking, telling his story. She cannot. She can only sit, fuming silently. Right now that has to be enough. She is here and she is not drinking. She doesn't even want a drink. She wants to blow up the family court building.

She sits in the back row and listens. All she cares about is getting her slip of paper signed.

The speaker ends his share by saying, "If you're eating a shit sandwich right now, it's probably because you ordered it."

The guy sitting next to Erin says under his breath, "There was nothing else on the menu." He chuckles softly. His breath smells of beer.

∞

In the parking lot, Erin gets into her car and takes out the CD set that arrived in the mail last week from Tanya. Maybe it was earlier than last week. She's losing track. The CDs contain words of wisdom from a guru who has a communal ranch an hour south of Dallas, somewhere in the wilds outside Waco. The guru is not publicly known. You have to know someone on the inside to receive an invitation to visit. Tanya knew someone and went for a weekend, not because she was seeking wisdom, but because she wanted to ride the palomino Akhal-Teke horses the guru kept on his ranch. The name Akhal-Teke meant free, according to the guru, though Tanya found nothing online to support his claim. Even so, the rides had been rapturous, the horse's stunning metallic sheen almost surreal in the afternoon sun. He was fast, agile, and powerful. Tanya rode the glorious horse and endured the guru's talks and purchased the CD in the gift shop. She came away from the weekend relaxed and was not disappointed that she felt no overwhelming sense of enlightenment.

Erin, much to her surprise, is finding the guru's talks helpful. She keeps the CDs in her ancient Toyota and listens every time she gets in the car. It helps her prepare for her mandatory AA meetings, her mandatory therapy appointments, her mandatory group sessions, her mandatory life. The guru says things like *you are here to enable the collective consciousness of the universe to manifest itself as an entity of collective bliss for all that is presently in existence.* Erin wants to believe the guru. But as she drives to her appointments and meetings, listening to his resonant, Hindi-inflected voice intoning words of infinite wisdom, she cannot understand how a stop sign or a strip of yellow paint on a county highway can morph into a state of collective bliss. Maybe she is taking the words too literally. Maybe the guru is speaking in metaphor. The first time she got to the end of the fourth CD, she determined to start over, to keep listening until it all made sense. She's trying to keep it together. Even if listening to the CD doesn't help, it occupies her mind, keeps it from going dark.

"When you have to make a choice," the guru intones, his words flowing from the Toyota's speakers as Erin idles in a long line of cars at an intersection, "You can choose to do nothing. Inaction as action. You will undoubtedly get results, as every action has results, sometimes consequences. Inaction can be as powerful a choice as action. You can choose to simply wait, and that waiting becomes the action you have chosen to take."

The blare of a car horn from behind her snaps her back to the intersection. But instead of continuing forward to the county road that will take her home, she cuts the wheel to the right and turns onto the road that leads to downtown Granite. Fuck inaction.

The Granite County Courthouse sits on what was once the town square, but it is surrounded now by rows of shops lining the streets on all four sides, as if a wall of commerce has been built around the two-story brick edifice, an impressive example of late Georgian architecture. Erin turns into a narrow driveway cut between a Dunkin' Donuts and Wells Fargo Financial Services. She presses a button on the ticket dispenser; the machine buzzes loudly and burps out a time-stamped rectangle of paper as the barrier gate snaps to attention. Erin drives past the reserved parking spaces—county court judges, supreme court judges, commissioner of jurors, clerks—and locates a spot.

The County Law Library is located on the second floor, behind a plain door with a small sign indicating the hours of operation. Erin's morning has been chewed up first with Dr. Cuevos, and then the meeting. The Law Librarian looks up from his reading as Erin enters.

"Can I help you, or do you know what you're after?"

"I think I know what I'm after," Erin says, "but I could probably use some help." The man does not seem at all put out as he places a marker in his book and closes it gently, almost reverently. He adjusts his black framed glasses and clasps his hands in front of him.

"Let me guess," he says. "Divorce? Foreclosure? Or Family Treatment Court?"

∞

A bright pink plastic bowl of chocolate kisses sits at the corner of the Nurse Practitioner's desk. The office is overheated to the point that Erin imagines the chocolate kisses must be gooey and soft. She unwraps one and puts it in her mouth. Her hypothesis was correct. At the meetings, they suggest that the newly sober should carry candy with them at all times. When the urge to drink hits, eat a piece of candy. Alcohol is, after all, a sugar. The chocolate melts across her tongue. She is being normal. One of the women at yesterday's meeting said, "Normal is a setting on the clothes dryer." Erin found herself laughing with the rest of the people in the room. A first.

Only, by the time she got home, when she opened the front door to her empty home, the tears returned. The people at the meetings tell her she has to find her spirit, that the only cure for her disease is a spiritual one, but she cannot begin to find it. Without her children, she has no spirit. Maybe that is the curse of motherhood. She hears the guru's voice, something about the end of the world as we know it. Something about bliss. The guru has escaped from the CD and gotten into her head. She invites him to join the chorus in her brain. Maybe he can talk some sense into them.

The Nurse Practitioner, a large woman with a cascade of dark brown ringlets falling across one side of her face, ushers a dog into the room. She looks like someone you might find at a weekend crafts fair, selling crocheted pillows that say things like *Karma is a bigger bitch than I am*, or *Today has been cancelled. Go back to bed.* Erin says hello to the dog before she says hello to the NP. Ginj would probably do the same. Erin misses Ginj. Though they traded contact info before going their separate ways, neither has reached out.

"How are we doing?" The Nurse Practitioner eases herself behind her desk as if she has a sore back.

"Okay." Erin wants to tell the truth, but it feels dangerous. She has to *seem* alright, whether she is or isn't.

The dog, a black and white mixed breed with basset hound ears, makes three tight circles and curls up on the floor in a corner of the small office. The Nurse Practitioner flips through the paperwork.

"You're on Effexor? Since the hospital? That working okay?" She pulls a prescription pad from a large pocket in her skirt and scribbles on it, rips the prescription off and holds it out.

"I don't need it," Erin says. "It's the Family Treatment Court, you know. Part of my Treatment Program."

"Ah. Well then it's probably best that you stick with it awhile longer. Is it bothering you?"

"I get dizzy. Sometimes it makes it difficult to think clearly."

"That could be anything, not just meds causing that." She peruses her chart. "You're not drinking, you're going to meetings?"

"I am not drinking. I go to meetings every day."

"Good for you! Are you able to see your kids?"

"They said I would have visitation, but . . ." Erin's throat tightens. She wonders what Lindsey and Paul are doing right now. In school, yes, but are they even missing her? She blinks quickly, squeezing the tears back. It is entirely possible that they never want to see her again. After what she did? What if she had succeeded? Her body could've lain there for hours. What if Paul had found her dead? The possibilities mortify her.

Loss. Regret. Erin swallows them daily, along with the ever-present question: What if? What if she died? What if her children buried her? In her darkest moments, she wonders if maybe Lindsey and Paul would have been better off. Children survive worse every day. After the shock and pain of their mother's death dissipated, they might have ended up more fortunate. Eddy would find a replacement, she was sure. Maybe Megan, or another version of Megan. A woman Eddy could rely on to act right and stay put.

"You have to be patient," the practitioner says.

"I really don't want the medication." Erin's resistance is not so much about bucking The Court as it is about trying to achieve some measure of stability. The meds are like a cloak of calm, shielding her when it's in place, but prone to slip off unexpectedly and reveal what's really going on inside. She is either crying uncontrollably or else she feels nothing, as if there's a switch in her brain with only two settings.

"Trust me," the nurse says. "Don't buck the orders. Do what they tell you to do and get out of there as fast as you can."

TWENTY-EIGHT

The barracks are quiet this evening. Erin sits cross-legged on her bunk, hugging herself, rocking and remembering home. The thing about parenthood that no one can prepare you for is how much you miss the child that disappears as she daily becomes someone new—wonderfully new, loved just as strongly, but different. And you never get to say a proper goodbye to the younger one that silently vanishes from your life. One day you wake up, and the baby is gone, replaced by the toddler; then the toddler too, disappears, never to return. Erin cherishes the memory of the hours she spent holding Lindsey and Paul, one in each arm, rocking her infants in front of the wood stove, wrapping them in love as fierce and beautiful as the snowstorms that buffeted the house deep in winter.

Candice strides in and throws herself on her bunk.

"Sergeant Drake wants to see you," she says. "He's waiting out front."

Erin slips into her shower shoes, grabs her jacket on the way out the door. She has managed to avoid having to speak to him since that night. Fucker.

"Okay then," Candice calls after her.

"Thank you," Erin calls back. "Sorry."

Drake is just inside the door, hands stuffed in his jacket pockets, cap pulled low on his forehead. Erin comes to attention two feet in front of him.

"Sergeant, Private Hill reports."

"At ease."

She goes to parade rest. She keeps her eyes level, refusing eye contact. She will not allow him to see that inside she is quaking. She maintains her military bearing.

"I'm afraid I have some bad news." Drake sounds sincere, but it's impossible to determine his inner state. Like she cares. It's taking everything she's got not to wrap her hands around his neck and plant a knee in his face.

"It's about your father."

He doesn't have to say it; Erin knows right away. She feels a vague flutter of loss, something like a small cloud skimming quickly overhead, a thin, wispy Cirrus flitting past so lightly it barely casts a shadow.

"He passed away last night." Drake waits for a response.

There will be no reaction. She will not let herself feel a goddamn thing, not for her father's passing, and certainly not over Drake's loathsome proximity.

"Is that all, Sergeant?" She keeps her tone even.

"I can put you in for compassionate leave."

"Thank you, Sergeant, but I'll pass." The words come out before she knows what she's saying.

"It might be best."

Erin maintains her position, silent, unmoving.

"I was drunk," he whispers.

From down the hall come the sounds of someone shrieking, followed by women laughing, as though they're in a college dorm or at a sleepover party.

"No shit, Sergeant." She will not give him anything. Nothing.

"I'm sorry," Drake says. "I'm not even sure what happened. But I'm very, very sorry." He pulls his hands from his pockets, folds his arms across his chest. "I'm not like that."

Erin keeps her focus on the plywood wall behind him, on the outline of a knot that is showing through the off-white paint.

"Hill?"

"Thank you for telling me about my father, Sergeant."

"Okay then. I'm sorry for your loss. Dismissed."

Erin salutes, backs away, does an about face, and heads for her room. Sorry for your loss. Does he remember her saying that to him? She can feel the heat rising in her face and is certain she's flushing bright red. Whatever. At least it didn't happen while she was eye to eye with him. The piece of garbage.

Back in her room, she goes straight to her bunk and cocoons herself in a blanket, though the room is warm. Candice is propped on her bunk reading *Warrior Skills Level 1*, a thick paperbound volume with an olive drab gray camo cover print. She slaps it down and sits up.

"Hey," she says, "you gonna talk about it, or what?"

"Not tonight," Erin says.

"Why not? When's better than now?"

"Candice, I can't. Not yet."

"No problem then. I got a feeling I already know. What'd he say?"

"My father died."

Candice crosses herself, says she's sorry for Erin. Erin thanks her. But they both know that's not what they were talking about. Erin knows she might feel better if she could bring herself to talk to Candice. But she's afraid Candice will insist that she file charges. She doesn't want to risk the shame involved in telling a story that would most likely get quietly squelched, if it were even believed in the first place. And nothing would happen. It never does.

"My mother's a good woman," Candice says. "A very smart woman. You know what she told me before I came over here? She told me not to worry about my son, she would take good care of him."

"You're lucky."

"I know. And then she said something else. She said as long as I was over here, I had to make sure and focus on fighting the battles in front of me, not the battles behind me."

Erin can't talk. If she talks, she will fall apart.

"Whatever." Candice sighs loudly. "I'm here, you know."

A moment later, a Snickers bar sails onto Erin's bunk.

"Gringa," Candice says, her face once again in the book, "Time may heal all wounds, but a little chocolate never hurts. You're gonna talk to me, no?"

"Just not right now, okay?" Erin rips the wrapper apart and bites off a chunk of Snickers, letting the chocolate goo melt over her tongue. She remembers the look of helpless consternation on her father's face as he lay in the hospital bed staring at the television, refusing to say goodbye when she visited him before shipping out. She remembers searching the bleachers at her basketball games, the staggered aluminum benches crowded with proud parents, supportive parents, and sometimes even obnoxious parents loudly throwing their arms up when the ref made what they thought was an unfair call. Her mom showed up once in a while, sitting silently, off to herself, as if by distancing herself she could avoid triggering a fresh round of tongue-clucking community gossip about her husband. Even after her mom had kicked her father out of the house, an event Erin, Tanya, and Daniel called The Final Bender, she didn't get out of the house except to go to her job. Monday through Friday she did data input for a large healthcare conglomerate that had, by some miracle, not outsourced its jobs to whatever distant country was offering the most slavish wages to its workers. Her mother hated the job, but she showed up religiously in order to support her family. She came to Erin's games when she could and sat alone, in the top row, with her back against the blue gymnasium wall, wondering what fresh hell she would face when her husband rolled in after another night at the bar.

Erin knew that her father wouldn't be there—not once in four years did he make it to a game—but she was always happy when her mother made it, happy to have at least one parent rooting for her.

Erin rewraps what's left of the candy and sticks it in her pocket. Gone. What was the last thing she'd said to him, before he left the planet? *See you in six months, Dad.*

She wonders if Tanya knows, or if their mother has gotten the news yet, but it won't much matter to her. He's been dead to her for more than a decade.

Last words. What had he said to her? *Don't go, little girl. Don't do it.* It comes back to her now, the hospital room, the yellow in his eyes, his ashen complexion. At least she'd told him she loved him; she remembers saying that, even if she hadn't been sure she meant it. The aching numbness that fills her now tells her that, however tangled the feeling might have been, her words were true. She had loved him and had been angry at herself for loving a father who could not love back, not fully, not unconditionally, the way a father should. His twisted version of love had tainted the whole family, left them wondering what it was about them that was so undeserving that he could not simply be there. With them. For them. How does she honor that? She doesn't know, but she takes a long moment and tries, lamenting that he couldn't find his way to a better life. She wishes to God he'd found a way to be there for her, for all of his family, while she was growing up. If you live in a small town, it's a cruel fate to be known as one of the fucked-up families, the ones who can't get it right, even when getting it right is completely out of your control.

Erin lets her head fall back on the pillow, wondering if her father's spirit is hovering somewhere close to where her mother sits, her head bent over a crossword, pondering a nine-letter word for *failure.*

TWENTY-NINE

B arb Copley pulls back the covers and shivers at the rush of cool that surrounds her. Thank God it's Friday. She prepares herself for the pain and lurches into her terrycloth robe, slipping her feet into matching Deerfoam slides. Glancing at the dresser against the far wall, she notices that Roy has left one of the drawers hanging open, one work sock dangling over the upper lip of the maple laminate drawer front. Barb eases over and stuffs the sock inside, closes the drawer. She has given up on asking him to close the drawers properly, accepting that it is an essential part of who he is rather than cause for divorce. She closes drawers. She picks up the crumpled napkins he leaves sitting on the end table next to his spot on the couch. He's a good man. He's a decent man. He works hard at one of the few remaining factories in the area, putting together stainless-steel machines that are used to process bovine innards into Lean Finely Textured Beef. Back in 2014, it seemed like he might lose his job after ABC News ran an exposé of LFTB, referring to it as pink slime. But the brouhaha disappeared into a lawsuit that would take years to settle, and the factory is still operational. Barb contemplates stopping at Burger King for lunch today. Though they claim not to use any filler, she has noticed a certain chewiness to the meat, and occasional bits of gristle that might indicate the stuff is in there. But it's the flavor she really likes. Something about that flame broiling really does it for her.

On the way to her first case, she reminds herself it's payday. At least there's that. But she doesn't look forward to her calls, worrying always about making a mistake. On her first day of training, Mrs. Hattelburg told her the unspoken policy is CYA: cover your ass. Barb removes the kids on almost every call she takes and leaves it to the courts and the parents to sort things out.

She has two morning calls on her schedule. The first is uneventful. The client, a teenaged mom on the methadone program who is actually managing to study for her high school equivalency degree, gives all the right answers to the questions Barb reads from her form. The house is clean, and the girl is well groomed. Barb is in and out in under an hour.

On her second call, the door is answered by an unwashed and fearful six-year-old girl wearing only a filthy, oversized *Finding Dory* sweatshirt. Her mother lies on a couch in the trashed living room, obviously zonked on pills, an open can of Pabst Blue Ribbon on the coffee table. Mid-thirties, maybe. And pregnant, her belly swollen. According to the paperwork, she already has six children, none of whom have been at school this month, thus Barb's visit. Barb hopes that the sheriff's office arrives quickly. This is not a case of taking a child just to make sure there's no blowback later.

Redeemable. That's the word. The one that stuck with her from orientation. A family court judge addressing the class had used the term to describe her decision-making rubric for determining whether to allow a parent to attempt regaining custody. "Bottom line," the judge said, "I have to ask myself whether the parent is *redeemable.* Because if they're not, it's better to pursue termination of parental rights as expeditiously as possible. There's no sense wasting resources if the parent is not *redeemable.*" Barb had wondered how anyone could make that determination, short of being able to predict the future. But she cannot afford to let herself feel guilty for the poverty she encounters, for the crying children who wail pitifully when she takes them from their mothers. She can't afford it emotionally, and she can't afford it financially. She's getting better at cutting off the feelings by reminding herself that if she weren't doing it, someone else would be.

During her lunch hour, instead of driving through Burger King, Barb drives to the Wemple Brothers Farm to Market grocery, on the north side of Granite. The picnic tables are still out under the long over-hang that runs the length of the building. A smattering of customers in fleece or denim jackets sit drinking coffee. Inside, Barb sails past the huge salad bar and the steam tables of prepared hot entrees, past the deli counter and on to the bakery at the rear of the store. She orders a pecan chocolate chunk cookie that's almost as large as an individual pizza, a rectangular slab of tiramisu, a fudge brownie, and a Nutella lava cupcake. She is exhausted from the paperwork and the morning removal. Some days it seems to her that there should be a check box somewhere on one of the zillions of DSS forms she is required to submit, a box in which she could place a big X to recom-mend involuntary sterilization. Six kids and another on the way, and the mother is downing Vicodin and chasing it with beer? What possi-ble argument can be made for allowing someone like that to maintain the ability to reproduce?

Sitting in the parking lot, she watches people going in and coming out of the grocery. She eats fast, chewing voraciously, and doesn't stop until nothing is left but some scattered crumbs of cookie and a few pieces of broken pecan on the center console, next to her thigh. She is as full as she has ever been, but wishes she'd bought another cookie. She wants to go home and curl up on the couch and watch a game show or maybe a few reruns of *The Big Bang Theory*. That's probably where that mother wishes she were right now. Back on her couch, watching TV through the glassy sheen of her warm, com-fortable Vicodin bubble, instead of locked in the psychiatric wing at St. Martin's. Barb crumples the empty paper bag, plucks a couple of the larger pieces of pecan from the console and pops them into her mouth. She dusts crumbs onto the floorboard and uses the rearview mirror to reapply her lipstick before checking her clipboard to see what's next.

On the front porch, she knocks loudly, remembering the first time she was here. The day she found Erin unconscious, near death, on the bedroom floor. She wonders if the other five kids from the earlier call have been located, makes a mental note to do a follow-up before leaving for the weekend. She's not on call and doesn't want any interruptions to her time off.

She always hesitates, in the moments between knocking on a door, seeing it open, bracing herself for what she'll see inside. Will the mother be sober? Stoned? Junked-out? Pissed off, hating, raging? Bruised and beaten? Will it be a father who opens the door? Rarely. Will the mother be polite and well-mannered? Ha. Good one. Grateful for her help? That happened. Once.

When the door opens, Barb sees the hostility right away. In black sweats, her brown hair uncombed, Erin holds her body in a fuck-you posture: shoulders back, chin up, hands in loose fists. Barb presses her clipboard against her stomach. "I need about a half hour."

Erin waves her in silently, spins and leads the way to the living room. Barb sinks into the couch, appreciating the relief in her knees. She should get comfortable shoes. But the comfy ones are like boats. "You have a nice home," she says.

Erin thanks her and folds herself on the couch, opposite Barb, who gets right to work asking the requisite questions: How is Erin feeling? Erin misses her children, when can she see them. Is Erin going to meetings? Every day. Is she going to the Early Recovery program? Every Wednesday evening. Are they testing her for drugs and alcohol? Yes, at Family Treatment Court. That's when? Every Tuesday afternoon. Has Erin come back dirty on any of the tests? No. Is she seeing the therapist? Once a week. Is she taking her medication? Yes, yes, and yes.

"The judge in family court said to talk to you about having a visit."

Barb thinks Erin is doing well enough for a visit but informs her that she cannot be alone with her children. An observer must be present. She tells Erin that a visit can be arranged at the DSS offices, or Erin can ask a friend to be at the house when the kids come to visit. The friend will have to be approved by the department.

Erin doesn't react visibly, but Barb senses that she's outraged. It has to be humiliating, to be told you can't be alone with your own children. Still, the agency can't be too careful.

"Have you spoken to your ex about it?"

"He says they don't want to talk to me, which is a lie I'm sure, but he won't let me talk to them so I have no way of knowing."

"They probably just need a little time."

"Well you can't know that unless you actually talk to them, can you?"

"I know it's hard. But try to keep the children's welfare in mind. If they're not ready to talk to you, we should respect that."

"He's lying. You know he left us, you know that. He barely visited them."

Barb looks up from writing, catches Erin brushing away a tear from the corner of her eye. At least the woman still has some pride, but Barb hates it when they get all teary. It's too late. If Erin is so concerned about her children, she shouldn't have . . . never mind. Just, never mind.

Erin doesn't mention the foreclosure proceedings. It would not be smart to let Mrs. Copley know. She fills out new paperwork every time the bank sends her a rejection, and as long as she keeps the paperwork flowing, they let it ride. Apply. Get rejected. Apply again. Get rejected. Apply yet again, and the cycle continues.

"I'm just trying to explain to you that he's lying. And he's probably lying to them, too. Keeping us apart. Don't tell me you've never seen that before."

"I'll look into it."

"Their attorney won't take my calls."

"Erin, it's probably not a good idea to harass people."

"I'm not harassing anyone. Don't I have a right to see my own children?"

"Yes. You have a right. You can try to compel a visit, but it's not a good idea. I'll talk to Eddy, talk to the children, see what I can do. But you have to be patient. What about a job? How's that going?"

"I'm doing everything I can."

This, Barb can sympathize with. She wouldn't be sitting here right now if she could find anything that paid as well. She really does have to get going on those courses. Maybe she could squeeze in an evening class for starters.

"What about the college? Didn't you work there?"

"They had to replace me when I was deployed. There aren't any openings right now."

"That doesn't seem right."

"It's contract work. They have no obligation to hire you from one semester to the next. Unless you're full-time, you're screwed."

"Where else have you tried?"

"Every business in the county has my résumé."

"Any interviews?"

"Two. They said they would get in touch. They haven't called."

"All you can do is keep at it," Mrs. Copley says. "How's the drinking? I mean, the sobriety?"

Erin wishes she didn't hate Mrs. Copley so much. She tries to separate the woman sitting across from her from the job the woman is doing.

"Thirty days."

"That's wonderful. That's a real start."

Even though it's a pat on the head from the enemy, Erin takes it.

"I have some good news for you." Mrs. Copley folds her hands over her clipboard. "We're transferring your case to Preventive. You'll have a new caseworker. It's a very good thing, a step forward. You'll receive all kinds of help. We're here to help you succeed. If someone is in Preventive and they need so much as a diaper and can't get out of the house to get it, the caseworker will bring them diapers. Free."

Erin sighs. "My kids are ten years old."

THIRTY

THIRTY

On a sleety Tuesday morning, the Family Court waiting area is cluttered with attorneys and clients. The waiting area smells worse than ever, or maybe it's just her amygdalae, those two tiny, almond-shaped clusters of nuclei, one in each hemisphere of her brain, gone into overdrive in spite of the 300 milligrams. of Effexor she downed with her morning coffee. She is complying with the Order issued by The Court to use all prescribed medications as directed by the prescribing physician. The Nurse Practitioner's advice to give it time has not proved helpful. The meds still leave her dizzy, with bloodshot eyes and medicine tongue as a bonus. The NP didn't seem to care much about side effects, but Erin has been doing her research, filling the emptiness of her home with time in front of her computer. The one constant she's found among psychotropic pharmaceuticals is that nobody seems to know how they work, or why (or even *if*, in many cases). The literature says simply that the mechanism of action is unknown. But six thousand Chinese rats have been virtually OD'd on this or that particular substance, and they didn't die or get cancer, so please, shut up and take your meds. At the least there's a placebo effect. When this one stops working, we'll try something new. Repeat as needed.

Mrs. Copley arrives and takes a seat near the courtroom door. She avoids looking at Erin.

Behind his Plexiglas window, the Court Clerk hangs up the phone and puts the paperwork into an Out tray, finding it by reach. Today he wears a dark lavender tie against a pale lavender shirt, pressed, as ever, to perfection. The day Erin filed the custody petition, he'd given her a wink of encouragement, a small but welcome crumb of kindness.

Erin hears forceful footsteps coming quickly up the stairs and recognizes Gavin's voice. At first she can't make out any words, though it sounds like an argument, and then she hears Gavin clearly, loudly, say, "I find your remarks inappropriate, Counselor, and I resent your characterization of my client!" He rounds the corner, almost wild-eyed, followed by Bagley, short and red-faced, his bow tie slightly askew. Bagley peels away and bustles through the open door of a conference room. Gavin spots Erin and adjusts his glasses, shrugs his suit jacket into place, motioning her to join him as he moves toward a conference room.

He closes the door behind them and leans on the desk. "It would have been helpful," he says, "if you'd told me you were filing a petition for return of custody. I could have, oh, I don't know, prepared a little?"

"I appreciate what you've done," Erin says, "But they're never going to give them back unless I make it happen."

"Okay." Gavin sniffs loudly. "Okay. I understand how you feel, but—"

"You don't know how I feel."

He takes off his glasses and trains angry blue eyes on her.

"You know what? You're right. I don't. I can't imagine. But here's what you've accomplished, by filing that petition without bothering to notify me. You have *seriously* pissed off the judge."

He slaps a stack of papers on the desk. The top sheet is splattered with CAPITAL LETTERS. The government font that says PAY ATTENTION, ASSHOLE.

"Your ex is standing fast, telling the court that the children aren't ready to go back to you right now. Child Protective Services doesn't think you're ready. And the attorney for the children, too. They all agree that you need more time in sobriety."

"And just what the fuck do they know about sobriety? Are any of them sober? I'm not drinking. I'm not going to."

Gavin looks at her hard. "Well there aren't really any guarantees in that department, are there?"

"Like what?" Erin glares right back. "Like there are guarantees about anything besides toasters or lawn mowers? No, I don't come with a warranty. Neither do wedding bands."

"He says he wants them to come back to you. But he doesn't think you're ready." Gavin sits on the edge of the desk, composing himself. "Are you?"

Erin sees him looking at her with one eyebrow raised, his forehead creased with concern.

"I'm doing the work, Gavin. I'm doing the work today, and tomorrow I'll do the same work, and the day after, and the day after that. Just like they say: one day at a time. You don't want to believe me? Then don't."

"And we all respect that. Look, Eddy says that before all this happened, he was planning to move to New Jersey. He doesn't want—"

"You mean before he had to actually start acting like a father to them? Give them a roof over their heads and feed them and get them to school, that kind of stuff?"

"He's trying."

"So as always it's all about him. Fuck everyone else. Give them back to me and let him move to New Jersey. Good riddance. It's not like he was in their lives. You see me. I'm sitting right here in front of you. Is there any reason you can see that they shouldn't come home today? They can come back to me right now. I'm fine. I want them home. That's why I filed the petition."

"The judge isn't going to let it happen."

"This is insane."

"She wants you to withdraw the petition."

Lungs, Erin recalls from some long-ago biology class, are paired organs. She coughs, inhales deeply, knowing full well that the air lacks sufficient oxygen to replenish her starving blood. She does not gasp. Quietly, sitting politely, she endures the process of suffocation.

"Erin. This is what you have to do. Keep showing up for your appointments. Keep coming to Family Treatment Court. Keep going to meetings. Show them that you're getting better. Focus on getting better." He stands and snugs his tie. "I'm on your side. Withdraw the petition."

Erin feels the blood coursing through her veins like a storm-swollen river, threatening to explode her. Anger, they say in the rooms, is a normal emotion, but not one you should sit with. It is essential to acknowledge it, and to deal with it before it mushrooms into full-blown rage.

"What did he say about me?"

"Who?"

"My children's so-called attorney. Coming up the stairs. What did he say that made you so angry?"

"That wasn't about you," Gavin says. "Different case."

They both know he's lying.

∞

Erin kneels in front of a mirror that runs the length of the wall; it must be forty feet long. It reaches six or seven feet up from the floor. Behind her is a cage, an octagon of black chain link set on thick wrestling mats. Outside it is an open work-out area, and next to that, four heavy bags hang from the steel beams of the exposed ceiling. She has to have the place cleaned before it opens at one. It's a cash money job. The landscape job is done; the boss was sympathetic when Erin asked if she could come back, but had no place for an employee who disappeared without notice and now, with all the therapy appointments and Family Treatment Court appearances, would have to leave mid-shift several times a week and not be available for regular daytime work. The owner here at the gym accepted her lie about why she'd missed a week and let her pick up as if nothing had happened.

179

She sprays glass cleaner on the mirror and wads up sheets of paper towel, sopping up the solution with large circular motions, wiping away sweat stains flung from the bodies of the MMA fighters who come to the club to assault each other. Ammonia prickles at her nostrils. Halfway down the wall, she steps back to eye her work. The mirror shines. She steps closer, sees a woman in gray sweatpants and a tee shirt, her hair frizzled, her skin ashen from insomnia, her green eyes dull with medication and circled with darkness, the whites heavily bloodshot.

She is thirty-six years old. She can't find a job. Her house is in foreclosure. Her children have been taken from her. Afghanistan haunts her. From some hidden alcove of her brain, Erin hears someone say, "You made your choices. Now live with them."

Then, unbidden, she sees in the reflection a woman sitting at a campfire on a spring night, watching a young man approach shyly, and saying yes when he asks her to dance. She sees a woman in a white nightgown, holding newborn twins. She sees the woman in uniform, full desert camo, rifle slung across her back. She sees the woman on her knees, drunk and praying for help: Dear God. "You," Erin says to the woman in the mirror, "you're just another worthless fucking burnout." It's too much, happening too fast and excruciatingly slowly at the same time.

She puts down her spray bottle and tosses the soggy paper towel to the floor. She goes to the rack on the back wall and tugs on a pair of boxing gloves, tightens the Velcro flaps with her teeth.

She walks to the closest heavy bag, gives it a shove. The chain holding it suspended from the ceiling creaks loudly, squeaking metallically against the hook. Back and forth. Back and forth. A pendulum, ticking away moments she will never get back. The baby disappears. The toddler disappears. The child disappears.

THIRTY-ONE

Fatima hears the news from a radio on the windowsill of a bakery as she waits for the shopkeeper to wrap up fragrant rectangles of naan. She'd been hungry. No more. She pays for the bread and tucks it into her beat-up backpack, which she lifted in the central market a week or so prior. There'd been no valuables inside, only a faded, wadded up camo sweatshirt and an empty water bottle.

She drives straight over from the bakery. Traffic is light on the pocked, narrow street where she used to live, but still she's glad to have the rearview mirrors on both sides of the motorcycle handlebars and grateful not to have been run off the road on the way over. The way men drive in Kabul, it's insane. She wonders if she would have felt something if she'd gotten the news of the bombing when it happened, while the blood was still warm. It's been three days now. The emergency vehicles and soldiers have come and gone.

She pulls the motorcycle to the curb in front of a plain apartment building. Most of the front wall is gone. On the second floor, there is her family's couch, seemingly untouched by the blast, still in its place in the middle of the living room.

∞

Fatima sits cross-legged on the ground, her motorcycle parked next to her, hidden in a copse of pines as the sun edges toward the horizon. The giant neoclassical Darul Aman Palace, in a state of ruin,

181

dominates a hilltop in the distance, surrounded by dusty plains dotted with scrub brush and modest thickets of pine trees like the one Fatima has taken refuge in. The latest renovation is supposed to begin soon. That the palace is there at all is a miracle. Its history exemplifies the history of the entire country. Gutted by fire. Rebuilt. Set on fire again. Shelled by the Mujahideen. Rebuilt as a refugee settlement a couple of years before Fatima was born. Later used as a battalion headquarters for the Afghan National Army. Her mother had lived through the Taliban and feared they would once again come to power and once again shut down the schools, rewrite history, force women indoors, and order that windows be blackened so nobody could see females from the streets. Fatima doesn't remember that time, or much of it. She was three by the time the Americans invaded and her mother was able to scrub the black from the windows and let sunshine once again into her household.

She searches her backpack. She misses her mother and wonders where her father is. She wonders where her brothers are. She supposes she should care, but she does not. They will get nothing more from her, not even anger or hatred. She will not be disappointed if she finds their names on the list of the dead.

She bites into the naan, wondering what her life would have been like if she had been born male. Though she occasionally gets a second look from someone who is perhaps struck by what a beautiful young man she is, for the most part she is ignored and so has experienced the liberation of being in public without restraint. Not that she wants to be a man. She thinks one day she would like to fall in love and have a family. But she knows that doesn't happen in real life. Not here. Maybe in America.

She's happy that she is a woman. She is not happy with the social constraints of being female. Some days it feels like a miracle that she's about to be eighteen years old and has not been sold off as a bride to some disgusting middle-aged pervert who happens to have a few dollars to pay for a wife. She thinks it's mostly because her father didn't want to give up his housekeeper.

A twig snaps behind her, bringing her to her feet instantly. She wheels around, ready to fight or run. But it's only a kid, a boy, maybe ten or twelve, looking as scared as she felt only a few seconds ago.

"What," she says, laughing.

He stares hungrily at the naan in her hands. She tears a piece off and holds it out to him. He grabs it and stuffs it in his mouth, chewing furiously. Fatima sits back down, motions for him to join her. He looks so lost. He lowers himself to the ground cautiously, like a hungry animal that cannot resist the sight of food but is prepared to bolt at the merest hint of danger.

The full moon lights the way as Fatima and the boy fly down the roadway, headlight off, the motorcycle engine straining on uphill stretches of roadway. He holds tight, his head pressed against her back. His arms feel slender and frail around her waist. He did not want to go back to the camp, but she persuaded him that he should at least say a proper goodbye to his family, so they would not spend time and tears hoping for his return. The boy's parents and siblings are dead, killed in a missile attack. She hopes that once he sees his aunt and uncle, he will want to stay with them. He's so young, around the age Fatima was when her mother and baby sister died. It feels like eons ago.

Fatima has heard of the IDP camps, the Internally Displaced People camps, but never seen one. Part of why she's taking the boy there is to see for herself if it would be an okay place to hide out, until she can plot how to get across the border.

183

THIRTY-TWO

The moon is full tonight, the ground snow-covered, glowing white. The limbs of leafless trees reach skyward like huge bony claws, casting shadows in the shapes of surgical instruments on the snow. The entire region has been hit with three days of record-breaking sub-freezing temperatures that began with nine inches of snow, and it's not even Halloween yet. The head meteorologist at the Department of Earth and Atmospheric Sciences at the University at Albany has predicted a return to normalcy later in the week. Erin listened to the forecast on the kitchen radio, a retro contraption with a crank handle she uses to power it when the electricity goes out. He expects a high of 47 degrees tomorrow. The snow glitters as if someone has scattered a million tiny diamonds on its smooth crusted white surface. It is bitter, so cold that the craters and ridges of the moon are easily visible. Though she tossed on only a down vest and fleece jacket before slipping out through the back door, Erin does not feel chilled. She looks skyward again, sees the ice-white halo as she bathes her face in the moonlight. The smiling mouth, it seems to be saying beware of those who speak frequently of karma. They will kill you with their own peculiar conception of kindness. The K-word is tossed about casually in the rocky, wooded slopes of Granite County. The hippies who've managed to survive are the real thing, throwbacks to the sixties, wandering through life in a haze of pot smoke and optimism, convinced that if humanity can only summon enough love, world peace will surely follow.

One of them is a dead ringer for Charles Manson. He walks every-where, walks all day every day, no matter the weather. He lives under some tarps in the woods near where the county highway department parks the snowplows and stores road salt in huge white piles beneath an open-faced igloo-shaped building, a kind of geodesic dome with the front chopped off. They call him Crazy Joey. Today, in front of the grocery store, Erin gave him two dollars. She still doesn't know why. He mumbled thank you but did not make eye contact. That is okay, that is fine. That is just the way she likes it.

On weekends, the hippies set up stalls in town and sell beads and candles and tie-died T-shirts to the day-trippers who drive up from NYC. When they count their cash on Sunday evening and it sums up to less than what was hoped for, they pack up and return to their dirt-floored yurts, muttering phrases like *The Universe Provides*.

It's dead-still quiet out here. Erin thinks it must be around five in the morning, not that she has any looming appointments and needs to be concerned with clock-time. Or maybe she does; perhaps she has an appointment or a court appearance or even one of each. What has slipped her mind? It doesn't matter. All she must do for the moment is get through the moment.

Her brother Daniel was fond of saying that the mentally ill could tell the correct time within two minutes of accurate, no timepiece necessary. He was completely intrigued with this alleged fact and mentioned it often when he was alive. Erin misses her brother. She stares at the laughing moon. Risible? Was that the word? Runcible? The runcible spoon, that was it. *The Owl and the Pussycat.* Reading to Lindsey and Paul. Reading children's rhymes at bedtime. Tucking them in. Telling them she loved them. Chasing away the bogeyman under the bed.

She can hear her heartbeat from within. Not even the owl, or the angry goose that squawks at odd hours . . . nothing is stirring out there in the shadows.

She wonders if the Judge is asleep right now, and Mrs. Copley. She hopes they are up wandering the halls of their houses, plagued by uncertainty over their cruel decisions. Fat chance. They are tucked in, she is sure, and sleeping like babes, all warm and snug in their comfortable, orderly, squeaky-clean, middle class homes, with flat-screen TVs in the den and, somewhere in the corner of a room, exercise equipment covered in clothes imported from Asian countries, destined for the discard bag.

She thinks about the soldiers still in Afghanistan, where true sleep comes only on the tail of exhaustion. Another American troop died last week. We're getting out, the recruiter had said. But still, US soldiers are over there, there and elsewhere, risking their lives for democracy and oil. And a madman is running for president. If the world one inhabits is insane, does it follow that the misfits, the crazies, the certifiables are the ones who are actually living sanely?

She sends love to her children, sends it bouncing off the moon, praying that it will find them in their dreams.

THIRTY-THREE

When Gavin rolls into the lawyer lounge, Todd Bagley stops mid-sentence, making it clear that Gavin has interrupted a private conversation. Gavin ignores this, taking in the curves of the woman facing Bagley, who—if Gavin's radar is on target—is no doubt conspiring with him. Small town lawyers thrive on manipulation. Gavin knows he's not immune but considers himself to be one of the few who is capable of taking a larger view. In his more reflective moments, he recognizes that it's his own sense of insignificance that drives him toward an inflated sense of importance, at least at the county court level, where his actions may seriously impact human lives. At last, the woman turns, glancing first at his face, but quickly scanning downward, checking out his package.

"Do you need privacy?" Gavin cocks his hip against the doorframe. Might as well give her an eyeful.

"Nope, we're done," Bagley says. "I was just leaving." He grabs his briefcase and nods goodbye as Gavin steps aside to let him through the door.

"So Ms. McClain," Gavin says. "How are we today?"

Chrystal McClain, lead attorney for the Granite County Department of Social Services, shifts from her sideways perch on the beaten leather couch and puts a sheaf of papers into her attaché. "I'm just lovely," she says, using manicured nails to flip a few long, dark curls over one shoulder.

"Yes, you are." Gavin moves to the coffee urn. A sign tacked on the bulletin board nearby reads *Nothing says 'I love you' like an order of protection.* "I've been meaning to call." He reaches for a coffee cup and is mildly, happily shocked to notice that they are made of paper instead of Styrofoam. Progress in Granite County!

"I'm sure," Chrystal says, relaxing on the couch, crossing her legs and stretching her arms across the back. But for the bow blouse and navy business suit, her pose could belong to someone sunning herself on a tropical beach.

Gavin grabs a cup and displays it.

"No thanks," Chrystal says. "I've hit my limit."

"You have limits?" He takes a slow sip of coffee.

"I think you know better than that."

"We should get together."

"I couldn't agree more." She checks her phone. "Dinner? Friday?"

"Date. I'll call you."

"No. I'll call you. And I suggest you answer."

"Honestly. I really *was* going to call." He sips again and gives her his look, the one that he's practiced in the mirror, the *I want you right now* look. He's glad he did almost three miles this morning and kept the cap on his little plastic vial. He's running low, carefully meting out the powder until he's sure he can get with his supplier. Just thinking about it stimulates the membranes in his nose.

"You caught that Hill case, am I right?" Chrystal uncrosses and re-crosses her legs, not giving Gavin a full crotch shot, but teasing at it.

He nods, lifts his eyes to hers. "That's what you and our esteemed colleague Mr. Bagley were chatting about? Is there something I should know?"

"Nothing. Just curious." She picks up her bag. "I mean, according to Todd she's a total fucking maniac, but it's understandable. Her ex is a piece of work, too."

"How's that?"

"Well he's got these kids just dumped in his lap out of nowhere, and now he's claiming that your client has been out of control since she got back from Afghanistan, which he didn't want her to go to in the first place. I mean she just out of the blue enlisted, according to him, and when she got back she just like, drank for four or five months, until he told her it had to stop."

"And it did, right? And what do you mean, dumped in his lap? They're his kids, too."

"Gavin. She tried to kill herself."

"A year—a pretty sober year—after he walked out on her. Left her on her own, with the kids no less, when she obviously had issues from the war. And wouldn't pay child support. I mean, come on. I'm surprised she didn't lose it a lot sooner than she did. Christ."

"And isn't it a good thing that most mothers, most sane mothers anyway, don't think that's a reason to do themselves in?"

"I don't think she intended to actually kill herself. It was a cry for help."

"One hell of a cry."

"Granted. But she's alive and she realizes the seriousness of what happened. And if he's complaining about having the kids, why doesn't DSS give them back to her? She seems to be doing fine now."

Chrystal brushes against him as she moves toward the door, sending a charge through him that's almost as good as coke.

"She tried to fucking kill herself, Gavin. You don't just pop back from that like nothing happened." She disappears around the corner.

Gavin downs the last of his coffee and crushes the paper cup. Friday. What the hell. He'll take her out to a nice dinner. And then try to fuck some sense into her.

THIRTY-FOUR

The closer she gets to the end of the deployment, the longer the days. On the really bad days, Erin fantasizes about confronting Sergeant Drake. Some days it ends with gunfire. They're all living with rifles strapped to their backs. The thoughts unsettle her; she knows she's not that kind of person. She does everything she can to stay clear of him, but he's their commander and there's no way to avoid him. He acts as if nothing happened. When Erin thinks about bringing charges, she quickly talks herself out of it. It's not worth it. She just wants out of here, and when she gets home to her life, to her kids, she will leave what happened here buried in the fine, powdery soil of Afghanistan, the moon dust.

So far, today at least, Drake has been nowhere in sight. He sent them off on their detail to pack and seal crates and hasn't bothered to check on them. Erin leans against an open plywood container full of computers and printers, trying to pull a plywood splinter from her thumb.

"Maybe you should wear gloves." Candice blows a large pink bubble and pops it loudly.

"Where'd you learn to do that?"

"You should see what my son can do." Candice laughs. "One time, I swear to you, he blew a bubble the size of his head."

"My son too! Same thing, got seriously into blowing huge bubbles. For about a month."

190

"Right? You find freaking bubblegum everywhere." Candice pops another bubble and pulls a mashed package of cinnamon rolls from her thigh pocket, peels back the wrapper and offers one.

Erin holds the sticky pastry by her fingertips, about to take a bite when Drake appears, walking briskly with another sergeant. He glances over at Erin and Candice, sees them standing around eating when they should be packing crates but ignores it, striding past without a second glance. When it's clear Drake isn't going to stop and harass them, Candice blows a huge bubble, pops it loudly.

"Fuckwad," Erin says.

"About time," Candice says. "Talk to me?" She puts an arm around Erin's shoulders and gives her a squeeze. "Buck up, soldier," she says. "We won't be here forever."

"Buck up?," Erin smirks. "Soldier? Seriously?"

Candice laughs but goes suddenly somber, almost whispering. "It's the ones who come after that you have to think about."

"There's nothing I can do." Erin stuffs the rest of the cinnamon roll in her mouth and chews, watching Drake until he disappears behind the chapel building. "And anyway, what about the ones who came before us? It's not like this shit is new."

"You're right of course. Still." Candice laughs and starts blowing another bubble, her eyes getting bigger as it enlarges.

Erin watches, frowning. "I just want to finish my tour and get the hell out of here, home to my family. And I'd rather be doing these shit details he keeps assigning than have to be out there driving around on the roads. If you can even call them that."

The bubble grows slowly into a giant pink balloon, almost as big as Candice's head. She holds perfectly still, motioning for Erin to take a picture. Erin fumbles her phone but manages to snap the shot just before a wind gust blasts in and plasters the bubble against Candice's face. Erin snaps a few more. Candice cracks up, begins blotting at the pink film on her cheeks, peeling it off carefully.

"Send it to me okay? When we've got wifi? Rodrigo will love it."

"Your son? Yeah I bet he will." Erin shades the phone screen from the sun glare with one hand, but she's not seeing anything. She's back in the bunker, tasting her own blood. Fuck Drake.

"Candice, I can't," Erin says. "I can't go through all that, with bringing charges. I can't."

"I get it," Candice says. "It's not like they'd do anything anyway."

"Right," Erin says, pulling her eyes from the phone.

"So let's just stand here," Candice says, "and think about how nice it's going to be when we get home, while we wait for someone to come nail this container shut. Right now, that's all we got to do."

The soldier with the hammer is still five containers away, banging away on a crate. Candice snugs her hat over her ears, turns up the collar of her jacket. Erin leans against the plywood container, pressing her back against it, trying to straighten her spine and take some of the tension out of her lower back. She knows what will happen if she files the paperwork. Drake will, of course, deny it. And she will still have to finish her tour and he will still be her commanding officer.

"You don't have to do anything," Candice says. "It's not your job. Where the hell is Ginj?"

Erin shrugs. Maybe he meant it when he apologized. Or maybe she's just looking for a way out.

Candice wads up the cinnamon rolls wrapper and stuffs it in her pocket. "I'ma run to the latrine," she says, trotting away easily.

This is the fourth container they've filled this morning. At least they're up close to a building, out of the full force of the wind that barrels down the steep slopes of the distant mountains and gathers speed rolling across the plains, delivering hard gusts of moon dust everywhere. In spite of the storage building's shelter, the sand is in Erin's teeth, in her hair, around her neck inside her jacket.

The soldier with the hammer is one container away now. Erin shifts the plywood top on the crate she and Candice were working on, lining up the edges. She's become an expert at fitting objects into containers. The lifting and carrying have strengthened her. When she gets home, unless she can get full-time work at the college, she'll apply at FedEx or UPS, anything with a steady paycheck. She'll take what she can get. Maybe she'll even consider moving, going where there are real jobs with decent pay. It feels good to make a plan.

"INCOMING! INCOMING!" The sudden voice-blare over the base PA system sends Erin and the hammer soldier scrambling. She snags her rifle from the metal wall of the supply building and grabs her helmet, strapping it tight as she runs for the bunker. She's almost to the entrance when the explosion goes off, somewhere behind her, distant, but close enough that she feels the percussion of the blast.

They're packed tightly in the gloom, raw sunshine filling the square openings at either end of the concrete barriers. The memories flash. Drake. Erin shudders. Fuck him. He's not in here now and maybe the rocket got him. Would that be just punishment? She's glad Candice left the area, and she's sure Ginj is nowhere close. Anyway the thing hadn't even landed inside the wire. Through the opening, she can see smoke rising in the distance, well outside the concrete perimeter wall.

"Missed me missed me," someone sings. "Off by a mile."

The bunker fills with nervous laughter.

"When Big Voice says move, you gotta move," someone says.

"What was that, did I hear a Fobbit talking? You ever even been off this base?"

"Not lately, and not planning to. I like it here just fine."

More laughter.

"Fucking towel-heads."

The siren blares again, then, "INCOMING! INCOMING!"

"Damn, time to go poo-hunting."

"Wait for it . . . wait for it . . ."

A moment later the sound of an F15 roaring into the sky scuds into the bunker.

"Fast-mover gonna get some today."

"Shut up, Geardo. You spent your entire paycheck on a bunch of shit you don't need and ain't ever gonna use."

KABOOM! This one lands inside the wire. Close. The concussion comes through the ground.

"Holy shit!" It's a chorus.

And then they hear it: soldiers moaning, soldiers crying out. The awful shrieking of injury.

The long moment of silent indecision. Erin bolts.

The sudden sunlight after the twilight of the bunker blinds her momentarily. She shades her eyes and scans. Smoke and dust hang in a cloud forty feet away. The front section of the supply building is torn open, metal walls curled wide, peeled back by the force of the explosion. Dusty smoke roils above the hole where the walls and roof had been. Three bodies lie twisted on the ground, sprawled, their limbs banked at horrible angles. Erin runs toward them, the awful sounds of their screams pulling and repelling her at once. She scans the sky and runs, praying it stays clear, half-expecting Big Voice to warn of more incoming but usually it's only one or two at a time, three at most, and suddenly she is standing over a body, the world gone silent as she kneels next to Candice, seeing and refusing to see. Dust floats slowly toward the ground, dull particles dancing in the sunlight, settling slowly back to earth, settling on the bodies that lay there, twisted and bleeding.

A roar fills Erin's ears and she thinks at first it is fighter jets but she is too stunned to move. The roar grows louder and Erin realizes it is coming from inside her, filling her ears and her brain and then her entire body as she looks for life in Candice's deep brown eyes.

Candice's right arm is broken. Her right foot is missing.

Blood pours from her ankle, spilling on moon dust.

There is a hole in her neck.

THIRTY-FIVE

Erin lies on the living room floor, staring at the ceiling. There is no reason at all for her to do anything. She remembers what it was like when Paul and Lindsey got wound up playing games upstairs, the thump of their feet as they chased each other around, the giggles, the squeals.

The sound of tires on gravel threatens to puncture her eardrums. A car pulling up the driveway. Backing up. Engine stops. Door shuts. Footsteps on gravel. Erin goes to the kitchen window.

She doesn't recognize the blue four door sedan parked nose-out, ready for a quick getaway. It looks like a government car. The trunk is open and she can't see who's behind it. A hand reaches up and pulls the trunk closed. A man in gray trousers and a white shirt wades through the jungle of dormant blackcap brambles that grew all summer at the edge of the driveway, providing berries for the birds, pollen for the bees. He has a clipboard in one hand. Erin wonders why he backed the car up so close to a snarl of thorny vines if he knew he had to get something out of the trunk. He has to stop several times and unsnag his trousers from the grip of the thorns. Erin enjoys watching, rooting for the thorn bushes. It serves him right. Guru voice interrupts, speaking softly and in well-modulated tones: *only through non-judgment can we hope to achieve inner peace.* She's not judging. She's observing. She grabs the broom from the kitchen corner and goes to the front door.

"Can I help you?" She keeps her voice neutral, neither threatening nor friendly.

"Bob Steele, Child Protective Services." He says this in the tone that TV detectives use when they show up unexpectedly to question a suspect. "I'm from Preventive." He shows his ID. "I believe Mrs. Copley told you to expect me."

Erin parks the broom in a corner of the kitchen. Mr. Steele places his vinyl-covered folder/clipboard combo on the table and opens it, moves some papers around.

"Doing a little housekeeping?" He clicks his pen. "That's healthy."

"Cleanliness is next to godliness." Erin guesses that it didn't occur to Mr. Steele that a broomstick can be an effective weapon. Some cop he is. It comforts her to have it nearby. She doesn't know this man at all.

"You completed Early Recovery? How long was that program?"

"Ten weeks."

Click. He makes a note of it. Erin got the cherished green piece of paper several weeks ago. But in spite of Mrs. Copley's assurances, completing the program had satisfied no one. And now Mrs. Copley is out of the picture. Erin's fate has been transferred to Preventive.

"And the program you're in now, how long is that one?" Click-click.

"There's no set time period."

Click. He jots more notes. Erin cannot make out his handwriting. His hands look soft, and he reeks of cheap men's cologne, or maybe the smell is because his shirt has enough starch in it to stand up by itself. He snaps his clipboard shut and extends a hand.

"Glad to see you're making progress," he says.

He's almost to the front door when he stops and turns abruptly. "One more thing," he says. "I'd like to have a look around the house."

Erin thinks she's misheard him.

"It's standard procedure."

Erin feels fatigue wash over her. These people are like mosquitos, buzzing around waiting to drain blood from a host. Evidently Mr. Steele likes to play detective.

"Just a quick look around. It's in your contract."

"There's not a drop of alcohol anywhere in this house."

"Are you refusing to comply with the terms of your agreement?"

Erin shakes her head. She will not give them cause to derail her progress, regardless of how humiliating they make the protocol.

"Why don't you have a seat on the couch?"

Erin does as she is told. She will sit on the couch and act as if there is nothing odd about a man you've just met coming into your home and rummaging through your belongings. She wonders if he's going to look in her underwear drawer. It happens every day. She reminds herself of that. It's nothing personal. And it's not just something you see on TV. It happens every day all across America to real people in real houses with real lives, living under the illusion that their homes are sacrosanct, that the Fourth Amendment will somehow shield them from violation.

She sits down and listens to Mr. Steele's footsteps on the stairway as he trudges up to the empty rooms where Paul and Lindsey used to sleep. Rock-Paper-Scissors. She used to play it with Paul at bedtime as he bargained for ten more minutes of Lego time.

He comes back downstairs.

"Very orderly," he says. "You keep a nice house." One of the signs that children may be neglected is a disorderly household. He proceeds to her bedroom. Erin forces herself to stay put. She hears him open her closet. She stares out the sliding glass door. The woods are peaceful. The woods are silent. His footsteps come back down the hall.

He walks over to her, holding the rifle. Erin feels the blood run out of her face. *Fuck.*

"Do you think this is a good idea?"

"It belongs to a friend. I've been meaning to return it."

"You had a suicide attempt."

"I'm not going to do anything stupid."

"I guess you should have thought about that before." He holds the Mannlicher delicately, as if he fears it could discharge by itself. "Is this thing loaded?"

"Of course not," Erin says. "I was deployed to Afghanistan, Mr. Steele. I'm an expert marksman. I know how to handle weapons."

He puts it down on the coffee table.

"Look," Erin says, "if you want, just take it with you, okay? It's not even mine."

She doesn't tell him that it wouldn't be here if Eddy's creepy friend Rico hadn't showed up and insisted that she take it. Jesus, how could she have been so stupid?

"Take it. Or I'll get rid of it. Whatever."

"I can't take it. But if you keep it, you're going to have to get a trigger lock for it if your kids come back."

Erin keys on the word *if*.

"Of course." She gets up, almost staggers but catches herself, resting a hand on the back of the couch. Mr. Steele seems not to notice. She follows him to the front door, closes it behind him and falls against it, listening to the sound of his car engine fading down the driveway. She waits a few minutes before pulling on a pair of boots and grabbing a coat.

Walking down the driveway, she hears the powerful hammering of a pileated woodpecker echo from somewhere in the woods. Lindsey and Paul were fascinated with them, especially after discovering Woody Woodpecker cartoons on YouTube.

At the end of the driveway, she opens the mailbox. It has been a long time since anything other than demands for payment has come out of there. When Eddy walked out, he walked out completely. She'd been through hearing after hearing trying to get child support. But he knew how to game the system: delaying hearings, filing petitions, not showing for hearings, then showing for hearings, then entering into an agreement, then not keeping the agreement. And when Erin dragged herself to the courthouse to file again, the process would start over. Though she knew the ordeal was pointless, if she stopped attempting to collect child support she would lose her food stamps.

Before opening the mailbox and its daily assault on her senses, she makes sure Mr. Steele is really gone. Erin wouldn't be surprised to see him parked down the road, playing at being a real detective doing surveillance. She hears a familiar rumbling coming from beyond the rise in the roadway, and then here comes the school bus on its afternoon run. It thrumbles past, not even slowing, leaving a gust of diesel-scented fumes in its wake. Its brake lights flash red just before it disappears around a sharp curve at the top of the rise in the road.

Erin yanks open the mailbox. There's one envelope. She rips it open. Inside is a letter from the SUPREME COURT—COUNTY OF GRANITE.

The people in the rooms are fond of saying that God will not give you more than you can handle. It's the kind of advice often found embroidered on a pillow or posted on Facebook.

The letter is titled: NOTICE OF SALE. The day after tomorrow, people will gather in the courthouse lobby and a referee will sell her house to the highest bidder. Day after tomorrow? Don't they have to give her more notice? What about her thirty day stay of execution?

She reads carefully, dread ballooning inside her. They are taking her house, her home. She will become one of the legions of homeless vets living under freeway overpasses all across America, listening to the hum of traffic as it sails past on the highways, the cars driven by motorists oblivious to the cardboard shantytowns full of veterans below.

She stares at the notice. The woodpecker jackhammers its long, pointed beak against a tree, much closer now. She scans the woods, searching for the red crown, the black wings, the white stripe along the neck, which should stand out easily against the pale browns and grays of the forest. They're large, as birds go, roughly the size of crows, but she can't find it. The birds' cries remind Erin of something you might hear in a jungle, an uninhibited keening both fearless and full of longing. They pair up for life and, should one partner die, the other will remain in the territory where the couple set up housekeeping.

She folds up the notice and jams it in her coat pocket. It isn't until the woodpecker hammers again that she's able to spot it, high up in a nearby hemlock, probing the bark for insects.

There are thirty-three foreclosures scheduled for sale in Granite County. There were as many last month. And more the month before.

Deutsche Bank is behind almost all of them. The bank has hired a local attorney to do the paperwork. His phone number is listed, and defendants can call to get further information. Erin's hands are shaking so badly she can barely press the buttons. Twice she has to stop and redial.

All across America, mortgages are being foreclosed. The media doesn't seem to be covering it so much anymore; they have a presidential candidate who likes to brag about grabbing pussy, and that seems to be all anyone can focus on, when they can focus at all.

PART III

PART III

THIRTY-SIX

Tiny infrared blackout lights glow in the darkness, marking the rear of the truck ahead. Red helmet lamps are the only source of light in the truck. They're on good road, a paved and level stretch.

"Stupid to say, but goddamn it's just not fair." Ginj stares at a gray-green world through her night vision goggles. She hasn't even bothered to buckle in. Erin should have noticed before they left, especially with Ginj being wound so tight.

"Hey," she says gently. "Seat belt?"

"Good looking-out, bae." Ginj yanks down the shoulder strap and snaps it. "Did you send me that photo yet?"

"Sorry. Forgot. When we get to Bagram." Erin sees the image: Candice with that big pink bubble covering her face. She grips the wheel and holds her foot steady on the gas pedal, following the devil eyes floating above the roadway in the black night. It seems at moments as if they're winking at her.

"I'd like to fuckin' punctuate the goddamn hajji that took her out. With a goddamn fitty."

"Ginj, try to take it easy."

"Turn him into pink mist."

"That's your grief talking."

"No, I'm serious, bae, I don't like what I'm feeling right now."

"I know." Erin wishes there were words. But there aren't. She knows this much about grief: the more you try to understand it, the deeper it sinks its teeth.

"Don't say it." Ginj bangs an arm against the window glass.

"Say what?"

"Some asshat platitude like *time heals all wounds* or some shit like that."

"Wasn't going to." Erin realizes she's gotten too close to the lights and slows to maintain proper spacing. Idiotic *what ifs* glide through her mind. What if Ginj had been there with her and Candice? What if Candice hadn't trotted off to the latrine? She despises the way her brain functions, looking for someone or something to blame under the guise of seeking reason. Do all the math you want: subtract, add, multiply, divide. Plan away. Just when you think you've got your balance, life will take you out at the knees.

"I don't know how to deal." Ginj sighs loudly. "I'm just not good at—"

The explosion sends the truck into the air, sailing like it's made of paper and balsa wood, like the little model car that Paul made for Erin when he was in elementary school, the one at home on Erin's bookshelf.

Ginj's arms fly up, her hands slam against the truck cabin roof. Slowly, time paused, time warped, the truck floats, rising, rising, the hood flies off and sails past the windshield, they are rolling through air, twisting and turning and rolling, Erin is upside down, the truck is upside down, Erin and Ginj strapped to their seats, suspended, hanging in the long slow curl of time, gravity broken, and then they are falling, falling, forever falling, turning and twisting until the slam and crash of breaking metal hitting the ground, the jolt of impact, and they are sideways, strapped in, and outside the window, black.

Smoke. Hot metal. Darkness.

"Fuck," Ginj whispers.

"Ginj?"

"Fuck." Ginj strains against her seat belt. Erin's fingers find one of the straps holding her in place, crawl along it until she reaches the buckle. She works at it and feels her head filling with cotton, the air goes yellow, lighting up the world, pinpricks of brown glittering in sick yellow. She smells smoke. She tries to speak. Her eyes close. Bursts of gunfire, *crak-kak-kak-kak-ak*, weapons stutter and spark like exploding strings of Black Cats, firecrackers on Independence Day. Someone is breathing heavily, panting, up close to her ear, right next to her ear. The brilliant yellow light flares again, inside her head, bursting onto the backs of her eyelids. Black.

∞

Sounds arrive first, in darkness, people talking, electronic beeps, a hum and bustle. Eyes still closed, Erin sees herself standing outside her car, her crappy little Toyota, pumping gas and making faces through the car window. On the other side of the glass, Lindsey and Paul, strapped into their booster seats, crane their little necks and bug their eyes, wrinkle their noses, twisting their mouths into clownish smiles. Silly Mommy.

She feels a hand on her wrist, a thumb pressing hard on the inside of it. Her eyelids tremble against the glare of light. A face appears. Nurse. Behind the nurse, Sergeant Drake, eyes narrowed as if he's squinting to shield against bright sunshine. The beeping blurs and fades. Erin falls back into nothingness.

∞

Pressure. On her shoulder. A hand on her shoulder, nudging gently. Erin strains to open her eyes. Lightglare. She brings a hand to her face, shielding against it.

"Erin?" The gentle voice of a woman. Kind. "Erin? Can you wake up? Can you sit up?"

Erin pushes herself back on the bed, foam mattress beneath thin sheet, edges herself upright.

The nurse hands her a cup of water. Erin sips through a straw, fights back a gag. Something flashes in her brain, a gray image, upside down, the truck, the explosion, Erin upside down in the truck and Ginj upside down next to her, the two of them strapped in place, hanging, suspended.

205

"Did Ginj . . ." She stops herself. Afraid to ask.

"You are so lucky," the nurse says.

Erin sips more water. A sheet covers her body, but she can tell both her feet are there beneath it. She has her arms. Thank God.

"Is Ginj here?"

"The one you came in with? Treated and released. We sent her back to the barracks. You have no idea how lucky you were."

Erin tries to remember. There are only brief flashes, disjointed bits, fragments.

"IED," the nurse adds. "They should just call them what they are. Roadside bombs."

∞

She's flat on her back, her head encased in a beige plastic cage. Her ears are plugged. She is trying to take the technician's advice, trying to think of something pleasant and relaxing. It is summer. She and Niki, a mom-bond friend since kindergarten orientation, sit on towels at the shore of Couillard Lake, whose calm waters take a dark blue hue from the surrounding hills. Their children splash near the shoreline. The afternoon sun has warmed the air; an occasional breeze flutters the leaves of tall oaks and maples in the woods behind them. Somewhere nearby, a chipmunk chatters to its mate. It is a perfect day. Perfect.

A mechanical hum intrudes. Erin feels the table beneath her rising slowly, then moving into the MRI machine, a tube of grayish-white plastic. She grips the plastic call button in one hand. Even with the ear plugs, she hears the whine and hum of the machine when it starts up. She closes her eyes and tries to go back to the lake.

∞

The lights are off, the room in shadows. Erin stops at the doorway, thinks she's hallucinating. Candice is back, lying in her bunk. Erin's eyes adjust to the gloom. The woman in Candice's bunk sits up. For the first time, Erin recognizes uncertainty on Ginj's face.

"Damn," Ginj whispers.

Erin goes to her own bunk and eases onto it.

"Wow." Ginj offers a hesitant shrug. "You're good? I thought . . ."

"What? I died or something?"

"Something. I thought maybe they'd be sending you home."

"Concussion," Erin says. "I'm here for the duration. Unless, you know, something else happens." Her ears ring as if there's a thin metal wire stretched tight between her ear drums, emitting a piercing, high-pitched tone that threatens to snap the filament in half. She presses her palms against her ears, but that only makes it sound as if the tone is coming through thick insulation.

"I guess I'm sorry to hear that. Sort of." Ginj shrugs one shoulder. "I mean, it would've been good for you, going home to your family and all." She pats the bunk sadly. "Feels kinda weird, lying here. Doctor's orders. No climbing, no jumping, no running. Can't even climb onto an upper bunk. So."

"Stranded in Puerto Rico."

"Yeah. At least they're not sending me home." Ginj's eyes seem a little unfocused. "I miss her."

"Stay there. Take the bunk. She wouldn't mind."

"Maybe I will." Ginj fluffs her pillow, lies back down. "When Drake dragged you out of the truck, I thought I was gonna be missing you, too."

"Wait. What?"

"He saved our lives, bae. Like, big time."

Erin tries to recall. Nothing. As if her brain is burying the memory deeper every time she tries to access it.

"Yeah, like fucking hajjis creeping on us, and we were out there stuck half upside down in that goddamn truck. You don't remember? Drake comes out of nowhere and takes out all three of them and cuts me out of my seat belt and you too and just like slings you over his shoulder and gets you to his MRAP, and didn't nobody know if there were more of them. He didn't give a shit. He got us the fuck out of there."

"Oh." Erin has a vague, unsettling awareness that she should be feeling something or saying more words. The ringing in her ears grows louder, painful, making it difficult to hear what Ginj is saying.

"He was awesome, man. A fucking animal, and it was some heavy fire. Like, seriously, if it hadn't been for him . . ." Ginj chokes, clears her throat. "We'd both be dead."

Erin wonders if they are, if they've both died and gone to a gray cinderblock hell. But it doesn't matter, really. Might as well get comfortable. She eases her boots off and slides them under her bunk, bending carefully. Lies down slowly. The closest thing she has to a feeling is emptiness. Pure emptiness. She wonders if Eddy would be relieved if she died. "How long have we been back?"

"Two days. I tried to wait for you. They ordered me back to barracks. Man. That shit was real."

"What'd they say? Your diagnosis."

"Concussion. Three more days bedrest before I can go light duty. You?"

Erin can't remember what the discharge nurse said. She takes the orders from her pocket, tries to make them out in the gloom.

"Doc said no lights for a few days. To help with the healing. Minimal stimulation or some shit like that."

"I guess that means you can't jerk off."

Ginj giggles, but quickly stops, pressing her temples with her palms. "Please bae. Don't make me laugh."

Erin tosses the paper aside. It doesn't matter yet. Neither of them is going anywhere for the next several days. They're punch drunk, oddly light-headed, loopy. Erin stares up at the peace sign carved into the paint of the upper bunk rack. Remembers seeing it the first time she lay down here, scared half witless. It feels like a century has passed.

THIRTY-SEVEN

Trauma and Anger, courtesy of DSS lead attorney Chrystal McClain, who just last week burst out of the courtroom, chasing after Gavin, yelling, "Wait. Wait a minute!" She grabbed Gavin's shoulder, announcing loudly. "I'm doing this for *her*, it's what she needs." Erin sat quietly in the waiting area, taking in the scene as if she were in front of a TV, viewing an afternoon soap.

"Yeah, right." Gavin jerked his shoulder free. "Give me a break." He stalked away, shaking his head with disgust. Erin supposed she should follow as he headed toward a conference room, but like everyone else in the waiting area, she was riveted.

"Oh my God!" Chrystal said. "Oh my God, I don't believe this!" She lunged toward the court officer. "Just, just, give me your gun right now so I can shoot myself!"

The Court Officer stepped back, his hand on his weapon, uncertain at first whether she was serious. Chrystal whipped her head around, lashing his face with her long curls, and disappeared back into the courtroom. It occurred to Erin that if she had behaved that way, they would have arrested her.

But Chrystal prevailed. Trauma and Anger is the fourth group the court has demanded Erin attend. The program starts tonight. A slender man in a Black Lives Matter T-shirt slouches on a wooden bench just inside the run-down strip mall entry. He nods at Erin and she says hey and continues down the long hallway. Stale, overheated air hangs in the corridor like the odor of burnt bacon.

Three women are there when Erin arrives, one at the large table in the center of the room and two others on a battered couch against the near wall. Erin positions herself at the far end of the table, closest to the room's rear exit. As women filter in, Erin recognizes some of them from AA and the Women's Group at Causeway Aftercare. She wonders if, like her, they are here because they have to be. Or maybe they have shifted their dependency from drugs and alcohol to meetings. Surely it's less harmful. There's no conversation. Phones are out, everyone is in her own comfortable—or uncomfortable—bubble of technology.

A middle-aged woman in a flowing skirt and colorful silk scarves bustles in holding an overstuffed loose-leaf notebook. Moving quickly around the table, she distributes hand-outs to the class.

"Hello everyone, are we all here for Women's Trauma and Anger?" This gets a few nods, but nobody says anything. The instructor flutters about the table, chirping "here you are" and "there you go" as she offers the papers. There's a diagram of the human body and a graphic with three labeled boxes: Emotions, Thoughts, Physical State. There is a page about triggers. Erin wonders if it's ironic that the word "trigger" is a trigger for her.

Ten minutes into the class, it is clear that the instructor is winging it. She drones on. The room is too warm. Erin fights to stay awake. "Okay then," the instructor says, "I'd like us all to share why we're here and how we got here."

Women take turns telling their stories. Different locations, different characters, different costumes, different words. Some of the women cry as they talk. Others are stoic. Others are pissed off. It is all the same story, really, and the story is this: every day, all over the world, women are getting the living shit kicked out of them. Women are terrified. Stalked. Raped. Murdered. Predators abound.

A woman on the couch is trying not to cry as she tells the story of how her boyfriend almost killed her. She uses her hands as she speaks, her voice barely above a whisper. Her hands swerve and dance in front of her as if she is conducting a string quartet, guiding them through Bach's *Jesu, Joy of Man's Desiring* as she says words like broken arm, six fractured ribs, and ruptured spleen.

Erin follows the woman's hands, and then all she can see are the hands, fluttering and floating, graceful, gentle. They stop suddenly, and fold into the woman's lap. At first it is only a trickle, and Erin isn't sure she's seeing it. But then the trickle grows, begins to flow, and another appears, and another. The woman's hands are bleeding, blood drips across her pale white skin, flowing out of her wrists. Erin looks away. She is dizzy and the room is too hot; she squeezes her eyes hard, looks again. It is still there, the blood, trickling across the pale white skin, dripping from the tips of the woman's fingers. That's when Erin realizes that the woman killed her abuser. The woman doesn't have to say it. Erin sees it in her eyes, on her hands.

Driving home, she tries to persuade herself that she didn't see what she most certainly saw. It was only the medication, a side effect, a chemical illusion. She merges onto the long straightaway stretch of county road that leads toward the winding country lanes in the hills, toward home, keeping an eye out for deer that might jump suddenly into the beams of her headlights. This requires her undivided attention, but she keeps seeing the hands. The blood. She shakes her head hard, shivers in her seat, trying to jar the image from her brain. She focuses on the white painted shoulder stripes as she guides the car along the black road in the black night. To the left and right of the roadway, the cornfields are hidden in darkness.

∞

The Department of Social Services parking area is jammed almost to capacity. Erin finally gets a spot in the back row, pulling up the hood on her rain jacket as she jogs across the lot, raindrops splattering sporadically at first, quickly becoming a downpour. She shouldn't be here, not without going through proper channels, but the channels are dysfunctional and what's driving her is not rational anyway. Gavin warned her against doing anything like this. Mrs. Copley, too, said just do what you're told. Questions of where her family will live and how she will provide for her children are pushed out of mind. Erin doesn't know if she's self-sabotaging or doing what any mother would do; the lines are as blurred as the rain-drenched glass doors in front of her. She pushes her way through, soaked.

The receptionist sits behind a Plexiglas window, her head down, her attention on something out of Erin's view, concentrating so hard that she doesn't see Erin standing in front of the window, next to a metal display rack stuffed with wilting brochures. Erin clears her throat. The woman ignores her.

Erin waits. The guru voice speaks in her brain: *Practice mindful waiting.*

Erin cannot determine whether she is waiting mindfully or mindlessly. Now a man joins the woman, peers over her shoulder, his big red tie dangling beneath a triple chin.

"Almost . . . almost . . ." he says, leaning in close, his lips near her ear. "Oh. That's it. Oh!" Their eyes move synchronously, tracking something. "Oh!" They moan in unison, as if in the throes of simultaneous orgasm. Their eyes meet. Erin sees it now, on the computer monitor, They are playing Angry Birds.

Are they fucking kidding?

Erin raps on the Plexiglas.

They look up blankly.

"Can I help you?" The woman's tone is stale with annoyance.

"My children were removed." Erin says the word slowly, enunciates it carefully. *Removed.* "I want to talk to someone about getting them back."

"We don't do that here," the woman says. "You have to go through the courts for that."

Erin rips off her rain jacket and shakes it vigorously, baptizing the room and splattering the Plexiglass. Dr. Cuevos' words come back to her: *Before every awakening comes a rude awakening.* The blue and red birds swim on the screen growing larger and more menacing, their baby birds out of reach in the tree. *You want an awakening? Look at how you got here: you tried to kill yourself. Stop all the raging and ask yourself why.* She will not answer. She can't.

"I want my children back!" Erin slams her hand against the Plexiglass again and again . . . "You can't keep doing this!"

A door at the rear of the receptionist's cubicle opens and a young woman enters, her see-through blouse wrinkled and stained. Her hair hangs on her shoulders in oily strands. Erin slams the Plexiglass once more, startling the woman before letting her hand fall to her side, useless. She laughs out loud, realizing it sounds a little crazy but she can't stop it, because she's laughing about wanting to tell the woman to wash her fucking hair. At least act like you give a shit. She glares at them. If she could, Erin would destroy all three of them, the creatures frozen behind the Plexiglass like taxidermied animals at a museum, their eyes gone marble with complacency. Erin despises them, her hatred as pure as motherhood. But if it would bring her children home to her, she would fall on her knees and beg these clods. She would beg them.

The receptionist has the receiver to her ear, punching in numbers from the safety of her cubicle. Erin hurtles toward the exit, kicking over a chair and sending it skidding across the floor as she flees from the building.

∞

Still shaking from the encounter at CPS, Erin sees the red light just in time to avoid running it. Her car jolts to a stop, rocks back on its chassis at the very edge of the intersection just as a large truck flies past. As it sails through the intersection, Erin realizes she's just missed being T-boned by a vehicle that would have crushed her.

For a moment, she wishes it had. Over and done with, no questions asked. Her hands tremble on the steering wheel. She has come to a stop in front of a run-down, old-school Irish bar, a watering hole with a green neon sign flashing in the dark window: OPEN. She can feel it. The pure burning-cold liquid of it. OPEN. Icy vodka slipping down her throat. OPEN. She can smell it. Taste it. Fuck it all. Eddy doesn't want to give the kids back? Fine. Let him take them. Maybe he should; maybe it's what's best. In the dark window, the green neon blinks: OPEN. OPEN. OPEN. It's too hard. The odds she'll make it are way, way long. She should park, go inside, and get it over with. The traffic signal leers at her. Red light? Green light?

A loud, long beep from the car behind her jolts her back to the intersection. She hits the accelerator hard, screeching away from the bar and weaving through traffic like she's driving in Afghanistan,

∞

The door won't budge. Erin tugs hard at the handle bolted to unpainted steel, scarred with key-scratch graffiti. Just as she manages to pull the thing open, her cell phone dings, indicating she has missed a call. She lets the door fall closed and takes out her phone.

"Erin, it's Gavin Costa, concerning your visit this morning to CPS. I want to talk about same; I've got some real concerns about it. Also I spoke to the children's attorney, Mr. Bagley, about visitation. He assures me he is working with your ex to arrange a visit. Please give me a call as soon as you can." She wonders who called him, and how they managed to get through to him so quickly. She dials. He's not available. She puts her phone away and yanks open the door.

In a small office at the end of a narrow hallway, Erin faces a hefty woman with dyed jet black hair pulled into a tight bun positioned at true north on her oversized head. A subtle hostility emanates from her, as if she's wearing a perfume called *Aggression*. Harriet is a Credentialed Alcoholism and Substance Abuse Counselor, having completed a minimum of 350 hours of education and passed a 150-question computer-generated multiple-choice examination to obtain her certification. She explains that she is a member of the Causeway Aftercare Team that will further evaluate Erin's recovery for the Family Treatment Court. Reading from the report in front of her, she notes that Erin completed the Causeway Aftercare Early Recovery program some weeks ago and congratulates her on that.

"So." Harriet folds her hands on the desktop. "How are you today?"

"Fine." Erin's voice is flat.

"Oh, that's nice to hear." Harriet nods her head slowly, up and down, up and down, like a life-size, animated bobblehead. She pulls a plastic tube from her desk drawer and hands it to Erin.

"I'll need a saliva sample."

"I get tested every week, at Family Treatment Court."

"You just open the tube, take out the swab and mush it around under your tongue. Be sure to get the insides of your cheeks as well." Harriet fans herself with her paperwork, watching Erin insert the sponge nub under her tongue. "Make sure you get it good and wet," Harriet says.

∞

Cindy, the Family Treatment Coordinator who collects the urine samples each week before court, stares into an industrial-size pot, stirring soup. One of Cindy's job responsibilities is to organize volunteer work for Family Treatment Court participants. Erin waits in the kitchen doorway, thinking that Cindy looks stoned; anyone can see that she's mesmerized by the soup swirling in the pot. But maybe that's just Cindy.

"Erin! Hi!" Cindy pulls the spoon from the soup and points to a squat man with a beautiful caramel complexion, a blue baseball cap tight on his head. "Meet Julio. He's in charge."

Julio nods and holds up a loaf of bread. "Cutting boards are over there, grab a knife."

Erin takes a serrated knife and grabs a thick multigrain baguette from a large brown bag of loaves, donations from a local restaurant. She cuts through the crust; the bread scent rises up in aromatic waves.

She feels, for the first time in a very long time, useful. Simply useful. Hungry people come here to get a meal. She puts the bread in a rattan basket, the kind used at linen-tablecloth restaurants. The soup kitchen has three servings each day, seven days a week, sit-down meals for people who have nowhere else to go: the jobless, the addicted, the homeless. Erin arranges the slices carefully and folds the white napkin over them.

She's not sure how much is left on her food stamps. She has to have her HEAP application in this week, or she will have no heating oil. If she has no heating oil, she will have to buy kerosene at the gas station and pour it into the tank two gallons at a time.

She has somehow managed not to call Eddy, not to go to Eddy's house, not to go to the school. It has taken every ounce of her willpower to stay away, but she is complying with the court order, fearing permanent removal. And no one, not Eddy, not Bagley, not Gavin, not Mr. Steele, and certainly not the judge, seems to care that it is taking an eternity to arrange even one simple visit, much less to seriously evaluate what kind of damage is being done by the separation of mother and child. Or maybe she has it all wrong. Maybe they are all doing exactly what they should be doing, protecting her children from their mother.

THIRTY-EIGHT

By the time they hit the outskirts of Kabul, the sun has warmed the cool air of a November night and morning traffic is stirring. Erin is forward in the driver's seat, gripping the wheel tightly, scanning the road for potholes and ridges as the convoy speeds into town. They're traveling empty, having delivered another shipment to Bagram for airlift back to the States. She follows directly behind a Cougar 4x4 MRAP, the fifty-caliber machine gun on top swiveling constantly, searching for insurgents.

A gaping pothole comes suddenly into view from beneath the MRAP in front as it clears the cratered pavement, seeming to materialize in the roadway as the vehicle muscles forward. Erin swerves, misses it, but her right front tire catches a hard curb of badly buckled pavement near the road edge, jolting her and Ginj against their seat belts.

"Nice driving," Ginj says, settling back in the seat.

They scan the street, the buildings, the tall concrete walls lining the sides of the battered pavement. It's different now, driving outside the wire. The possibility of attack, of death, is no longer conceptual, no longer only a thing they've heard lectures about or read about in Army training manuals. They both feel it constantly now, whether inside the wire or out: it's fucking real. Every nerve in their skin vibrates, scanning for threat.

Local cars surge madly onto the main road, darting out of side streets from behind corner buildings, trees, parked cars, hidden until they're already halfway into the traffic lane. It's video-game driving. A truck loaded with mattresses chugs by, blocking the view to the right. A white on yellow taxi—they're everywhere—recklessly threads the needle and seconds later another one swings out of nowhere, swerving dangerously close to the truck.

The convoy slows momentarily, and Erin hears Drake's voice coming through the speaker in her helmet. "Close the gap to four seconds. Do not stop at the traffic circle, roll straight through. Repeat, do not stop at the traffic circle." She hates when it comes unexpectedly through her helmet earpiece. It's like he's right there. Like he was that night. She mashes the accelerator, gets on the tail of the MRAP in front of her as the convoy picks up speed. Nearing the traffic circle, she hears a cacophony of horns, growing louder. A 6x6 MRAP has stationed itself across the lanes, blocking traffic and backing up civilian vehicles around the far loop of the circle and all the way down the connecting feeder street. Standing at their open car doors, drivers shout furiously, reaching in to lean on their horns as they curse the American soldiers who seem to think they run the place.

The convoy blows through the circle, engines roaring, and Erin holds the wheel tight as centrifugal force pulls at the two and a half tons of metal she steers through the tight arc. She swings a hard right onto the straightaway, gunning it again to maintain proper distance from the vehicle ahead.

A clump of men in orange safety suits, some in hard hats, some in baseball caps, stop their work on the sidewalk to lean on their shovels and stare at the convoy rolling past. They spit and shake their heads. On the straightaway again, Erin quickly searches the top of a large billboard that stretches across the roadway, scanning for snipers. The image of a young Afghani in a gray shirt, his arms outstretched and reaching across four lanes of traffic, beams down at her beneath English and Arabic lettering: *Best network coverage. The future is yours.*

As the sun begins to sink, the convoy is southeast of Gardez. They've made good time, rolling on narrow but mostly paved highways past the miles after miles of relatively even landscape. The vast expanse of light brown soil that stretches toward the mountains is cut into squares and rectangles of sprouting, cultivated green. The highway starts to climb, and Erin knows the hard part is up ahead, the treacherous, winding road that runs up alongside a sheer, stone-faced mountain on one side and a steep, seemingly bottomless, ravine on the other. It's a prime location for a trap. The convoy is halted while drones and sappers check out the territory ahead.

They pull to the side of the road and sit.

And sit.

Dusk has come on full and shadowy. Ginj dozed off half an hour into the wait. She looks peaceful in sleep, contented as a napping puppy. Erin wishes they could get moving instead of sitting here as stationary targets. She's relieved when Ginj stirs, stretching in the cramped space. Half asleep, Ginj leans toward the window, still getting her bearings when something darts in front of the truck.

"Oh my god! A dog! It's hurt!" Without hesitation, she grabs her rifle and bails out, shutting the door against Erin's shouted *NO* and the next thing Erin sees is Ginj crouching around the front of the vehicle and sneaking between the truck and the MRAP in front of them, scrambling down an embankment.

The rule is: do not exit your vehicle without authorization. Erin lowers her window and watches as Ginj moves toward an odd stand of juniper jutting up from the dark soil that slopes down from the roadway. She'll get slammed if she's caught. Erin grabs her rifle and jumps from the truck, racing after her.

"Ginj!" Erin hisses.

Ginj winds through sparse clumps of ash and juniper and quickly scoops up the wounded animal, shushing and soothing as she tries to get a hand around its muzzle. The dog jerks back, twists its head, growling a sharp warning before it sinks its teeth into Ginj's cheek.

"Motherfucker!" Ginj releases the animal, pressing a hand to her face. Erin moves toward Ginj's voice and hears the sound of the dog limp-running away, disappearing into the dusk as Ginj lets loose with a stream of expletives, whisper-yelling in the brush.

"Ginj? Are you okay?" Erin moves over the rocky terrain toward her, past clumps of scraggly grasses spiking out of the earth.

That's when she sees him.

A kid, a child, he can't be even twelve years old. He steps out from behind the twin trunks of a low growing ash tree, not even ten feet away. Erin stares, certain that she should be doing something, but the thought won't connect. *Where did he come from? Where did he come from?* Shock jolts through her and it's not words in her head, it's something deeper, hitting her again, she was looking right at him and did not see him, and now she sees him, this ghost boy, and really sees him, and Jesus Christ she's staring at his hands and he's got a goddamn grenade, a US military-issue hand grenade, and he's standing there looking at her while behind her Ginj keeps it up: *fuck, fuck, fuck, fuck.* The kid is barely older than Erin's son, and he's about to blow them all up, himself and her, and Ginj, who's oblivious, applying pressure to her face with a bandana. Time slows like some huge machine with gears the size of buildings, grating and groaning against its own momentum. Erin feels the safety lever against her thumb, hears the click of it.

The boy doesn't move.

She sucks in a breath, tries to squeeze the trigger. Sweat trickles from her armpits.

Erin hears the sound and sees red blossom on the boy's shirt as his hand loosens and the grenade thuds dully against dirt. His slender body straightens, slumps slightly, then folds, crumpling to the earth.

Ginj brushes past from behind Erin, keeping her rifle trained on the boy's body, ready to shoot again. There's no need. The two women back away, turn silently toward the truck. Erin glances over her shoulder, searching for the thing he was holding. Her eyes fall next to his lifeless hand. Now she sees it, the perfect shade of green. An avocado.

THIRTY-NINE

Umbrella in hand, Erin plods down cracked concrete steps to the basement of the Old Stone Church and pushes open the battered oak door. Inside, the scent of coffee cuts through the odor of mold. It is damp and dark, one reason she doesn't often come to this meeting, though she goes every day to a meeting somewhere, whether she feels up to it or not. She just goes.

She takes a place at the table, surrounded by men in their fifties and sixties, and one woman who sits knitting a hat of pink yarn. A man with cloudy eyes and a Vietnam baseball cap, his face covered with gray stubble, gives her a friendly wink and says *welcome*.

She wants a drink. It's barely noon. No, she doesn't. She doesn't really want a drink. She just wants out of her head. Her recognition of this fact is progress. The topic is One Day at a Time. For the first time—even though her voice quavers—Erin participates. She says that it's difficult not to let her mind hurl her into the future, where horrible things await. It is difficult not to let her brain drag her back to the past. She does not say anything sarcastic like, "I don't have to drag myself into the past, I have judges and therapists who do it for me."

She's unsure how anyone could benefit from her sordid confessions, if she could bring herself to utter the awful specifics, like the times she drove drunk, the highway stripe undulating like a strip of yellow ribbon bobbing on the rolling swells of a dark, unknowable ocean. She cannot tell this roomful of strangers her secrets. She doesn't want to be here, surrounded by people who have dropped the

221

façade, who aren't afraid to tell anyone who'll listen that the rooms are the only solace from the cruelty that goes on out there in the world. Erin doesn't like the fear that grows in her stomach as she listens to how important it is to attend meetings. She keeps wondering when her life will go back to normal. And then she remembers what normal was, and hopes to God it doesn't.

Coming up the stairs after the meeting, confused, jealous of the people who are able to rely on faith for their salvation from booze, she feels her phone buzz. It is Mr. Steele, from CPS Preventive: a visit has been arranged. She can see her children next week. She should report to the CPS building at 3:00 p.m. on Wednesday, December 28. She thanks him and hangs up quickly, before he can reverse the decision. She will not protest that Christmas will be days past before the visit. She will take her lawyer's advice: play the game, don't try to fight CPS. She is dizzy with anticipation, and scared out of her mind. She needs a gift. She has to bring them a gift. She knows what to get them, but she's almost completely stone cold broke. She hears a chorus of AAers: *Let go, let God.* She raises her eyes to the sky. A raindrop splats, right in the middle of her forehead.

She walks down the block, away from the church, away from the post-meeting crowd gathered at the entrance, some lighting cigarettes, many still sipping coffee. The sidewalk is made of bluestone, four-foot square slabs laid edge to edge, worn smooth by decades of foot traffic. Slick with rain, it shines dark blue-gray, almost black in some sections. December used to bring only snow, but it's oddly warm today, near sixty. There's a winter storm watch for tomorrow morning, predictions of ice and sleet. Erin pushes open the scarred storefront door of a dusty pawn shop. The guy behind the counter shoves shoulder-length frizz off his forehead and yanks at the neck of a white T-shirt that says Vote for Pedro. Erin puts her wedding ring on the counter. Isolated on the linty black jewelry tray, the simple band of hammered gold looks alone and foreign, like something lost, something she's never seen before.

"Okay then," the pawnbroker says, turning the ring in his fingers, testing its weight in his palm. Erin doesn't want to remember that day: friends gathered around the stone altar Eddy had built in the woods near their house site. The sky was pale blue and cloudless on a summer afternoon; occasional breezes whispered through the trees, unsettling the deep green leaves. Erin's father showed up sober, proudly offering his arm and walking her along a petal-strewn path while Big Gordy from the Visser Kok played the Prelude from *Bach's Cello Suite No. 1.* on his guitar. Eddy beamed at her, love in his eyes, pride in his eyes, about to marry the girl he'd had a crush on in high school. But it had grown into something bigger, something deeper and stronger: he was her lover, and he was her best friend. They would be family.

"I can go forty," the pawnbroker says.

SALE! SALE! SALE! Christmas specials abound. Erin walks past aisles of polyester toward the far end of the Walmart, past the plastic and chemical scent of the pharmaceutical section, past hardware, past seasonal, past toys. Last summer, they had asked for a tent. She hadn't been able to swing it, hadn't been able to swing anything. She's got two crumpled twenties from the pawn shop stuffed in her pocket. She finds a tent for $34.99. It's not the nicest one, but it's good enough and the price is right.

∞

On Christmas Day, Erin gets the wrapping paper from its spot in the upstairs closet. She wraps the tent and puts a ribbon on it and puts it in the entryway near the front door. An AA Christmas dinner is marked on the kitchen calendar. Erin thinks about going. She thinks about going to a meeting. She should try to be around people. She does not want to be around people.

It's pitch dark by 5:30. Good. Tonight, it is welcome. She goes to the kitchen and takes her medication. She should eat something.

Instead she goes to her computer and willingly lets herself get sucked into the internet timesink, clicking and scrolling mindlessly until she somehow lands on a YouTube video of spectacular glacial calvings. In it, towering ice faces, masses of ice the size of buildings, break free and implode into the sea, churning up huge clouds of white mist, generating surfing-sized waves that roll toward the tourist boats as people clap and cheer, capturing iPhone videos of the spectacle.

At some point she slouches into the living room and puts tea candles all around, on the bookshelf, on the coffee table, on the floor by the big sliding glass door. She is careful to move the drapery aside before lighting the candles, one after the other, and folding herself onto the rug in the middle of the living room.

The flames are lovely in the dark, dancing with the smallest fluctuations of air, the minor disturbances so subtle that, hard as she tries, Erin cannot feel them on her skin. The room seems completely, perfectly still, but the tiny flames quiver in the darkness, their shadows dancing on the walls.

∞

She is barely settled in the office at Causeway Aftercare when Harriet says, "So. The Team has decided that you should attend the Women's Group."

Erin feels heat rising into her face. "I really don't think I need another group."

"If you choose not to attend, I'll have to notify the Family Treatment Court that you're not being cooperative."

"That's not a choice. If you tell them I'm not cooperating they'll kick me out of the program."

"It's up to you."

"Are you serious?"

"The Team feels—"

"Can I meet with the Team? I don't even know the Team. I've never met them."

"It's only one night a week."

"How do you expect me to get a job with all these meetings and appointments?"

"Surely you can see the difference between the therapeutic groups here and an AA meeting."

"Actually I can't. They're identical."

"But the Women's Group is only women."

"AA has those, too. I go every Wednesday."

"Hmmm. Well. You're going to be compliant, aren't you?"

This is one of Harriet's words. Erin detests it. She hates it so much that she Googled it. Compliant: inclined to agree with others or obey rules, especially to an excessive degree; acquiescent: good-humored: *eagerly compliant girls*. See note at obedient. The note at obedient: complying or willing to comply with orders or requests; submissive to another's will: *she was totally obedient to him*. The examples, curiously or not, note female compliance. Even the goddamn dictionaries are biased. The shit's everywhere, fucking embedded in the culture. One of the oldest (and still living) meanings of compliant is reshaping under pressure, as in the conversion of the gel to a much less compliant glass. Comply, or we will shatter you. Guru voice says *what goes around comes around*. Erin leans back and offers a compliant nod, listening silently as one of the other voices in her brain replies, *Shut the fuck up, guru. This is real life, not some dilettante's ranch with exotic horses running around on it.*

∞

"Mrs. Hill?" The caseworker flings a clump of brown hair over her shoulder and jerks her head in the direction of the door.

Erin doesn't bother to correct her. She picks up the tent, in its silver paper and red curlicued ribbons, left over from last year when Tanya and Stephen had come for Christmas.

She walks behind the caseworker, focusing on the roll of flab that hangs over the back of the woman's bra, bulging beneath a tight, thin, polyester blouse that is stretched almost to the point of translucence. The black leggings, too, are at maximum capacity. Tanya would be having a field day doing fashion commentary, but Erin hears the guru crooning something about how remaining non-judgmental is essential to good mental health. She reminds herself that she is just a human walking behind another human down a long, badly lit hallway painted a sad shade of pale blue. This woman has done nothing to deserve her wrath. And what Erin is feeling really has nothing to do with the woman leading her down the hall. Erin is about to see her children and does not know how to face them. She is terrified.

The woman stops outside a closed door.

"What's in the box?"

"A tent."

"Nothing else?"

"It's a Christmas present."

"Nothing else?"

"No. It's still in the box, unopened. From the factory."

"Hmm." The woman peers at her, suspicious. "I guess it's all right if it's still in original packaging." She opens the door wide, motions Erin in.

There they are. Lindsey and Paul, standing next to a table with some kind of activity center on top of it, a garish green and pink and orange maze of wires and plastic objects designed for toddlers, not ten-year-olds.

Erin doesn't know what to do. Her children are four feet away from her, but the distance feels infinite. They are taller, their faces slenderer. Erin is afraid if she moves she will frighten them. Paul edges backward, plucks at the wire maze, keeping his eyes on the floor. He is challenging her, his body stiff with anger, hurt.

"Hey," the woman says, too loudly, too happily, "How about a hug for Mom?"

Erin takes a step toward them and opens her arms. They stand uncertainly. A tear rolls down Lindsey's cheek. Erin can't move, feels like she might be having a panic attack. Paul's face is stricken, Erin sees in his unwavering stare that he is afraid of how much he hates her. All three of them stand frozen, paralyzed.

"I'm so, so sorry," Erin whispers. "I've missed you so much." Erin feels like a monster, a towering, menacing adult in a small room with two children who are afraid of what the grownup might do next. She kneels down, rests back on her heels. She's afraid she'll collapse right here in front of them. Lindsey swipes quickly at the tear and folds her hands tightly together. Paul's eyes are still narrow with suspicion, his lip trembling.

"I'm so sorry I hurt you." Erin chokes. "I'm really so, so sorry. I love you both. Both of you. So, so much."

They look past her, at the woman standing just inside the doorway. Erin gets up and faces her, pleading with her eyes. Can she please, please just have this one moment alone with them? She has been unbearably selfish, and unless they will let her back into their lives, she is doomed to live the rest of her own knowing that she is the one who destroyed the most sacred bond of all: she has destroyed their trust, broken their family. She has broken her own children's hearts. No penance will ever be sufficient.

"I'll be right outside," the woman says. She leaves the door slightly open.

Erin turns back to her children. "Please believe me." She opens her arms again, struggling not to cry. "Can you forgive me?"

It is Lindsey who takes the first step. Erin feels a flood of relief and gratitude as she bends to hug her daughter, folding Lindsey into her arms, kissing her cheek, hoping she will remember how things used to be.

"I love you, sweetie, and I will make all of this up to you. I'm so sorry." She feels Lindsey's arms around her neck, loosely at first, uncertain, and then tighter, and she pulls her closer.

Paul watches them, his whole body trembling. Erin can no longer blink back her tears.

"I love you," she says, "both of you, more than anyone or anything else I have ever loved in my life. Paul. Please."

At first, he looks confused, like he's seeing something he can't make sense of. He frowns suddenly and rushes for the door, but as he brushes past Erin she slips an arm around his waist and pulls him to her. He struggles, but she refuses to let go, and then slowly he stops pulling away and lets her hold him. Erin searches for words, something, anything. His whole body is taut, trying again to tear away and run for the door.

"I'm here," Erin says. "I love you."

"Mom," he whispers, and collapses against her. He wraps his arms around her neck, and Lindsey snuggles in tighter, all three of them sobbing.

FORTY

The sky is just beginning to lighten as Eddy clamps on his cleats and treads onto the frozen surface of the reservoir. The sled, loaded with gear, glides across the ice behind him, its smooth swooshing sound steady beneath the friction swishes of his coveralls and the metallic clicks of his cleats biting the ice.

He is the lone soul on the vast, frozen gray-white surface. Most winter fishers hit the ice in late afternoon, figuring to haul up some dinner during the sundown feeding, but Eddy has always caught his biggest fish during the sunrise feed. It's plenty cold in the morning, but Eddy accepts it like he accepts most of what life has offered him: if you want the big ones, you gotta be willing to suffer. And sometimes you gotta suffer just because somehow, you've found yourself in a relationship with somebody you'd once cared about, but no longer know, which makes you feel like a fool for thinking you knew them in the first place. Two in a row now, for him. First his wife, and now his business partner. He's wondering if it's a pattern.

He's getting tired of always having to prod Nick to work harder. Nick likes comfortable, doesn't want to take risks. But since deciding to go all in, Eddy is pushing him to expand the business. He's shown Nick how to safely run their profits through construction jobs that exist only on paper. They keep most of what they make completely off the books, claiming just enough to be able to file believable tax returns. Fuck the IRS. In spite of how he feels about Nick, Eddy wishes they'd reconnected in the weeks after the knife factory pink-slipped him. Maybe if he'd been able to keep bringing in money back then, Erin might not have lost her mind. He still can't make sense of it. She should've known he'd do what had to be done. That's why it hurt so bad. Eddy is not the type to speak up about pain. *If wishes were horses then beggars would ride.* The old man had been fond of that one. Eddy had never been afraid of work, and still isn't. Erin shouldn't have run off and tried to save the family from ruin. She should have had some faith in him.

He's not sure what he would do without Megan around to help with the kids. But she doesn't have a clue that Eddy and Nick are anything but construction contractors, and he plans to keep it that way. This time around, he's not going to let love cloud his judgment. He's still trying to talk Nick into a move to New Jersey, closer to their main customer base. And Megan might be an even tougher sell than Nick. She's a hometown girl, close to her mother, which is nice when Eddy wants time alone with her because they can leave Lindsey and Paul there on overnights. And he wants time alone with her a lot. It's all fresh and new, like it used to be with Erin.

After the twins, things had changed. The babies became her sole focus, and he felt somehow that her love for him suffered as a result. Being a mom came so naturally to her that some days, in the twins' early years, he felt like the unwitting victim of a bait-and-switch operation. He loves them, of course, but sometimes it doesn't feel like enough. His longing for something bigger, newer, more exciting, reminds him of the way he'd felt as a kid when, after waiting weeks for the county fair to open and finally getting to go on all the midway rides, he trudged back to the car feeling like the annual event hadn't lived up to its billing. His family sometimes left him feeling tacked on, as if Erin and the twins had an exclusive club and he was only occasionally allowed in, like a weekend visitor.

And then she'd come home from the war a completely different person, lost in her own head, barely functioning, drinking herself to sleep every night. He could hardly be blamed for leaving. All the child support nonsense didn't help matters. He planned to pay, eventually, but right now he needs to keep the business going, buy a new truck, pay Nick for his share of the buy in. She made her choices and he doesn't owe her a damn thing. How does he even know she's not still drinking? He's not going to give her money every month so she can waste it all on booze.

He finds the hole he was fishing yesterday when the sun disappeared behind the mountains. He uses his father's ice spud, the one he'd pulled out of the barn before the tax man came to claim the farm less than a month after his father passed. He spikes the heavy bar repeatedly against the frozen surface, chipping through the fresh ice that has formed since yesterday evening. His anger gives him strength. By the time the sun crests the rounded peaks on the east side of the reservoir, Eddy has his jigging line in the water and is sitting on his camp stool, bobbing the short pole up and down, making the bait dance enticingly in the hidden waters beneath the frozen surface.

He'd driven out after picking the kids up at CPS and dropping them home with Megan. He could tell they'd been crying when the social worker brought them out to the waiting room after the visit, and right away he suggested stopping for ice cream, which seemed to brighten things up. In the truck on the way home, he didn't ask how the visit went and they didn't volunteer anything, concentrating on their ice cream cones in silence. He pushed aside the reality that they missed their mother, needed her. Harder to admit, sometimes he missed her too. Once upon a time they were a team. And a family. It was impossible to know what was going through his children's heads. He wasn't sure what he was going to do, not in the long run. That was a good enough reason to go fishing. It calmed him. It gave him time to think. He'd stayed on the ice until the last possible minute, leaving only enough time to gather his gear and trek back to his truck before it got too dark. He hadn't caught any fish, and he hadn't figured out what his next move would be.

This morning, he feels the sun warming his back and wishes he could stay out here all day, alone with the peaceful sky. The kids are getting on the school bus about now. He hopes Megan won't be angry.

Usually she's not, and if she gets that way she gets over it quickly enough. But he's noticed it more and more often, the tension in her jaw when she's packing lunches and telling Paul and Lindsey to hurry-hurry or they'll miss the bus while he leans against the refrigerator, watching her and sipping coffee. Come on though, it's not like she's got something better waiting for her. She dropped out of high school, was working at the Home Depot in Granite when Eddy hooked up with her that night at the Visser Kok. Erin had been deployed two entire months by then.

Now, Megan doesn't have to work at all, except taking care of the house and the kids. She should appreciate that he appreciates her. And the kid situation is temporary. As soon as Erin gets herself together the twins will go home to her and things between him and Megan will move forward for real. Megan thinks he's punishing Erin. He'd prefer she keep her theories to herself. He's a good guy; he takes good care of her. She's even said as much. He gives her cash for the bills, and extra to spend on herself. But lately she's talking babies. He's definitely not ready for that.

At the edge of the reservoir, he turns for a reluctant last glance at the morning. The sun is full up now, poised at pretty close to 9:00 a.m. If it weren't seventeen degrees out here, he'd take a moment for a long, satisfying leak, arcing his stream right into the reservoir. He finds it satisfying to piss directly into a prime source of New York City's drinking water.

232

FORTY-ONE

The guru tells Erin to be aware of her spirit, to feel it inside her body as a part of a powerful living universal entity.

She parks in front of the ugly brown building, waiting for her inner body to calm down. There is no collective bliss to be found in Causeway Aftercare. The guru is saying something about time being an arbitrary construct created by man to control the common population. If there were no linear concept of time, no one could ever be late to work. Erin turns off the CD player. At Family Treatment Court last week, the judge said, yet again, "We just want you to become a productive member of society." It seems to be her go-to phrase. Erin wishes the people who use that phrase would be more specific, more honest: we want you to become a tax-revenue-producing member of society.

Walking across the pocked and littered parking lot, Erin doesn't care what she is supposed to produce. At yesterday's visit, Lindsey and Paul said they wanted to come home. That is all she cares about. They don't like living with Dad and Megan. They want their mom. Erin told them she was working on it, that it would take time. They asked if they could stay with Aunt Tanya, and Erin had to explain that nothing could happen right away, that another hearing would be coming up soon. She tried to keep resentment from her voice. When the caseworker slipped back through the open door and said the visit was over, she had to physically hold the children back, force them to stay in the room. Erin had practically run from the building, her eyes filled with tears, and past Eddy's truck in the parking lot. She refused to acknowledge he was there as she hurried to her car and drove away, cursing him from the safety of her vehicle, praying that his self-righteousness would turn on him like a wounded animal.

She passes a sad tree surrounded by tips of brittle weeds poking out through snowmelt, stranded on a parking lot island in the sea of snowplowed blacktop. Anxiety bubbles inside her like a thick, simmering liquid. She pictures Tanya riding a glorious golden horse, abandoning herself to the moment. It doesn't help.

Inside, Christmas decorations remain taped to the receptionist's window, hanging on glumly though the holiday has passed. The receptionist wears a brand new sweater and a shiny gold necklace with a tiny blue gemstone dangling from it, something a high school boyfriend might buy for his high school girlfriend when they are in love and certain it will last forever.

Harriet comes out right away and calls Erin's name cheerfully. Erin fakes a smile, determined to do whatever it takes to get Harriet to fax over a glowing report, an amazing report, a report that will assure DSS and the Family Court Judge that Erin has been redeemed. At her office door, Harriet motions for Erin to enter first, saying, "After you."

Confused by Harriet's courtesy, Erin slips past. That's when she smells it. She thinks it must be an olfactory hallucination. She sniffs again. Gin.

It's real. Harriet has booze on her breath. Erin wants to take her to the ground and stick one of those white plastic swabs down her throat and run to the front desk waving it like a miniature torch, demanding that they send it to the lab, STAT. Harriet isn't drunk. At least not yet. Erin wonders where she stashes her bottle.

"So." Harriet seats herself and folds her hands. "How are we?"

Erin chokes back a snicker. She is courteous and optimistic, careful not to seem smug. Although she knows Harriet's secret, she will not let hypocrisy derail her. She tells Harriet how grateful she is to be sober and how she never wants to go back to the hell of alcohol.

She tells Harriet that she's continuing her job hunt and will keep on until she finds something. She will do whatever it takes to support her children on her own. She will no longer ask for child support. She's reasonably sure that it was the accusation that Eddy wouldn't provide for his family that made Eddy so mad in the first place, mad enough to call the police on Erin. Because if he actually cared about his kids and thought they were in danger because their mother was such a fuckup, wouldn't he have come and gotten them?

"You still need to pursue child support," Harriet says. "For the kids' sake. But your attitude is healthy."

The room seems smaller. Erin marvels silently about the change in her perception. Somewhere in the rooms she heard someone say that, for the alcoholic, sobriety is like an acid trip. She's starting to believe it. Things grow and shrink according to her mood. She is Alice *sans champignons*, able to adjust herself to the right size as circumstances demand, without even nibbling on fungi. She remembers reading the story to Lindsey, who had been unsettled by the tale, leading them to abandon it. Maybe they'll try it again when Lindsey comes home, but only if she wants to. Erin wants her children's homecoming to be magical.

When she walks out into the parking lot, she sees it almost immediately.

She has a flat tire.

They say in the rooms that it's not the major calamities that send people in recovery back to the bottle. It's the little thing, when you least expect it, that will tank your sobriety. Something as insignificant as a shoelace snapping.

A man has come outside and stepped away from the building to light a cigarette. He inhales, watching her, but turns his attention to the smoke as it drifts skyward.

Erin feels no need to drink. It's only a flat tire. She takes out the vehicle instruction manual, remembering an early meeting, only a few weeks in, when a woman came up to her at the coffee urn and practically pressed herself against her and crooned, "Don't you just love Jesus? I love Jesus sooo much." Erin had stepped away with her coffee cup half-filled. She checks the index at the back of the manual, finds the page. Jesus is not going to stroll up and miraculously inflate the tire, though she's sure he would want to if he were anywhere in the vicinity.

One of the bolts on the jack is tightened to the point that she cannot turn it. She tells herself, rationally, that she is stuck and needs help. She reminds herself that it is okay to ask for help. She gets to her feet and carries the jack toward the man. He tries to turn away, but she approaches him directly. When she gets close enough to offer him the jack and ask him to loosen the bolt, she sees the lettering on his red baseball cap: Make America Great Again.

∞

Erin and Gavin enter the courtroom and take their place at the defense table. The Bailiff is at his post near the bench. At the rear of the courtroom, Tanya sits reading a paperback. With his usual fifteen minutes of prep time, Gavin has readied her to testify. Erin is filled with gratitude for her sister. Dear, sweet warrior Tanya has once again dropped everything and jumped on a plane.

"All rise." The Bailiff opens the door and the judge flows into the room, draped in black. She settles at the bench, cupping one hand gently to the side of her crisply cut and well lacquered auburn hair, which hugs her head like a helmet. Her eyebrows are darkened and impeccably plucked. She is what Erin's mother would call well-groomed.

The Bailiff calls the court to order and moves to his position, one thumb tucked into his gun belt. "Be seated."

Her Honor calls the case and casts her attention to Gavin. "Mr. Costa?"

"Your Honor." Gavin rises. "We have tried repeatedly to negotiate with DSS and with Mr. Hill for the return of the children to their mother's custody. Erin has fully complied with all requirements of Family Treatment Court, and she continues to do so. She has accumulated more than six months of sobriety, and in addition to the activities required by her treatment program, she regularly attends AA meetings. At her last visit with the children, they expressed that they would like to return home to her. We ask that you grant our petition for return of custody of the children to Erin Hill. It's time for them to go home to their mother."

Bagley stands. "Your Honor, if I may?"

"Go ahead."

"My understanding is that it is not Mr. Hill's intention to interfere with the relationship his ex-wife might be able to re-establish with the children, once she has properly dealt with her issues, which, as the Court knows, are significant. But I cannot stress strongly enough that, in my opinion as Attorney for the Children, I feel it is too early, and in fact would be dangerous, to allow the children to be returned to the mother's custody at this time. We are looking at a situation where a mother tried to commit suicide, in her home, and I'm sure I do not need to remind the Court of the dire consequences and loss of life that have occurred in cases where children were either left in custody of, or returned to, parents who were not fully fit to care for them or who suffered from mental health issues or substance abuse issues. While I'm pleased that Ms. Hill has complied with her treatment program and shown some progress, there are troubling issues that remain, and these convince me, as well as the children's father, that the mother is far from ready to have the children back in her custody."

"Your Honor?" Gavin stands. The judge motions him to sit back down.

Bagley glares at Gavin, raises his volume. "Additionally, Your Honor, it has been brought to my attention by CPS Preventive that Ms. Hill was found to be in possession of a weapon, specifically a 6.5 Mannlicher, a very powerful rifle. While this is not illegal, it is plainly ill-advised for someone suffering from Ms. Hill's conditions. I wish to state clearly and on the record that I am adamantly opposed to the children being returned to the custody of Erin Hill at this time."

Erin can't move. Eddy leans forward, looking past Bagley, past Gavin, directly at her. Their eyes lock, and Erin wants to look away but she can't. A dark gray cloud roils out of his eyes, growing darker as it flows toward her, black bits of agitated matter swimming and spinning in the thing rushing toward her and then she is lost in it. She feels herself stand, move toward him, knowing she will strangle him where he sits. She feels her hands around his neck, her thumbs on his throat, in utter blackness. She cannot see; she is drowning in black, consumed by it. Blinded.

"All rise." The voice arrives from somewhere far away. Erin feels a hand on her arm, urging her up.

Slowly, slowly, the black fades to gray, the gray dwindles, evaporates, and the room comes back into focus. Erin waits, hearing a jumble of voices until the last shades of gray lingering at the edges of her view clear completely. She is standing in a courtroom, at a wooden table. She doesn't remember standing up. Everyone is standing. The judge is rising from her bench and moving toward her private exit. Erin runs her fingers across the wooden tabletop. The oak came from trees, gorgeous, magnificent trees. It is smooth and beautiful, holding decades of pain and anguish in the shading of its grain.

The door opens slowly. Gavin closes it and sits down, placing the file folders carefully on his knees. He sniffs loudly. Anyone can see it: he is pissed. He sniffs again. And then he slams a hand against the file folders, hard, and the *fwap* of it hits Erin right in the face.

"Why didn't you tell me?" *Fwap!* He slaps the folders again. "You had a goddamn rifle at your house? Really?" *Fwap!* "Why didn't you tell me?!"

Erin can't move. Can't breathe. She has to get out of here but her body won't move. FWAP!

"Erin! Are you listening? Why didn't you tell me?! Do you even really want them back?" FWAP! "Do you?" FWAP-FWAP-FWAP!

238

Erin sits perfectly still as the walls edge in, squeezing and squeezing, and the room goes yellow, a cloud of yellow materializing from somewhere in front of Gavin and Tanya, filling the room like poison gas saturating a chamber in some secret government laboratory.

Her sister's voice echoes in the yellow haze, something about *I'll be right back*, and Gavin is leafing through paperwork. He digs out a pink slip of paper, the court form with the date of the next hearing written on it, and jabs it at Erin, making no attempt to hide his anger.

"Get rid of it," he says. "Today."

At the conference room door, Tanya sees Eddy exiting the courtroom. She leaves Erin with Gavin and takes off after him, down the hall, past the Lawyers Lounge, the room as worn out as the rest of the tired building. Two mustached men look up from where they sit gossiping on an old leather couch as Tanya rushes past.

She's several yards behind him as he veers around the hulking plastic Magnetron, past a forlorn line of petitioners and respondents waiting to be scanned. Eddy pushes open the glass-and-steel front door and emerges into the sunshine. Behind him, closer now, Tanya slams the steel bar and flings the door wide as she exits. He's almost to his truck when she catches up.

"Hey! Eddy!"

He turns slowly, removes his sunglasses.

"What." Dismissive. Rude.

"You can't do this. I won't let you do this."

"Evidently I can, and evidently I just did. Are we done?"

"What?!" Tanya wants to slap him.

"Excuse me." Eddy leans in close, "I meant to say fuck off."

"Eddy. Stop. Just, wait a minute. I know we don't get along, and hey, whatever, but Jesus."

He jostles his keys in one fist, lets out a long sigh. "She's a mess, Tanya. Okay? I don't know what happened to her and I really don't care. Not anymore. She was fucked up enough when she went over, or she never would have gone in the first place."

"She's their mother. She loves them. You're killing her."

"Me? Oh no, no, no." He leans in. "I'm not taking that. Listen to me and listen good. If that fucked-up bitch had her shit together, none of this would've happened. Neither one of you has any sense. She tried to kill herself! Drink herself to death. And Paul found her. Paul!"

"And how did that happen?! Where the fuck were you?"

Eddy takes a menacing step toward her but stops. Tanya moves back, sees his arm trembling, his fist at his side. "I'm their father," he says. "So why don't you just stay out of this. Take yourself home to where you belong."

"She has PTSD, you asshole."

"Whatever." He wheels around and walks toward his truck. Tanya waits until he's far enough away before yelling after him.

"She was raped!"

At his door, Eddy turns. "What did you say?"

Already walking away, Tanya doubles back. "Nothing."

Eddy throws his truck in gear, eying Tanya like she's Satan.

"Where were you, Eddy? Huh?! When she needed you?" She gives him the finger.

Wheeling out of the parking lot, he rolls down his window and responds in kind, punching the gas as he does.

FORTY-TWO

Erin opens her eyes to sand and low brush, level and stretching all the way to the gray-blue mass of mountains. The line of jagged white peaks looks sharp enough to slit the wrists of any god who dares reach down with loving hands to pluck up stray souls and hoist them into the heavens.

The world is sideways and silent. Sun-glare and sand. Moondust—silty, powdery, gray—hangs in the air, blows in the wind; it's in her eyes, in her mouth. Her back is on fire. The images come at her slowly first, slithering through the fog of memory like a black snake until it whips into a tight coil and strikes: the boy beneath the tree. The roadside explosion. Eddy, his clenched hand. Drake, entering her forcibly. The bruise and blood of it, of all of it, written forever in her skin, etched in the folds of her brain.

She gags, retches, spits saliva and grit. Stares at the utterly insignificant wet slime on the vast sands that blanket the earth, spread flat and relentless to the distant horizon. A spot of moisture, soaking into the sand, evaporating rapidly into dry air.

She spits again. Pushes herself upright and hugs her knees, rocking, rocking, a high-pitched beam of lightsound shooting through her brain. As the sun cooks her back, she smells her own fear-tainted sweat. She is disgusting. A sharp pain stabs her left kidney. Water. And shade. She needs shade.

In front of her is chain link topped off with barbed wire; behind her, the wooden walls of buildings, the concrete and machines and trucks and aircraft and weapons, all of it glimmering like a mirage in hell. Dizziness hits and she sinks back to the ground, and that is when she sees it. She reaches for the fencing in front of her and tries to stand up. She cannot.

A motorcycle churns a plume of dust in its wake as it speeds across the rutted and broken landscape, cutting through heat-warped air, seeming to materialize out of the earth. The driver's *shalwar kameez* and *keffiyeh* flap wildly as the motorcycle approaches, its screaming engine cutting through the noise in Erin's head. She reaches around and slips her rifle off her back. It's so hot it burns her fingers. She's lived with this rifle for months now. She maintains her grip.

The front wheel of the motorcycle stops at the fence, mere inches from where she sits. The stench of hot rubber fills her nostrils. Ripped bits of brown plants are packed into the rough black nubs of the front tire. The rider unwinds the *keffiyeh*, revealing deep brown skin and a tumble of thick black hair that falls over her shoulders. Her face is slender, her eyes a piercing green blue.

Erin thinks at first her mind is tricking her, but then realizes that no, the woman facing her is the young man from the rec center. He'd been working the desk the morning Erin called Lindsey and Paul. Thanksgiving. She's sure of it. Erin shakes her head, uncertain again whether the woman is real or imaginary, some vision cooked up in the heat that is boiling her brain. She doesn't know how she got here. She's sure she shouldn't be here. Last night in the barracks, Ginj produced, like magic, a bottle of industrial green Crest Scope Outlast Mouthwash that was not mouthwash at all. Erin doesn't remember after that. She sits there like a fool, staring up at the rider.

The grit in her teeth, though, the grit on her tongue, she can taste it. She grabs a fistful of sand, lets it slip through her fingers. She can feel it; this must be real.

Erin looks down the razor wire to the distant tower. She tries to move, tries to shift her rifle around to a usable position, but her arms remain limp, exhausted. The thought that this woman might be about to blow both of them up drifts somewhere in the back of her head, but her body does not respond.

The woman leans forward, resting her arms on the handlebars. "Do you need help?"

Erin rubs at her face, the moondust scrapes against her cheeks as her eyes tear up, trying to wash out the grit.

"I remember you. You work here."

"I had to quit." The woman straightens, grips the handles. "My father, my brothers, they had me put in prison. If they knew I was out, they would try to kill me. I saved some money. I'm getting out of here."

Erin wonders again if this is illusion, hallucination. This cannot be real. It can't but it is.

"It is their law," the woman says. "But already I escaped from prison. I will go to América."

Erin nods, and feels tears trickling out, irritation from the grit in her eyes. "I hope you make it."

The woman leans back and opens her palms to the sky. "My brothers are lazy. They will give up looking for me. But even if they catch me, I will still be free." She grips the handlebars, rises from the seat and kick-starts the bike, cranking the throttle with rapid twists of her wrist, gunning the engine loudly. She lets it fall back to an idle and stares straight into Erin's eyes. "My father's god is not my god. My brothers' god is not my god. I hope you make it, too." She eases the bike away slowly first, until some distance has opened, and then she cranks the throttle wide, churning a plume of sand behind the bike as it fades toward the mountains.

FORTY-THREE

Erin's bed is covered with the scattered entrails she ripped from the desk drawers in her search for Social Security cards. She needs passports. She's had enough of court. She's had enough of treatment. She's had enough of all of it. She never would've had the rifle if Eddy's friend Rico hadn't insisted she take it. She thinks maybe Eddy sent him with it, but decides she is being paranoid. It doesn't matter anyway. She needs options. She has looked everywhere but found nothing. She gives up, goes online. The government must've hired the same people to design their sites that they use to design their forms. Keywords: needless complication/lack of clarity/pointless repetition/superciliously authoritative language, Orwellian fucking language.

Stacks of papers cover the comforter. Fighting foreclosure, fighting the courts, divorce proceedings, child support claims, the detritus of two years of struggle since she set foot back on American soil. She could bury herself under legal and administrative proceedings, conceal her body beneath a sheath of paperwork several inches thick. Fuel for a funeral pyre. Which page should she light first?

She goes downstairs to the basement and finds herself in front of the washing machine, as if she's been programmed to come here. There's no laundry to be done. She did it all days ago, when she was preparing for Lindsey and Paul to come home. She washed their sheets and blankets. She washed the towels that had been sitting in the closet since August, wanting them to smell fresh for her children. She

244

:hought they would be with her. She thought they would be allowed to come home. It is forty days until the next hearing. Forty days. She does not like feeling this angry. She waits for the guru voice. Hah. She mashes her palms against her temples, trying to contain the pressure. She has forgotten why she came down here.

FORTY-FOUR

E rin's rifle rests against her thigh. At long last she is on a C-17 headed in the right direction. Home. She's going home. She is three seats in, with row upon row in front of her, the plane packed to capacity. The darkened interior reeks of sweaty soldiers. Her helmet chin strap is tight on her jaw. They are still in the war zone. It feels as if it will go on forever. She grips the butt of her rifle and tries to relax. *Please God let me make it home to them.* She doesn't let herself remember. It's done. Over. She leans forward to look past the sleeping soldiers next to her to the row of seats that line the wall of the fuselage. Ginj gives her a somber nod. The plane is suddenly buffeted by a cross-wind, and just then the interior lights flicker. Erin stifles a gasp, feels an unwelcome swell of pressure in her head. *No missiles. Please. Yes God, I'm talking to you. I'm begging. Begging. I'll do anything.*

She holds her breath, praying, as the lights flicker repeatedly. Finally, the flickering stops and the lights come up full. Ginj gives Erin a thumbs-up and makes a little dance move with her arms. *Yeah, girlfriend, we made it.* They have left combat zone air space.

They've survived, yes, but home still feels a million miles away. Erin wants to lean on the idea of a moral universe, its arc bending toward justice, for reassurance that they will make it. But she quickly dismisses the thought, fearing that a truly moral universe might bend toward knocking this plane from the sky while quoting Joseph Conrad: the horror. The horror. Justice and moral arcs be damned; that's out of her league: all in the world Erin wants is to get home to

Lindsey and Paul and what may or may not be left of her marriage. She glances at the sleeping soldier sitting next to her, eyes not quite all the way closed, his jaw slack. What a gift, to be able to sleep right now. She adjusts her earplugs to blunt the roar of the engines and leans back.

∞

Her hands feel empty as she stands at attention in company formation outside the looming steel doors of the hangar, shivering in the cold February evening. It is the first time in more than six months that she has not had a rifle with her, day and night. The evening is brittle with quiet, the sky uninterrupted by the strain and whoosh of aircraft landing and departing, the scorch of tires hitting the runway.

As the hanger doors glide slowly open, the cheers of the crowd spill out, riding on light from the brightly illuminated interior and falling across the lines of troops column by column as the doors open wider. Inside, the families hold signs and balloons, craning their necks in efforts to locate their loved ones. They are shouting, cheering, clapping, delirious with happiness. Ginj is three rows in front of her. Candice should be here. Erin feels tears well up, fights them back. Candice had seemed so at ease at the deployment ceremony, laughing and joking with her son.

The company steps off and marches into the hangar. Erin stares at the head of the soldier in front of her, his neck dark brown from the Asian sun. She cannot look left or right, though everything in her is telling her to find Lindsey and Paul. She knows Tanya flew up yesterday to bring them to the return ceremony, but whether Eddy will be with them is unclear. Erin wants him to be there, wants the fairy tale ending where their time apart has led them both to realize they should try to save the marriage.

The company halts at attention, front and center, facing the stage. The backdropped flag behind the podium and stiff row of chairs seems even larger to Erin than it did at the deployment ceremony.

It is huge, practically covering the entire rear wall. The sight of it brings to mind another ceremony, the one they'd held at J-bad: caskets loaded into the back of the transport plane, Candice's, like the others, draped in an American flag much smaller than the one Erin now faces. There is a special size. Somewhere, a company manufactures government-spec flags measured and cut specifically for draping caskets. Candice's son Rodrigo probably has it by now, the one draped over his mother's casket when the Air Force brought home her remains. Angel flights, they call them. It's accidental that Erin is standing here instead of Candice. Accidental that her brother Daniel was at his desk that morning. In a sense—in spite of the inevitability of death itself—they're all somehow randomly circumstantial. Even in suicides, the when and how may be simple matters of opportunity, chance, and coincidence.

Marching music plays. Erin does not know the name of the song. She stays at attention, careful to keep her knees slightly flexed so she doesn't cut off her circulation and faint. She learned that at basic training, a couple of eons ago. She can feel the tension in the ranks; they all want this part over with. They want to find their families. The image of the boy under the tree flares in her brain. She erases it immediately, focusing on the massive flag hanging in front of the troops.

Finally, the music ends, and Sergeant Drake steps to the podium. Erin bites her lip, bites her tongue, chews on it until it hurts. She will not go back to that night. It's gone. Done. Over. She will leave it where it happened, in a foreign country roughly seven thousand miles from her home, light-years away. She hears Drake's voice, but not his words; his speech is a blur, an incantation, echoing off the metal walls of the huge enclosure.

The sound of cheering and applause snaps her back. A general has taken the stage. He praises them. Erin can't make out the words. She doesn't want to make out the words. Words won't change what happened. The general says, ". . .from a grateful nation, welcome home!" The music comes up again; this one she knows—"The Army Goes

Marching Along"—but the families won't wait any longer, they move, only a few at first, and then a scramble as the crowd flows into the center of the hangar, parents and spouses and children, searching for their soldier, and people are pushing past Erin as she scans frantically, anticipation rushing up inside her as it did at the first pangs of labor. Where are her babies? Where are they?

A woman in spike heels, her boobs hanging halfway out of a tight black dress, bumps into Erin and says, "Oh, I'm so sorry," as she rushes toward the thick center of the formation, which is rapidly dispersing as soldiers locate their loved ones and weave through the throngs to get to them. A text from Tanya was waiting for her when she turned on her phone after deplaning: *Will b there w/ kids can't wait to c u*, followed by a string of emojis: hearts and a plane, party symbols and a clown face, punctuated with the image of a unicorn. There'd been no mention of Eddy. Erin searches the crowd, wondering if she will be one of the unfortunates who have arrived home with nobody there to greet them.

She stands on tiptoe, bumped and jostled by happily shrieking humans. And then out of the noise comes the sound of her sister's voice, Tanya's unmistakable drawl.

"Here! Here! We're right here!" Tanya has her huge bag slung over one shoulder as she weaves Lindsey and Paul through the crowd. Erin sees their faces light up and rushes toward them.

PART IV

FORTY-FIVE

At the end of the driveway, holding Lindsey's hand and shivering, Erin still can't believe she's home. The woods are exquisite, every glint of sunlight and every shadow adding surreal depth to the landscape. The air is clear and still.

"Mom! My Valentine's cards!" Lindsey starts to pull away but Erin hangs on, squeezing Lindsey's little hand in its red mitten.

"It's fine, hon, they're in your backpack."

"Paul?" Lindsey tilts her head at her brother. "You got yours?"

"Yep." He scoops up a handful of snow. "Mom? Where's Dad?"

"He's working, hon." Erin doesn't have a clue where Eddy is. He'd told Tanya to go ahead and take the kids, that he'd join them at the base if he could make it. But he hadn't been home when Erin and the kids got back from the return ceremony after dropping Tanya at the airport. Erin doesn't know if he came in last night after she was asleep—gloriously asleep in her own bed for the first time in six solid months—and left early this morning, or if he didn't come home at all.

Paul works on the snowball, scooping up more snow and packing.

Don't you dare," Erin says.

He grins at her.

"It's so cold!" Erin says. "I'm freezing!"

"Was it hot? Where you were?" Lindsey looks up at her, her glasses lopsided on her nose, visible on the small part of her face that isn't covered with the stocking cap and scarf.

"It was hot sometimes and sometimes it was pretty cold," Erin says. "But never cold like this. This is serious cold."

"Nah," Paul says. "Fourteen degrees. I checked."

"You're not cold?"

"No way." Paul holds the snowball like a baseball. "I don't get cold till it's at least zero."

"Don't throw that at me. I'm telling you."

Paul creeps closer, aiming.

"I mean it." But she doesn't, and he can tell from her laughter.

He rears back like a pitcher on the mound and hurls the snowball; Erin sees it arcing toward her and readies to dodge it, still laughing, but suddenly there are two of them coming at her. Her world goes yellow, flashes brilliant white, then BOOM! Black. Something slams into her head; icy wet cold dribbles onto her face. She feels herself staggering, hears their voices from somewhere far away, "Mommy? Mommy?" and then she can see again, she is standing there at the end of the driveway, right where she was, a circle of snow caked on her cap where the snowball landed, her children staring at her uncertainly. Trembling from adrenaline, she forces out a laugh and quickly scoops up some snow and begins shaping a snowball, grinning at Paul in a way she hopes is convincing. Inside, she is quaking.

She is saved by the school bus, rumbling down the road belching diesel fumes, churning to stop in front of the mailbox.

"Hugs, hugs." Erin gives them a squeeze before they clunk up the metal steps, weighted down by their backpacks. She waves to Bob, the driver who has been picking them up since kindergarten.

"Welcome home!" he says.

Maybe it's the haze of jet lag but, inside, the kitchen seems to glow. The sink is full of dirty dishes. Erin laughs out loud. They're beautiful.

In Lindsey's room, as she tidies up, the walls beam cheerful yellow. She arranges the many stuffed animals Tanya has sent over the years. Horse posters, also courtesy of Tanya, hang on the wall. Horse statues, frozen in mid-prance, dance on the bookshelf. From the shelf below them, Erin picks up a composition book covered in shiny horse stickers, labeled Diary Private Do Not Touch. She wants to open it in the worst way but makes herself return it to its place.

Paul's room—red, red, red—has been invaded by a giant Lego sculpture that takes up a fourth of the room. Erin isn't sure what it is, but it's impressive, towering like an architectural model for some vast, Brutalist-inspired government structure. The drum set she'd found at a yard sale takes up another quarter of the room. Erin makes up Paul's bed and tidies the books spilling out of the bookcase—*The Maze, The Giver, The Chronicles of Narnia*. She reminds herself to check for the date of the annual spring library fair, the primary source of her children's books.

She goes back downstairs to the small desk in the corner of the bedroom. Stacks of unopened mail and piles of papers. Unpaid bills. Eddy has left it all for her to deal with: six months' worth of mail. At least he kept the electricity on.

Even the chaos on the desk can't dampen her mood. She is home. She'll deal with all of it. She'll get back to her job. Maybe there are some summer courses available. She'll buy groceries and do laundry and vacuum and dust and all of that. Apparently, the house hasn't really been cleaned since the day she deployed.

It doesn't matter. She tells herself everything is fine, even if she's walking around in a haze of pink happiness, amazed and grateful not to be carrying a rifle and saluting. Now that she's away from it, she doesn't know even what it was or how she got there. It's like she has awoken from a nightmare, opened her eyes to realize that no, she is not at the bottom of a deep hole being buried alive in sand by faceless creatures with shovels; she is at home and her children are safe. But the ground beneath her feet feels porous, less than solid. She realizes, in a way that she was not capable of before going away, that her world is completely and utterly perishable. And that it can disappear in an instant.

She goes to the sink and starts the dishes. She doesn't want to think about why Eddy hadn't been home when she and the kids arrived late last night after dropping Tanya at the airport. Right now, it's pointless to speculate. She will not let herself descend into the suck and whirl of imaginary conversations with her husband. Next week she will go to the base and begin her official separation from the Army. Her contract is up. She'll figure out the rest of it later.

By the time she finishes the dishes, she is shaking. She doesn't know what is wrong. She's home, goddamit. What can be wrong? All she knows is that she feels like she is about to die. She doesn't know how, what direction the attack will come from, but she knows it will come.

In the freezer, she finds a half empty bottle of vodka. Eddy always did like keeping it cold.

∞

Her jeans are covered in dirt stains, large ovals on the knees, streaks of black where she wiped the soil from her landscape knife as she worked is gashed across the thighs. She has been at it since 9:00 a.m., digging holes and planting flowers and pulling weeds and shoveling mulch from the huge load delivered to the job site by a dump truck earlier this morning. She's grateful for the work, glad they were able to start the season ahead of schedule because winter disappeared early this year. After that one icy Nor'easter that came through in February, the week she got back from her deployment, there wasn't much snow; the rest of the month was warm. They started in March, and so far, she has been able to get several days of work each week. There are no openings at the college. She is on the list, in case something opens up, but the secretary said that most likely wouldn't happen for several months, until the Fall 2015 semester at the earliest. But at least she got her landscape job back.

She likes the plants: their silent beauty, their energy. They simply are. She removes a Velvet Cloak Smoke Tree from its container and gently loosens the roots before putting it in the ground and filling the hole with soil, connecting the shrub to Earth. She presses the dirt firmly around the base of the plant, letting her palms rest momentarily on the surface of the planet, feeling its tranquility. But then reality jolts into her fingers, electric. She can feel it: all around the globe, war is this minute gnawing at the planet, migrating from one place to the next and eating at the skin, leaving behind festering wounds that never really heal, as if it were some kind of deadly, drug-resistant bacteria.

She has read that the sound of plant roots being ripped out of the soil is a balm to the human psyche, and that the smell of soil releases endorphins in the brain. She listens carefully as she pulls weeds. She breathes deeply the scent of the soil. She works daily to forget.

They do weekend homes mostly, large, often estate-like houses set well back off the country lanes and gated against intrusion. There are swimming pools. There are tennis courts. There are elaborately designed patios and decks and sun porches. The recession didn't hit Wall Street the same way it did Granite County. Weekends and summers, the bankers and brokers and moguls, the art collectors and museum directors and filmmakers, the deans of private colleges, the internet millionaires, they flee NYC and escape to the bucolic hills of upstate New York. Life is good.

It is almost time to leave to pick up the kids at school. On Wednesdays, they stay after for an art program. The other days, they take the bus to Niki's, a few miles down the road from home, happy to play with their pals until Erin comes by after work to pick them up. Erin sometimes brings plants salvaged from jobs where the owners have tired of them and decided to replace them with something newer, more colorful or exotic. Niki has a gift for nursing the scraggly, neglected plants back to their former lives as beauty queens.

The house they are working on today buzzes with activity. Caterers are setting up for a big Memorial Day celebration that will last all weekend. It saddens Erin to think that the people at the party won't have a clue about Candice. Or any of the others, most likely. It's just another three-day weekend, and it's May: winter is gone and upstate is gorgeous. Party on. A pool crew does a maintenance check on the natural swimming pool that shines clear and inviting, surrounded by cedar decking and bluestone. The gardens are stunning.

Erin carries her shovel and rake and edger to the van and says goodbye to the women on the crew. She likes all six of them, but they've been working together for years, and Erin still isn't sure how she fits into the puzzle. They respect that she works so hard. Several other women have already come and gone since Erin came on board, a few of them lasting less than a week. It takes stamina and strength. It is physically exhausting, but that's a good thing. It helps her sleep at night. She dusts the dirt from her jeans before getting into her Toyota and driving to Granite Elementary.

Children wander into the cafeteria, some lighting up when they spot Mom or Dad, some reluctant to join their parents. Lindsey arrives skipping, holding hands with Niki's daughter Amanda; they rush up to Erin.

"Can I go to Amanda's, can I go to Amanda's? She invited me for a playdate!" Lindsey bounces in place. Amanda joins in. "Please-please-please?"

"Does your mom know about this plan?"

Amanda rushes past Erin to Niki and drags her mother back by the wrist. Lindsey and Amanda continue their bouncing until Niki shrugs and says, "It's fine," laughing as she adds, "I'll give them pizza for dinner and call it a vegetable. Paul can come too."

Though Niki's son Greg is a year older than Paul, the boys get along well. Niki's house is where the twins went after school while Erin was deployed, at least on the days Eddy happened to be working. It's their second home.

Driving home alone, Erin is thankful Niki has taken the kids again. She can sit in the living room and drink in peace, catch an hour or two of relief before bedtime reading. She will be careful not to overdo it. She'll need to go pick them up after dinner, because there's no way Eddy will be around.

∞

By summer, Erin finds a routine. They say it's important to establish one after the disruption of a deployment. She rises before the sun hits the horizon at around five-thirty each morning. The light comes up well before that, the sky going a slow lavender blue in advance of full daybreak. She gets outside as soon as it's light enough to see, while the kids are still sleeping, to weed around the house and water the flowers salvaged from jobs. Sometimes Eddy is on the couch; most times he's not. She keeps thinking that at some point it will get easier, that they'll learn how to at least talk to one another again.

This morning, a Monday in late June, she returns home from picking Lindsey and Paul up from a slumber party to find a note from Eddy on the kitchen table. He's out with Nick, estimating a possible job. Like always. At least he left a note. Usually he's just gone. The note says he'll meet her for their appointment. Lindsey and Paul are in a post-slumber-party stupor. They don't argue when Erin suggests a nap, but want to stay in the same room, like they did when they were little. She walks them upstairs to Lindsey's room and tucks them in.

∞

Eddy throws himself into a waiting room chair while Erin goes to the window and writes a check for the co-pay. Neither of them wants to be there. They've been going at it all summer, cycling through fights and into silence that lasts days, until the next angry exchange blossoms between them.

She hopes there's enough in her account to cover the check. Because she was never officially in combat she does not have the priority rating, whatever that is, that provides services without a co-pay. Maybe she can pick up an extra cleaning job this week, to supplement her pay from landscaping. Eddy keeps saying he's out looking at construction jobs, he and Nick pricing up estimates for potential customers. But the jobs never seem to materialize.

Each morning, weekends included, he gets in his truck and drives away, going to meet Nick. Every night, well after the kids are asleep, he comes home reeking of alcohol and pot. Some nights he doesn't come home at all. Erin thinks maybe he's dealing, but if he is, most of the money is being smoked up or spent in bars in the evenings She wonders who he's fucking, but she doesn't care enough to ask.

Every couple of weeks, she finds a few hundred-dollar bills on the kitchen counter, next to the coffee maker. Sometimes she finds more than a few. She never knows. At least the electricity is on. She keeps up her job search, online late at night, afraid to go to sleep. There are minimum wage positions; that seems to be it. She does better working landscape. Maybe she really should consider relocating. But she doesn't want to upend Lindsey and Paul unless there's no other choice. And she's on the wait list at FedEx and UPS. Something will open up.

She takes a seat and opens her phone. Her Reminder List has twenty-seven items on it. Groceries and bills and job search, house repairs—Eddy's too busy. Her car inspection is due next month. She's got a degree, dammit. Where are the jobs? The landscape work will last another four months, until November, but after that she'll have to go on unemployment. She doesn't know how she'll make it through the winter. She doesn't know why she insisted that they come here today to try marriage counseling, except that she wants to know she tried everything. Eddy is obnoxious to her except when the kids are around. Screaming arguments that go around and around in circles until the war rushes into her brain and she feels like her head is going to explode. She's told him he can leave, anything would be better than this, but he refuses. She is his wife and he loves his kids and he is going to watch them grow up and she has no right to interfere with that. He barely even sees them. He's never home. She has pleaded. She has demanded. She has begged until she understood perfectly why he has come to hate her. He has taught her how to hate herself.

The doctor comes out and calls their names.

The office has a ficus plant near a small, high window that lets daylight trickle into the room. Erin hears a faint buzzing noise coming from above. The light fixture is at an odd angle, as if one end of the rectangular fluorescent strip has disconnected from the ceiling.

"Okay, so. Welcome. I'm Dr. Kloeten. Why don't we start with you, Erin. You were in Afghanistan, let's see, says here August 2014 deployment?" He squints at his paperwork. "Returned in February?"

"Yes."

"Thank you for your service. So, five months back. How's it going for you?"

Erin hates that. She hates it when people say that. Thank you for your service. Like they have a clue. Like they care enough to do more than put a yellow ribbon magnet on their car bumper.

"It's been a little rough," she says. "I was drinking for a while. I've stopped now."

"Like, yesterday," Eddy says, his legs crossed as he fiddles with the shoelace on his work boot. "Tell the truth," he says. "Things haven't been good since you deployed. Since before that even."

"Have you been screened for PTSD? Did you suffer any injuries over there?"

"There was an IED."

"Did they give you a diagnosis?"

"Concussion. I returned to duty a week or so later."

"They did an MRI?"

"The hospital at Bagram."

"Are you having any physical symptoms? These days?"

"No." She is lying. Or at least she thinks she is. She's not sure. What is a physical symptom? Her trembling hands? The jagged electric shock that jolts her when someone touches her unexpectedly? The shadows that turn into Afghanis among the trees and then vanish before she can truly see them?

"Well, that's good. Without a diagnosis of PTSD or TBI—"

"What's that, TBI?" Eddy glances at Erin as if he's afraid it's a contagious disease.

261

"Traumatic brain injury. But if she wasn't diagnosed within a year of the injury, preferably in the immediate aftermath, the VA isn't going to cover treatment. It doesn't sound like that's the problem anyway." Dr. Kloeten shifts his attention to Erin. "What about psychological? Nightmares? Flashbacks?"

"How can you not, with stuff like that?"

"And you've stopped drinking completely, or just cut back?"

"No, I've stopped."

"Are you going to meetings?"

"I went to one," Erin says. "I'm doing okay. With the not drinking thing."

"Any history of alcoholism in your family?"

Eddy laughs. "Yeah. Like her dad was one of the biggest drunks in town."

"My father died from it." Erin gazes at the ficus tree, wanting to put her attention anywhere but on Eddy. What does he know about her father? It's not like Eddy ever once tried to talk her dad out of taking a drink. They got drunk together plenty of times.

"That's not the real problem," Eddy says.

Dr. Kloeten shifts his attention. "Do you feel like you might know what the problem is?"

"The problem is she took it on herself to make decisions that affected our entire family and she never even asked me about it, she just signed up, and left me stuck me with taking care of two kids which I can tell you is not the reason I got married. I'm the father. Not the mother." He plants his boots on the ground and leans toward the doctor. "I would never have agreed to that."

"And I'm sorry for that," Erin says. "I've told you more than once, and I really am."

Eddy scoffs, slaps his hands against his knees.

"I never thought I would go. Be deployed. I made a horrible decision. But we needed the money and I did it to—"

"You did it to be the hero." He leans toward her, jabbing the air with an index finger. "You did it because being a mother wasn't enough,

262

not for you. You know I would have pulled it together. Nick and I . . ." He turns away from her. "Let me tell you something, doctor. This woman is the most fucked up, twisted person I have ever met in my entire life, and if it weren't for the fact that she is the mother of my children I would never have anything to do with her at all, ever again. She betrayed all of us."

Dr. Kloeten nods thoughtfully. "So what do you see as the solution?"

"Divorce," Eddy says. "Plain and simple."

Wow. Out of nowhere. Erin has been trying to talk about this for months, and Eddy always said no way, and now, suddenly, it's the magic solution.

Erin stares at the floor. Maybe Eddy is right. Maybe she is twisted and fucked up. In fact, she's sure he is right. He is one hundred percent correct. Whatever. Let him hate her. That started before she put on a uniform.

"You know," the doctor says, "things like this happen. It's very difficult to return from deployment, and sometimes couples find that they are unable to re-establish the lives they had prior to one, or in some cases both of them, being sent to a war zone. It's nothing you should blame yourselves for."

"Oh, I'm not blaming myself," Eddy says. "Be sure of that. This is all on her."

"Okay," Dr. Kloeten presses a palm in Eddy's direction, a visual suggestion that Eddy calm down. "Erin. I think you could benefit from maybe a few more appointments. Not couples counseling, just you on your own. When is your contract up?"

"I only had a couple of weeks left when I got back. I separated the end of February."

"Well, that's not a problem. You were deployed. Your medical benefits continue for five years."

"I'm not sure I can afford the co-pays."

"How about this. Why don't you look into your situation, and if you get it worked out where you can make the co-pays, call and make an appointment. In the meantime, well, first, let me ask you this." He looks at Eddy. "Is there any way, do you see any possibility, of working things out? As far as the marriage? Do you feel like you should maybe give things a chance to settle a bit before making such a permanent decision?"

"You mean about divorce?" Eddy shakes his head. "I don't see the point of dragging things out. What we had is gone."

"Do you maybe want some time to think about it?" Dr. Kloeten tries a smile.

Eddy shakes his head. "Nope."

Dr. Kloeten sits back in his chair, letting out a long, uncomfortable sigh. "If that's the case, I would advise both of you, before you proceed on any kind of divorce action, to think about using a lawyer. They can make things easier, help you get to some basic terms of agreement regarding custody and child support, that kind of thing."

Eddy shakes hands with Dr. Kloeten and walks down the hall. Dr. Kloeten hesitates at the door, waiting for Erin to get up, waiting to see her out.

When he realizes she's not ready to leave, he closes the door.

"You can make an appointment for this week," he says. "I'll work with you while you figure out the insurance thing."

"Thank you," Erin says. "But I think I need to see a medical doctor, or a psychiatrist."

"Tell you what. Let's get you set up for an evaluation, just so we can make sure they didn't miss something when you were injured. You can figure out the co-pays later."

"But I still need to see someone. Today."

"You're having a crisis? You need medication?"

Erin nods. "Yes. Please. Today."

∞

The doctor gives her pills. Xanax. When things are really bad, she takes one. But she doesn't like taking them and sometimes waits too long, until she's having trouble breathing and has to hide in the bath-room so Paul and Lindsey won't see that their mother is falling apart. Some days she sits on the edge of the bathtub and cries into a towel so they won't hear her. Some days it feels as if her head will explode. It's not pain. It's pressure, as if the memories are swelling, pressing against each other, pushing against her skull. But she doesn't drink. She doesn't drink and she doesn't drink and she doesn't drink.

She digs holes in the ground and puts plants in them. The flowers are beautiful.

∞

Erin pulls into the driveway and there it is again: the front yard needs mowing. She is dog-tired. But it's easier to do it herself than to ask Eddy, as she's done all summer long. It'll only be taller and that much harder to mow by the time she asks, then pleads, and then fights with him over it. Anyway, this might be the last mow of the season. Halloween is approaching. She's already dirty from work, she might as well just do it. Since the counseling session with Dr. Kloeten, when the word divorce crystalized between them, they're supposed to be communicating about it, working out terms. They barely speak. He stays gone, claiming to be working with Nick.

She grabs her lunch box, goes to the kitchen to refill her water bot-tle. The first thing she sees when she walks in is a half-empty bottle of wine, set out near the toaster. It's just sitting there, in the middle of the counter, like the *Drink Me* potion from Alice in Wonderland. Erin doesn't have to consider how small it might make her. She knows by now that the very first sip can make her disappear completely.

A few hours later, she is parking the mower in the shed when Eddy roars up the driveway and jerks to a stop, his truck leaving a trail of gravel dust hanging behind it because he doesn't care about coating the cars, coating the porch railings, coating the siding on the house, coating everything, even the inside of the house, with dust. When

Erin brings it up, he goes buggy. She hears his voice in her head, has the exact intonation down. "It's just a little dust! Stop flipping out over it. You're crazy!" She wonders if he's right. But if she is, it's not something that shows up on any kind of scan. She's seen the neurologist. She's had the scans. Dr. Kloeten has assured her that there is nothing neurologically wrong with her brain. All that's happened is she owes a bunch of money in co-pays and all she knows is that her brain wasn't bruised. Maybe she's just batshit.

He bails out of his truck, a Yankees cap pulled low on his forehead, his clothing clean, no sign of manual labor. He goes straight into the house, not even acknowledging her presence on the lawn. Fine. Whatever. Let's just agree to leave each other alone. She's got this. She will find a way out. And she will try to keep things civil, for the kids.

When she walks into the kitchen he is there, holding up the now empty wine bottle, examining it as if it were evidence at a crime scene.

"You're drinking again."

"Isn't that why you left it there?"

It is, and they both know it.

"You're drunk," he says.

"No. I'm not. I didn't touch it. I poured it out and mowed the lawn, because gee, you're always so pressed for time."

"Bullshit." He puts the bottle down hard on the counter.

Erin feels something shift in her head, sensing the controlled violence in the movement of his hand. He did not slam the bottle on the counter, but he put it down hard. Escalation is imminent.

"Neither of us needs this shit." Erin tries to keep her voice level. "Okay? So why don't we just deal with it."

"You're not the person I married."

"Thank God. And you've got a girlfriend. Why didn't you just tell me?"

He moves so quickly that Erin doesn't realize what's happening until she sees the bottle rushing toward her, hurled at her, and she is barely able to duck before it smashes against the cabinet behind her, shattering, and Eddy is inches away, screaming, his face contorted with rage, "You fucking alcoholic bitch! I'm out of here! And you can go straight to hell!"

He blows past her and she's left standing in the kitchen, trying to breathe, hearing the sounds of dresser drawers being open and slammed shut, a suitcase zipping shut, the stomp of his work boots approaching the front door. "This is all on you! IT'S ON YOU!" The door slams.

Erin stays put, shards of glass on the counter behind her, on the floor in front of her. She hears an explosion, smells gunpowder and hot metal. It is as real to her as the sunset glaring through the kitchen window.

The truck engine starts. Tires fling gravel.

The sound of a vehicle roaring away.

Dust.

FORTY-SIX

It's a Saturday night at Bagram, and Ginj is off duty, but it's hot as hell outside and she doesn't much feel like hanging in the rec center. She's not sure why she finds herself thinking back to Erin and Candice, but she decides to go old school and actually write a letter. With like, an envelope and a stamp and everything. She isn't sure of the right form. She's never actually written a letter before, but she's written some emails, and that's probably close. And she remembers reading letters from one of the books assigned in her high school English class, *Frankenstein*, the year before she took her GED and escaped from that hellhole. She'd been surprised to learn that Frankenstein wasn't actually the monster. Frankenstein was the name of the guy who created the monster.

She sits at the tiny desk in her tiny barracks room and writes carefully. She goes for script. At least they taught her that much. She has a cousin in fourth grade who's been using a Chromebook issued by his elementary school and hasn't written on paper almost at all for the entire school year. Her cousin and aunt and uncle had met her at the return ceremony and driven her to her mom's apartment in South Plainfield. She found herself staring out the window as they sped south on I-95 in the dark, rolling past the quiet, snow-covered February fields. She wished her night-vision goggles weren't sitting in her luggage in the trunk of the car. She knew already, only a few hours after the C-17 landed, that she wouldn't fit in with her friends anymore. She never did, really, preferring to be in the country with her aunt and uncle, where she could run free in the woods. Her thoughts were still half a world away. She made up her mind well before they exited the interstate that like, tomorrow, she would begin the process of transferring to active duty. With any luck and a sufficient amount of paperwork, she could be somewhere far away from home within six months.

Sergeant Drake had stepped up big league. He'd actually encouraged her. She wasn't sure why, after her monumental fuckup, but he helped her get the signatures she needed and gave her a solid recommendation. Maybe that's why she's thinking about Erin tonight. She feels responsible for what Erin went through after that day. That's what it is for Ginj: that day. For herself, though, it isn't an issue. The little fucker. He should have known better than to be out there like that. He should have showed them what he had in his hand. How could you know? No sense looking back. She's sure the Special Forces guys who showed up to take care of the body weren't losing any sleep over it, and neither was Drake. They know what has to be done and they do it. They're warriors. Ginj counts herself in the club and intends to get even better at it. You got a job to do. You do it. World keeps turning.

She's not sure how to start the thing, so she finally just writes *Yo Professor . . .*

Yeah, it's me lol. I'm like at Bagram. I went active duty and came back over almost as soon as I got home, and here it is like a year and a half later and I'm still here, like, advising, haha, but it's a lot better than J-Bad ever was. And I think maybe I'll take your advice and enroll in college when I get back. Rank up, go for Officer. Anyway it got me thinking about you. Just checking in to see how you're doing and all. I guess by now you're back to teaching and putting up with your little ones. I saw my cousin when I got home and he's pretty cool. Going into fifth grade and making straight A's, not like me lol. I let my mom keep the dog. She was psyched. My mom I mean.

I guess what I really want to say is that I'm sorry for putting you in that situation, you know. Like I shouldn't have got out of the truck. I hope you can let

it go, cause it seriously wasn't your fault, bae. I mean, what are you gonna do in a
situation like that. We did what had to be done, and you gotta be okay with that.
So just know that and chill, right? I owe you.
XO and all that, bae.
Ginger McCarty
Bagram, Afghanistan
August 15, 2016

FORTY-SEVEN

E rin folds up the letter and sticks it in her pocket. She's not sure why she brought it with her, why she keeps pulling it out and reading it. She's grateful to Ginj for the attempted absolution, and afraid of what Ginj may become. She's grateful that she failed, that she froze up. Ginj never mentioned that, not once. But though Erin did not pull the trigger, she carries within her a deep remorse. She cannot help thinking about the boy's parents, how one day their son simply disappeared and how at some point their hope will fade to hopelessness. They will make the correct assumption: their son is gone forever.

She cannot dwell. She will get back to work, stay busy. The MMA studio opens at one.

In front of the wall-length, ceiling high mirror, she inspects carefully, looking for smudges. There cannot be any smudges. It has to be perfect. The boxing gloves are sorted and stacked in the rack. The jump ropes hang in a row, the ends perfectly aligned. Nothing is off-center. She has wiped down the heavy bags and mopped the mat in the cage. She has dusted the front desk, arranged the business cards and brochures on the counter. The bathrooms sparkle. The showers smell disinfectant clean. She goes to the storage closet and pulls out the vacuum, plugs it in and goes to work.

When she finishes, she gathers the two large plastic garbage bags of empty drink containers—Monsters and Red Bulls and Dasanis—and goes to the front to lock up. She takes the envelope with her name scribbled on the front from its hiding place under the computer keyboard and pockets the cash. She will not report the income to the Department of Social Services. She is one of those mothers, one of those single moms, those welfare moms, who knows how to work the system. Ha. She will use the money to buy groceries, because her food stamps for the month of August have almost run out, in spite of her best efforts to stretch every entitlement dollar which, for Erin and her two children, works out to about $4.20 per meal. She thinks she has about twelve dollars left on the card, with replenishment still two weeks away.

Every couple of months since October, when Eddy threw the bottle at her and stomped out the door, disappearing from his family, she has gone to court to file for child support. Nothing ever happens. He's is very good at hiding whatever income he has. It could be that most of it is cash, most of it is illegal. She doesn't care, and no longer expects him to start supporting his kids. But she has to file for child support in order to keep her food stamps. It's a regulation.

Her job at the college never materialized, not last fall, and not in spring. Enrollment was down, they'd had to let some adjuncts go. She works landscape or cleaning jobs whenever they are available. She is starting to believe there is something about her that frightens people, and she will never be able to find a real job anywhere. Interviewers are cordial; they always say *we'll be in touch*. But they never are.

A bag over each shoulder, she walks beneath the overhang past Subway and RiteAid and Wells Fargo Financial, around a corner to where the strip mall widens out to accommodate the supermarket. The recycling machines are just inside the entrance, in an alcove that reeks of beer and sugar syrup and cigarette stubs. She feeds in the cans, feeds in the bottles, listens to the crackling plastic and crunching aluminum as the machines eat the containers. She stuffs the empty bags into the recycle bin and takes her receipts to Customer Service for redemption. $4.85. She won't report that either.

Since school let out at the end of June, Paul and Lindsey stay at Niki's when Erin has work. She knows it's getting to be a strain. She tries to reciprocate on weekends, having all the kids at her house. And she tries not to envy the big, messy, extended families that are able to pass their kids around to grandparents and uncles and aunts.

After she gets the groceries, Erin will stop to buy two gallons of diesel at the gas station. She will carry it home in a blue container and pour it into the feeder pipe for the furnace in the basement. The container is heavy, bulky, and if she loses her grip while struggling to pour fuel into the pipe the diesel smell stays in her clothes through two or three washings. But the federal program for heating oil only gives the state a certain amount of money each year and, once it's gone? Tough luck folks. Get a job, why don't you? At minimum wage, she would only have to work a little over a week and a half to fill the tank. Before taxes. And leaving nothing for food or gas or anything else. The term disposable income is not part of her vocabulary.

The grocery store is full of genetically modified vegetables and insecticide-laced fruit. There are eight million varieties of children's cereal; Erin can smell the sugar when she turns into the aisle. Everything else is full of high fructose corn syrup or partially hydrogenated oil.

Where the hell is the food?

She gets peanut butter and bread, some jelly. No added sugar! Like it's a gift. She gets milk and hates herself for considering Cheerios but that's what Paul and Lindsey want and why can't they have it, Daddy always lets them have it, on the rare occasions when he begrudgingly takes them for an overnight. The last two times Erin asked, he said he couldn't do it; he was working. Twenty miles away, in a neighboring town, he has a new life, new house, a new girlfriend, a new everything. He's gone. He has walked away. He walked away from the house, the kids, from everything, and does not want any reminders of the life he has shed like a rooster molting feathers in fall.

Cheerios. Fuck it. She buys the biggest box on the shelf. As she turns onto the pasta aisle she can feel it coming on, anxiety churning inside, growing and spreading in her torso. She's got to hurry. She wants to make sauce from scratch but knows she won't be able to manage it. It will burn. It will be over-or-under-seasoned. The kids won't like it, preferring store-bought.

She stares at row upon row of glass bottles, garish labels glowing in the perfect grocery store fluorescence, and finally she is able to focus on a single jar of sauce, America's favorite brand, or so the label says. It's red. She grips her cart. The store is suddenly huge. Steel beams criss-cross the ceiling, painted the color of sand. The muzak invades her brain, swelling and swirling. She lets go of the cart, paces, feeling the thing inside her. No one else is in the aisle. It stretches forever in either direction. She feels herself choking, she can't breathe. Someone is going to see her; there's still no one on the aisle but it's only a matter of minutes now, it has to be. Someone will turn the corner and see her there, falling apart. Back and forth in front of the noodles—spaghetti, linguine, fettuccine, penne, farfalle, campanelle—which one? Which one? She snatches a bag of penne. Penne, yes, the kids like that and maybe they'll eat dinner tonight without crying when they ask about Daddy. Daddy said he'd come pick them up for a visit but where is he? They don't talk about Daddy's house or Daddy's girlfriend, and Erin doesn't tell them that Daddy is fighting her in court, saying he will rot in hell before he'll ever pay her a dime of child support. She clutches the bag, feels the dry noodles breaking inside it. She can't breathe. She should just run, leave the cart and run down the aisle and out of the cavernous store and outside to where there is air and sunshine. What kind of mother goes to the grocery store and comes home empty-handed? She grabs the cart handle and hurries toward the pharmacy section.

She can't do this. How long has she been doing this? Linear time has disconnected. There is the summer she went to war, and that divides her life into before and after.

She doesn't take the Xanax often, but sometimes she has to. She has not been able to explain her situation, her condition, to the family practice doctor Kloeten referred her to. He doesn't want to hear it, any of it; the guy writes off her symptoms as easily as he scribbles out the prescriptions. He chalks it up to anxiety and lets it go. It doesn't matter, though, because there's no way this doctor can understand what this thing is in her head. She doesn't understand it herself. All she knows is that something isn't right, even if nothing showed up on the scans.

Xanax tucked in her bag, she waits in line in front of a perfect woman who comes up behind her at the main registers, her cart loaded with fresh vegetables and the expensive bread and free-range chicken and lots of organic navel oranges. The oranges look delicious. Goddammit, it wasn't supposed to be like this. She was supposed to come home and get a good job and reunite with her family. But she's about to lose her house and she can't find a job and her children are confused and angry about Daddy leaving and never coming to see them anymore. Their lives are full of broken promises, month after month after month, and what the fuck is wrong with her brain?

She can't do this anymore. She can't. Yesterday, after she opened Ginj's letter and felt momentarily hopeful that Ginj would find some kind of future for herself, she opened the next envelope in the stack to discover a bright blue notice inside: Foreclosure. Eddy's driving around in a seventy-thousand-dollar truck but he hasn't got a dime for child support and he hasn't got an hour to come visit his kids. Her heart pounds. Her brain sloshes against her skull when she picks up the bag of groceries to load it into the cart. She can't do this. Can't.

She practically runs to the car, pushing the cart over the bumpy blacktop, and puts the groceries in the back seat. She is getting in, halfway behind the steering wheel when she sees the sign. Hanging in the window of the store right next to the grocery store. The liquor store. She hasn't had a drink since before she and Eddy went to counseling, a year ago now. The sign is bright red: End of Summer Sale! Big Savings!

FORTY-EIGHT

Fatima walks a narrow, guttered pathway between a row of make-shift, weathered tents, many of them consisting of nothing more than blue tarps tied to spindly wooden frames by twisted plastic bags instead of rope. The afternoon is August hot, but she keeps her *shemagh* pulled about her face. Her sunglasses and the loose *shalwar kameez* she wears allow her to move freely, walking as a man through the sprawling IDP camp on the outskirts of Kabul. She wonders if the boy is still here, if he stayed with his aunt and uncle.

In a while, she will get on her motorcycle and leave this place. She is not sure where she is going. Maybe Pakistan. Eventually, she will make it to America, or die trying. She's promised herself that.

But first she is going to say goodbye to the Sad Mother. She feels a momentary grief, but does not let her mind stay there. She has much to be grateful for, though it has come at a cost. Her brothers are not chasing her. Their names, and her father's too, were on the list of those killed by the bomb that exploded on the street where she used to live. Fatima hopes they did not suffer, but that is the extent of what she allows herself to feel for them.

She doesn't know how many people are in this camp and the other fifty or so spread around Kabul, and the other camps cast throughout the country. People. Thousands. Hundreds of thousands. Millions. The government calls them IDPs, Internally Displaced Persons. The Taliban has blown up their homes. NATO, led by the Americans, has blown up their homes. ISIS has blown up their homes. ISIL-K, from

276

Iraq, is here now. The militaries and the insurgents blow up their homes, their mosques, their hospitals. No one is winning. There is nowhere to go but here, to the camps.

She pulls back the blue tarp.

The Sad Mother sits on a rug in the center of the tent, rocking and weeping in the blue-tinted light. She is in a black, loose-fitting abaya, and the black hijab covering her head is knotted loosely at the neck. No one knows where she came from, or whom she has lost. No one knows her name. No one remembers ever hearing her speak. People bring her rice or lentils, maybe some raisins or yogurt, whatever is available, when food is available. No one has ever seen her eat, but she must be eating enough to survive. Bone thin, she continues to breathe and cry.

There is no furniture to speak of in the tent, or anywhere in the camp. The water tastes foul; the facilities are inadequate to handle the continuous influx of human beings.

Fatima steps inside and lets the tarp fall closed behind her. She pulls out a cellophane package of raisins and crouches before the Sad Mother. She sees the quiet tears rolling down the woman's emaciated cheeks and holds out the package. The Sad Mother's eyes lift to Fatima's.

Fatima puts the food on the carpet in front of the woman, nods respectfully and retreats to the front wall tarp. She is about to push open the blue vinyl when the Sad Mother coughs quietly, and chokes out, "*Astagfirullah.*"

Fatima goes back, folds herself onto her knees, propping herself at eye level in front of the woman. She keeps her voice low, betraying no anger.

"Why do you seek forgiveness from Allah?"

The woman repeats herself, whispering, "*Astagfirullah.*"

"Do not ask him for that," Fatima says. "Look around you. Remember all who have been slaughtered. And offer *your* forgiveness to Allah. He is the one who needs it. He and all the other gods."

The Sad Mother picks up the package of raisins. Fatima hears the crinkle of the transparent wrapping as the woman picks out one raisin, puts it in her mouth, and chews silently.

"Enjoy them," Fatima says. "They're especially sweet."

She rises and ducks out of the tent, marches along the dirt path, hearing the sounds of children, the sounds of mothers and fathers, the subdued conversations from within the blue tarp walls, words of those who have—by the grace of Allah, if they can still believe such as thing as grace exists—survived the bombings.

FORTY-NINE

The smell of beer and skunkweed wafts out of Nick's truck as the window glides down, hitting Erin right in the face. In the passenger seat, unable to see the way Nick looks at Erin, Eddy snickers. Erin feels her face burning. Eddy seems to think it's okay to show up unannounced—and stoned, and drunk. Erin despises hypocrisy.

Mrs. Copley had been surprised when Erin called her to ask why Mr. Steele searched her home. Mrs. Copley said that it was highly unusual, as CPS did not make a habit of conducting searches, not without some indication that there was something amiss in a household. Erin wonders if Eddy had something to do with it. And now, she considers calling the cops herself. She could take down Nick's plate number and dial before these two made it down the driveway.

"Where are the kids?" She has to work to keep anger out of her voice.

"They're fine, they're fine," Eddy says. "How are you doing?"

"Like you care?"

Eddy finds this hilarious. "They're good," he says. "Really. They're with Megan."

"Does CPS know about Megan?"

"Of course. They've been to the house, checked it all out." Eddy's speech is slurred.

"When can I see them?"

Eddy fiddles with the glove box handle. "Maybe we can set something up next week."

"I miss them," Erin says. "I want them to come home."

"We just came to get a chain saw," Nick says.

"Okay then," Erin says. "So get it." She goes back to the porch as they practically tumble out of Nick's slick black truck and stagger toward the shed.

Erin knows why they came. They didn't come for a chainsaw. They came to humiliate her. She goes inside but does not slam the door. She won't give them the satisfaction of knowing they've gotten to her.

Inside, she goes straight to her closet and grabs down the rifle, tossing the blanket onto the floor and working the combination on her lock box. She hears the throaty rattle-crack diesel engine of Nick's truck idling in the driveway, as if it's clicking off the seconds, timing her.

She jams the ammo into the Mannlicher, works the bolt to chamber a round. There. Got it. She heads upstairs.

In the country, no one thinks twice when they hear a gunshot. People shoot rifles in the woods year-round. During hunting season, it sometimes sounds as if there's a war going on out there.

Erin peeks out the window. She feels a stillness inside that has not been there for ages. She is filled with a glittering golden light. The guru's got nothing on her. She's not going to kill them. Though it wouldn't be hard, the mere physical aspect of it: the aim and trajectory. The velocity. They're still at the shed door, examining Eddy's bright orange Husqvarna with the eighteen-inch chain guide. Erin wonders why he didn't take it with him any of the several times he snuck back over to the house and grabbed his belongings while she was working and the kids were at school. It doesn't matter. He's got CPS firmly on his side and he's pushing her around, just because he can. He's showing off for Nick. He's putting her in her place.

She cranks the bedroom window slowly open. The cold air flowing into the room kicks on the furnace, but she doesn't care. She pulls the clips on the screen and eases it out of the frame, leans it against the wall. It's easy to forget how high up the second story of a house is. Look at them down there, so small. They have no idea she's there.

They have no idea she could take them out before they even knew where the attack was coming from.

She clicks off the safety. Why are they in her life, how it is that the three of them have collided, like billiard balls on smooth green felt, knocked this way or that, bending to the rules of geometry?

They get in the truck, Eddy stopping to put the chainsaw in the back before he slams the passenger door shut. Then they get back out of the truck, and Nick hands Eddy the keys. Eddy gets behind the wheel. Erin considers, momentarily, calling Mr. Steele, or even Mrs. Copley. But she knows what would happen: voicemail. Even if she reached them, they wouldn't do anything. *She's* the alcoholic, not Eddy. *She's* the one who can't be trusted.

Even from this far away, she can hear the music thumping from inside the truck. Eddy backs into the turn-around and eases down the driveway, moving at a pace barely above idle.

Erin props herself against the window ledge and pulls the rifle to her shoulder, holding it tight, lining up the sights, aiming carefully.

She loops her finger over the trigger, pressing until her flesh has given all it will give, and continues the squeeze smoothly, feeling the trigger tighten, tighten, until CRACK! and the kick against her shoulder, and the recoil. The driver's side taillight on Nick's truck goes out. Erin lowers the rifle as Nick's remaining brake light flares in the evening and the truck comes to a stop. It sits there, idling for a moment, and then the brake light goes off and the truck continues down the drive, its lone taillight glowing red in the dusk. She laughs. They don't even know. Maybe Nick will have a moment, waiting at the dealership while the taillight is replaced, when he remembers hearing a loud pop beneath the music blasting in the truck cab. Maybe the mechanic will show him the lens from the casing, and they'll ponder whether that really is a bullet hole.

She closes the window and replaces the screen. Her ears ring. The room smells of gun smoke. But the war does not come rushing at her. She never knows when it will happen, or why, but right now it doesn't. It drifts somewhere out there in the atmosphere, like an orbiting military satellite, programmed to zap its signal to her brain at the speed of light just when she least expects it.

∞

Eddy sucks in a healthy hit and passes the joint to Nick just before turning off the reservoir road.

"I'm done," Nick says. "You want more?"

Eddy waves him off, and Nick pinches the joint out and pops it into the empty Altoids tin where he keeps his stash. He likes how it adds a nice mint aroma to the pot. Plus it helps cover the smell. He tosses the tin into the glove box as Eddy makes the turn onto the state highway.

"Shit." Eddy brakes hard and the truck rocks to a stop.

State police patrol cars are parked on either shoulder of the two-lane road, lights going, and four troopers stand on the highway stripes, stopping vehicles one by one, running a DUI checkpoint.

"Fuck." Nick digs in the glove box and comes out with a spray can of Ozium, popping the cap and filling the cab with fumes. Eddy cranks the car heater fan to max and Nick rolls down his window, fanning frantically with his hands.

"Damn." Eddy edges the truck forward as a tall trooper with a stern face waves him up and then offers a flat-palm instruction: stop the vehicle. He peers in the window. Eddy smiles at him. The trooper tilts his head, gazing through the glass at Eddy. Finally, he raises an index finger and twirls it in a circle: roll down the window, idiot.

Eddy hits the button and the window glides down.

"License, registration, and insurance, please." The trooper wrinkles his nose, then leans in for a serious inhale.

"You had anything to drink this evening?"

"I had a beer," Eddy says.

"Just one?"

"Just one."

Nick leans toward the open window, resting an arm on the console.

"Travis?"

A flutter of recognition crosses the trooper's face.

"Nick. How you doing tonight?"

"Good, good. Heading over to the Visser Kok. When do you get off? You could join us."

Eddy hands the trooper his papers and the trooper examines the driver's license under his flashlight.

"Sit tight," he says, and walks to the rear of the truck, and around the other side, and back to the driver window. While the trooper inspects the vehicle, Nick relaxes into his plush leather seat.

"It's cool," he says. "He used to date my sister."

"I hope they split on good terms," Eddy says.

"Unlike some couples." Nick laughs.

The trooper returns and almost leans through the open window. He inhales again.

"Looks like you've got a brake light out," he says. "I'm gonna need you to pull over there onto the shoulder, right behind my vehicle there." He points to the police car, the Visibar strobing red, white, and blue against the night.

∞

A banging on the front door. Erin opens her eyes. She's lying on her bed, on top of the covers, still in her cleaning clothes, old sweats, a sock in one hand. She arrived home so tired last night that was as far as she'd gotten before falling asleep. In addition to the MMA studio, she has almost ten houses a week now. She is dependable and does good work. More banging, forcefully on the storm door, rattling the glass in its metal frame. She pulls herself up and goes to the window. She doesn't recognize the crappy Hyundai parked there.

Through the storm door, a man smiles at her, but it's a fake one and he's not so good at it. He looks kind of sketchy, but it's not like the glass can protect her. She opens the door.

"Morning," the man says. He is missing a front tooth. He hasn't shaved for a couple of days. His clothes are clean, jeans and a navy-blue golf shirt. "Erin Hill?" He holds an envelope at his side.

"Who are you?"

He hands her the envelope.

"Sorry to do this to you," he says. "I know how it is. You've been served." He turns away quickly and hops down the steps. "Really," he says. "I'm sorry. Just trying to make a living."

Erin closes the door, hears the car start up and pull away. The envelope is plain manila, oversized, with a thick document inside. She rips open the flap.

Her house has, after several false starts, been sold at auction. She had managed to get the sale postponed several times but, in the end, she ran out of paperwork. There was nothing left to file with the court, no legal reasons she could give for why they should let her stay in her home. She should be feeling something, she guesses, wondering if she missed anthing, if there might have been some way to postpone it again. After so many months, though, it was inevitable she would run out of options. The notice is probably somewhere in the stack of unopened envelopes on her desk. Or maybe she overlooked it, tossed it out with the junk. It doesn't matter. She has ten days to vacate the premises.

She walks upstairs to Paul's room. Across the hall to Lindsey's room. She will pack the things she knows they treasure. Stuffed animals. Legos. Posters and hats and books. They already have their clothes, their sports stuff, and a few favorite toys at Eddy's house. Suitcases won't do. For this, she will need boxes. As she's leaving the room, she spots Lindsey's diary, tucked on a low shelf in the bookcase, next to *Mrs. Frisby and the Rats of NIMH*. She knows she shouldn't but cannot stop herself.

She flips through pages of neatly printed pencil text. There are colored-pencil drawings: friends' faces, flowers, mermaids, and trees. One catches her eye; she stops, pins the diary open. On the left page is a plain pencil drawing of a child's face. A large tear covers most of one cheek. Opposite that, handwriting, also in pencil, neatly printed: *Warning. This is sad. My parents are getting a divorce.*

Something breaks; something eggshell-delicate in Erin's chest is crushed. She closes the notebook.

It's the late afternoon rush at Granite Wine & Spirits, the hours between 3:00 and 5:00 p.m, where people who have spent the morning miserably hungover, swearing never to drink again, or at least not to drink today, find themselves once again standing at the sale bin. All the way through the eternal afternoon they have fought the craving, trying valiantly to keep their promises, but when the long evening creeps onto the horizon, a thirsty doppelgänger urges them to surrender. They promise themselves to start fresh tomorrow. Their determination is fierce. Their commitment is real. Just, right now? They need this.

Erin sits in the parking lot for a long time, afraid to go in. How many times had she sat here like this, trying to talk herself out of walking through that door? Everyone has told her, everyone—the people in the rooms, the counselors, the doctors, the shrinks—they've all said the same thing: don't take that first drink. Don't do it. If you do, you are doomed. What do they know, really? She's being evicted from her home. The home her children no longer live in. God will not give you more than you can handle. Bullshit. What do they know about anything? What advice can they give her? *It is what it is?*

She gets out of the car and walks across the parking lot. There is no snow here. The blacktop melts it quickly. Pine bark mulch crunches beneath her snow boots as she short-cuts across an island that holds nothing living, not even a shrub. Soil wants plants, don't these people know that? Soil wants plants and plants want soil. They live together as mother and child.

The little brass bell on the door chimes as she walks in. The wall to her right is lined with bottles, glistening colored glass, clean, clear glass, bright labels, subtle labels. Some of the bottles wear necklaces, dangling miniature breastplates. In front, three rows of crates, dark green wine bottles stacked neatly inside. Erin's brain goes electric, humming, buzzing, the air around her hollows out, leaves her standing in a vacuum.

She steps up to the counter. The clerk is early twenties, with a hipster beard and wire-frame glasses. He's handsome like a movie star.

"Know what you want?" His tone makes it apparent that he's used to dealing with people like her. He doesn't particularly like them.

On the counter, a clear plastic box sits filled to the top with nips: vodka, whiskey, rum, gin, even miniature brown Kahluas with their bright yellow labels. The clerk waits not-so-patiently. No one is at home. No one would know. One little bottle. She won't lose anything. There is nothing to lose.

"Uhm, what can I get you?" The clerk regards her suspiciously.

"I'm moving," Erin says. "I was wondering if you have any spare boxes."

"Oh." The clerk hustles from behind the counter and heads toward the back of the store. "Sure. Follow me. We got tons of 'em."

Back in her car, boxes tumbled behind her, Erin lets her head rest on the steering wheel. She waits until she thinks she can form a sentence, and then she takes out her phone and scrolls through the numbers.

The call connects and a recording comes over the speakerphone, "Welcome to Granite County Alcoholics Anonymous. For a list of meetings, press 1. If you need to speak to someone, press 2 . . ." Erin presses 1 and leans back in her seat, listening for a nearby location. Maybe she'll have to drive across the river. No matter. She'll drive.

∞

Her phone wakes her. She is lying on the floor in the middle of Lindsey's room, next to one final box that needed taping shut. After the meeting, she'd come home and pushed herself into exhaustion, packing until she was staggering. The phone trills loudly, again and again.

She hits speakerphone and lets her head settle back onto the carpet.

"Erin?"

"Yes."

"Are you there? Are you okay?"

"Who's this?"

"It's Gavin Costa. You don't sound good."

"I'm fine." Erin forces herself to sit up, shakes herself awake. "I'm fucking peachy."

Something shimmers on the carpet, Erin reaches for it but it shifts away before she can touch it, slipping from beneath her fingers. It's only lightplay, the sunlight casting shadows through the branches of the big sugar maple outside the window.

"Something's come up," Gavin says. "It's not exactly good news, but it might work in your favor."

∞

Erin's entire body is shaking, as if she's been caught outdoors in bitter cold and gotten deeply chilled. She snugs her jacket tighter in the small, freezing, glass-enclosed visitor booth and waits for the deputies to bring in the prisoner.

Eddy arrives wearing a Granite County Jail canvas jumpsuit that is not white or gray, but some color in between. His dark hair is uncombed. He needs a shave. He waits at the edge of the countertop on the other side of the glass, his head down, while the deputy removes his handcuffs. When he finally sits down he folds his hands on the plastic laminate and waits for Erin to speak.

Erin waits right back at him. She's afraid to make eye contact, afraid of what might come at her if she attempts any kind of connection, even with the glass shield between them. Finally she makes herself look up. He's scowling, angry that she's seeing him in this place, this situation.

"Why'd you come here?"

287

Erin won't let him make her angry. Not again. Not ever, if she can help it. He does not know how to say, "I'm sorry." He lacks the capacity, or the humility, or whatever connection it is that enables one human being to apologize to another. What a lonely way to exist. Sitting across from him, looking at him through the transparent wall of an outside authority, Erin feels as if she's watching him on a computer screen, the image beamed from a 24/7 webcam on some voyeuristic reality TV show. It's one of the coping strategies Dr. Cuevos taught her, looking at whatever situation she's in as if it's not really her that's in it, as if she's observing it from outside herself. He is just a man in a room, a man she once loved. The boy who was never her high school sweetheart. The man who did not know how to be a husband and father. Beneath his anger, he is lonely and frightened and insecure, and Erin can trace when it all overtook him: when he lost his job, when no one would hire him and he couldn't face the bills, the kids, her. She had hoped, for a long time, that the love of their small family was harvest enough, but she had hoped too hard, too long, suffering her way into the thankless role of victim.

"They're with Megan," he says, leaning forward to speak through the perforated metal disc in the center of the glass. His voice comes through sounding hollow, electronic.

Erin nods, already aware. Gavin told her when he called this morning.

"She takes good care of them." Eddy picks at an imaginary spot on the beige countertop.

Erin nods again, determined to keep the peace, no matter how fragile it feels. She wills herself to feel nothing, because to feel anything right now is dangerous. But just as with addiction, willpower is insufficient to the task. The thing that Erin has felt lurking inside her reveals itself suddenly and silently, like a bear emerging from a heavy fog on some desolate country road, causing you to swerve so violently you almost lose control of the car. It is not a sharp, raw-nerve signal or the stinging sensation of an unexpected slap to the face. The pain declaring its presence as Erin stares through the glass at Eddy is dark and silent and empty, like the interior of a deep-but-long-dry water well, left for useless. Abandoned.

"I've no doubt," she says. She will say whatever she has to say. She had loved him, truly and faithfully, and yes, she had fucked things up royally when she enlisted without so much as mentioning it to him beforehand, but by then he'd been unreachable, sunk in the depression of long-term unemployment, venting on Facebook and snarling at her every suggestion. She couldn't stand to see him like that, month after month. She couldn't bear his anger any longer. Maybe she wanted to jolt both of them into some kind of recognition that there was always something that could be done, even if that something was desperate. And yes, she should have found a way to get her shit together when she came back from Afghanistan. But she hadn't, and by then he'd grown so distant that she couldn't even ask him for help. When he walked out on her, it was nothing short of instinct, the need to survive, that convinced her that it didn't hurt, that she didn't care. She'd been *left*. With sole responsibility for two innocent young lives, marooned with her in their own home. They'd been left, too.

She wonders now, as the pain moves in and gets comfortable, if that is part of what drove her to try to obliterate herself, even if doing so meant leaving her children to navigate a motherless reality. She was not strong enough to bear the ache and humiliation of being rejected, scorned.

Eddy gazes at the ceiling as if he thinks someone has tacked an emotional cheat sheet up there. Neither of them knows what to say. Outside authorities have swooped them up like fireflies caught in a net, tossed carelessly into a jar and forgotten.

Erin remembers the day they'd finally finished painting the interior of their home, early on a summer Saturday afternoon. Pulling up the last of the dropcloths, Eddy asked her if she'd ever done the rock scramble to the top of the Boorland Crag. A couple of hours later, they were halfway up the massive tumble of huge granite boulders that spilled and piled at a steep angle against the sheer gray-veined white rockface. The boulders looked precariously balanced, as though tossed onto one another by some careless giant, but the stones were immovable by anything less than an earthquake. Erin followed Eddy up, crawling, stretching to reach for solid grips on rough stone edges, prodding and poking with her feet to find places to wedge a sneaker for a foothold, always maintaining at least three points of contact with the rockface. The few times she dared to look down, she'd been mortified to realize that a slip could result in falling twenty or thirty feet onto boulders and broken stones. Death was a possibility, serious injury almost a certainty. But there was something magical about being on the rockface; the sheer mass and weight and solidity of the boulders emanated a timeless energy.

At the top, Eddy took Erin's hand and they ventured over sheer stone dotted with scrub pine to the very edge at the tip of the crag, which offered a stunning 360-degree view. They could see much of Granite County from where they stood. Hawks and vultures sailed past, gliding far above the forests and emerald green pastures and farmlands far below. In that moment, Erin had felt certain that their love would last forever, as timeless as the sheer stone ledge on which they stood, surrounded by nothing but sky.

That love brought Lindsey and Paul into the world. That is still beautiful. That will always be beautiful.

"They want to come home, Eddy." Erin leans toward the glass. "Will you tell Bagley, please, that it's okay with you?"

Eddy's hands hang at his sides, a posture of utter defeat. Erin thinks maybe, just maybe, she understands now. The only way Eddy could defend his battered pride was with anger.

He walked out because she couldn't love him enough to make him feel whole. Even his own children could never love him enough. Nobody could, leaving him no choice but to despise her. He didn't even consciously know why.

It no longer matters. For Eddy, it was never about the children. The children were collateral damage.

∞

Gavin is waiting outside the courtroom when she arrives. He steers her into a conference room.

"You've got a very real shot at getting them back. Today."

Erin starts to tell him about the eviction notice but catches herself. Not a word. First, get them back. Deal with the rest later.

"What's wrong?"

"Nothing," Erin says. "I just can't believe it."

"Got to ask one question, not that I care about it. But." Gavin bounces his satchel against his knees, ready to get into the courtroom. "Did you know?"

"No," Erin says. If Gavin thinks she's lying, he doesn't show it. And she's not. Not really. She suspected, of course, but she has no issues with pot dealers. In any case, she didn't know what Eddy was up to. She didn't want to. She wonders whether, if she had, she would have taken out that taillight. She's really not sure.

The judge is already at the bench when Gavin leads the way into the courtroom. Bagley is at his usual spot. Erin can't tell for sure, but the Bailiff seems happy today. Maybe he's been rooting for her all along.

The judge calls the case and, no sooner does she finish than Bagley is on his feet. "If I may, Your Honor?"

The judge nods, giving him permission to continue.

"In light of Mr. Hill's detainment, I believe we've worked out an arrangement that would be in the best interest of the children. I feel strongly that minimal disruption is essential to their continued well-being, and that they should stay in the home where they're presently living."

"NO!" Erin shouts, slamming her hands against the table, glaring at Bagley as the Bailiff moves toward her. The judge rocks back, fumbles for her gavel and bangs it hard, not once, but three times, glaring at Erin.

"I'm sorry." Shocked to realize she's standing, Erin raises her palms to the Bailiff and quickly sits down. *Fuck.*

291

"As I was saying," Bagley continues, "Mr. Hill's fiancé resides with the family in the home, and she has agreed to take sole responsibility for their care until Mr. Hill returns."

"Your Honor." Gavin stands. "This is the first we've heard of this arrangement, and I deeply resent council's failure to communicate with me." He tosses a look of disgust at Bagley. "I have acted in good faith from the beginning of these proceedings, and there is no excuse for counsel's secretive behavior. Mr. Hill has been arrested. This makes it all the more reasonable and definitely in the best interest of the children that they be returned home to their mother, not left with a pot dealer's girlfriend."

The judge eyes Bagley.

"Your Honor," he says, "this is a very recent development and I apologize to Mr. Costa if he thinks I intentionally kept anything from him. I only learned of the situation this morning."

"Didn't we all." The judge picks up a piece of paper and lets it fall back to the desk, clearly exasperated.

"I did manage to speak with Mr. Hill personally. He is firmly in agreement that the children should stay with his fiancé until his current situation is resolved."

Erin fumes silently, working to keep her expression from betraying her.

"Apparently he is not firmly in agreement with laws against driving around with twenty-three pounds of marijuana in his truck." Gavin waves his arms dramatically. "I mean, come on!"

"It wasn't his truck, Your Honor."

"He was driving it, wasn't he, Mr. Bagley?"

"Your Honor, I respect the Court's position, but it's important to remember that Mr. Hill has only been accused of the activity. Nothing has been proven. He should be considered innocent at this point."

Gavin puts a hand on Erin's shoulder; she gets the message: stay seated and quiet. She's not sure she can.

"Your Honor," he says, "Innocence notwithstanding, it would appear that Mr. Hill is in fact engaged in criminal activity, apparently on a regular basis. I think we should consider what kind of risk that puts the children in. For God's sake, let them go home to their mother."

"Mr. Costa, your client has just displayed an inability to control herself right before my eyes. What am I to make of that?"

"Perhaps the Court can consider the frustration that Erin is experiencing. She has been totally compliant with the Court's orders, she has maintained sobriety and attended all her programs. Her ex, meanwhile, has made it extremely difficult for her to visit her children on a regular basis and, it would seem, is engaged in commercial distribution of an illegal substance." Gavin flashes on the image of the vial in his jacket pocket. He doesn't allow himself to dwell on it. Guilt is not productive.

"Your Honor, as the Court pointed out, we just witnessed a prime example of the fact that Ms. Hill is in need of further treatment. Additionally, I really don't believe that disrupting the children's living arrangements yet again is what's best." Bagley makes a weird, gloating movement with his head, as if tossing an imaginary ponytail off his shoulder. "I told Mr. Hill I would have no objection to keeping the children where they are, but that we would need to get approval from the Court, seeing as we are in the middle of a neglect proceeding against the children's mother."

"And now," Gavin interjects, "against the father as well."

Neglect. Erin cringes at the word. What does Mr. Good Girl know of it?

"CPS has been to the home, checking on the welfare of the children?"

"Yes, Your Honor. There would be no need for any additional verification of the suitability of the home or of Mr. Hill's fiancé. It's all been done."

Gavin glances over his shoulder. Where the fuck are they, anyway? He stands.

"Your Honor?"

"Mr. Costa?"

293

"Noting the absence of the DSS attorney?"

"She called. She has the flu. We'll conference her in if necessary." The judge sighs loudly, wearily. "Okay. Here's what I'm willing to do. I'm assuming here that if DSS hasn't already done so, they will be filing a neglect case against Mr. Hill due to his arrest. If Mr. Hill will agree to voluntarily place the children in foster care, which means they will legally be in the custody of DSS while they reside with his fiancé, I will permit them to remain there for the time being in spite of his absence. We'll revisit the situation in six weeks. Has bail been set?"

"Not yet, Your Honor."

"The guardian will have to sign a contract that spells out specific terms for the mother to visit, every week, until such time as she completes her program and we determine some kind of permanent custody arrangement."

"Your Honor, this is—"

"Mr. Costa. Enough. Mr. Bagley, I'm sure you'll be seeing the children no later than this afternoon to ascertain their well-being in light of this change in circumstances?"

"I will, Your Honor."

Erin does not recall ever, in her entire life, despising anyone as much as she hates this judge, right here, right now, in this place. Sitting up there all high and mighty, ruling over her subjects, completely out of touch with the consequences of her actions. For her, it's just another day at work.

"Your Honor?" Bagley digs through his satchel. "When I visited with Mr. Hill this morning, I took the liberty of having him fill out the necessary paperwork. May I approach?"

Erin listens as the judge says more words, words like adoption and permanency hearing. Appeal and fair hearing. Her Honor is signing papers.

That's it. All it takes. He has given them up. He has given them up and no one will listen to her. No one. Erin is not presently fit to be a mother. His girlfriend Megan—and who knows whether she's in on his dealing—has been promoted to fiancé and will, for the time being, continue to care for the twins. CPS can change its mind and move them wherever it wants, whenever it wants. Lindsey and Paul are officially in foster care.

Erin feels as if she is dangling from a thread, like a fallen leaf caught in a single strand of spider silk deep in the woods, fluttering beneath the trees. In an instant, she understands completely. They talk about it in the rooms: the moment of clarity. She knows. Her children have been taken from her for a reason, and she will never get them back, no matter what she does. This is not random. This is not the system, however fucked up it may be. This is no less than the glorious and eternal Universe in action. It is a Goddamned red flower blossoming on the shirt of a twelve-year-old boy, right where his heart used to beat.

The judge stacks the papers, lays them on the bench and folds her hands over them. Her fair and unbiased hands. Her honorable hands. Her hands that know so well the intimate touch of the pen, the power of ink on paper.

Erin feels Gavin's grip on her arm, helping her stay upright as they walk from the courtroom. He tightens his grip and guides her to the elevator.

"Easy," he says. "Almost there."

It takes forever to arrive. When the doors open, he helps her into the stainless-steel box. Erin sees his finger press the button labeled 1. One. That is her now. Erin Hill, family of one.

"You can appeal," he says. "But first we need to see where this thing is going. If Eddy gets prison time—"

"No." Erin swipes away tears. "Tanya said she would help. They can go to her. How do I do that, make a motion or whatever, to give custody to Tanya?"

Gavin hesitates. "You shouldn't be the one to file. The best course of action, if you really want to do that, would be for Tanya to file the motion."

The elevator doors open and he guides her out and down the long hallway, still holding her arm, directing her to the exit.

"Look. Erin. Before you get Tanya involved, let's wait and see what the charges against Eddy are, how that all shakes out. I'll talk to Bagley, see if I can get him to come around." His sentences come to her broken, like a stutter. He's been saying the same things all along. Do your program. Be patient. She's trying very hard to push away the image of that black cloud of anger that came out of Eddy's eyes in the courtroom that day, the day Gavin was hopeful things would be over. Just like he was today. It's never going to be over. She is certain the cloud is inside her now. It got in through her eyes. It is inside her and lurking there, waiting for its moment.

As they approach the Magnatron, Gavin asks her if she'll be okay. Busy day. He's up on another case.

"Patience," he says. "Maybe you should catch a meeting."

"Maybe you should, too." Erin taps her nose.

She steps out into the afternoon. Though snow is piled high in one corner of the parking lot and banked in white rows between the street and the sidewalk, the sun is shining, the temperature is mild, the sky is deep blue and cloudless. She digs for her keys as she walks toward her car. When she looks up, Mrs. Copley is approaching, smiling as if they are old friends.

"Hello!" Mrs. Copley says. "How are you? You're doing okay?"

"Yes," Erin replies, too brightly. "How are you?"

"Oh, I'm good, thank you." Mrs. Copley twirls just a bit, flaring her long skirt, almost like she's dancing. It must be the sunshine. "I mean I got called out late last night, but at least I'm not on the dead baby squad."

It takes a moment for the words to sink in. Erin tries not to let her mouth fall open.

"Enjoy your day." Mrs. Copley turns and clomps toward the courthouse.

∞

Tanya smiles brightly at the security guard, practicing for the flight ahead as she shoves her bag onto the belt and passes through the metal detector. She grabs the rollaway, snaps the handle up and heads for the gate. At least there won't be any passengers to deal with on the flight out. Today is easy: she's deadheading to 29 Palms to pick up a planeload of Marines and bring them from training camp to San Diego for deployment. The military passengers are so much easier to deal with than the general public. They know how to mind their manners, at least while they're on the plane. She'll overnight in San Diego and be home in time for lunch tomorrow. She'll talk to Stephen. She'll try hard to be encouraging instead of bossy, though lately that's how he seems to see her, regardless of her efforts.

At the gate, she checks her phone one last time and sends a quick text to her son: *LUV U 4ever&always.* She's about to power-off when the phone dings. The text isn't from Stephen. It's from Erin: *Promise me you will get them. Eddy got busted but they still won't let me have them. Promise me you will get them. Please?*

There's a woman's name, Megan, and a phone number. And Gavin's number as well. Jesus God almighty. Welcome to Shitstorm Central.

Tanya hits the keypad: *WTF of course I will. About to take off will call u the minute I land. LvU.*

The empty plane is a blessing, even reeking as it does with the scent of chemical air freshener. Tanya greets the pilots and enters the cabin, vacant but for the other two flight attendants on crew. Thank God her pal Vince is working. He's been around Renegade Airways almost as long as Tanya has, long enough to share her amazement at the airhead mentality of the new hires, whose faces are always in their phones. She grabs a seat next to him, belts herself in.

"Talk to me," she says. "I'm on the ledge."

∞

Sometimes, it happens that way. There you are, driving down the road in your beat-up Toyota, running errands, taking four large garbage bags of your remaining household goods to the Salvation Army, where they can be sold to the poverty-stricken. Maybe it's because you are doing the next right thing. You have packed up all your children's belongings and mailed them to your sister's house. It's far away, but that is okay, you know she'll take care of them. You've thought about having a yard sale, but you've got six days left to get out of your house, get out of your home. You've already posted the furniture on Freecycle.com and people have come and carried away the big stuff. They showed up within forty-eight hours of the posting and loaded things into old pickups and station wagons and vans. Watching one couple load your children's bunk beds into the back of a pickup that was leaking oil onto the driveway, you were reminded of something you heard while standing in line at the grocery store. The woman in front of you, her cart loaded to the hilt with processed foods from the middle area of the store, is talking on her iPhone, and she's saying, "I know, I know! It's like nobody gives a damn about the environment anymore, the damn thing was spewing a cloud of exhaust all over the road. I'm like, why don't they just take it to the damn mechanic and get the damn thing fixed?" And you want to tap her on the shoulder politely and then scream at the top of your lungs, "MAYBE THEY'RE TOO DAMNED POOR! Maybe they don't have enough money to get the thing fixed!!!"

But you didn't, you just stood there in line until it was your turn and you used your EBT card to pay. You know your brain isn't right. All it took was one little explosion. But now, today, you decide you must have made the correct, conscientious decision while standing in the checkout line because whatever, just, wow, here comes The Universe, providing.

What it is providing is one lane over, less than a car length in front of Erin: a shit brown Volvo carrying the arrogant, self-righteous bitch who stole her children and gave them to Eddy, the man who walked out on them, who now sits in a jail cell waiting for a bail hearing, who has given them over to the custody of DSS and left them with his girlfriend. Her children are in foster care. It's not right. It's not fair to Lindsey and Paul. Erin is sure that unless Tanya can get them they will be given to a couple somewhere in the 54,526 square miles that comprise the Empire State. Maybe they're perfectly nice people or maybe they're a couple of functional addict layabouts who are in it for the monthly check. Her children do not deserve that. But she has no home to bring them to, not in six more days. And it doesn't seem to matter how many programs she completes, how much therapy she does, the court just keeps saying more treatment, more programs, see you in sixty days, see you in ninety days, see you in six months, see you when we have time to squeeze you in, like it's nothing, like her children aren't growing up fast while Erin slogs through the system. Mrs. Copley's words echo in her brain: *You will not be allowed to have so much as a school picture of them.*

Erin keeps her distance, following the Volvo.

∞

Dusk is coming and Tanya still hasn't called. Erin walks—kitchen, dining room, living room, foyer, back to the kitchen and do it again—walking in circles through her empty house, her footsteps knocking loudly in the hollow rooms. Her voice mutters curses but it's someone else talking. It's not her; she's only listening. A comic-book zap sound slices through her brain, vibrating between her ears like a sudden and unexpected cell phone notification. Brrrrt. Brrrrt-brrrt. *Rude. Listen to me!* Someone is laughing, she hears Mr. Steele, but no, it's not him, not his voice. Oh it's her, her voice, there she is saying, "Mr. Steele! How are things at Preventive? How many children did you kidnap today?" Please, come in, have a seat, oh, wait, you'll have to sit on the floor because I gave the couch away day before yesterday. Please, please though, come in. Would you like an avocado? The refrigerator is full of them. Meet Sergeant Drake. He'll tell you all about it. What it's like to walk on moon dust. To live with sand in your teeth and explosions in your brain. You can't even hear them, can you? The explosions? That's okay, the doctors can't hear them either.

They don't show up on an MRI.

They don't show up until the autopsy.

The scars on the brain tissue—look into the microscope now—the scars look like dust.

She walks, circling, walking in circles, scared of the looming front door. Maybe she won't leave. Maybe she'll make the sheriff physically force her out. Will he loft her in his arms and carry her over the threshold, or will four of them take her, one on each limb—she's still got her arms and legs, unlike so many others—will they each take one appendage and deposit her body on the lawn? Will they take her to jail or to the psych ward?

"Private Hill!"

Get out of my head get out of my head get out of my head!

"Hill!"

Get the fuck out of my head, Sergeant.

Out through the sliding glass door, the door her children used to tumble through laughing with friends, so much laughter, so much hilarity, ha-ha-ha-ha-ha who's that laughing? Are they singing? Erin goes outside and across the back yard, to the fire pit.

She positions twigs beneath the split logs, strikes a match. The crackle of ignition, she kneels on stone and watches the flame gnaw its way up a twig, leap to another, and another.

Warmth. Heat. Fire. So beautiful. She holds her hands close, feeling the air grow hot as the flames get stronger, crawling up into the logs, igniting the splinters where the axe split the wood.

Who? Whoo-whoo? Whoo-whoo-whoo-whoo. Whoo-awww. The call brings her back. Fire. Burning bright now. Bits of ash flutter and jump in the shimmering air above the flames, hurled skyward by radiance. The bird calls again, closer this time. Erin scans the edge of the woods, searching for the barred owl. She is sure she's looking right at it, but she cannot see it. They are masters of camouflage, the owls.

Silence. She keeps searching. A sudden scream pierces the air, from deep in the woods, jolting fear straight through her. Someone is out there, a child screaming in pain, out there in the woods, injured or trapped. She bolts for the house, throws open the door, retrieves the rifle, lock and load, she is across the yard to the edge of the woods, listening, gulping air. It comes again, the scream painfully wild, frighteningly wild.

Erin recognizes the sound now, though she has not heard it for years, not since Lindsey and Paul were small. It is the cry of a fisher cat. She waits, hearing only the thudding of her pulse. Even the owl has gone quiet. An evening moon hangs in the sky, frowning down at her in shades of white and gray. She drops the rifle to her side and weeps.

She walks back to the fire.

There is no past. There is no future.

Ah. Guru voice. Where have you been?

She pulls a burning beech log from the fire, a sapling log that fits easily in her hand. The wood is warm against her skin as she grips it, holding it aloft like a torch, the end flaming high above her. She walks toward the house. Her empty, empty house.

FIFTY

Only the trees are real, worshipping the sun with their upraised branches. The trail is narrow, pocked with deer tracks. Erin walks fast but looks deep into the maples and oaks and beeches as she goes, passing shallow hollows in the snow where rabbits have hopped across the trail. Her snowshoe crampons crunch in the silence, cutting the hard-crusted top layer of icy white snow. She digs a gloved hand through the crust, scoops up a palmful and tosses it into her mouth; it goes immediately to ice water.

She walks steadily, her pace even. Above her, the tiniest of buds vibrate silently on their branches, waiting for spring. The trail widens out to an old logging road that passes an abandoned bluestone quarry. Industry was here, a hundred years ago. The early sidewalks of New York City were laid with this stone. The scars remain, cut into the earth, squarish wounds in dark blue sandstone cliffs, bleeding chunky rock rubble that spills onto the forest floor.

She heads off the logging road and climbs an embankment, grabbing beech saplings as she pulls herself up toward the crest of the snow-covered stone ridge. Near the top, the rock outcropping harbors a spot of bare brown earth, almost a cave. Animals have taken shelter here; the earth is packed hard. Maybe a bear has slept here in the warm months. The fisher cat wouldn't choose this place. Fishers choose hollowed-out trees.

From here, she can see what is left of the house she and Eddy built: a rectangle of blackened concrete set into the ground—the

302

basement—filled with a few feet of water and the imploded rubble of charred wood and scorched appliances from the building collapse.

The fire investigator has come and gone. There wasn't much left by the time he arrived. He asked her point blank if she set her house on fire. It took several weeks for him to finish his investigation, to determine that the fire started next to the furnace and was not suspicious. He didn't exactly throw himself into the investigation; it was a routine matter for him, but he did his job. It's not like folks in the country have huge respect for big banks and insurance companies. Whichever international entity was holding the mortgage when the house burned will get the insurance money but, in the meantime, Erin has emergency lodging funds to keep a roof over her head while she continues on the treatment conveyor belt that takes her to meetings and appointments.

Though she will not fully believe it until the documents are made official, she is willing, for the moment, to trust that the games are over. Gavin has assured her that the paperwork is prepared and everyone is in agreement. Bagley has agreed. DSS has agreed. The judge approved the settlement. Eddy, facing fifteen years in prison and a devastated fiancée, has cooperatively signed off. The Court will grant custody to Tanya. In a way, Erin feels bad for Eddy, but only in the way she would feel bad for anyone caught in his circumstance. Fifteen years. For a plant. What kind of karma is that?

She winds around the side of the cropping and scrambles up to the ridge. She's not quite at canopy level, but the sparse tree growth on the slope affords a good view. Tanya has already given her a flight pass. As soon as Erin is released from Family Treatment Court, she will get on the first plane there, and she will scoop her children into her arms and never let them go. Yesterday, when she visited them at Megan's, they cried at the news that they would be going to stay with Tanya for a while, and that mommy would be joining them there as soon as she could. Lindsey explained that she was crying happiness tears, and Paul quickly nodded his agreement.

Erin doesn't know whether they'll be able to stay permanently; Eddy still has some say in whether she can relocate the family. But she will deal with it when the time comes. For now, her children are safe and she will work hard to stay sane. When she got in her car after the visit, she had to adjust her rearview mirror. She realized it had been months since she had last sat up straight in her car, or anywhere.

Movement just over the tree line catches her eye. A red-tailed hawk rides the currents, circling slowly, its wings tipping lightly against the drafts in the pale afternoon sky. An approaching breeze whispers as it moves through the forest like a ghost, an entity of nothingness, a wave of pure movement. Even leafless, the trees respond. She has worked hard, works every day, to recognize when the storm is on the horizon, to prepare for its inevitable surges. She understands: there is no getting over the experience of war. There is no getting over the returning, no way to undo the plunge into despair that followed her tour of duty. The drinking. The ripping apart of her family. The loss. There is only this: learning how to live with it. Erin hears the keening of a partially fallen tree, caught in the branches of a still-standing neighbor somewhere behind her, the friction-call of wood creaking against wood as the trees lean and sway, standing their ground in the quiet afternoon.

ACKNOWLEDGMENTS

My heartfelt thanks go out to my exceptional and insightful agent, Betsy Lerner, of Dunow, Carlson & Lerner Literary Agency in New York, whose support and persistence led me across the finish line. Thanks also to my wonderful editors, Mark Gompertz and Caroline Russomano, at Arcade, and to Jeannine Hanscom for her excellent proofreading. I want to offer my gratitude to Abigail Thomas for sharing her wisdom and encouragement early on, when I was lost in the story, and for reading when I'd found my way back to the edge of the forest. I'm grateful as well to early readers and advisors Blair Breard, Claudia Davenport, Lisa Fabiano, Thomas Impola, Judith Hakam, Robert Leaver, Mary Mendola, Dolores Quiles, Frank Reggero, Sylvie Rabineau, Gordon Wemp, and Andrew Wyant. And as always, thanks and love to my family for their encouragement and support.